DATE DUE

R

N. V. Gogol

РЕВИЗОР
(The Government Inspector)
A Comedy in Five Acts

Edited by
M. BERESFORD

Studies in Slavic Language and Literature
Volume 9

The Edwin Mellen Press
Lewiston/Queenston/Lampeter

Library of Congress Cataloging-in-Publication Data

Gogol′, Nikolaî Vasil ′evich, 1809-1852.
[Revizor] = The Government inspector : a comedy in five acts / N.V. Gogol ; edited by M. Beresford.
p. cm. -- (Studies in Slavic language and literature ; v. 9)
Preface and introduction in English; text of play in Russian.
Includes bibliographical references.
ISBN 0-7734-8840-5 (hc)
I. Beresford, Michael. II. Title. III. Series.
PG3332.R4 1996
891.72'3--dc20 95-35519
CIP

This is volume 9 in the continuing series
Studies in Slavic Language and Literature
Volume 9 ISBN 0-7734-8840-5
SSLL Series ISBN 0-88946-290-9

A CIP catalog record for this book is available from the British Library.

The Edwin Mellen Press
Box 450
Lewiston, New York
USA 14092-0450

The Edwin Mellen Press
Box 67
Queenston, Ontario
CANADA L0S 1L0

The Edwin Mellen Press, Ltd.
Lampeter, Dyfed, Wales
UNITED KINGDOM SA48 7DY

Printed in the United States of America

This book is dedicated to my mother and father.

CONTENTS

PREFACE

The Government Inspector, a work of enormous comic power, with penetrating shafts of satire and a gallery of unforgettable characters, is the greatest play in the Russian language and one of the acknowledged masterpieces of world drama.

Probably no other play has had such a long, complex history of misunderstandings and misinterpretations. Gogol maintained that his purpose in writing it was to exert a moral influence on corrupt officials. Convinced of the redemptive power of art, he believed he could move public servants to mend their ways by exposing them to ridicule on the stage. His comedy, first presented in 1836, was laughed off by many of his contemporaries as an improbable farce, and most of them saw it, erroneously, as an implicit attack on the whole tsarist system.

Gogol's reforming purpose was not fulfilled but his drama, because of its universal theme of human corruption and its artistic excellence as much as the denunciatory significance attached to it, outlived its own time to become firmly established as a literary classic and as the leading play in the Russian dramatic repertoire. Outside Russia, too, it has acquired lasting popularity through its numerous translations and adaptations. It continues to amuse and delight audiences in many parts of the world, and to challenge the skill of producers and actors alike, offering great scope for diverse kinds of treatment.

In *The Government Inspector* Gogol departed from the tradition of comedy that had grown up in Russia from the eighteenth century. He retained the structure and many of the technical devices of conventional comedy, but purged it of much of its artificiality and extended its range, freeing it from the limitations of the love-plot with a happy ending. There is no trace in Gogol's play of the didacticism that characterizes earlier Russian comedies. There are no champions of virtue, no knights in shining moral armour. His characters, unlike those of his predecessors, are not neatly divided into good and bad, but are living people who, though mostly rogues, all display a mixture of qualities, some good, some bad. His comedy, both in its characterization and in its language, is much nearer to real life than any previous Russian play. He thus gave to Russian drama a new orientation, preparing the ground for later playwrights, such as Ostrovsky, Chekhov and Gorky.

The present edition is designed to provide the reader with all that is required for a full understanding and appreciation of *The Government Inspector*, which has been woefully mutilated in many of its English translations, even the best of which fail to match the stylistic subtlety, variety and eccentricity of the original. Of all Russia's great writers Gogol has proved the most elusive, the most difficult to render effectively. Yet such is the sheer force and humour of his play that it has been a success on the stages of the English-speaking world despite the inferior quality of its translations and despite the fact that, notwithstanding all that Gogol wrote to the contrary, it has been represented almost invariably as a farce and its characters have all too often been treated as grotesque.

The Russian text reproduced here is based on the edition of 1842, incorporating some minor amendments which Gogol made subsequently, and modified to conform with present-day spelling and punctuation. The text is accompanied by a lengthy introduction and copious notes on points of linguistic, historical or ethnographical interest. Words and expressions are glossed only if they are not given, or not given with a meaning appropriate to the text, in *The Oxford Russian-English Dictionary* or Smirnitsky's *Russian-English Dictionary*. Words and phrases quoted from earlier versions of the play in order to elucidate the meaning or illuminate the creative process are taken from the Academy edition of Gogol's works, Moscow and Leningrad, 1937–52, Vol. IV. Stresses marked in the text follow the pronunciation of Gogol's time, where it differs from that of today. Works referred to in the notes are included in the full bibliography given at the end. All translations from the Russian are my own.

For their generous help and advice in the preparation of this book I wish to thank my colleagues Professor J. C. Dumbreck, Dr. P. Doyle, Dr. D. G. B. Piper, Mr. V. I. Rosman and Mr. V. L. Vishniak.

INTRODUCTION

The Plot

The plot of *The Government Inspector* is simple and unoriginal. Khlestakov, a vain, feather-brained young man who works in the capital, St. Petersburg, is returning to his father's country estate when, having lost all his money gambling at cards, he becomes stranded in a small provincial town. He is taken by the local officials to be a government inspector who, they are led to believe, is travelling incognito in their province. Finding himself fawned upon and treated as an important personage, Khlestakov begins to live up to the part and after being wined and dined he indulges in extravagant lies and shameless fanfaronade, making himself out to be a grand Petersburg celebrity who is both a highly respected official and a prolific man of letters. He exploits the situation with relish, accepting gifts and money offered to him as bribes. In rapid succession he woos the Governor's daughter and wife, becomes engaged to the former, then abruptly departs. Shortly afterwards the townspeople discover his true identity from a letter, opened by the local postmaster, in which Khlestakov makes most unflattering remarks about all the officials. Before they have time to recover from their shocked sense of outrage they are plunged into consternation by the announcement that the real inspector has arrived.

This comedy plot, based on the age-old theatrical device of mistaken identity, was transformed by Gogol's literary genius into a consummate work of drama. *The Government Inspector* is an indictment of dishonest officials not only in tsarist Russia but everywhere, at all times, and its satire goes beyond the sphere of bribery and corruption, striking at the vulgarity, triviality and philistinism found in many human beings. First and foremost, however, it is a brilliant, amusing exposure of the jobbery and skulduggery practised by Russian bureaucrats in the time of Nicholas I. It is only in the context of this historical period that the play can be fully understood and appreciated.

Historical background

The reign of Nicholas I (1825–55) began with the Decembrist Revolt, in which a group of noblemen, most of them serving in the army, tried to seize the reins of power. The rebellion of 14 December[1] was swiftly crushed and the insurgents, after a lengthy investigation, were severely punished. The leading conspirators were hanged and most of the others were either banished to Siberia or condemned to serve in the ranks in remote parts of the empire. This attempted *coup d'état* left an indelible impression on Nicholas, who dedicated himself to defend the established order by imposing the strictest discipline on his realm. Fearing treason and subversion, he ruled Russia for thirty years with a rod of iron, introducing repressive measures and multiplying the agencies of inspection in every sphere of life.

The Tsar, a stern, majestic figure, dominated his country. He was trained as a soldier and possessed the soul of a martinet. He nearly always wore military uniform in public, was frequently present at parades and reviews, and drilled his Household Guards in person. He gave preference to army men over civilians and demanded unquestioning obedience from all his subjects. Under him the Russian people were regimented and their country, in the words of one contemporary, resembled a huge barracks. Punishments were generally inflicted with great harshness and cruelty. Common criminals had the Russian letters B–O–P stamped on their faces with branding-irons[2] and soldiers often died after being made to run the gauntlet several times through lines of hundreds of men. So widespread was the practice of beating subordinates that the Tsar earned the popular nickname of 'Nicholas the Rod' (Николай Палкин). In foreign affairs he became the head of the ultra-conservative powers in Europe, allying himself with the monarchs of Austria and Prussia. He maintained a large standing army which was used to suppress rebellion both at home and abroad. His soldiers quelled the Polish uprising of 1830–1 and brought Hungary back into submission to the Austrian crown in 1849, so that Russia came to acquire the reputation of being 'the gendarme of Europe'.

Compared with the states of Western Europe, Russia was a backward country. Its economy, almost entirely agrarian, was beset with difficulties, including inadequate means of transport, a shortage of capital, a scarcity of skilled labour, and the extremely low purchasing power of the masses. The chief obstacle to progress was the fact that more than three-quarters of the population were peasants belonging either to the state or, as serfs, to the landowning gentry, who treated them as chattels. For quite minor offences

[1] All dates are given in the Old Style, i.e. according to the Julian calendar, which in the nineteenth century was twelve days behind the Gregorian calendar used in the West.

[2] The word 'вор' then signified not only 'thief', but was applied to any criminal. The first letter was branded on the forehead and the other two on the right and left cheek respectively. In 1846 the brand B-O-P was replaced by K-A-T, an abbreviation of каторжник ('convict').

male serfs could be flogged, deported to Siberia or sent into the army by their masters. Even the Tsar realized the iniquity of this system and disapproved of it, but feared the consequences of abolishing it at a stroke. In 1842 he observed at a meeting of the Council of State: "There is no doubt that serfdom, as it exists in our country today, is an evil palpable and obvious to everyone, but to touch it *at present* would be even more disastrous". In the same year he declared that the land belonged in perpetuity to the landowners and that he would never grant the serfs freedom. There was, it is true, some improvement in the lot of the peasantry during his reign, inasmuch as some of the worst abuses of the serf system were removed. Landowners were forbidden to sell serfs without land as a means of settling private debts, or to sell them by public auction, so as not to split peasant families. Serfs whose owners had gone bankrupt were given the right to buy their liberty. State peasants were given larger plots of land and provided with some welfare facilities, such as schools and a medical service. But these reforms, owing to the malpractices of local bureaucrats, were not put into full effect and thus did little to improve the condition of most peasants. Discontent was rife among them and there was a steady increase in the number of incidents in which manor-houses were burnt down and landlords, together with their bailiffs, assaulted or murdered. Such outbreaks of violence were put down by the military with great cruelty.

The administrative machine of the Russian Empire under Nicholas was based on the system instituted by Peter the Great and later modified by Catherine II. Both central and local organs of government were run by officials, who were appointed by the authorities and graded according to a hierarchy of ranks corresponding to those in the army. The holder of each rank had his own privileges, bore a special title, and was required to wear uniform when on duty. Promotion was much sought after, as was the prestige attaching to membership of various honorary orders, each with its own insignia and ceremonial. The civil service was staffed by members of the gentry, who were organized at local level into their own corporations and allowed to elect certain officials from among their number. In the provinces town councils were elected on the basis of a restricted franchise and in practice they became bodies of merchants whose scope of action was severely circumscribed. Real power lay with the police and other officials, who were responsible not to the local population but to the governor of the province and ultimately to the authorities in St. Petersburg. Under Nicholas this administrative organization remained substantially unchanged, despite the fact that a special committee spent several years studying it and produced various proposals for reform.

The outstanding feature of Nicholas's regime was the centralization of the state apparatus, accompanied by a great increase in bureaucracy. The Tsar, a firm believer in autocrácy, kept as much political power as possible in his own hands. He considered that the tasks of government, especially policy decisions, were for him alone, not for the Council of State or the Senate, still less for the Committee of Ministers. Accordingly, a fundamental change was made in the machinery of central government – the most significant change in the entire reign of Nicholas. In 1826 the Imperial Chancellery, which had been relatively unimportant until that time, was transformed into a key organ of state and expanded into several sections, each of which acted independently and was answerable only to the Tsar.

The First Section continued the original function of the Chancellery, dealing with court matters, the appointment and supervision of senior officials, and the management of the crown estates. The Second Section undertook the formidable task of compiling and codifying all existing laws, a genuine achievement in the sphere of jurisprudence. The administration of law, however, remained deplorably slow and cumbersome. All cases were heard *in camera*, with the proceedings conducted entirely in writing. Litigation dragged on interminably and arrested persons were often held in custody for years before their cases were tried.

The Third Section, together with the Corps of Gendarmes, a special armed police force formed at the same time, constituted the real centre of political power. Its functions included the collecting of information relating to state security, the surveillance of all politically suspect persons, religious dissidents and foreigners, the supervision of prisons and places of exile, and the eradication of corrupt practices in administration. It rapidly grew into a powerful intelligence organization controlling a vast network of spies, agents and informers. So wide-ranging were its powers that it became a state within the state. It was independent of ordinary legal procedures and frequently acted as a judicial body with powers to detain and punish. People were arbitrarily arrested and beaten for quite minor offences, and their correspondence was opened and perused. Absolute secrecy prevailed in all branches of administration and fear of inspection or denunciation became widespread, although Russian officials were traditionally well practised in the art of concealing the true state of affairs from their superiors and from inquisitive foreigners. The Marquis de Custine, a Frenchman who visited Russia in 1839, described it as a country of mutes in which fear replaced, or rather paralyzed thought. "The Tsar," he wrote, "is the only man in the empire to whom one can speak without fear of informers."

Despite the numerous agencies of supervision and inspection it proved impossible to exercise effective control over all the outposts of administration, owing to the enormous size of the empire and its grossly inadequate system of communications. Bribery and extortion, which had become deeply entrenched in all departments of the administration, both civil and military, continued to thrive. In 1827 General Benkendorf, Head of the Third Section, received a report from his second in command, M. von Vock, in which officials were castigated as the most corrupt element in society. "Among them honest men are rarely to be found. Plunder, fraud, and perverse interpretation of the laws – these are their trade." A similar picture of this period is given by the anonymous author of a political document which circulated secretly at the time of the Crimean War. "The letter of the law was observed, but negligence and crime were allowed to go unpunished. While grovelling in the dust before ministers and directors of departments, in the hope of receiving *tchins*[3] and decorations, the officials stole unblushingly; and theft became so common that he who stole the most was the most respected."[4] Some officials, to be sure, were honest and conscientious, but most of them tyrannized over the local population, extracting bribes and gifts in order to line their own pockets. No petitioner would appear empty-handed, and if he was too poor to offer money he would present a cake, a pot of honey, a towel or some other inducement. The venality that prevailed in the dispensation of justice found expression in the popular saying: "If you have a hundred roubles the law is on your side" (Сто рублей есть, так и правда твоя).

The administration of the Russian Empire was thus both corrupt and incompetent. An important cause of corruption among officials was the fact that all of them, save the highest, were miserably underpaid. The real value of their salaries had declined owing to severe inflation, especially during the Napoleonic wars, and was not restored even when increases were granted by Nicholas in the mid-1830s. Administrative incompetence, on the other hand, was largely the consequence of Russia's backwardness, for its standards of education and professional training were considerably lower than those in Western countries. Many of the landed gentry, after generations of property division by equal inheritance, had fallen on hard times, so much so that by 1836 two-thirds of all their estates were mortgaged to the government. As a result more and more of their sons moved into the towns to take up official posts which offered the prospect of supplementing a low income by taking bribes and of tasting the fashionable pleasures of urban life. The ranks of the bureaucracy, except in the top posts, were filled with men of poor education,

[3] *tchins* (чины), i.e. high rank.
[4] Quoted by D. Mackenzie Wallace in his book *Russia*, London, 1877, p. 445.

which prevented Russia from developing a reliable, efficient civil service. The country was governed by an army of remote, anonymous functionaries operating a rigid, formalistic system of administration in which precedent and routine were paramount. In the capital, St. Petersburg, there was a complex of offices that flooded the country with orders, decrees and circulars. The whole of this immense empire was strangled by red tape, cramped by administrative fetters, and oppressed by a monstrous tyranny of paper over people.

In the field of education the Russian government sought to impose strict discipline and a pattern of conformity in behaviour and thought. A law of 1828 extended the period of compulsory schooling and confirmed the existing system of public education, at the same time defining the social composition of each type of school. In principle, parish schools were to be attended by children belonging to the lowest social classes, chiefly the peasantry, district schools were intended for children of petty officials, merchants and artisans, while high schools (гимназии) and universities were reserved almost exclusively for children of the gentry. By laws enacted in 1835 all forms of state education were brought under the direction of regional overseers, and strict supervision was introduced over discipline in both schools and universities. Religious instruction was made compulsory for students as well as schoolchildren. Universities, whose teachers were already regarded as state officials, lost nearly all their autonomy, since the Minister of Education was given the power to make appointments without consulting the academic boards. Further restrictions were imposed by introducing tuition fees in universities in 1839, and then raising the fees at both high schools and universities twice in the following decade. Finally, after 1848 university curricula were curtailed. The teaching of philosophy was restricted to courses in logic and psychology, which were handed over to the clergy, and courses in constitutional law were abolished altogether.

Education under Nicholas I was pursued in the spirit of 'official nationality', a doctrine first formulated in 1832 by Sergei Uvarov, shortly before he became Minister of Education. According to Uvarov, the only way to counteract the influence of West European ideas was to establish an educational system based on 'the truly Russian conservative principles of *Orthodoxy, autocracy and nationality*, which are our ultimate sheet-anchor and the surest guarantee of our country's strength and greatness'. Autocracy was the most important element in this triple formula, as the Tsar exercised supremacy over the Orthodox Church, and 'nationality', or rather 'national spirit' (народность), was taken in practice to mean unconditional loyalty to throne and altar. This doctrine, inculcated in all educational establishments, even found its literary apologists in Nikolai Grech and Faddei Bulgarin, two writers who were connected with the Third Section and jointly edited the journal *A Son of the Fatherland* and later the daily newspaper *The Northern Bee*.

The small minority of educated upper-class Russians suffered from the increasingly harsh measures imposed by the authorities. Travel abroad was made more and more difficult and finally stopped altogether. Nicholas, deeply suspicious of liberalism and freethinking, tightened the controls over all kinds of literature in an attempt to prevent the spread of subversive ideas. Foreign publications were admitted into the country only after the most rigorous examination, and the possession of a forbidden book was considered a grave offence, punishable with exile. A statute on censorship, issued in 1826, prohibited the publication of any matter that was deemed to disparage the monarchy or the church or which criticized, even indirectly, the existing order of society. Works of logic and philosophy, other than textbooks, were not to be published. Under a slightly more lenient decree, enacted in 1828, censors were relieved of the responsibility for guiding public opinion and correcting 'mistakes' of fact, and even style, in works submitted for publication.

The censorship system operated through a multiplicity of agencies. The general censorship was administered by boards nominally supervised by the Ministry of Education, but in practice largely dominated by the Third Section. In addition powers of censorship were exercised by each government ministry and at times by the Tsar himself. In 1837 a system of dual control was instituted, which required that each work should be examined by two censors. And when in 1848 a secret committee headed by Count D. Buturlin, the so-called 'censorship of the censors', went into operation almost every word of print was subjected to the closest scrutiny. The writer A. V. Nikitenko, himself a censor, observed in 1850 that 'if one counts all the persons in charge of censorship they will exceed the number of books printed in a year'.

Editors of literary journals were constantly harried and hounded. They required special permission to publish their periodicals, which could be closed down for giving offence to the authorities. Several journals were so banned and their editors either exiled or barred for a time from practising their profession. Thus in 1836, the year in which *The Government Inspector* first appeared, the journal *Telescope* was suppressed because its editor had published a *Philosophical Letter* in which the author, Petr Chaadayev, expressed the view that Russia was an intellectually barren country which had made no contribution to civilization and that she should draw closer to

Western Europe. The editor of *Telescope* was sent into exile, the censor who passed the article was dismissed, and the unfortunate Chaadayev, officially declared insane, was placed under medical observation.

The intelligentsia emerging in the 1830s became passionately concerned with Russia's national identity and historical destiny. Chaadayev's famous 'Letter' gave rise to a protracted dispute between the Westernizers, who believed that Russia should adopt West European culture and institutions, and the Slavophils, who held that Russia was a country apart, which should continue to cultivate its own native traditions. For all their differences of outlook, however, the men of both ideological camps were united in their detestation of the regime and opposition to the system of serfdom. They also shared a desire to be given freedom of speech and publication. But there was no freedom of expression in Russia and the discussion of ideas, which could not take place openly, was conducted through the medium of imaginative literature. In this way literature came more and more to reflect Russia's social problems and was turned into a weapon in the struggle for enlightenment and progress.

Writers naturally had to use great caution and often resorted to subterfuge, employing the so-called 'Aesopian language' of hints, allusions and circumlocutions in order to disguise their ideas. At the same time works which had been banned by the censors were freely circulated in manuscript copies. Thus, despite the shackles of censorship, literature flourished under Nicholas I. Indeed by a curious paradox of history his reign, which was one of reaction and stagnation in most spheres of life, produced a great ferment of ideas and a remarkable burgeoning of literary talent. Pushkin, Gogol and Lermontov were all at the height of their creative powers in the 1830s and in the latter part of the reign Turgenev, Dostoyevsky and Tolstoy made their literary debut. Of these great writers none was endowed with such fertile creative powers or displayed such extraordinary originality in the use of language as Gogol, one of the most complex and elusive figures in all Russian literature.

Biography

Nikolai Vasilievich Gogol was born on 20 March 1809 in the little market town of Sorochintsy, near Poltava, in the heart of the Ukraine. His father, a small landowner, was a sociable man with literary leanings, who wrote a number of comedies which he produced in the domestic theatre of a wealthy, distantly related neighbour. His mother was a simple, gentle creature who married young and bore twelve children, of whom only four survived childhood, Nikolai and three younger sisters. It was she who had the strongest influence on him in his earliest years and she retained his life-long devotion. She was a pious person, who loved the ritual of the Orthodox Church, and a superstitious one, believing in all sorts of omens and premonitions. She instilled in Nikolai her own primitive kind of Christianity, grounded in a fear of the devil and a fatalistic acceptance of everything that happened as 'the will of God'. She doted on her son when he was a puny infant and spoiled him all his life. At times she idolized him to the point of absurdity and in later years embarrassed him by crediting him with other writers' works and even, so it is reported, with the latest inventions, such as the steamship and the railway train. It seems probable that he inherited from her his exceptional powers of imagination.

His childhood was spent on the small family estate of Vasilievka and he received his first tuition from a student of divinity. For about a year he attended the district school in Poltava and then at the age of twelve he was sent as a boarder to the high school in Nezhin, some 150 miles from his home. Besides being small and rather gauche he was extremely self-conscious and secretive, living much of the time in a world of his own, and his schoolfellows aptly nicknamed him 'the mysterious dwarf'. His scholastic record was undistinguished and he was often berated for laziness, slovenliness and tomfoolery. He disliked mathematics and outdoor games, but was fond of art, history and above all poetry. Much of his time was spent reading and he contributed to various school magazines, but very little has survived of his juvenilia, which included several poems, a verse tragedy called *The Robbers*, and his first prose tale, *The Tverdoslavich Brothers*, which he tore up and burnt after it was condemned by his fellow-pupils. He possessed a sharp tongue and a remarkable gift of mimicry which he used to entertain the other boys, giving lively and amusing imitations of their teachers. But his dramatic talents came to the fore most of all in his passion for the theatre. He took part enthusiastically in the production of several school plays, painted the scenery and played various roles, the most successful of which was that of Prostakova, the stupid, domineering mother in Fonvizin's comedy *The Minor* (1782).

He was deeply distressed at his father's death in 1825, after which he began to think seriously about his future. He had vague dreams of serving his country in some lofty endeavour and spoke of taking up a career in law, although it is likely that even then he aspired to become a man of letters. Proud and ambitious, he was determined to make his mark on the world, dreading the thought of being condemned to live a life of mediocrity and obscurity, buried in some provincial backwater. In December 1828, a few months after leaving school, he set out for St. Petersburg, full of hope and bent on achieving fame.

For some time he met severe setbacks and could not find employment in the capital, despite the letters of introduction he had brought with him. St. Petersburg failed to live up to his romantic expectations. "There is not a spark of spirit in the people," he wrote to his mother, "they are all office workers and civil servants who talk about their departments and ministries; they are all oppressed and bogged down in the futile, paltry labours on which their lives are squandered."

His first published work, a poem entitled *Italy*, appeared anonymously and went entirely unnoticed. This was followed by *Hans Küchelgarten*, a sentimental idyll which he published at his own expense under the pseudonym of V. Alov. This poem, most of which was probably written at school, received only three reviews. The first two were extremely unflattering, while the third was distinctly encouraging. Before this last notice had appeared, however, Gogol reacted in characteristic fashion. He went round the bookshops with his servant, bought up all the unsold copies of the poem he could lay hands on, and promptly burnt them in a hotel room hired for the purpose. This was not the first work he had consigned to the flames, nor was it to be the last. His hopes of becoming a famous poet were completely dashed and after that he never wrote another line of verse. In a letter to his mother, written in July 1829, he unburdened his feelings. "Everywhere, without exception, I have met with nothing but failure . . . utterly incompetent people with no one to pull strings for them have easily acquired what I could not obtain with the help of my patrons. Was this not a clear indication of God's providence at work? Was He not manifestly punishing me with all these failures in order to set me on the right path?" This strong conviction of God's personal intervention in his life was to be expressed in many of his later letters.

Shortly after burning the printed copies of his poem he made a brief trip to Germany. He visited Lübeck and Travemünde, then returned to St. Petersburg by way of Hamburg. For this journey he used a sum of money which his mother had sent him to pay the interest on her mortgage, and in return he formally renounced his share of the family estate in her favour. His reason for making the trip was probably quite simple: to escape for a time from the scene of his failure. But he explained matters differently to his mother in order to excuse himself for embezzling her money. He attributed his abrupt departure to his tragic infatuation for a Petersburg beauty whom he had idolized, only to be shattered by the discovery that she was a prostitute or, to use his quaint euphemism, 'a divinity lightly clothed with human passions'. Whilst in Germany, however, he wrote to his mother explaining that he had gone there on medical advice to get a cure for a rash he had acquired. To his horror his mother, putting two and two together and making five, concluded that he had contracted a venereal disease. Both his explanations were, in all probability, falsehoods of the kind that he invented quite often to conceal his real motives and intentions.

He returned to St. Petersburg penniless, but did not yet admit defeat. Unable or unwilling to find work in the civil service, he made an attempt to go on the stage. One morning he called at the office of Prince Sergei Gagarin, Director of the Imperial Theatres, and announced that he wished to become an actor. He was later given an audition, at which he was asked to read monologues from several classical plays. Nervous and embarrassed, he read in a flat, timid voice and stumbled over his lines. His chief offence in the eyes of his examiner, Alexander Khrapovitsky, was that he spoke naturally and did not adopt the conventional style of histrionic declamation, which consisted of ranting, howling and sobbing, and was known in the profession as 'dramatic hiccups'. His slight build and his unprepossessing appearance, with short legs and a long, pointed nose, also told against him and consequently he was considered unsuitable for anything but walking-on parts. Certain that he had failed, he did not even bother to enquire about the result of his audition. It was a humiliating experience for an ambitious young man who had distinguished himself in amateur dramatics at school and believed he had considerable talents as an actor. Nor was his belief mere youthful vanity, for he was later to astonish and delight his contemporaries with the masterly readings of his own works that he gave at private gatherings.

Towards the end of 1829, thwarted in his attempts to become a poet or actor, he reluctantly entered the civil service as a minor official of the lowest grade. His salary was meagre and he suffered considerable hardship in St. Petersburg, where life was very expensive. In the following April he obtained a better-paid post in another government department, but found the work there no less tedious. Much of his spare time was spent attending classes at the Academy of Arts and associating with Ukrainian friends, most of them old schoolfellows. At the same time he persisted with his literary endeavours. Taking advantage of the growing interest among the reading public in folklore, especially in things Ukrainian, he began to write stories about the life and legends of his native Ukraine or 'Little Russia', as it was then called. For these he drew on his memories of tales heard in childhood, scholarly works on the Ukraine, and information about its dress, customs and beliefs supplied by his mother and friends.

His first tale, *Bisavryuk, or St. John's Eve*, which was published anonymously in 1830, attracted little attention. His next prose pieces were published in *Northern Flowers* and the *Literary Gazette* by Baron Anton Delvig, a poet and close friend of Pushkin. From Delvig, it is believed, he obtained a letter of introduction to Vasily Zhukovsky, the famous romantic poet and tutor to the Tsar's eldest son. Through Zhukovsky he was introduced to Petr Pletnev, a minor poet and critic who later became Professor of Russian Literature at the University of St. Petersburg. In 1831 Pletnev procured him a post as history teacher at the Patriotic Institute, a boarding-school for officers' daughters, and work as a private tutor in a few wealthy households. He was now acquainted with many of the leading literary lights in St. Petersburg, including Pushkin, whom he first met at a soiree given by Pletnev in May. He had a new vocation, which he took up with enthusiasm, and he put behind him for ever his 'stupid, senseless' work in the civil service, where, as he later observed, the only useful thing he learnt was how to stitch loose pages together.

In September 1831 he published the first volume of *Evenings on a Farm near Dikanka*, which won him immediate recognition. Pushkin, in a short published comment on it, expressed his delight at 'the genuine gaiety' of the tales, which were 'devoid of affectation or prudery' and touched in places with 'poetry' and 'sensibility'. When the second volume appeared in the following year Gogol's literary success was assured. His colourful tales of Ukrainian life and legend, told by the fictitious narrator Rudy Panko, revealed a world still relatively unknown to the Russian reader. The stories, which are peopled with earthy peasants, witches, demons, nymphs, goblins and all kinds of supernatural phenomena, abound in exuberant vitality and contain a poetic blend of the fantastic and realistic, the lyrical and farcical, a mixture of arch humour and stark horror. Gogol, at the age of twenty-three, was a famous writer. The doors of all the salons were now open to him and his circle of literary acquaintances rapidly grew larger. In the summer of 1832 he returned to Vasilievka by way of Moscow, where he met some of the literary and theatrical celebrities, including the historian Mikhail Pogodin, the writer Sergei Aksakov, and the distinguished actor Mikhail Shchepkin, all of whom were to remain his lifelong friends.

Despite the success of his first book he had misgivings about his literary ability and was still uncertain of his calling as a writer. Spurred by intense ambition, he secretly yearned to achieve lasting fame by producing a great work of literature and dismissed all that he had written so far as trivial and inconsequential. He strove to overcome his doubts by undertaking new literary ventures. At the beginning of 1833 he turned to drama, which had interested him from an early age, and began to write a comedy entitled *The Order of Vladimir, Third Class*. Foreseeing difficulties with the censor, however, he abandoned it in the second act and took it up again only several years later, when he turned it into four separate sketches. In the middle of 1833 he started a more light-hearted comedy, *The Suitors*, which was finished in less than a year but put aside as unsatisfactory and not published until several years later, after much revision, under the title of *Marriage*.

Still undecided about his future, he became more and more immersed in the study of history, which had interested him since 1831. He devoted himself energetically to historical studies, read avidly, and seriously considered becoming a professional historian. Full of confidence and optimism, he announced grandiose plans to publish vast historical works, none of which ever materialized. Towards the end of 1833 he applied for the chair of history at the newly-founded University of Kiev. He composed *A Plan for the Teaching of World History* and sent it to Uvarov, the Minister of Education, who approved of the article and had it published in the official organ of his ministry. Gogol failed to obtain the coveted post at Kiev, but in July 1834 he was appointed Adjunct Professor[5] of History at St. Petersburg University with the help of influential literary friends.

In September he began a course of lectures on the Middle Ages. He gave a brilliant opening lecture and later produced another impressive *tour de force* when Pushkin and Zhukovsky attended one of his classes. For the rest, however, he skimped his preparation, often arrived late, and delivered brief lectures in a perfunctory manner. His career as a lecturer was an unmitigated disaster, as he later acknowledged. He had neither the qualifications nor the temperament needed for scholarly work. He knew insufficient history and failed to fill the gaps in his knowledge. He relied on inspiration and worked as the mood took him, bursts of energy and enthusiasm alternating with periods of indolence and apathy. At the end of 1835 he was forced to resign when a ministerial circular decreed that henceforth all history professors must possess at least a doctorate, a requirement he could not possibly comply with. His pride had received another severe blow and he took his revenge by cocking a snook at the academic world. "I have spat farewell to the university," he wrote to Pogodin, "and in a month I shall be a carefree Cossack again. Without recognition I mounted the rostrum and without recognition I step down from it."

Meanwhile his pen had not been idle. In the first months of 1835 he published *Arabesques* and *Mirgorod*, both of which appeared in two parts. *Arabesques* was a miscellaneous collection of essays on history and the arts,

[5] A senior academic post equivalent to that of Associate Professor in American universities and Reader in British universities.

together with three of his 'Petersburg Tales', *The Portrait*, *Nevsky Prospekt*, and *The Diary of a Madman*, all of which reveal a gulf between appearance and reality, showing the disastrous consequences which befall man when, seduced by Satan's wiles to pursue earthly love or beauty, he discovers them to be mere masks concealing the moral squalor beneath.

Mirgorod contained four tales of Ukrainian life and legend. *Vii*, a fantastic, gruesome story, supposedly drawn from folklore, and *Taras Bulba*, an epic tale of the Cossack struggle against the Poles, are predominantly romantic works. Side by side with these are two much more realistic narratives, *The Story of the Quarrel between Ivan Ivanovich and Ivan Nikiforovich*, in which a petty insult leads to a lengthy lawsuit, and *The Old-fashioned Landowners*, a picture of an aged couple who vegetate contentedly on their small estate. In both these tales the patriarchal way of life in the Russian countryside is depicted with a mixture of satirical irony and gentle good humour, tinged with sadness at the tragic and absurd waste of human lives. Pushkin described *The Old-fashioned Landowners* as 'a humorous, touching idyll that makes you laugh through tears of sadness and tenderness'. This remark gave rise to the celebrated expression 'laughter through tears', which was later widely used to characterize Gogol's artistic perception of life. And the tears that Pushkin discerned behind Gogol's laughter betokened something more than pathos or compassion; they sprang from a deep sense of what Virgil called the *lacrimae rerum*.

Vissarion Belinsky, soon to become the outstanding Russian critic of his time, enthusiastically praised *Arabesques* and *Mirgorod*, declaring that Gogol possessed 'an extraordinary, powerful and lofty talent' and was now the country's foremost living writer. Belinsky's article, which did more than anything else to establish Gogol's literary reputation, made a great impression on him and gave him much-needed comfort at a time when he was depressed by the poor sales of his two latest books and still felt very unsure of himself, being under heavy attack from many critics for showing the seamy side of life in some of his tales.

During his time at St. Petersburg University he had continued his attempts to write a drama. In the summer of 1835, whilst preparing his lectures on Anglo-Saxon England, he began a play about Alfred the Great, but got no further than the beginning of the second act.[6] Then in the autumn of 1835, or possibly earlier, he started to write his chief dramatic work, *The*

[6] Even if it had been completed, the play would most likely have been banned since the censorship, under Nicholas I, rarely countenanced the representation of any monarch on the stage.

Government Inspector, and completed the original version early in December. The play, when it appeared on the stage in the following April, achieved a *succès de scandale*, provoking great controversy among critics and theatre-goers. The playwright, deeply disturbed by the savage criticism and bitter hostility it met in some quarters, felt persecuted and misunderstood; he had reached a turning-point in his life and decided to leave Russia. In a letter to Pogodin he wrote: "I am going away to dispel my gloom, to think deeply about my responsibilities as an author and about my future works. . . . Everything that has befallen me has been salutary for me. All the insults and unpleasantness have been inflicted on me by lofty Providence for my education. And I feel now that it is no earthly will that guides me along my path." Once again, as in all the critical moments of his life, he saw the hand of God controlling his fate.

He left his native land and went to Western Europe, where he remained in voluntary exile for the next twelve years, returning only twice to spend the winters of 1839–40 and 1841–42 in Russia. During this period of European wanderings he suffered much of the time from financial hardship and ill-health. His greatest solace was travelling, which he deemed necessary for his creative work and once described as his 'only medicine'. He visited Germany, Switzerland, France and Italy, finding his spiritual home in Rome, which enchanted him with the beauty and grandeur of its historical monuments. He made the city his principal abode and usually spent his summers visiting various German watering-places in search of cures for his ailments.

Once abroad, Gogol turned his back on all his former works, which he regarded with shame and contempt. In a letter he wrote from Paris early in 1837 to his friend and old schoolfellow Nikolai Prokopovich, he dismissed them as 'scribblings' which he recalled with horror. "They appear before my eyes," he wrote, "like stern accusers. My soul craves oblivion, a long oblivion. If some moth were to appear and suddenly devour all the copies of *The Government Inspector*, together with *Arabesques*, *Evenings* and all the rest of the rubbish, and no one were to say or print a single word about me for a long time, I should thank fate for it." Like many creative artists, Gogol was a perfectionist who experienced a kind of post-parturient revulsion against the progeny of his own mind.

He now applied himself to the chief task of his life, the book with which he hoped to achieve lasting fame. This was his novel *Dead Souls*, which he had begun not long before leaving Russia. It was Pushkin who had urged him to undertake a major literary work and supplied him with the theme for this novel. The news that the great poet had been killed in a duel at the end of January 1837 was a crushing blow to him. Without Pushkin, who had been his mentor and guide, he felt lost. He expressed his feeling of desolation in a letter to Pogodin. "My life, my highest pleasure has died with him. The bright moments of my life have been moments of creation. When I created I saw only Pushkin before me ... I never undertook anything, I never wrote anything without his advice. Everything good that I have done I owe to him." The mantle of leadership in Russian literature had now passed from Pushkin to him, but it sat uneasily upon his shoulders.

Dead Souls, the fruit of more than six years' toil, was published in May 1842. In Russia it provoked even greater controversy than *The Government Inspector* had done and was received with a similar mixture of acclaim and vituperation. The critics of the left hailed it as a brilliant, fearless satire, while the right-wing journalists denounced it as a distorted picture of Russian life. In fact it presented a remarkable portrait gallery of provincial landowners: the sentimental hypocrite Manilov, the canny crone Korobochka, the cheating braggart Nozdrev, the coarse, crafty Sobakevich, and the miserly 'tatter of humanity' Plyushkin – all of them living mean and meaningless lives. The hero of this diffuse work is the smooth, acquisitive Chichikov who sets out to buy cheaply the 'dead souls' of various landowners, that is to say their male serfs who have died since the previous census and for whom they are still required to pay a poll-tax. By mortgaging the souls at the normal price Chichikov aims to build up a large estate for himself. The tale is told with ironic humour, punctuated with bold hyperbole, bizarre enumerations and involved comparisons, and it is interspersed with lyrical and didactic passages in which various symbolic themes are elaborated. It was Gogol's *magnum opus*, which earned him a place among the immortals in Russian literature.

Towards the end of 1842 a four-volume edition of his collected works was printed, including two previously unpublished comedies. The first of these was *Marriage*, which exposes the snobbery and sordid bargaining associated with match-making, and incidentally also reflects Gogol's deep fear of sexuality in women. The second was *The Gamblers*, a short, amusing piece in which a card-sharper is outwitted by a gang of professional confidence tricksters. In addition, the collection contained revised versions of *Taras Bulba* and *The Portrait*, the final text of *The Government Inspector*, and the most famous of his shorter works, *The Overcoat*, a poignant tale about a humble clerk who is robbed of his most prized possession, a new winter coat, which he has scrimped and saved for months to buy.

Gogol's life as a creative writer was now effectively finished. All the works which established his reputation as one of Russia's greatest writers were produced during the twelve years between the beginning of 1830 and the end of 1841. The last ten years of his life, darkened by a prolonged inner conflict, were barren of artistic achievement.

He continued to write, but regarded himself more and more as a preacher and prophet than as an artist. Absorbed in his own spiritual problems and subject to fits of depression, he became tormented by guilt feelings and preoccupied with the salvation of his soul. He was afflicted by deep misgivings about the moral effect of his writings and came to look upon them as 'sins' for which he must atone. His artistic gifts, which lay in an extraordinary capacity to satirize human folly and vulgarity, had been given free reign in the belief that ridicule would serve as a means of correction. But when the moral improvement he looked for failed to appear he was seized by doubts and concluded that he had sinned against his fellow-men by denigrating them. He now sought to expiate his sins as a writer by creating a lofty, positive work of literature which would, he believed, have a wholesome influence on morals. The resulting conflict between his moralizing urge and the nature of his artistic talents brought him to a creative impasse from which he was never to escape.

During the first years following his departure from Russia in June 1836 his outlook on life became increasingly dominated by religion. This change in him was almost certainly the result of a long and gradual inner process, not of a momentary revelation or sudden spiritual crisis, as some of his biographers believe, and its origins are to be found in his early upbringing. Many of his acquaintances noticed the change during these years. One of his friends, Ivan Zolotarev, who lived with him in Rome during 1837–8, observed that even then he was 'extremely religious'. He fell under the spell of the Eternal City and was undoubtedly influenced by some of the religious people he associated with there. In Rome, too, he was profoundly affected by witnessing death at close quarters when in May 1839 Joseph Vielgorsky, a gifted young nobleman to whom he had formed a brief but very strong attachment, literally expired in his arms after Gogol had spent many sleepless nights at his bedside. Before dying, Vielgorsky had presented him with a copy of the Bible, inscribed "To my friend Nikolai", which Gogol said was 'doubly sacred' to him.

More than once after this experience Gogol believed he was about to die. During the summer of 1840 he fell ill with a grave nervous complaint in Vienna. He had gone there to take the waters and felt so invigorated that he threw himself into a feverish bout of creative activity, as a consequence of which he overtaxed his frail body. At that time he was chiefly engaged in writing a historical drama about the Zaporozhian Cossacks, entitled *The Shaved Moustache*, which he hoped to finish in a few weeks. But his characters failed to come to life and his impotence drove him to despair, finally bringing about a nervous collapse in which he came near to the point of death. Even the doctors gave up all hope of his recovery, and he hastily made out a will. In fact he recovered quite soon after leaving Vienna, but less than a year later he had a nervous breakdown in Rome. He talked morbidly about death and was so afraid he was going to die that he frequently spent most of the night on a sofa in a friend's room.

When he visited Moscow in the autumn of 1841 Sergei Aksakov saw a great change in him. "He had grown thin and pale, and a gentle acquiescence in God's will could be heard in every word he uttered." By now he was convinced that he was an instrument of the Almighty, a sacred vessel which his friends should treat as something infinitely precious. A few months before his visit to Moscow he wrote to Aksakov: "A wonderful creation is forming and taking shape inside me, and my eyes are now quite often filled with tears of gratitude. The holy will of God is clearly apparent to me in this: such inspiration does not come from man; no man could ever invent such a theme!"

This 'wonderful creation' was to be a continuation of *Dead Souls*. Before he completed the first volume his conception of the work had already broadened into a monumental trilogy, a kind of prose counterpart to Dante's *Divine Comedy*. In the first part he had shown only the darker side of Russian life, the 'Inferno' of the soul. In the 'Purgatory' and 'Paradise' he intended to introduce 'colossal figures' and reveal the noble qualities of the Russian people. The second part would show the characters caught up in the conflict between good and evil, while the third would celebrate the triumph of righteousness and the redemption of his hero Chichikov. The volume already completed was, as he wrote to his old friend Alexander Danilevsky, 'a somewhat pale introduction to the great epic which is taking shape in my mind and which will finally solve the riddle of my existence'. By this he meant the fulfilment of his God-given mission to produce a great work that would bring about the moral regeneration of Russia and thereby enable her to achieve the high destiny which he believed history had assigned to her. This was the vastly ambitious goal he had set himself and it was to prove his tragic undoing both as an artist and as a man.

In order to accomplish his sacred task he concluded that he could not rely on his imaginative powers, but must acquire some of the virtuous qualities he wished to embody in the continuation of his novel. Just as he had imparted his own 'nastiness' and 'vices' to the negative characters in the first part, so he would imbue his positive characters with the goodness he now hoped to attain. Thus, wishing to purge himself of his faults and become a better man, he embarked on a lengthy course of introspection and spiritual education. The quest for personal perfection tormented him for the rest of his life. He withdrew more and more from society and spent much of his time reading religious works, especially the Gospels, the writings of the Church Fathers, and Thomas à Kempis's *Imitation of Christ*. As a means of purifying his soul he resorted to prayer, meditation, and finally to ascetic practices. In his letters he began to refer to himself as a pilgrim and a stranger on this earth. When writing to his relatives and friends he continually urged them to point out his faults and to pray for him. In return he gave them solemn advice and admonished them for their shortcomings in such an arrogant, sanctimonious tone that his relations with them became severely strained at times. Small wonder that Pogodin and his friend Shevyrev predicted he would end up in a monastery or a madhouse.

Gogol started writing the second part of *Dead Souls*, it is believed, towards the end of 1840, before the first volume was completed. For the next three years he was busy 'throwing chaos down on paper', as he put it in a letter to Zhukovsky. Then he spent a further two years trying to reduce this chaos to order. But progress was painfully slow and his creative powers forsook him for long periods. "Several times," he wrote later in his *Author's Confession*, "I sat down to write ... but could not produce anything. My efforts nearly always resulted in illness and suffering and finally in attacks which forced me to give up my work for a long time." He remained dissatisfied with what he had written and burnt much or all of it in 1843, and a second time he reduced it to ashes in the summer of 1845, after a grave illness. His health had been deteriorating for some months and broke down completely in Frankfurt, where he was again seized with the fear that he was dying and even sent for a priest to administer the last rites to him. But by the autumn he was well again and he saw his recovery as a miracle, interpreting it as a sign that God wished him to go on living in order to fulfil his mission of saving Russia.

Meanwhile, disabused of his belief that men's hearts could be changed by works of satire and unable to embody his ideals satisfactorily in the continuation of *Dead Souls*, he decided to reveal the truths he had discovered about life in a straightforward, didactic fashion. For several months in 1846 he worked intensively on this new book, comprising thirty-two articles, some based on letters addressed to various acquaintances, but most of them specially written for publication. The work, entitled *Selected Passages from Correspondence with Friends*, was published at the beginning of 1847, after the censor had expunged five articles entirely and deleted portions from some of the others. More than half the book was devoted to literary and artistic themes, which Gogol treated with considerable originality and critical acumen. In the remainder of the letters he expounded his political views and assumed the role of spiritual guide, preaching personal austerity, humility, and submission to the established powers, both temporal and ecclesiastical. He upheld the institutions of autocracy, Orthodoxy and serfdom, believing the existing social order to be sacrosanct. He justified the class system on the grounds that each man should serve his country in the station to which his Maker had called him. He opposed the education of the illiterate peasants and maintained that they should bow to the will of their masters, whose authority derived from God. The bribery and corruption so prevalent among officials were caused, he claimed, either by the extravagance of their wives or by the emptiness of their domestic lives.

In Gogol's view each person's actions should be directed to serving God, his country and his fellow-men. Russia, in her parlous spiritual condition, needed not judicial or administrative reforms, but a radical transformation brought about by each member of society striving to become a better person. His central vision was of a Russia truly united in the spirit of Christian love. The instrument of her salvation was to be the Orthodox Church, which was uniquely fitted to realize the brotherhood of man since it alone, he believed, had preserved Christ's teaching in all its pristine purity. Men strayed from the path of virtue through ignorance and pride, but they could be persuaded to turn from their sinful ways by personal example, moral precept and noble works of art. Convinced that his own literary works had failed to exert the moral influence he had intended, Gogol repudiated them and pronounced this new book to be his most important work, one which he hoped would bring about a spiritual regeneration of the Russian people.

Selected Passages created a sensation in the Russian literary world. It provoked an outburst of hostile press comment from liberal and radical intellectuals, and even some of Gogol's closest Slavophil friends were disgusted by the sententious, oracular manner in which he had pronounced his opinions and the sycophantic attitude he had shown to authority. The most passionate protest came from Belinsky in a letter he wrote as he was ailing desperately with consumption in Salzbrunn. The distinguished critic, a dedicated Westernizer, rounded on Gogol with a torrent of abuse, calling him a 'preacher of the knout, apostle of ignorance, champion of obscurantism, panegyrist of Tatar morals'. He castigated Russian officialdom as 'huge syndicates of sundry bureaucratic thieves and robbers', and accused Gogol of perverting Christ's message by advocating a state based on fear and repression. What Russia needed, he said, was the abolition of serfdom, the spread of enlightenment, and respect for human dignity. His anger sprang from the wounded feeling of being personally betrayed by the great writer whose work he had exalted for so long and who had now forsworn his earlier progressive ideals. He was seriously mistaken, however, for in fact Gogol had never shared his political and social outlook. Belinsky believed in institutional reforms as a means of achieving social justice, whereas Gogol, always a supporter of the established secular order, had arrived at a theocratic view of society and sought to convert his fellow-Russians to a practical expression of Christian ideals in everyday life.

Belinsky's famous letter, which was widely circulated in manuscript copies and soon became a manifesto of the liberal intelligentsia, came as a profound shock to Gogol. He realized that his attempt to convert and improve others by preaching to them had been a disastrous mistake. While refusing to recant, he admitted that he had struck the wrong note and conceded that there was some truth in Belinsky's strictures, in particular that he had lost touch with his own country after leaving it. He decided to return to Russia, but before doing so he made a long-delayed pilgrimage to Jerusalem in search of spiritual succour. Unfortunately, in the Church of the Holy Sepulchre his heart remained cold and his soul failed to soar aloft. This experience only increased his morbid fears and strengthened his growing belief that he was irrevocably damned to eternal perdition.

His last years were spent mainly in Moscow, where he lived on the hospitality of his friends. He renounced all attempts at moralizing. "It is not my job to teach people by preaching," he wrote to Zhukovsky. "Art teaches men without that. My task is to speak through *living images*, not with arguments." He resumed his labours on the second volume of *Dead Souls*, which now assumed an even greater importance in his eyes, but his work progressed with agonizing slowness. His health was undermined with frequent fasting and he was often silent and withdrawn. His spiritual travail was aggravated by a fanatical priest, Matvei Konstantinovsky, who urged him to even greater asceticism and increased his fear of everlasting torment in hellfire. Konstantinovsky exhorted him to abandon literature as the work of the devil. Gogol held out for a time, but finally succumbed to the desire to placate the Supreme Judge. Having lost the will to live, he took almost no nourishment and resisted the ministrations of his doctors. One night, shortly before his death, he burnt some of his manuscripts, including all the second part of *Dead Souls* that he had written since 1845. After a fortnight of almost total abstinence from food, exhausted in body and spirit, he died on 21 February 1852.

Productions, reviews and revisions

The theme of the stranger mistaken for an investigating official, on which the plot of *The Government Inspector* is based, was by no means fanciful or far-fetched, given the conditions prevailing in the empire of Nicholas I. Contemporary records mention several authentic cases of visitors to the Russian provinces being taken for inspectors from the capital and received with great deference by the local officials, who had good reason to fear the long arm of the authorities in St. Petersburg. Nor was the theme a new one in literature. The German dramatist August von Kotzebue, whose plays were very popular in Russia, where he lived for several years, treated the subject of the impostor in his satirical comedy *Die deutschen Kleinstädter* (1803), and the same theme was used, although without any satirical purpose, in A. F. Veltman's tale *The Provincial Actors* (1835). But the closest parallel to Gogol's plot is to be found in a didactic comedy, *The Visitor from the Capital*, by the Ukrainian writer Grigory Kvitka, who used the pen-name of Osnoviyanenko. This play, although not published until 1840, was written in 1827 and its plot is so strikingly similar to that of *The Government Inspector* in certain details that it seems reasonable to assume that Gogol at least knew of it and may even have read it in manuscript. However, none of these works is mentioned by Gogol as a source of inspiration and whatever thematic elements they have in common with his play, they are artistically almost as far removed from it as Holinshed's *Chronicles* are from Shakespeare's historical dramas.

In his *Author's Confession*, written in 1847, Gogol states that he was indebted to Pushkin for his plot, and this is corroborated by several of his contemporaries, including the critic and literary historian Pavel Annenkov. Count Vladimir Sollogub, a writer who knew Gogol for many years, states in his memoirs that the plot of *The Government Inspector* was based on two incidents recounted by Pushkin, who is said to have called himself the 'godfather' of the play. The first anecdote concerned a gentleman who visited the town of Ustyuzhna in Novgorod province, where he passed himself off as a ministry official and fleeced the local inhabitants. The second incident involved Pushkin himself, when he was visiting Orenburg province in the summer of 1833 to collect material for his *History of the Pugachev Rebellion*. At Nizhny Novgorod he dined with the governor of the province, M. P. Buturlin, who received him most courteously but found some of his enquiries rather disquieting. From there Pushkin went to the fortress town of Orenburg, where he stayed with the military governor, V. A. Perovsky, an old friend of his. One morning a letter from Buturlin arrived, warning the count to be on his guard with Pushkin, whom the writer suspected of being an inspector in disguise. Perovsky roared with laughter on reading the letter and showed it to the poet, who was quick to share his amusement.[7]

A quite different story is given by O. M. Bodyansky, Professor of Slavonic Studies at Moscow University, who was a friend of Gogol for many years. In his diary Bodyansky states that Gogol told him, during an evening at the Aksakovs in the autumn of 1851, that Pushkin supplied the original idea for the play. The poet had recounted how in the 1820s Pavel Svinyin, a prominent journalist, posed in Bessarabia as an important official from St. Petersburg and even began to accept petitions from prisoners before he was exposed as an impostor. Gogol added that he had heard subsequently of several similar escapades, one of them involving a man named Volkov.[8]

Apparently Pushkin himself intended at one time to write a tale or play on the theme of mistaken identity. The brief outline of his plot, written on paper bearing the watermark 1832, came to light only three-quarters of a century after his death. It reads as follows: "(Svinyin: *deleted*) Crispin arrives in the Province (NB for the fair) – he is taken for an Ambas[sador]. The Govern[or] is a worthy fool – the Gov[ernor's wife] flirts with him – Crispin asks for the daughter's hand."[9] Pushkin may well have decided that the theme was better suited to Gogol's talents than his own and gratuitously presented it to him. It is possible, however, that Gogol simply appropriated the theme from Pushkin, judging from a remark the latter is reported to have made in reference to *The Government Inspector* and *Dead Souls*. According to Annenkov, Pushkin did not give Gogol these subjects entirely of his own free will and laughingly observed to some of his intimates: "One has to be very wary with this Ukrainian; he robs me before I have time to shout for help."

It is not known which of the several anecdotes Gogol used for his play, nor is it possible to say exactly when he heard them from Pushkin, although clearly it must have been some time during the period 1833–35. In most modern editions of Gogol's work it is stated that *The Government Inspector* was written following a request made in a letter to Pushkin which Gogol wrote from St. Petersburg on 7 October 1835. "Do me a favour," he asked,

[7] V. A. Sollogub, 'Из воспоминаний', *Русский архив*, 1865, p. 744.

[8] O. M. Bodyansky, 'Дневник', *Русская старина*, Oct. 1889, No. 10, p. 134. It has been discovered from local archives that a retired second lieutenant, Platon Volkov, was the person who masqueraded as an inspector in Ustyuzhna. Gogol probably heard of this incident when he worked as a tutor in the house of General P. I. Balabin, who had received confidential information about Volkov's activities. See V. Panov, 'Ещё о прототипе Хлестакова ...', *Север*, 1970, No. 11, pp. 125–7.

[9] A. S. Pushkin, *Полное собрание сочинений*, Moscow & Leningrad, 1937–49, Vol. 8, Book 1, p. 431.

"give me some plot, it doesn't matter whether it is amusing or not, so long as it is a purely Russian anecdote. Meanwhile my hand is trembling to write a comedy . . . Do please give me a plot; I'll produce a five-act comedy in one burst and I swear it will be funnier than the devil!" No reply to this letter exists, and since Pushkin did not return from his country estate to St. Petersburg until 23 October he could not have answered Gogol's request verbally much before the end of that month. And we know, from a letter Gogol wrote to Pogodin, that the play was finished on 4 December. "I have been so preoccupied all this time," he wrote two days later, "that I only just managed to finish the play the day before yesterday."

From the evidence of these two letters it is generally assumed that the play, at least in its original version, was written between the end of October and 4 December 1835, that is in just over a month. There are grounds for suspecting, however, that Gogol may have begun to write the play before October 1835, as his earlier biographers believed. One of them, V. I. Shenrok, reports a story told to him in 1884 by Alexander Danilevsky, who was then seventy-five. The old man recalled that when they were once travelling from Kiev to Moscow with Ivan Pashchenko, another old schoolfellow, Gogol staged a real-life rehearsal of *The Government Inspector*, 'on which he was then working intensively'. He sent Pashchenko ahead to announce at all the post-stations that an inspector was on his way, travelling incognito. The stratagem worked perfectly. Gogol, whose travel document showed him to be an associate professor (адъюнкт-профессор), was taken by most of the postmasters to be someone scarcely less exalted than an aide-de-camp (адъютант) to the Tsar. He asked various seemingly innocent questions and was treated with exceptional courtesy, being given fresh horses without delay. The journey proceeded very smoothly, a most unusual thing in Russia at that time.[10]

If Danilevsky's story was true, this incident could only have occurred in August 1835 while Gogol was still a university professor and when, as we know from other sources, he did in fact travel from Kiev to Moscow. This conflicting evidence makes it impossible to determine exactly when Gogol began his play, but the first draft cannot have been started much before the beginning of 1835, since it contains a reference to Meyerbeer's opera *Robert le Diable*, which was first performed in St. Petersburg in December 1834.

Soon after *The Government Inspector* was completed Gogol tried it out on a private audience, as he did with many of his writings. On 18 January 1836 he read the play before a literary gathering at Zhukovsky's home and it was

[10] V. I. Shenrok, *Материалы для биографии Гоголя*, Moscow, 1892–7, Vol. 1, p. 364.

acclaimed with enthusiasm, especially by Pushkin, who laughed uproariously. Only one person failed to share the general amusement, namely Baron Yegor Rozen, a prolific but mediocre writer who thought himself a great dramatist and regarded Gogol as a mere caricaturist. Prince P. Vyazemsky, an eminent poet and critic who was present at the reading, doubted whether the play would be as successful on the stage since few actors would be able to match Gogol's masterly solo performance of his own work.

Contemporary accounts vary as to how the play reached the stage, but Gogol was certainly fortunate in having influential friends to help him in the difficult task of obtaining approval from the censors. Only a few years earlier, in 1828, a new system of censorship had been introduced, whereby playwrights were required to submit their works to the ordinary censor for publication and to the Third Section for permission to have them performed. Whether Gogol submitted his play to the censors immediately is not certain. A. I. Wolf, a theatre historian, states that Gogol sent the text of his play to the ordinary censors, who were so alarmed at its contents that they flatly refused to pass it for publication.[11] As there is no contemporary evidence to support this, however, it is quite possible that Gogol tried to circumvent the censorship in the first instance. At all events he decided to appeal through his friends to the supreme censor, the Tsar himself.

According to Wolf's account Zhukovsky, supported by Vyazemsky and a wealthy courtier, Count Mikhail Vielgorsky, interceded on Gogol's behalf and succeeded in obtaining royal patronage for the play. A different and generally discredited account of all this is given by Alexandra Smirnova, a celebrated court beauty, who states in her memoirs that Gogol read his play at one of her soirees and that Pushkin asked her to use her influence with the Tsar to secure its approval for performance on the stage.[12] Whether the Tsar read the play in manuscript, as Vyazemsky states, or whether it was read aloud to him at court, as Wolf maintains, in either case it found favour with the Emperor, who authorized its public performance. On 27 February a copy of the manuscript reached the censor of the Third Section, E. Oldekop, who deemed it suitable for the stage. In his lengthy report, written in French, Oldekop described the play as witty and excellently written, and after summarizing its plot he pronounced that it contained nothing objectionable. The only important change he made was to exclude the N.C.O.'s wife from the second petitioning scene in Act IV, although, curiously enough, two of the Governor's allusions to her flogging were left uncensored. A number of

[11] A. I. Wolf, *Хроника петербургских театров*, St. Petersburg, 1877, Part I, p. 49.

[12] A. O. Smirnova, *Автобиография*, Moscow, 1931, p. 331.

minor textual alterations and deletions were made on moral or religious grounds. Thus, in Act V Khlestakov was not allowed to boast, in his letter to Tryapichkin, that he intended to cuckold the Governor, and the latter's revelation that he had lied to a priest at confession was suppressed. A few invocations to God and the saints of the church were allowed to stand, but many were modified or removed so as not to offend pious feelings. For example, the interjection ей-богу ('I swear to God') was frequently toned down to ей-ей ('I swear') or deleted altogether. Similarly, the Governor's ejaculation Батюшки, сватушки! Выносите, святые угодники! ('Holy fathers! Saints of heaven preserve us!') was replaced by the feebler Ай-ай-ай! ('Oh dear! Oh dear!').[13]

Acting on Oldekop's report General Dubbelt, a senior official in the Third Section, granted permission on 2 March for the play to be performed. Soon after this, on 13 March, the play, with substantially the same changes, was approved for publication by the censor A. V. Nikitenko. Meanwhile, with the Tsar's prior assent, rehearsals had already begun towards the end of February at the Alexandrinsky Theatre, the finest playhouse in St. Petersburg.[14] The production was under the general supervision of Alexander Khrapovitsky, a bureaucrat quite devoid of any artistic sense. The author, following a common theatrical practice of the time, took an active part in the rehearsals, acting as co-producer. Gogol, who made alterations in the stage text until a few days before the play opened, was present in the theatre giving advice on decor, costume and the interpretation of roles, most of which went unheeded. Special sets were designed, something most unusual for a new production in those days. But Gogol insisted that the opulent furnishings provided for the opening scene should be replaced by something more modest. He also made the actor playing Osip change from livery resplendent with gold braid into a grimy old frock-coat.

The management refused Gogol's request for a dress rehearsal on the grounds that it was not customary and in any case was quite unnecessary, since the actors knew their job. Unfortunately, however, most of the actors, trained to perform highly stylized plays far removed from real life, were puzzled by this new kind of comedy. It conformed neither to the canons of neo-classical comedy nor to the type of vaudeville which dominated the Russian stage at that time. Petr Karatygin, a prolific vaudevillist and a

[13] See N. V. Drizen, *Драматическая цензура двух эпох, 1825–1881*, Petrograd, 1917, pp. 41–3.

[14] The theatre, designed by the architect Carlo Rossi and named after the Emperor's consort Alexandra, was opened in 1832. It is now called the Pushkin State Academic Theatre (Государственный академический театр им. Пушкина).

member of the company, tells us that when Gogol first read his play to the actors they did not know what to make of it. "'What is this?' his listeners whispered to each other after the reading had finished. 'Is it supposed to be a comedy? He certainly reads well, but what language he uses! The manservant actually speaks like a servant and the locksmith's wife Poshlepkina is nothing but a common peasant woman taken straight from Haymarket Square. . . .[15] What do Zhukovsky and Pushkin see in it?'"

Karatygin has left us a vivid description of Gogol at the final rehearsal. Some of the younger actors were evidently less amused by the play than by its author, who cut a strange, comical figure. "Gogol was greatly agitated and obviously upset . . . He was a short man with fair hair piled up enormously at the front, gold-rimmed spectacles perched on his long, beaky nose, screwed-up little eyes and tightly pursed lips . . . His green coat with long tails and tiny pearl buttons, his brown trousers and the tall top-hat which Gogol would now doff with a jerk, running his fingers through his topknot, then twirl around in his hands – all this made him look something of a caricature."[16]

At the first performance of the play, given on 19 April 1836, the auditorium of the Alexandrinsky Theatre was packed with a glittering assembly. The stalls were occupied by nobles, men of letters and several ministers of state, while the gallery was filled with lesser mortals – junior officials, shopkeepers, students and others. Just before the curtain rose the Tsar appeared in the royal box, accompanied by the Crown Prince. Nicholas seems to have thoroughly enjoyed the spectacle. He laughed heartily and applauded several times during the performance, and his obedient ministers followed suit. On leaving his box he is said to have remarked to those near him: "That was quite a play! Everyone has taken a knocking, myself most of all!"[17] Nicholas, who had an open contempt for the whole of his vast bureaucracy and was well aware of the bribery and corruption that permeated it, was no doubt well pleased to see dishonest officials publicly pilloried. But he evidently did not foresee the social and political impact the play would make on educated audiences, otherwise he would certainly have banned it. In fact he commanded the rest of the royal family and his other ministers to go and see it, and made presents of money to three of the actors. Gogol himself was given 800 roubles as a mark of appreciation for presenting the Tsar with a copy of the play. He received a further 2,500 roubles from the director of the St. Petersburg theatres for the performing rights.

[15] Сенная площадь, at that time the haymarket of St. Petersburg.

[16] *Исторический вестник*, Sept. 1883, p. 735. Curiously enough, no topknot appears in Karatygin's portrait of Gogol, sketched at the same time.

[17] Many scholars treat this remark as apocryphal.

The most reliable and substantial account of the premiere is that given by Pavel Annenkov in his memoirs. "Even after the first act everyone was looking puzzled (it was a select audience in the full sense of the word), as if no one knew what to make of what he had just seen. After this the bewilderment increased with each act. Most of the spectators, unaccustomed to expect this sort of thing in the theatre, were thrown off balance by it and seemed to take comfort in assuming that they were watching a farce, an opinion they clung to with unshakeable determination. Yet there were some features and scenes in this farce which rang so true that once or twice there was a burst of general laughter, especially in the parts that were least at variance with the conception of a comedy held by most of the spectators. Things took a different turn in the fourth act: laughter still echoed across the auditorium from time to time, but it was a rather timid laughter that died away in an instant. There was hardly any applause at all, but the rapt attention, the intense concentration with which the audience followed every subtlety of the action, and the dead silence that occasionally reigned, showed that they were passionately gripped by what was happening on the stage. By the end of the act the earlier bewilderment had turned into an almost unanimous feeling of indignation, which was brought to a climax by the fifth act. Many people called for the author at the end because he had written a real comedy, others because some of the scenes showed talent, and the ordinary spectators because the play had made them laugh. But the general opinion expressed on all sides amongst this select audience could be summed up in the words: 'This is impossible, it's a slander and a farce'."[18]

Gogol, who shared a box with Zhukovsky, Vyazemsky and Vielgorsky, had arrived in the theatre with a deep sense of foreboding and he suffered agonies throughout the evening. He expressed his feelings on this occasion in 'a letter to a certain writer'. "*The Government Inspector* has been played," he wrote, "and I feel so down at heart,[19] so strange . . . I knew before it started how things would go, yet for all that a sad and disagreeable feeling of oppression overcame me. My own work seemed repugnant and outlandish to me, as if it were not mine at all . . . From the very beginning of the performance I sat in the theatre feeling downcast. I was not worried about the audience's reaction or whether it would be enthusiastic. Of all those present in the house there was only one judge I feared, – and that was myself. Inwardly I could hear reproaches and grumbles about my play which

[18] P. V. Annenkov, *Воспоминания и критические очерки*, Vol. I, St. Petersburg, 1877, p. 193.

[19] Gogol wrote 'у меня на душе так смутно', using the word 'смутный', as he often did in his earlier writings, in its Ukrainian sense of 'sad'.

drowned out everything else. However, the audience was pleased on the whole. Half of them even gave the play a sympathetic reception; the other half, as is usual, abused it, but for reasons which have nothing to do with art."[20]

The author was well pleased with Sosnitsky, who acted the part of the Governor, and with Afanasiev, who played Osip, but found the rest of the players woefully inadequate. The celebrated vaudeville actor Dyur (Dure) had utterly failed to grasp the character of Khlestakov, whom he portrayed as a typical stage villain and calculating trickster, quite contrary to the sense of the text, which clearly shows that the hero does not set out deliberately to dupe or cheat the town officials. Gogol was also dissatisfied with most of the costumes, and simply gasped with horror at the ridiculous garb in which Bobchinsky and Dobchinsky were attired. These pot-bellied squires, who should be neat and well groomed, appeared untidy and dishevelled in very tall grey wigs, with enormous shirt-fronts sticking out of their breeches. Finally, the dumb scene at the end of the play was badly mismanaged. The curtain was rung down at the wrong moment, so that the play seemed to be left hanging in mid-air. Gogol blamed the theatre people for this failure, complaining bitterly that they would not listen to him. This scene, to which he attached great importance, could only succeed, he said, if it was presented as a *tableau vivant* in which each of the actors adopts a pose that reflects an individual reaction appropriate to the character he is portraying.

At the end of the performance Gogol left the theatre immediately, without taking a bow. He went to call on Pletnev, who was not at home, and then visited Nikolai Prokopovich, arriving at his house in an irritable mood. His host handed him a copy of the play, which had appeared in print that same day, with the words: "Take an admiring look at your little son." Gogol flung the book on the floor, went over to the table and leaning on it, said pensively:

[20] *An Extract from a letter written by the author to a certain writer shortly after the performance of "The Government Inspector"* was first published in *Москвитянин* in 1841. Writing to Sergei Aksakov from Rome in the same year, Gogol stated that this was part of a letter he wrote on 25 May 1836 to Pushkin, who had missed the premiere, being out of the capital (he had gone to bury his mother near the family estate of Mikhailovskoye, but was back in St. Petersburg, probably unknown to Gogol, between 24–29 April, when he left for Moscow). The letter was not dispatched at the time, Gogol explained, because the poet had returned to St. Petersburg shortly afterwards (he returned from Moscow on the night of 23 May). Some scholars, following Tikhonravov, claim that the bulk of this extract was written early in 1841, and hence not addressed to Pushkin. On balance it seems more likely that Gogol wrote the letter in 1836 and merely polished it up in 1841 for publication. See A. G. Gukasova, 'Отрывок из письма, писанного автором вскоре после первого представления «Ревизора» к одному литератору', *Известия АН СССР, отделение литературы и языка*, 1957, Vol. 16, No. 4, pp. 335–45.

"Lord! If just one or two people had abused it I wouldn't have cared, but everyone, everyone . . ."

Despite the fact that *The Government Inspector* was played in the style of a vaudeville, it made a great impact on the audiences and caused a great stir in the capital. Every performance was booked out in advance and the play provoked lively and sometimes heated controversy. In this sense it was a success. In Gogol's eyes, however, it was a failure, indeed a twofold disaster, because the actors, or most of them, had presented a complete travesty of his artistic intentions, and because his moral purpose had not been understood at all. The reception of the play by public and critics alike was a mixture of violent obloquy and enthusiastic praise. Some, like the popular playwright Kukolnik and the finance minister Kankrin, dismissed it as a cheap farce unworthy of serious consideration. At the same time many people saw in this 'farce', as it was then generally taken to be, an implicit denunciation of the whole social and political system of their country. Liberals and progressives applauded Gogol's exposure of the vices of provincial officialdom as a bold, albeit indirect attack on those in power at the top. On the other hand, the conservatives and most of those in high official positions regarded it as an impudent, outrageous calumny against Russia and her government, a calculated attempt at subversion. This attitude was epitomized by Khrapovitsky in his diary entry on the evening of the premiere. "The play is extremely amusing," he noted, "only there is intolerable abuse of the gentry, officials and merchants." In short, few people saw in the play what Gogol had intended, namely a moral satire aimed at exposing and correcting the abuses practised by all but a mere handful of Russian officials.

The play was a great success with the majority of ordinary theatre-goers in St. Petersburg, and especially with the younger generation, but most of the members of high society were displeased or even scandalized by what they regarded as its vulgar tone and its subversive tenor. Writing to his friend Alexander Turgenev on 8 May, Prince Vyazemsky said: "Everyone tries to be more of a monarchist than the Tsar, and they are all angry that permission was given to perform this play which was, nevertheless, a brilliant and total success on the stage, though not in the sense of winning universal approval. It is incredible what stupid opinions you hear about it, especially in the higher circles of society! 'As if such a town existed in Russia.' 'How is it possible not to present on the stage a single honest, decent man? Are we to believe there are no such people in Russia?'" Typical of this kind of reaction was an indignant outburst by a prominent official, F. F. Vigel, who, before he had even seen or read the play, described it in a letter to the playwright Mikhail Zagoskin as a slander in five acts. "The author," he wrote, "has created a fictitious Russia and a particular small town in which he has dumped all the loathsome things you occasionally find on the surface of the real Russia: what a heap of knavery, baseness and ignorance he has piled up ... I know this gentleman who is the author of *The Government Inspector* – he typifies young Russia with all its impudence and cynicism."[21]

A similar attitude no doubt lay behind the refusal by members of the Academy of Sciences to award Gogol a gold medal for his play. The proposal to confer this distinction on him was made by Pavel Demidov, a wealthy manufacturer and patron of the arts who donated 25,000 roubles each year to be distributed in prizes by a special committee of the Academy. Demidov warmly commended Gogol to the committee for having graced Russian literature with a new work which 'may be regarded as a model of its kind in the depiction of characters'. At a plenary meeting of academicians held on 13 May the proposal was rejected on the grounds that the rules of the competition specifically excluded literary works. And when Demidov later asked that the clause in question should be deleted, his request was refused.[22]

The reviewers in the St. Petersburg press for the most part treated Gogol's play as a farce, at best amusing and at worst positively harmful. Petr Serebreny, writing in the literary supplement to *The Russian Invalid*,[23] described it as an innocent, light-hearted piece which would 'cure many a sorrow and banish many a depression'. Its harshest critics were Faddei Bulgarin and Osip Senkovsky, both of them zealous apologists for the government and dedicated literary enemies of Gogol. Bulgarin, in a long article which he published in two consecutive issues of his newspaper *The Northern Bee*,[24] said that Gogol was undoubtedly a talented writer and his play was vastly amusing, but it was no comedy, for a real comedy, he dogmatically asserted, could not be based on administrative malpractices. The play was no more than a hilarious farce on a hackneyed theme, with a plot that was both trivial and highly improbable. In his view Osip, Bobchinsky and Dobchinsky were masterly, life-like portrayals of character, but the rest of the *dramatis personae* seemed to him ludicrous caricatures lacking all human attributes except the gift of speech, which they employed to indulge in idle chatter. In no small town, and rarely even in large cities, would

[21] *Русская старина*, 1902, No. 7, pp. 100–1. The term 'young Russia' refers to the young writers of the time, especially those who contributed to Pushkin's journal *The Contemporary*. It was doubtless suggested by the names 'Jeune France' and 'Junges Deutschland', used to describe French and German literary movements in the 1830s.

[22] See E. S. Kulyabko, 'Из архива АН СССР. Несостоявшееся премирование Гоголя', *Русская литература*, 1967, No. 4, pp. 170–3.

[23] *Литературные прибавления к Русскому инвалиду*, 1836, No. 59–60, pp. 475–80.

[24] *Северная пчела*, 1836, No. 97, pp. 385–8 and No. 98, pp. 389–92.

one find such flirts as Anna Andreyevna and her daughter – such coquetry was quite un-Russian. His moral sensibilities were offended by the spectacle of the two women treating Khlestakov as fair game and shamelessly squabbling about which of them he preferred. Such behaviour, commented the critic acidly, was just like that displayed by the savages of the Sandwich Islands when Captain Cook landed there.[25]

Bulgarin complained that the play provided no contrast between good and evil, but presented only rogues and fools. Moreover, the characters and customs shown in it bore no resemblance to anything in contemporary Russia but belonged to an age long past. "It would be a great pity," he remarked, "if any of the spectators, unfamiliar with our provinces, thought that such morals and manners *really* existed in Russia or that there could be a town without a single honest soul in it . . ." Gogol's intention had been to describe a Russian district town, but in fact he had depicted a small town in the Ukraine or Belorussia. Finally, Bulgarin asserted that the play was larded with crudities of language such as he had never known on the Russian stage or in literature and said it was unforgivable of Gogol to resort to the kind of coarse double entendres found in *The Government Inspector*. Bulgarin's general verdict on the play was that it made an unpleasant impression, for it offered 'no food for the mind or heart, neither ideas nor feelings'. In short, he considered that Gogol's comedy was devoid of social significance or artistic distinction and failed to reflect contemporary Russian reality.

Senkovsky, in his *Library for Reading*, published an unsigned review which contained substantially the same criticisms of the play as had been made by Bulgarin.[26] The reviewer approached the comedy somewhat differently, however, adopting an ostensibly sympathetic tone and showing himself eager to give helpful advice to the budding young dramatist. He acknowledged Gogol's exceptional comic gifts and commended several scenes in the play, quoting some of them at length, but warned its author to be on his guard against the excessive praise bestowed on him by some of his admirers. *The*

[25] V. I. Shenrok, in his *Материалы для биографии Гоголя*, Moscow, 1892–7, Vol. 3, p. 483, incorrectly interprets Bulgarin's remark as applying to the whole play. N. A. Kotlyarevsky, in his *Н. В. Гоголь*, Petersburg, 1908, p. 330, and E. L. Voitolovskaya, in her *Комментарий*, 1971, p. 44, repeat the same error.

[26] *Библиотека для чтения*, May 1836, Vol. 16, No. 5, pp. 1–44. The review was long considered to be Senkovsky's own, but his authorship has been questioned by two scholars. L. Ya. Ginzburg ascribes it to the critic Nikolai Polevoi (*Очерки по истории русской журналистики и критики*, Leningrad University, 1950, Vol. 1, p. 334); A. S. Dolinin suggests it was written by Vasily Ushakov, a close friend of Polevoi (*Ученые записки Ленинградского пед. института, факультет литературы и языка*, Vol. 18, 1956, No. 5, p. 55). Both scholars agree, however, that Senkovsky edited the article to suit his own purposes.

Government Inspector, albeit highly amusing, was a sordid drama which at times plumbed greater depths of vulgarity than the crudest of farces. Respect for his readers, the critic added, prevented him from quoting any of the offending passages. Though it showed promise for the future, the play had no literary merit and was devoid of any idea or message. It had no plot, he complained, meaning by this that it lacked the love interest which was an essential ingredient in traditional comedy, and he suggested that Gogol should remedy this defect by introducing a rival to Maria for Khlestakov's affections. Nor had the play any real characters, he observed, for the *dramatis personae* had been made to fit the requirements of the story. It was peopled throughout with scoundrels and fools whose actions were not inspired by human passions. Furthermore, the bad characters were not counterbalanced by any good ones, which was wholly at variance with what one found in real life.

Gogol's play, the reviewer claimed, was merely a dramatized version of a trite foreign anecdote told many times before in various languages, whereas a true comedy should treat the mores of a particular society (for him the word comedy was evidently synonymous with comedy of manners). "Abuses cannot be the subject of a comedy," he wrote, "for they are not the morals of the people, nor are they characteristic of society as a whole but the crimes of a few individuals, and they should evoke in honest citizens indignation rather than laughter." His patriotic sentiments were outraged by the way in which the play, while describing a local incident, purported to give a typical picture of the whole country. After admitting that corrupt practices existed among officials in remote provincial places, the critic concluded with the patently absurd objection that there was no reason to attribute them solely to Russia by transferring this international story to a Russian setting.

Two months later, after Gogol had left Russia, Vyazemsky refuted these criticisms point by point in a long article, which appeared in Pushkin's journal *The Contemporary*.[27] The play, in Vyazemsky's view, was a worthy successor to the satirical comedies of Fonvizin, Kapnist and Griboyedov. He defended the author's right to choose any subject he wished, however sordid or distasteful it might be, and pointed out that the language of the play, though vulgar and shocking at times to some ears, was entirely appropriate to the characters it presented. It was not a farce, he said, although there was an element of caricature in the portrayal. Its plot was perfectly credible, for similar cases of mistaken identity had been known to occur in actuality. The Governor's error concerning Khlestakov's identity, which Bulgarin had

[27] *Современник*, July 1836, Vol. 2, pp. 285–309.

found a totally inconceivable blunder on his part, was quite understandable if one remembered the popular saying that 'fear has big eyes'.[28] The Governor and his fellow-officials learn of Khlestakov's arrival when they are in a state of panic. In this situation their mistake is entirely plausible.

Gogol's detractors had alleged that his play was immoral because it presented no virtuous characters and thus left out the better side of human nature. Vyazemsky objected that a work of literature could only be called immoral if it tended to corrupt people. But Gogol had merely presented immoral behaviour in a detached manner and shown only a part of life, not the whole of it. The comedy could not be said to slander Russia, for such people as those in the play existed in real life. All that Gogol had done was to assemble them in one imaginary place, using the artistic method of selection, in order to produce a typical, generalized picture. He was not in any way implying that there were no good people in Russia. In any case, the immorality of Gogol's characters should not be exaggerated, since they were 'more ridiculous than villainous' and displayed 'more ignorance and lack of education than depravity'. Nor was the plot of the play based on any criminal act or perversion of justice. "It is said that there is not a single intelligent person in Gogol's comedy," he concluded. "This is not true – the author is intelligent. It is said that there is not a single honest and right-thinking person in Gogol's comedy. This is untrue: the honest and right-thinking person is the government which, while striking at abuses with all the force of the law, allows a writer of talent to correct them by using the weapon of ridicule." For Vyazemsky, as for Gogol, *The Government Inspector* embodied not a political protest, but a moral indictment.

Gogol was not only distressed by the way his play was burlesqued on the stage, but also deeply perturbed by the public reaction to it. What alarmed him most was the political interpretation put on it – something he had not expected at all. He had hoped it would evoke a positive response and exert a beneficial influence on morals. Instead it had stirred up a violent controversy and brought down a storm of abuse from high officials and influential conservatives who considered it to be an attack on the whole system. He was equally embarrassed by the praise showered on it by liberals and progressives. He realized that he had badly miscalculated the effect his play would have and his correspondence at this time reflects his bitterness and disillusionment.[29]

[28] The complete saying runs: 'Fear has big eyes, but they see nothing' (У страха глаза велики, да ничего не видят).

[29] D. Magarshack, in his *Gogol: A Life*, 1957, p. 148, writes that Gogol 'was fortified by the storm his play had raised' and 'his faith in the moral influence of art now seemed to have been

In two letters to Pogodin he complained, more in sorrow than in anger, about the way *The Government Inspector* had been so widely misinterpreted. On 10 May he wrote: "I am not disturbed by the fact that positively every single class of society is now up in arms against me, but it is somehow distressing and sad to see your own countrymen, whom you love with all your heart, unjustly turned against you, to see how they pervert and misconstrue everything, taking the particular for the general and the exception for the rule. What is spoken truthfully and vividly actually seems to them a lampoon. Put two or three scoundrels on the stage and a thousand honest people say angrily: 'We are not scoundrels' . . . It is time that I wrote with greater deliberation," he concluded, clearly referring to the unfortunate misunderstandings his play had caused.

Five days later he took up the same theme again. "It makes you sad," he wrote, "to see what a sorry plight the writer still finds himself in here in our country. Everyone is against him, and there is no countervailing force at all on his side. 'He's an incendiary! He's a rebel!' And who says so? Men in high offices of state, men who have risen in the service, men of experience who should have sufficient intelligence to understand the true position, people who are considered to be educated and whom society, at least Russian society, calls educated – they are the ones who say this. Scoundrels appear on the stage and everyone is furious, demanding to know why they should appear. I don't mind scoundrels getting angry, but people I never took to be scoundrels are angry. I am saddened by this ignorant petulance, a sign of the profound, stubborn ignorance that pervades all classes of our society . . . Something that enlightened people would receive with loud laughter and sympathy provokes a splenetic outburst of ignorance, and this ignorance is found in everyone. If you call a crook a crook they consider you are undermining the foundations of the state; if you say something that is merely true to life it is interpreted as defaming a whole class of society and inciting its subordinates or others to turn against it."

Meanwhile preparations were in hand to present *The Government Inspector* in Moscow, but Gogol, who had originally intended to go there and help with the production, now changed his mind. He was so shaken and disheartened by the reception given to his play in St. Petersburg that he firmly resisted all efforts to persuade him to go to Moscow. On 29 April he sent a letter and several copies of the play to his friend Shchepkin, the distinguished actor who was to play a leading role in the Moscow production. In this letter

confirmed'. The opposite is the case; Gogol's faith in the moral power of art was badly shaken by the way his play was received.

he again voiced his strong feelings, which amounted almost to persecution mania. He persisted in believing, quite erroneously, that *everyone* was against him. "Having made the acquaintance of the theatre managers here," he wrote, "I have become so disgusted with the theatre that the mere thought of the 'pleasantness' in store for me at the Moscow theatre too is enough to deter me from making the trip to Moscow . . . Finally, to crown all the dirty tricks that could be possibly played on me, I understand the management here, that is to say the director Gedeonov, actuated by a petty personal dislike of some of the chief actors in my play, such as Sosnitsky and Dyur, has seen fit to give the main roles to other actors after four performances. It's all too much for me. Do what you like with my play, but I won't bother with it. I'm fed up with the play itself, as I am with all the fuss over it. The effect it had was to create a great furore. Everyone is against me. Elderly and respectable officials cry out, saying that nothing is sacred to me, daring to speak as I have done about civil servants. The police are against me, the merchants are against me, the literary men are against me . . . Now I realize what it means to be a comic writer. At the slightest whiff of truth they are up in arms against you – not just individuals, but whole classes of people."

Gogol entrusted the Moscow production to Shchepkin, informing his friend that he had lost interest in the play and was dissatisfied with many things in it, though not the ones his critics had found fault with. When Shchepkin encountered resentment and lack of co-operation from his fellow-actors he asked Gogol to hand over the task of supervision, nominally at least, to Sergei Aksakov. Gogol would agree to this only if it was absolutely necessary, still preferring Shchepkin to be in charge. In the end, however, the production was taken over by the playwright Mikhail Zagoskin, who was Director of the Moscow Theatres. It was mounted in a slapdash fashion after only about ten days of rehearsal, with little understanding and less enthusiasm on the part of Zagoskin, who was a literary rival of Gogol. New scenery was provided, but the costumes were antiquated and ridiculous. It was announced that the comedy would open at the Bolshoi Theatre on 24 May, but the management, fearing a public reaction similar to that in St. Petersburg, transferred it to the smaller Maly Theatre on the pretext that the Bolshoi was undergoing alterations.

The first performance in Moscow was given on 25 May to an audience composed, in the main, of people belonging to high society. Nearly all the actors at the Maly, like those at the Alexandrinsky Theatre, treated the play as a vaudeville and most of them failed to get under the skin of the characters they were playing. A few were successful in their parts, notably Potanchikov as the Postmaster, Stepanov as the Judge, Orlov as Osip, and above all

Shchepkin, who made the Governor a more earthy, robust rogue than Sosnitsky had done. But Lensky, though superior to Dyur, was still a long way from interpreting the central role of Khlestakov as Gogol conceived it.

The play was given a cool reception by the predominantly aristocratic audience at this premiere and there were no curtain calls for any of the actors. The reaction of the spectators was described by Shchepkin in a letter he wrote to Sosnitsky on 3 June. "The audience was amazed at its novelty," he said, "and roared with laughter a great deal, but I had expected it to get a much bigger reception. I was extremely surprised by this, but an acquaintance of mine gave me the following amusing explanation for it: 'Come now,' he said, 'how could it have been better received when half the audience were bribees and the other half bribers?'"

After its first performance in Moscow the play was received with greater acclaim than in the capital and was a great success with the general public. In Moscow, as in St. Petersburg, it soon became the talk of the town and aroused violent hostility in some quarters. Sergei Aksakov tells us in his memoirs that the most malicious rumours were spread about Gogol in the highest official circles of Moscow and some even reached the ears of the Sovereign. Aksakov further states that Count Fedor Tolstoy, a prominent aristocrat, was heard to declare at a large private gathering that Gogol was 'an enemy of Russia who should be clapped in irons and sent to Siberia' and there were many people, especially in St. Petersburg, who were of the same opinion.[30]

The critical reviews of *The Government Inspector* published in Moscow were much more favourable than those which had appeared in the press of St. Petersburg. The first review was published in the journal *Moscow Observer* by its editor Vasily Androsov, a moderate Slavophil.[31] Androsov judged Gogol's comedy to be worthy of a high place among the few truly original dramatic works Russia had so far produced and described it as 'an exceptionally important phenomenon in our literature'. He distinguished between light comedy, in which the petty frailties of individuals are held up to ridicule, and high comedy, 'the comedy of civilization' as he called it, which depicts common social vices. Light comedy serves as an idle distraction, inviting us to laugh at the folly and foibles a man exhibits in his private life, at the plight of some wretched miser, jealous husband, or an old man madly in love. High comedy attacks vices indulged in by man acting in a social capacity, and the

[30] S. T. Aksakov, *История моего знакомства с Гоголем*, Moscow, 1960, pp. 40–1. Tolstoy, nicknamed 'the American', was a notorious gambler and swashbuckler, satirized in Griboyedov's *Горе от ума* (Act IV, Sc. 4) and by Pushkin in his second verse epistle *К Чаадаеву* (1821).

[31] *Московский наблюдатель*, May 1836, Part 7, No. 1, pp. 120–31.

laughter it produces is quite different, being commingled with a sense of shame arising from self-recognition. Such laughter, directed not at the offender but at the offence, is socially beneficial; the louder and more maliciously people laugh at public vices, the better for morality. The writer of a social comedy, far from undermining authority, actually increases people's respect for it by exposing abuses. Gogol's play belonged to the second category. In fact it was a new kind of comedy, very different from the classical comedy of manners which reflected the social climate of earlier times.

Androsov went on to draw a distinction in drama between literal truth, or absolute fidelity to real life, and literary truth, which consists in presenting people as human types and showing how, being what they are, they would think and act in particular circumstances, but without any attempt to explain why they so behave, since that is not the dramatist's function. Gogol's comedy was of the latter kind, for it conveyed this inner truth and expressed the essential nature of his fictitious characters, who exemplified the various forms of morals and manners found in provincial Russia. Then, sensing perhaps the political risk involved in accepting Gogol's picture of Russian reality, Androsov asserted, quite against the sense of what he had written before, that it was not in any way typical. He could not understand, he said, why officials and others should take offence at *The Government Inspector*, since its author was attacking individual abuses and presenting characters who were exceptions. Like Gogol himself, Androsov refused to admit the typicality of these characters, hoping thereby to reassure his readers that the play did not in any way pose a threat to the regime.

In *Rumour*, a weekly supplement to the journal *Telescope*, a sympathetic and perceptive review of the Moscow production was published by the editor Nikolai Nadezhdin, under the initials A.B.V.[32] Nadezhdin affirmed that the comedy, despite the malicious attempts of Bulgarin and Senkovsky to discredit it, and notwithstanding the obvious signs of haste in the production, was nevertheless a great success with the general public because Gogol was a writer of talent and his play was wholly relevant to contemporary life. He had not written a domestic comedy based on the conventional love intrigue, but a social comedy which dealt with real life and real people. It was a thoroughly Russian play, a product not of imitation but of Gogol's bitter feelings about his country. Furthermore, it was a more serious and profound work than many people realized. "Those who think that this comedy is amusing and

[32] 'Театральная хроника', *Молва*, 1836, No. 9, pp. 250–64. This article was formerly attributed to Belinsky, although he explicitly disclaimed its authorship, while expressing his agreement with most of the reviewer's observations. See S. Osovtsov, 'А. Б. В. и другие', *Русская литература*, 1962, No. 3, pp. 75–101.

nothing more are mistaken," he wrote. "Certainly it is amusing, on the surface, so to speak; but inside it is a thing of grief and woe, a poor creature clad in rags and tatters."[33] The players had mistakenly tried to be funny, whereas they should have acted simply, truthfully and good-naturedly. This quality of good humour, profoundly characteristic of all Gogol's works, was almost entirely missing in the Moscow production. Finally the actors, with the notable exception of Potanchikov (playing the Postmaster), were criticized for gabbling their lines and taking the play altogether too briskly, thus failing to reproduce the leisurely speech and sluggish pace of life one found in the provinces.[34] Even in a grave emergency, such as the one they face in the play, the townspeople would not change the habits of a lifetime: they would still move about quietly and sedately.

Meanwhile, following the uproar his play had caused in St. Petersburg, Gogol decided to leave Russia. In his letter to Pogodin of 10 May he wrote: "I am going abroad to dispel the anguish that my countrymen are causing me each day. A modern writer, a comic writer, a writer concerned with morals and manners should be as far away from his native land as possible. A prophet is without honour in his own country." He was in a state of inner turmoil, unable to resolve the deep conflict within him. He felt that he must escape from Russia, for a time at least, in order to see it more clearly from a distance and to reflect on his role as a writer. On 6 June 1836, accompanied by his old school-friend Danilevsky, he left for Western Europe.

* * *

Even before Gogol left Russia attempts were made by influential officials and journalists to have his play banned from the stage or at least performed as infrequently as possible. These attempts came to naught, but soon afterwards the authorities, alarmed by the success of the play, sought to counteract its political impact by arranging for it to be followed by a three-act sequel written, apparently, by a certain Prince Tsitsianov, if not to order at least with official blessing.[35]

[33] Nadezhdin's words, which defy exact translation, are: "но внутри это горе-гореваньице, лыком подпоясано, мочалами испутано."

[34] This criticism, though sound in general, does not apply in the case of Bobchinsky and Dobchinsky, who are supposed to speak rapidly, as Gogol makes clear in his notes on characters and costumes.

[35] See A. Petrov, 'Николай I как репертуарный цензор: «Настоящий Ревизор»', *Советский театр*, 1930, No. 5, p. 44, and S. S. Danilov, *«Ревизор» на сцене*, Kharkov, 1933, p. 43.

In this crudely unrealistic denouement, entitled *The Real Inspector*, justice is seen to be done and the wrongdoers are duly punished, as the dramatic conventions of the time demanded. The real government inspector, a certain Provodov, has been staying in the district town for some time under an assumed name and is acquainted with all that has happened there. In the final scene Provodov announces his engagement to the Governor's daughter and then, after revealing his true identity, proceeds to pronounce sentence on the various officials. The Governor is barred from office for five years and the rest are forced to resign. Most severely dealt with is Zemlyanika, who is to be taken to court for informing on his colleagues. Khlestakov, who returns to town, is condemned to serve as an ensign in a remote province. This sequel, first played on 14 July, was taken off the stage after only a few performances, having been loudly hissed by the audiences.

Gogol saw the Moscow production of *The Government Inspector* on 17 October 1839, during his first visit to Russia after leaving three years earlier. Sergei Aksakov persuaded the director, Mikhail Zagoskin, to put on a special performance in honour of Gogol, who was spending a short time in Moscow. The play was given at the Bolshoi Theatre, to which the Maly production had been transferred in May of the previous year. Many Muscovite notables attended the theatre that evening, among them quite a number of literary figures, and the actors, who included Shchepkin, did their best to excel in the presence of the author. The performance went down well with the audience but not, apparently, with Gogol who sat, or rather slumped, in a box on the pit-tier. At the end of the second act some of the spectators rose and applauded, calling for the author.[36] But Gogol did not show himself. He had earlier asked Sergei Aksakov to inform Zagoskin that he was not in the theatre. This piece of deception annoyed Zagoskin, who knew full well that Gogol was present. Taking him at his word, Zagoskin made no attempt to invite him to the director's box, from which it was customary for authors to take a bow. As the tumultuous cries continued Gogol sank lower in his seat and, after almost crawling out of the box, hurriedly departed. The curtain rose and the actor taking Khlestakov came forward to announce that the author was not in the house. At the theatre exit Gogol was overtaken by Aksakov, who had seen him leave, but he could not prevail upon him to return. The following day he wrote a letter of apology to Zagoskin in which he stated, quite untruthfully, that he had received distressing news from home

[36] Some eye-witnesses put this at the end of the second act, others at the end of the third. See *Литературное наследство*, Vol. 58, Moscow, 1952, pp. 568–73; I. I. Panayev, *Литературные воспоминания*, Leningrad, 1950, pp. 175–6; S. T. Aksakov, *История моего знакомства с Гоголем*, Moscow, 1960, p. 59.

just before the performance. He was fortunately dissuaded from sending the letter, but his sudden departure from the theatre caused something of a scandal and made a bad impression on the public, who saw it as a sign of vanity on his part. There can be little doubt that Gogol felt piqued at the way Zagoskin had snubbed him, but he probably used this as a convenient excuse for making his escape. Despite his thirst for fame he had a genuine horror of public acclaim. This is borne out by the fact that he reacted in exactly the same way twelve years later when he slipped out of the Maly Theatre half-way through a performance of his play to evade the plaudits.

The Government Inspector steadily gained in popularity, especially in Moscow, where the production was greatly superior to that being shown in St. Petersburg, except when Shchepkin appeared there in April 1838 as a guest artist. By 1839 it was an established theatrical attraction, despite the continued hostility displayed towards it by many people in official circles. Both its popularity and its more frequent appearance on the stage were due in no small measure to the praise bestowed on it by Belinsky.

In a short anonymous article written in 1836 Belinsky referred to the play as 'a genuine work of art' which exhibited qualities already apparent in Gogol's earlier writings, his 'original view of things, his ability to capture character traits and stamp them with the mark of typicality, his inexhaustible humour'. Two years later Belinsky again praised the comedy as 'a profound work of genius' and 'a great work of dramatic genius'. His main critique, however, was embodied in a long article on Griboyedov's *Woe from Wit* which he wrote in the autumn of 1839 and published early the following year in *Notes of the Fatherland*.[37] This detailed study of Gogol's play, the first to appear in Russian critical literature, was written before Belinsky had embraced the philosophy of materialism, at a time when he was still largely committed to the Hegelian concept of reconciliation with reality and believed in the autonomy of art. He staunchly maintained that the creative artist should be objective and not allow his moral or political opinions to intrude in his work.

Comedy and tragedy, Belinsky declared, are both based on some dramatic conflict, but whereas tragedy deals with lofty passions and great crimes, comedy is concerned with more trivial passions and misdeeds. A tragic conflict evokes horror, compassion, or a feeling of pride in the dignity of human nature. In comedy, on the other hand, the conflict provokes laughter, a reaction which is not just an expression of mirth on the part of the spectators, but a way of taking revenge at witnessing the degradation of

[37] *Отечественные записки*, 1840, Vol. 8, No. 1, pp. 1–56.

human dignity. Thus the moral law triumphs in comedy, just as it does in tragedy, albeit in a different way. Drama, like all works of art, must be based on an idea. Gogol's play, in Belinsky's view, expressed the idea of 'the negation of life', since it was concerned with 'illusions', by which he meant all that is bad, ugly or unworthy of man's highest spiritual aspirations.[38] What we are shown in *The Government Inspector* is 'a void filled with the activity of petty passions and petty egoism'. Gogol's comedy is a statement of the ideal through its negation – a wholly Hegelian concept. All the feverish activity in the play is illusory; it is a purely negative force, the chaotic element in life struggling against a higher, 'rational' reality.

All the actions in the play, Belinsky observed, are strictly motivated by the characters of the people involved. These people are taken at a critical point in their lives and reveal the essence of their being, so that we can deduce from this one chapter the whole of their previous life-history. Gogol's characters are not puppets, but real people drawn from Russian life. Khlestakov is a shallow, foolish person, foppish in both dress and manners, exactly the kind of dandified figure that adorned signs hanging outside inns, barbers' and tailors' shops in Moscow (aptly described by Belinsky as a денди трактирный). This young man, who reacts unthinkingly to each new situation, is quite innocent of any design to defraud the town officials and at the Governor's house, after a copious lunch and flushed with wine, he prattles away hardly aware that all he says is pure invention. In this role of presumed inspector he is 'a creature of the Governor's frightened imagination, a phantom, a shadow of his conscience'.[39] It is the Governor's fear that sets the play in motion, therefore the Governor is its central character. He is 'no caricature ... but an extremely clever person in his own way and very effective in his own sphere of life'. However, his normally shrewd mind is so clouded by fear of exposure and retribution that he 'inhabits a world of phantoms'. His fear is increased by the fact that the inspector has been sent from St. Petersburg, a remote and mysterious world beyond his ken. We are not told anything about his earlier life, but it is clear that he was poorly educated and in his childhood had received no moral or religious guidance. As a youth he was given 'lessons in worldly wisdom, that is to say in the art of *feathering his nest* and *covering his tracks*'. His philosophy is simple and pragmatic. He believes the aim of human life is happiness, which can only be assured by the possession of wealth and rank. To attain these one may use

[38] Belinsky used the term 'illusions' or 'illusoriness' (призрачность) to denote 'the negative aspects of reality', not 'unreality', as some critics have assumed.

[39] V. Erlich, in his *Gogol*, 1969, p. 105, makes nonsense of this observation by taking it to mean that Belinsky was 'questioning Khlestakov's very existence'.

any means to hand, including bribery, peculation and servility towards those with money and power. He is the product of a society that condones such practices and he considers his behaviour to be justified by the fact that everyone else resorts to them.

In Belinsky's judgement, there were no scenes in the play which could be singled out as better than the rest, because there were no inferior ones. It was a true work of art with a unity imposed not by the external form, but by the content. It constituted a self-contained world in which each element formed an indispensable part of an integrated whole. The play thus fulfilled Belinsky's chief requirement of a work of art, namely that it should contain nothing arbitrary or accidental, that everything in it should proceed inevitably from some basic idea and unfold logically from its inner rationale. By contrast, Griboyedov's play *Woe from Wit* had no unifying idea and its dramatic conflict was not inevitable but fortuitous. Although it was highly poetic and contained many fine scenes, *Woe from Wit* did not present a self-contained world but had an extrinsic purpose, namely to ridicule contemporary society. Being a satire, it could not be regarded as a work of art since, according to Hegel's aesthetic, all satire is artistically flawed by its tendentiousness. Similarly Molière's plays, despite their undoubted merits, were not true comedies but satires, for they too were not artistic ends in themselves but 'a means of correcting society by mocking at vices'. Belinsky failed to note that Gogol's play was also a satire, since it was written with the intention of eradicating social abuses by holding them up to ridicule. It is true that Gogol, unlike Griboyedov and Molière, eschewed overt didacticism in his comedy, but his purpose was the same as theirs – to effect a moral reform by means of ridicule. Apparently it did not occur to Belinsky that a satire might be conveyed objectively, as is the case with *The Government Inspector*. Nor does he seem to have considered whether dramas that lacked objectivity, like those of Molière, might nevertheless be works of art. Having ruled out satire, Belinsky took the view that Gogol's play was essentially a psychological study.

Nikolai Grech, a close literary associate of Bulgarin, strongly disagreed with the opinions Belinsky expounded in his article. During the winter of 1839–40 Grech delivered a series of public lectures which were published shortly afterwards under the title *Readings on the Russian Language*. In his tenth lecture he took Belinsky to task for pronouncing *The Government Inspector* greatly superior to *Woe from Wit* and to all of Molière's comedies, a judgement which he described as 'a bitter mockery of both the public and Gogol'. In Grech's estimation *The Government Inspector* was not a comedy but 'a caricature in dialogue' (карикатура в разговорах), in which no ideas and no noble or lofty emotions were expressed. But he was more indulgent towards its author than Bulgarin and Senkovsky had been because he found the play, for all its shortcomings, to be not only amusing, as they had readily allowed, but also witty and gay, with characters that were vividly portrayed and true to life.[40]

Gogol was greatly flattered by Belinsky's article and in his later writings on *The Government Inspector* he developed some of the views first expressed about it by the critic, notably the idea that the Governor's error in mistaking Khlestakov for an inspector springs from an uneasy conscience.[41] But Gogol disagreed fundamentally with Belinsky's opinion that the Governor is the main character in the play. Two years later, in a letter of 20 April 1842, Belinsky withdrew this and conceded that Gogol was right in maintaining that Khlestakov was the central character.[42] Gogol would not have agreed either that there were no inferior scenes in the play. On the contrary, he was far from satisfied with a great deal in the first version of 1836 and completely revised the play in the course of the next six years. He was particularly dissatisfied with the fourth act and he tells us in his *Extract from a Letter* that he sat down immediately after the premiere and began to rewrite the beginning of it, after observing during the performance that the play appeared lifeless at this point and the pace of the action dragged rather limply.[43]

For the next two and a half years he left the text of the play untouched, being preoccupied with his main work, *Dead Souls*. Then towards the end of 1838 he began to alter and correct some of the scenes in Act IV, but completed this revision only in January and February of 1841, whilst he was living in Rome. He asked Sergei Aksakov to supervise the publication of a new edition of the play, incorporating these changes. Aksakov, having just suffered the loss of his youngest son, felt unable to participate in the enterprise and handed it over

[40] N. Grech, *Чтения о русском языке*, St. Petersburg, 1840, Part 2, pp. 138–42.

[41] This was first pointed out by Pavel Annenkov in his *Замечательное десятилетие* (1880); see P. V. Annenkov, *Литературные воспоминания*, Moscow, 1960, p. 184. But Annenkov was wrong in stating that Gogol was also indebted to Belinsky for the suggestion that laughter plays a positive role in the comedy. Gogol's conception of 'serious' laughter was developed from an observation made by Vyazemsky on Fonvizin's plays and more especially from Androsov's comments on *The Government Inspector*.

[42] In making his original assessment of the relative importance of the two characters Belinsky was no doubt influenced by the poor showing made by the actors playing Khlestakov at that time. Gogol himself complained to Sergei Aksakov that he could find no actor suitable for this part, that consequently the play lost its point and should be entitled *The Governor*, rather than *The Government Inspector*.

[43] Some of Gogol's biographers are sceptical about his statement that he set about this revision straight after the performance and believe that he started it later.

entirely to Pogodin. The latter, eager to include contributions by Gogol in his new journal *The Muscovite*, took the liberty of publishing the amendments to Act IV in the March issue of 1841, thereby incurring the author's displeasure. Pogodin then pressed ahead and brought out the second edition of the play in the summer of the same year, disregarding Gogol's express wish that it should be delayed until the autumn, when he believed it would attract better sales. In the new version of the play the opening scenes of Act IV were modified and new material was added to them. The most significant change was the addition of a new scene at the beginning of the act, in which the officials are shown conspiring to bribe Khlestakov.

During June and the first half of July 1842, whilst he was staying in Berlin and Bad Gastein, Gogol thoroughly revised his play, using a copy of the first edition specially printed with wide margins. He meticulously worked over the lines, pruning away all superfluous matter to achieve a dense, compact texture and produce 'a pearl of creation', to borrow an expression he used in *Dead Souls*. Having read and heard many comments on his play, he decided to underline its serious social implications. Accordingly he eliminated most of the farcical incidents, which had been grossly overplayed in the original production, and increased the satirical content, thereby giving the play a broader social significance. The comedy in its final form gained considerably in dramatic dynamism and was greatly superior as a work of art to the earlier versions.

The textual changes that Gogol made chiefly affected the speeches of Khlestakov and the Governor, adding greater subtlety and depth to their characterization. The Governor's speeches in Act I were made shorter and crisper by eliminating extraneous details. So, too, were Khlestakov's speeches in the sixth scene of Act III. On the other hand, Khlestakov's lies and exaggerations were made even more extravagant and the Governor's last main speech in Act V was expanded into a magnificent tirade, culminating in the famous words addressed to the audience: "What are you laughing at? – You are laughing at yourselves!" The short interview with the N.C.O.'s wife in Act IV, which had been deleted by the censor from the text published in 1836, was restored. Gogol also included detailed directions for presenting the final dumb scene, which had been bungled on the stage, and appended an epigraph as a riposte to his critics. This version of the play appeared in the fourth volume of his collected works, published by Nikolai Prokopovich and dated 1842.[44] Finally, while preparing a second edition of his works in 1851,

[44] The edition, printed in 1842, was not published until the end of January 1843. Volumes III and IV were held up by the censorship committee which took alarm when Nikitenko, who had passed the collected works, was put under token arrest for one night after allowing the publication of a tale that contained passages considered disrespectful to the army.

Gogol made a few minor stylistic changes which are incorporated in the standard text of the play.

In addition to the three published versions of *The Government Inspector* there are numerous manuscripts of all or part of the text, written at various stages of its composition. Among the extant manuscripts are two versions of the play which antedate the first published text of 1836. The work thus exists in five different versions, which will be referred to hereafter as R1, R2 etc., the letter R being used to denote 'Revizor' (the Russian title). These versions, in chronological order, are as follows:

R1 First manuscript draft.
R2 Stage text.[45]
R3 First published text of 1836.
R4 Second published text of 1841.
R5 Third published text of 1842.

Gogol's commentaries

Besides altering and revising the text of *The Government Inspector* several times, Gogol took considerable pains to answer his critics and to elucidate the play for the benefit of the public and the acting profession. His first comments appeared in a spirited defence of it made in a short dramatic sketch entitled *Leaving the Theatre after the Performance of a New Comedy*. He wrote the original draft of this piece, it is believed, in May 1836, and completely revised it in the summer of 1842 for publication in the first edition of his collected works, printed at the end of the same year.

The scene of the sketch is a theatre foyer. The author stands discreetly on one side listening to remarks made about his comedy by the spectators as they leave the theatre. Various people from different walks of life express their opinion in turn. Some of them give the views of the ordinary members of the audience, some voice objections made by Gogol's literary opponents Bulgarin and Senkovsky, others serve as mouthpieces of the author. *The*

[45] This exists only in copies, not in Gogol's own hand. From these copies Nikolai Tikhonravov reconstructed the 'original stage text', published in 1886. Tikhonravov believed that two different versions were written between R1 and R3, but V. L. Komarovich, the textual editor of the Soviet Academy edition of the play, established that the various manuscripts belonging to this stage of its composition constitute essentially one version. The texts of this version (R2), used for the original productions in St. Petersburg and Moscow, differ in some details because Gogol made some amendments after he had sent it to Moscow. These slightly divergent texts, and not the published version (R3), were used in the theatres of the two capitals for many years. The final published version (R5), banned from public performance by the censor of the Third Section, was first used on the St. Petersburg stage in 1870, and in Moscow not until 1883.

Government Inspector is generally agreed to be amusing, but is variously condemned as a silly, improbable farce or as a sordid spectacle presenting caricatures of humanity. Society's sores, it is argued, should be concealed from the public gaze and are not a fit subject for a comedy. By exposing corrupt officials to general ridicule the author is undermining the confidence of ordinary people in their government.

There are two main criticisms that Gogol is concerned to answer here, the first being that his play has no real plot. His reply to this objection is given by the Second Art-lover, who says that audiences have grown accustomed to a conventional type of comedy based on a love intrigue which inevitably ends in marriage. His play has no plot in that sense, because he believes the scope of comedy should be broadened to include new themes, such as the pursuit of wealth, position or an advantageous match. The action of a play, he says (echoing Belinsky), should be governed by some idea, some conflict which gives the work a unity and involves not only the main protagonists, as in classical comedy, but all the characters. Comedy can thus be just as suitable a vehicle as tragedy for expressing lofty ideas. He then draws a parallel between the role played by Fate in ancient Greek tragedy and that of the government in modern comedy. Firmly believing that governments exercise authority with divine sanction, Gogol elaborates Vyazemsky's remark that the Russian government was an honest character in the play, although by this Vyazemsky had meant no more than that the Tsar was to be praised for allowing the comedy to appear on the stage. "A kind of secret faith in the government is harboured in our hearts," says the Second Art-lover. "Well, there is nothing wrong in that: God grant that the government may, at all times and in all places, be mindful of its mission to be the representative of Providence on earth and that we may believe in it as the ancients believed in a Fate which overtook transgressors."

This idea is further developed by a Very Modestly Dressed Man, another mouthpiece of the author, who argues that the play, by exposing corrupt officials, will strengthen the trust of the people in their government. "Let them dissociate the government from its bad executives," he says. "Let them see that abuses come not from the government, but from those who do not understand its requirements and who do not want to be answerable to it. Let them see that the government is noble, that its unslumbering eye watches over all alike, that sooner or later it will catch up with those who have violated the law, honour and man's sacred duty, and that those with guilty consciences will blanch before it." Clearly Gogol intended the ending of *The Government Inspector* to be seen as a victory for the authorities.

The second main charge which Gogol answers is that there is not a single decent or virtuous character in his play. The reason for this, he explains, is that an honest figure would attract all the sympathy of the spectators and make them forget the wickedness of the other characters, thus spoiling the whole effect. The image of the honest man is presented indirectly or implicitly, by showing his opposite. The Second Art-lover asks: "Does not all the deviousness of heart, even the slightest, in an ignoble and dishonest person of itself show us what an honest man should be like? Does not all this accumulation of base actions and breaches of law and justice show clearly what is required of us by law, duty and justice?"[46]

At the end the author steps forward and speaks in his own person. Taking up an observation made by Androsov, he expresses regret that the spectators have failed to notice the one truly honest character in the play, namely *laughter*, not the kind that serves merely as an idle distraction, but 'the laughter that springs wholly from man's better nature, . . . which goes to the heart of things and highlights something that would have gone unnoticed otherwise, and without whose penetrating force man would not be so appalled by the triviality and emptiness of life'. Such laughter does not make us feel angry or vindictive towards the wrongdoer whose baseness is held up to ridicule, but tends to reconcile us with him by moving us to compassion. The wrongdoer himself will not join in the laughter but he will be affected by it, for mockery is something men fear above all else. The concept of laughter as a moral force was for many years a cornerstone in Gogol's aesthetic credo. At this time he still believed that abuses could be corrected by exposing them to ridicule on the stage. Only four years later, however, he expressed a different view in his *Selected Passages*. In one of his letters he declared pessimistically that 'you can achieve nothing by satire', and in another that in Russia 'bribery has reached such proportions that there are no human means of stamping it out'.[47]

Some time after completing his dramatic apologia *Leaving the Theatre* Gogol wrote *A Warning to those who would play "The Government Inspector" properly*, an essay which was not published until 1886.[48] His chief

[46] Belinsky made the same point when he wrote in 1841: "In a comedy we are shown life as it is in order that we might clearly conceive life as it should be." He went on to cite *The Government Inspector* as a superb example of an artistic comedy (*Разделение поэзии на роды и виды*).

[47] The same despairing view of bribery is expressed in the last fragment of the unfinished second part of *Dead Souls*, by the Governor-General. "I know," he says, "that wrongdoing cannot be eradicated by any means, by any terrors or punishments; it is too deeply entrenched. The dishonest business of taking bribes has become a need and a necessity, even for people who were not born to be dishonest."

[48] This essay was probably written about 1846, not in 1842 as Gogol's earlier biographers believed.

advice to actors is that they should not caricature their parts but play them naturally, indeed even underplay them, in order to achieve the right comic effect. "The main thing to guard against is caricature," he wrote. "There should be nothing exaggerated or trite, even in the minor roles. On the contrary, the actor should try particularly to be more modest, more simple and noble, so to speak, than the person he is playing really is. The less the actor tries to play for laughs, the more he will reveal the comic nature of the part he is playing. The humour will emerge spontaneously from the very seriousness with which each of the persons portrayed in the comedy is occupied with his own concerns. They are all busily, even feverishly pursuing their own affairs as if these were the most important things in their lives. Only the spectator, from his detached position, can see how futile their concerns are." Gogol was doing something more here than advising actors how to tackle their parts; he was enunciating one of his fundamental dramatic principles – that the characters should be exposed not by others but by themselves.

The actor's primary task, Gogol continues, is to get under the skin of the character he is playing and find out what makes him tick. "An intelligent actor," he writes, "before seizing on the minor oddities and the minor outward peculiarities of the person he is playing should strive to grasp the *universal human* expression of the character.[49] He should consider why this part was created, examine the principal and overriding concern of each person, the thing he spends his life on and which is the permanent object of his thoughts, his constant preoccupation . . . He should not worry too much about particular scenes and small details. These will succeed by themselves and be skilfully done provided he concentrates all the time on this preoccupation that possesses the mind of his character."

The Governor is primarily interested in personal gain, in 'not missing anything that floats into his hands', as his friend Chmykhov puts it in the letter read out at the beginning of the play. Because he has always had an eye to the main chance he has never taken a hard look at life or at himself. For the same reason he has turned into an oppressor almost without realizing it, since he is not actuated by any malicious desire to tyrannize over others. Nor is he vindictive, for he forgives the merchants who have informed against him to Khlestakov. Aware of his sins, he prays, goes to church and believes himself to be a devout Christian. He even contemplates reforming some day, but the

[49] In a letter to Shchepkin, written in December 1846, Gogol offered advice to actors in almost exactly the same words, saying that they should perceive 'the universal human expression' (общечеловеческое выражение) of their parts. The close similarity of the wording supports the view that *A Warning* was written about 1846.

lure of worldly possessions is too great to resist and the urge to acquire them has become an ingrained habit with him. Confronted in the play with a trickier situation than he has handled before, he oscillates between panic and elation, and his nerves are strained. This affects his judgement and makes it possible for him to be deceived, something most unlikely to happen when he was not under such emotional stress. "Thus, when it is suddenly announced that a real inspector has arrived, the shock of this thunderbolt is greater for him than for everyone else and his position becomes truly tragic."

The most difficult role in the play is that of the main character, Khlestakov, whose paramount urge is to show off and impress everyone as the important person he would like to be. The fear of the officials that they may be exposed gives this nonentity a golden opportunity to appear important, but he has no thought of swindling or deceiving them. Even the subjects on which he dilates so extravagantly are all suggested in the first place by his listeners. He is impulsive in everything, and when he talks he is simply carried away by his own imagination, so much so that he believes his own fantasies. "In short," writes Gogol, "he is a phantasmagorical person, the embodiment of lies and deception, who sweeps off in his troika God knows where." This last remark may well have been suggested by Belinsky's description of Khlestakov as a phantom.

These observations tally with the comments Gogol made earlier in his *Extract from a Letter*, where he wrote: "Khlestakov is not an impostor at all; he is not a professional liar; he forgets that he is lying and almost believes his own words. He is uninhibited and in high spirits. He sees that everything is going well, that he is being listened to – and for that reasons alone he speaks with greater fluency and familiarity, he speaks with an open heart, absolutely frankly, and in his lying he reveals himself for what he is. . . . Khlestakov does not tell lies at all coldly or in a theatrically boastful way; he lies with passion and his eyes express the pleasure he derives from it. All in all, this is the finest and most poetic moment of his life – almost a kind of inspiration."

Khlestakov's character, Gogol continues, is fluid and elusive. In appearance he is perfectly ordinary and does not differ in any way from other young men. "He even behaves well occasionally and speaks at times with gravity. It is only in situations demanding either presence of mind or strength of character that the mean and insignificant side of his nature is revealed . . . If you analyze Khlestakov, what is he in fact? A young man, a civil servant, and a shallow fellow, as they say, but one who has many qualities possessed by people whom the world does not deem to be shallow . . . In short, this man should be a type embodying many things found separately in different Russian characters, but here combined fortuitously in one person, as very often happens in real life. Each of us becomes or has become a Khlestakov at least for a moment, if not several moments, only naturally we do not care to admit it. We even like to make fun of the fact, but of course only when we see Khlestakov in someone else, not in ourselves." [50]

These and other comments on the *dramatis personae* which Gogol published in the two articles quoted above, together with the brief character sketches with which he prefaced the play, and various observations he made in letters to Shchepkin and Sosnitsky, are an invaluable source of guidance for actor and reader alike.

In the autumn of 1846 Gogol wrote *The Denouement of "The Government Inspector"*, in which he put forward an entirely new interpretation of his comedy. This dramatic tailpiece was written whilst he was finishing his *Selected Passages*, at a time when he was preoccupied with religion and believed he had a messianic destiny to fulfil. He now began to reinterpret his earlier writings retrospectively. In *The Denouement* he asserts that his comedy is not a social satire, but a moral allegory. The provincial town in the play, he explains, is in reality the spiritual city which exists within each one of us. The dishonest officials represent various human passions which dwell there and 'plunder the treasury of our soul', while Khlestakov is the incarnation of our volatile worldly conscience. The play as a whole is intended to arouse in us fear of the real inspector, who symbolizes our true conscience and is the voice not of the government, but of the Eternal Judge whom we all have to face in the hour of death.[51] This view of *The Government Inspector* as a kind of secular morality play was clearly an *a posteriori* revaluation of the work on Gogol's part, for he certainly had no such conception of the comedy in mind when he wrote it ten years earlier.

The cast of this dramatic epilogue comprises the players themselves and a few spectators. It opens with 'the leading comic actor' (i.e. Shchepkin or Sosnitsky) being offered a laurel wreath by his fellow-actors and urged to crown himself.[52] The rest of the scene consists of a discussion about the

[50] The radical publicist Alexander Herzen wrote in similar vein of 'the eternal type of Khlestakov, recurring from the rural district clerk right up to the Tsar' (Diary, 20 February 1843). The novelist Ivan Goncharov went further, seeing Khlestakov as a universal type. "Khlestakovs still exist today," he wrote, "and perhaps always will exist, not just in Russian society but in human societies everywhere, only in a new form" (***Воспоминания***, II, 5).

[51] Gogol's deep, almost morbid concern with the question of man's ultimate accountability to God first appears in a letter he wrote to his mother on 2 October 1833, where he recalls the profound impression made on him as a boy by her vivid, terrifying account of the Last Judgement.

[52] When he introduced this gesture of tribute, Gogol may well have recalled attending a performance at the Théâtre-Français, Paris, in January 1837 to mark the anniversary of

nature of comedy between the leading comic actor and the spectators. One of the latter protests that *The Government Inspector* is of no real benefit to society. Another condemns it as positively harmful and takes particular exception to the Governor's words: "What are you laughing at? – You are laughing at yourselves!" as an impertinence and a sign of disrespect to the audience. Finally, when one of the spectators asks to know the meaning of the play, the leading comic actor provides the key, explaining that it is not to be taken literally, but as an allegory.

Many of Gogol's friends and admirers strongly objected to this interpretation of *The Government Inspector*. Sergei Aksakov sought to prevent the scene from being published because, as he wrote to his son Ivan, "It is all ridiculous and absurd nonsense from beginning to end, and if it is published it will make Gogol the laughing-stock of all Russia." Shchepkin, who had a great affection for both the play and its author, indignantly rejected this new interpretation. After failing, through illness, to answer three of Gogol's letters from abroad he eventually sent a reply on 22 May 1847, in which he protested vehemently that Gogol had reduced the flesh-and-blood characters of his comedy to lifeless abstractions. "After reading your ending of *The Government Inspector*," he wrote, "I was furious with myself at my own short-sightedness, because up till now I have studied all the characters in *The Government Inspector* as living people . . . Leave them me as they are. I love them, love them with all their weaknesses . . . You want to take them away from me. But I won't let you have them, not as long as I live! After I've gone you can turn them into goats if you like, but till then I won't part with Derzhimorda, because even he is dear to me."

Gogol, in reply to Shchepkin's letter, which caused him considerable embarrassment, claimed that the symbolic interpretation referred only to *The Denouement* itself. He admitted, however, that this was a clumsily written piece which would give spectators the mistaken impression that he wished to turn *The Government Inspector* into an allegory. "That is not what I have in mind," he wrote. "*The Government Inspector* is *The Government Inspector*, but the essential thing is for each spectator to relate the play to himself, and this applies to every other play besides *The Government Inspector*, though it is more appropriate in the case of *The Government Inspector*." The whole point of the epigraph was to make the spectator examine himself and see whether his own mug was crooked.

Two months later, in a further attempt to answer Shchepkin's criticism,

Molière's birth. At the end of the play the actors had come on the stage in pairs and placed wreaths on a bust of the famous French dramatist.

Gogol rewrote the last part of *The Denouement*. In this so-called *Supplement to The Denouement* the leading comic actor is now made to explain that he is not seeking to impose his own allegorical interpretation of the play on his audience. Nor could the author, had he any such idea in mind when writing the play, have made this obvious, for the result would have been an insipid homily. In fact the author's purpose had been to describe the horror induced by abuses in the real world, not in some ideal or abstract town of the soul, and to show that evil should not be regarded as an essential complement to good, as shade is to light in a picture. His aim was 'to gather together in one pile all the worst things on our earth' and 'to depict the dark side so vividly that everyone should feel it necessary to do battle against it and the spectator be made to tremble, filled with horror at the sight of lawless acts'.

Gogol insists that we should examine our own hearts and apply the moral of the play to ourselves. He bears witness to the wholesome, cathartic power of laughter that is born of love for one's fellow-men. This kind of laughter is a scourge that shames us and drives out the base impulses which steal into our hearts under a noble guise. "It has been given to us," he concludes, "so that we might laugh at ourselves, not at others. And anyone who lacks the courage to laugh at his own failings would do well never to laugh at all. Otherwise laughter will be turned into slander, a crime for which he will be answerable . . ." This last remark clearly reflects Gogol's sense of guilt, born of the belief that he had sinned by using laughter as a weapon to attack others. He sought to assuage his guilt feelings by suggesting that he had acted charitably towards his fellow-men in showing them their faults and thus enabling them to become better human beings. However, fearing perhaps that this rationalization would not carry much conviction, he eventually decided not to send the *Supplement* to Shchepkin.

It had been Gogol's intention that *The Denouement* should be given, together with the final version of the play, at benefit performances in Moscow and St. Petersburg for Shchepkin and Sosnitsky respectively. But this was not to be, since Shchepkin flatly refused to act in *The Denouement* and it never reached the censor of the Third Section, having been rejected by the Director of the Imperial Theatres, A. M. Gedeonov, who declared it quite unacceptable for the leading player to be offered a crown by his fellows, since the rules forbade any such demonstration of approval on the stage. Gogol had also planned to bring out a new edition of *The Government Inspector*, including *The Denouement*. He wrote a preface for the edition, in which he announced that the proceeds from its sale would be donated to the poor and gave a list of influential acquaintances in Moscow and St. Petersburg whom he nominated to collect the money and distribute it in accordance with his wishes. In the event, however, he was so disheartened by the opposition of his friends to this plan that he abandoned the idea of publishing the new edition, even though it was passed by the literary censor Nikitenko. In fact *The Denouement* did not appear in print until 1856, when it was included in the second edition of his collected works.

Later productions and adaptations

The Government Inspector maintained its place on the Russian stage but continued to divide the public for many years. It was especially popular with the younger playgoers. Vladimir Stasov, an eminent art and music critic, recalled in later life the enthusiasm it had aroused among his fellow-students at the School of Law in St. Petersburg when he was a youth. They even put on an amateur performance of the play in October 1839, without costumes or scenery. And some of them, he tells us, went to see it on the professional stage. "We were all in raptures over it," he reports, "as indeed all the young people were at that time. We would then recite whole scenes and long dialogues from it by heart, correcting and prompting each other. In our own and other people's homes we quite often got involved in heated debate with various elderly people (and sometimes, to their shame, not so elderly people) who waxed indignant about the new idol of youth and tried to make out that Gogol's works bore no resemblance to real life, that it was all invention and caricature on his part, and that such people just did not exist, or if they did there were far fewer of them in a whole town than in this comedy of his. Our exchanges were heated and prolonged . . . but the old people could not budge us one inch, and our fanatical worship of Gogol only grew stronger and stronger."[53]

Amongst officials *The Government Inspector* sometimes produced the most hostile and violent reactions. On one occasion it gave rise to a scene of such comic absurdity that it might have come straight from the pen of Gogol himself. In 1848 it was playing in Rostov-on-Don to a packed house. Among those present was the local governor, who happened to have a double-barrelled surname like his counterpart in the play. The worthy gentleman was soon bristling with anger at the guffaws of the other spectators, who were looking significantly in his direction. At the end of the first act, unable to contain himself, he leapt on the stage and began to hurl abuse at the actors for daring to lampoon the authorities in public. It was politely explained to him that the comedy was the work of Nikolai Gogol, a famous writer, and that it

[53] *Русская старина*, 1881, No. 2, pp. 417–18.

was played in St. Petersburg. He was even shown a copy of the text but refused to believe these assurances and threatened to have the actors put in prison unless they stopped the play at once and put on something else instead. By now the theatre was in uproar. At this point the manager appeared, set about the governor with a stick and drove him out of the theatre, calling him a churl and an ignorant brute, much to the amusement of the audience. After the governor and his police officers had gone, the performance continued and was a great success. The governor later lodged an official complaint against the actors, but the affair had become so notorious that his superiors rewarded him with a reprimand and subsequently removed him from his post.

A further incident reveals the accuracy with which Gogol had portrayed provincial officials. In a letter he received from Sergei Aksakov in 1849 his friend referred to a performance of *The Government Inspector* in the town of Rybinsk which his son Ivan had recently attended. The actors had been struck by the similarity beween the stage characters and the local dignitaries who were occupying the front stalls, whereupon a reversal of roles suddenly took place. "In the middle of the play," wrote Aksakov, "the actors, seeing that the spectators resembled the people in the play more than they did themselves, all split their sides with laughter."

In the provinces prominent officials continued to look upon the play as a seditious work. In 1856 Count A. G. Stroganov, the Governor-General of Novorossiisk and Bessarabia, expressed his view of it in a private letter to the Minister of Education, A. S. Norov: "I do not know what your Excellency's opinion is of the comedy *The Government Inspector*, but I believe, with the deepest conviction, that in origin, content and spirit it is a copy, *au petit pied*, of Beaumarchais' *Marriage of Figaro*.[54] I do not know whether it has had any beneficial influence or reformed one single briber or cheat. But I am sure that if *The Government Inspector* and its hundreds of followers[55] have not yet, thank God, had such melancholy consequences for Russia as Beaumarchais' work had for France, nevertheless the translations of them have already given rise to many unfavourable criticisms and false judgements of Russia abroad."[56] Stroganov was alarmed at the pernicious effect he considered Gogol and other writers were having on French attitudes to Russia. In 1854,

[54] *The Marriage of Figaro* (1784), in which Beaumarchais exposed dishonesty and incompetence in high places, was often referred to as 'the prologue to the French Revolution'.

[55] The followers referred to were all admirers of Gogol's literary talent and particularly the writers who belonged to what the critic Chernyshevsky called 'The Natural School'.

[56] *«Литературный музеум». Цензурные материалы*, ed. by A. S. Nikolayev and Yu. G. Oksman, 1921, Vol. I, p. 352.

soon after the outbreak of the Crimean War, *The Government Inspector* had its first foreign performance in Paris, under the title *Les Russes peints par eux-mêmes*. The translator, Eugène Moreau, had taken many liberties with the text and the play was such a flop that it emptied the theatre of every single spectator. This caused something of a scandal in Parisian society at the time, but it was soon forgotten.[57] Stroganov thus greatly exaggerated the effect the play had on public opinion in France. French hostility towards Russia, especially marked since the early 1830s, was fanned rather by such books as the Marquis de Custine's *La Russie en 1839*, Ivan Golovin's *La Russie sous Nicolas Ier*, and Frédéric Lacroix's *Les Mystères de la Russie*, works published in Paris in the 1840s which all presented an extremely unflattering picture of contemporary Russia.

Perhaps the most noteworthy amateur performance of the play was that given on 14 April 1860 by a group of writers, led by P. I. Weinberg, to raise money for the Russian Literary Fund, a society recently founded to assist needy authors and scholars. The role of Khlestakov was taken by Weinberg himself, and the Governor was played by Pisemsky. Dostoyevsky played the Postmaster, F. A. Koni took Abdulin, and amongst the other literary figures appearing as merchants were Apollon Maikov, Dmitry Grigorovich and Turgenev – the last wearing a frock-coat and pince-nez. The comedy, acted on a specially constructed stage at a private house in St. Petersburg, was given to a packed house and received with general acclaim.

A landmark in the stage history of *The Government Inspector* was its revival at the Alexandrinsky Theatre in October 1870, when it was given for the first time according to the final published version of 1842. This production, mounted with scrupulous concern for historical detail, established the play in its classic form, but at the same time turned it into a kind of theatrical museum-piece, something which could be admired but scarcely enjoyed. Moreover, the production lacked harmonious teamwork by the actors, a thing that Gogol always considered essential to success in the theatre. In fact the show was entirely stolen by the brilliant comedy actor Vasily Samoilov, who played the minor role of Rastakovsky.[58]

[57] A detailed account is given of its reception in E. S. Nekrasova, 'Гоголь пред судом иностранной литературы 1845–1885', *Русская старина*, Sept. 1887, pp. 562–6.

[58] In the two main published versions of the play (R3 and R5) this part consists of only a few lines, but Gogol originally included in Act IV a whole scene between Rastakovsky and Khlestakov. He later deleted it because, as he said himself, it slowed down the action, and probably also because Khlestakov, uncharacteristically, came off second best in the encounter. In 1841 this scene was published in *The Muscovite* and as an appendix to the second edition (R4), being intended for reading only. But when it was first introduced on stage in the 1870 production it found such favour with the actors that they kept it in the play for many years.

Gogol's definitive text was used again at the Maly Theatre in 1883 and thereafter was adopted in playhouses throughout the country. Producers began to pay more attention to historical accuracy in presenting the comedy, which was now firmly established as the chief classic of the Russian stage. Such was the case when the Alexandrinsky and Maly Theatres, the two main exponents of *The Government Inspector*, mounted jubilee productions in 1886 to celebrate fifty years since its premiere. These were distinguished only by the large number of well-known actors who took part, even in the minor roles. The production at the Alexandrinsky in 1897 again underlined the period flavour of the work. By now nearly all the satirical sting had been taken out of the play, which was treated merely as a picture of the moeurs of a bygone age.

This dry, academic approach to the comedy also characterized the production given at the Alexandrinsky in 1908 to mark the centenary of Gogol's birth. A break with this tradition came later in the same year, however, when the play was put on at the Moscow Art Theatre by Konstantin Stanislavsky, assisted by V. Nemirovich-Danchenko and I. M. Moskvin. The producers sought to breathe new life into the play by exploring it in greater psychological depth. But, despite some good acting, the production was dominated by the meticulous care that was taken to reproduce the *realia* of Russian provincial life in the early 1830s and the result was rather lifeless. For all that it had two features which marked a significant shift in the play's interpretation and which were taken up by later producers. For the first time Khlestakov was given pride of place over the Governor, who had been treated previously as the central figure, quite contrary to Gogol's intention. And there was an attempt to bring out the symbolic aspect of the work, especially in the finale, showing that the producers had taken note of the radical reinterpretation of Gogol's writings propounded by some of the literary decadents and symbolists. Whereas Belinsky, Chernyshevsky and their followers had treated Gogol as a realist, at the turn of the century Rozanov and Merezhkovsky, followed by the poets Annensky, Bely and Bryusov, put forward a completely different view of him as a master of the grotesque, the hyperbolic and the fantastic, whose works had little to do with reality.

After the Revolution of 1917 the theatres opened their doors to audiences of workers and soldiers. In the first few years of the Soviet period producers made no concessions to the new proletarian spectators, but clung to the well-tried method of presenting Gogol's play and continued to give prominence to external features, especially the decor.

The 1920s saw a great revival of interest in Gogol and with it a whole spate of productions of *The Government Inspector*, among them some of the most striking and memorable ever presented. In 1921 a new production was put on at the Moscow Art Theatre by Stanislavsky, who now staged it as a satire without any emphasis on the historical setting. He compressed the action into a single day and introduced a new spatial conception of the play by presenting it on a narrow strip of platform that gradually expanded as the action unfolded. The outstanding feature, however, was the novel interpretation of Khlestakov by Mikhail Chekhov, a nephew of the famous playwright. Chekhov's Khlestakov was a fantastic character with pronounced pathological tendencies. His face was made up to resemble that of a clown. He made strange, jerky gestures, he slavered, spoke incoherently at times, made long pauses in odd places, then shouted almost hysterically. He gnawed enthusiastically at a table-leg during the wooing scenes, dived under the table when the Judge dropped his banknotes, grabbing them with a smile of joy, hid in panic behind Anna's skirts when the Governor appeared in Act IV, went over to a life-size portrait of Nicholas I in the Governor's parlour and adopted the same regal pose. The effect of this *tour de force* was hypnotic. Khlestakov was transformed into a universal symbol of evil, a grotesque embodiment of the spiritual void that Gogol so deeply abhorred. This interpretation owed much to Merezhkovsky's metaphysical view of Khlestakov as a manifestation of the devil, and Chekhov's brilliant but eccentric performance aroused great controversy. It was out of keeping with the rest of the production, but gave a quite new dimension to the part that could not be ignored by other actors cast in the same role.

In 1922 an updated version of *The Government Inspector* entitled *Comrade Khlestakov* was given at the State Theatre of Comedy and Drama in Moscow. Gogol's original was condensed by D. Smolin into three acts, interspersed with other material, including poems by Mayakovsky, while the characters were given functions appropriate to Soviet society. This rather tasteless attempt to modernize the play was not a success with the public. After that came other experimental productions of *The Government Inspector*: a constructivist version by V. M. Bebutov in 1924 and a pantomimic version by N. V. Petrov two years later. But these theatrical curiosities were completely eclipsed by Vsevolod Meyerhold's stupendous production, first staged in December 1926.

This was a lavish spectacle in fifteen episodes, drawn from the different versions of the play and bodied out with material from Gogol's other works. It included vaudeville elements taken from the first draft of the comedy and freely expanded. For example, in the original Act III, Scene 3 Anna Andreyevna boasts to her daughter that a cavalry captain was once so bewitched by her eyes that he almost blew his brains out. This was incorporated into a boudoir scene where Anna changed dresses numerous times behind a screen while Dobchinsky played peeping Tom; after his departure her fantasies were extravagantly illustrated when a shot rang out and up sprang a group of handsome young officers, who proceeded to serenade her on imaginary guitars. With another shot one of them burst out of a cupboard and dropped to his knees before her, brandishing a bouquet of flowers; then another officer, rejected when he fell at her feet, drew a pistol and shot himself. Also restored were the comic scene in Act IV where Khlestakov converses in a mixture of Russian and German with Dr. Hiebner, and the incident, later in the same act, in which the N.C.O.'s wife makes to lift her skirt in order to show Khlestakov the bruises caused by her flogging. Gogol's text was refashioned to create a vast symbolic picture of tsarist Russia, with heavy emphasis on the satire, but at the expense of psychological realism. The scope of the play was widened to embrace all types of corruption in Imperial Russia and the scene was transferred from a small provincial town to a large city, with strong overtones of St. Petersburg.

Most of the action took place on a pair of small truck stages, the first of which was rolled forward in near-darkness with actors and props ready in position, then drawn back at the end of the scene to be replaced by a second one, similarly prepared. The full stage was left bare and used in only four episodes, most effectively in a composite bribery scene. At the rear was an arc of panels containing a row of doors, at which eleven figures appeared simultaneously. With mechanical gestures they proffered envelopes full of banknotes to a befuddled Khlestakov, who stepped forward and took each of the packets in turn, also with the movements of a robot. Great stress was laid on everything physical. Costumes, furnishings and scenery were rich and resplendent: heavy silk drapery and solid-looking furniture in imitation mahogany were used, and plentiful dishes of succulent food were displayed in several scenes. All of this bore little resemblance to the domestic conditions Gogol had portrayed.

Great liberties were taken not only with the text but also with the *dramatis personae*, who were much increased in number and sometimes formed into a chorus. Gogol's originals were altered and adapted, some of them becoming an amalgam of various characters he had created of the same type. The Governor was turned into a high-ranking officer who struck quasi-Napoleonic poses, while his wife disported herself as a voluptuous society beauty of dubious morals, a kind of provincial Cleopatra. The elderly, taciturn Osip appeared as a sprightly country lad who sang a duet with a maid at the inn. Khlestakov assumed a variety of guises: he was by turns a timid clerk, dreamy poet, astute swindler, imperious general, and dissolute dandy with a hankering after the fleshpots. In the inn scene he cut a demonic, Hoffmannesque figure, dressed in black, with sinister-looking spectacles in square frames and an old-fashioned tall hat. Most of the time he moved silently but rather unsteadily on his spindly legs, and he was accompanied by a wan-faced officer who acted as a silent commentator.[59] When Khlestakov realized that he had been taken for a man of high position he borrowed the officer's uniform and demonstrated in mime the importance of his person. The two of them danced a quadrille with Anna and Maria in the episode where Khlestakov plays the gallent wooer to both women, his amorous antics being surveyed by his companion with sullen disdain. When Anna scolds her daughter for arriving inopportunely and then holds herself up as a paragon of propriety, another silent officer walked upstage, clasping his head in despair at the thought of the mother's 'virtue'.

In the last scene Anna collapsed in a swoon and was borne away, like the heroine of some Racinian tragedy, by her band of devoted officers. Thereupon the Governor, now hysterically demented, was put in a straitjacket by the doctor, with the assistance of the police, and carried off the stage on a stretcher. A mad dance ensued, to the sound of galloping music, drum rolls, police whistles and a crescendo of church bells, belatedly ringing to celebrate Maria's 'betrothal'. The players joined hands and in a dancing file, led by a fiddler, swept into the auditorium, whooping wildly. Then all fell silent as a huge white curtain rose before the stage, bearing the Gendarme's announcement inscribed in large gold letters. It slowly vanished to reveal fully clothed, life-size effigies of the townspeople, arranged exactly according to Gogol's directions for the dumb scene. The substitution of puppets for real people was meant to show the characters of the play as 'dead souls', and the finale was presented in such a way as to symbolize the downfall of the old regime. The production, elaborately orchestrated and mounted with great panache, incorporated the most striking use of decor and lighting, as well as music, dancing and mime. It was a brilliant realization of the Wagnerian ideal of total theatre, embracing all the arts.

Meyerhold's version of *The Government Inspector*, by far the most striking ever produced, made theatrical history and inspired a voluminous output of critical literature, probably more than any other production of a play before

[59] Meyerhold was criticized for introducing, in this shadowy figure, a 'mystical' element into the play. In fact the officer, who was the infantry captain mentioned in Act II, Sc. 3, was included simply as a means of overcoming the artificiality of the soliloquy by providing a listener. See Erast Garin, *С Мейерхольдом*, Moscow, 1974, pp. 127–8.

or since.[60] He himself called it 'a grandiose suite on Gogolian themes' and defined its genre as 'musical realism'. In fact it was a sort of *tragédie bouffe* in which the grotesque traits were grossly overdone and the acting overshadowed by the powerful scenic effects. The production toured the provinces and in 1930 was taken to several German towns, then to Paris. Everywhere it provoked great controversy in the press and among the public, greater indeed than the premiere of 1836, and it attracted a good deal more censure than praise. Its director was condemned by leading organs of the Communist Party and denounced on all sides for committing a sacrilege against one of Russia's literary masterpieces, but the production remained in the repertoire right up to 1938, when Meyerhold's theatre was closed.

Other experimental versions of *The Government Inspector* followed in the wake of Meyerhold's bold and imaginative venture. The most bizarre of these was I. Terentiev's futuristic production of 1927, in which Gogol's characters were dressed in emblematic costumes. The Postmaster wore trousers bearing envelopes and stamps, the Doctor had a skull painted on his sleeve, and the Director of Charities bore on his back an image of two strawberries – a reminder of his surname. A new twist was given to the plot by making Khlestakov reappear at the end as the real inspector. But what predominated was the frankly scatological tone, deliberately calculated to scandalize the spectators. Thus, at the centre of the stage was a water-closet to which the actors retired, in Khlestakov's case with a candle and to the strains of Beethoven's *Moonlight Sonata*. This lavatorial approach betrayed the influence of a Freudian study by I. D. Yermakov, who claimed to have discovered in Gogol anal-erotic tendencies.[61]

In the late 1920s a reaction set in against experimental art and in 1934 socialist realism was adopted as the official literary doctrine. With this return to realism modernized versions of *The Government Inspector* fell into disfavour and the play was presented as a brilliant satire on the corrupt tsarist regime. The Maly Theatre production by L. A. Volkov in 1938, a deliberate counterblast to the avant-garde adaptations of the play, was typical of this realistic approach that became the hallmark of nearly all its subsequent appearances on the Soviet stage. An isolated exception was the unsuccessful version presented in 1939 at the Vakhtangov Theatre, in which Gogol's

[60] Besides numerous articles three books are devoted solely to this production, viz., A. A. Gvozdev *et al.*, *«Ревизор» в Театре имени Вс. Мейерхольда*, Leningrad, 1927; E. F. Nikitina (ed.), *Гоголь и Мейерхольд*, Moscow, 1927; D. L. Tal'nikov, *Новая ревизия «Ревизора»*, Moscow-Leningrad, 1927. For the fullest account in English see N. Worrall, 'Meyerhold directs Gogol's "Government Inspector"', *Theatre Quarterly*, Vol. 2, No. 7 (1972), pp. 75–95.

[61] I. D. Yermakov, *Очерки по анализу творчества Н. В. Гоголя*, Moscow–Petrograd, 1924.

satire was distorted by being treated playfully in an attempt to give the play modern appeal.

To this day *The Government Inspector* has maintained its place as the greatest Russian theatre classic and has had many sucessful revivals, notably at the Maly in 1949 and again in 1952 to celebrate the centenary of Gogol's death. Perhaps the most imaginative production of recent years was that put on at the Maly in 1966 by Igor Ilyinsky, an accomplished Gogolian actor. Appreciating that the vices satirized in Gogol's play are still prevalent in the world today, Ilyinsky sought to bring out its contemporary relevance. He was the first producer to give outward and visible expression to the proverb "Don't blame the mirror if your mug is crooked", which Gogol took as the epigraph of *The Government Inspector*. These words were broadcast in the foyer and cloak-room of the theatre and repeated, in the same impassive voice, from loudspeakers in the auditorium before the play started. To reinforce the message, the curtain used at the beginning and end of the show took the form of a huge old-fashioned looking-glass, in which the spectators saw their own reflections. Mirrors of various kinds were also placed on the set to create a somewhat grotesque, confused impression. Thus, the actors were reflected in a distorting mirror as they entered the Governor's reception-room. And at the beginning of Act V the Governor, relishing the prospect of high rank, went up to what appeared to be a mirror and saw in it the figure he dreamt of being, in a fine uniform resplendent with epaulettes and a blue cordon across his chest.

The dumb scene was staged in a novel fashion, allowing it to run the full length of time Gogol had prescribed. The curtain fell on the usual tableau after some 10–12 seconds, then the town police-officers appeared on the proscenium in poses similar to those of the main characters, except that they appeared to be falling. This effect, designed to symbolize the tottering tsarist regime, was achieved by means of special clips which secured the actors' boots to the floor. Shortly afterwards the curtain rose again to reveal the principal players against a backdrop of black velvet, and above them appeared replicas in identical poses, expanding and shrinking in size in what seemed like invisible mirrors. Finally the images dissolved and vanished together with the actors, who descended below stage through traps, still frozen in their various postures.

Many generations of Russian actors have been brought up on the play and its roles are treated as touchstones of acting ability. From Sosnitsky and Shchepkin stemmed quite different interpretations of the Governor, to which various modifications were added by later actors. Among the most memorable later interpreters of this role are Vladimir Davydov, Nikolai Yakovlev and Fedor Grigoriev. The part of Khlestakov, one of the most difficult in the Russian dramatic repertoire, was poorly played in the early years, gained in stature with Sergei Shumsky in 1851, and was successfully realized first by Mikhail Sadovsky in 1877. Since that time the most accomplished exponents of this elusive, chameleon-like character have been Mikhail Chekhov, Stepan Kuznetsov, Erast Garin and Igor Ilyinsky, the last of whom subsequently played the Governor, also with great success. Yet despite all its long experience of *The Government Inspector* the Russian theatre has evolved no generally accepted style of playing Gogol, as it has in the case of Ostrovsky and Chekhov. The play and its characters are still interpreted very differently even within the prevailing realistic tradition.

In addition to its frequent stage appearances *The Government Inspector* has been turned into a film several times. In 1916, during the era of the silent cinema, a Maly Theatre production of the play was filmed by V. Sashin. In 1952 V. Petrov directed a most successful screen version, in which Igor Gorbachev gave a notable peformance as Khlestakov. In 1978 a film adaptation, entitled *The Incognito from Petersburg*, was produced by L. Gaidai. Foreign versions include a Czechoslovak film made in 1933 and one produced in Bombay in 1950, this being an adaptation of the comedy to modern Indian life.[62] The play has also been turned into an opera by composers of various nationalities: by the Czech K. Weis in 1907; by the Russian composer K. N. Shvedov and the Hungarian E. Zádor, both in 1935; by the Italian A. Zanella in 1940, and the German W. Egk in 1957.

The first translation of *The Government Inspector* was Jan Chełmikowski's Polish version, which appeared in 1846. A French translation by Prosper Mérimée was published in 1853[63] and the following year a German one by August von Viedert. The first English translation, by T. Hart-Davies, came out in 1890, followed two years later by that of A. A. Sykes, which included some useful notes and comments. A shortened three-act version of Sykes's rendering was used by the Stage Society in London for the first English performances of the play, given at the Scala Theatre on 17 and 18 June 1906. The first major presentation of the comedy in England was produced by Theodore Komisarjevsky in April 1920 at the Duke of York's Theatre, London, and a few years later at Barnes, using an unpublished

[62] The play was adapted for the cinema in 1934 by Mikhail Bulgakov, in collaboration with a producer named Korostin, but this version was never filmed. The script was published in *Новый журнал*, New York, 1977, No. 127, pp.5–45.

[63] The French novelist did not really understand the play and his translation was later subjected to much criticism and correction. See H. Stolze, 'Mérimées «Inspecteur Général»', in his *Die französische Gogolrezeption*, 1974, pp. 21–32.

translation by T. H. Hall. In America the comedy was first performed in October 1922 at the Yiddish Art Theatre in New York under the direction of Maurice Schwartz, who played the title-role. After this production there followed an English version, given in April 1923 by the Classic Stage Company, with Schwartz again taking the leading part.

Since that time the play has seen many revivals on the stages of the English-speaking world and has been especially popular with amateur companies. Many other translations of it have been made, several specially commissioned for a new production, but the majority of them remain unpublished. Some of the translators have abridged Gogol's five acts to three, and others have even added new characters and inserted material of their own, to such an extent that many acting versions are sheer travesties of the original and descend into pure knockabout farce.

Numerous other translations and adaptations of *The Government Inspector* have appeared in all the major languages of the world and many of the minor ones too. The play has thus attained, in the twentieth century, the status of a great stage classic that belongs to world literature.

The play's character and purpose

The Russian stage in Gogol's time was dominated by the virtual monopoly of the Imperial Theatres in St. Petersburg and Moscow. These theatres, which came under the Ministry of the Court, were bureaucratic institutions, in effect an arm of the state. They received a government subsidy, were administered by functionaries and even hired their actors as civil servants.

The spirit prevailing in the Russian theatre was one of almost unrelieved philistinism. For the most part the public was offered a choice between crude vaudevilles, lurid melodramas and turgid historical pieces. Taste was dictated partly by the authorities who promoted plays that fostered public patriotism and loyalty to the crown, and partly by theatre-goers seeking only entertainment. The Tsar himself, who often patronized the theatre, had a great liking for vaudeville, especially for what Turgenev later called 'pseudo-sublime' dramas, though he detested melodrama. The theatrical offerings were mostly translations and adaptations of light comedies by lesser French playwrights such as Ducange, Scribe, Dumas and Marivaux. Audiences also flocked to see the romantic historical dramas of Nestor Kukolnik and Nikolai Polevoi, and above all the pieces of Prince Shakhovskoi and Mikhail Zagoskin, the leading Russian comedy-writers of the period. Seldom did the theatres present plays by Shakespeare, Molière, Schiller and other great dramatists of Western Europe. With the few native plays of real merit things were even worse. The two outstanding romantic dramas of the time, Pushkin's *Boris Godunov* (1825) and Lermontov's *Masquerade* (1835) had to wait many years for their first public performances, while Griboyedov's *Woe from Wit* (1824), a brilliant satire on Moscow society, was permitted on the stage only in a grossly mutilated form until 1869.

Gogol condemned the vaudeville with its inconsequential trivialities and the melodrama with its cheap sensationalism. He voiced his complaints in two articles he wrote just after *The Government Inspector*, one of which was published in *The Contemporary*. Like Belinsky and others before him, Gogol deplored the fact that the theatre was inundated with foreign works and called for a genuinely national repertoire of plays based on Russian life. "For God's sake," he wrote, "give us Russian characters, give us our own people, our rogues and our eccentrics! Onto the stage with them, for everyone to laugh at!" He repudiated the concept of drama as a kind of aesthetic toy, believing it to be a powerful moral force that should be used to influence men for good. "The theatre," he declared, "is a great school and it has a deep purpose: it teaches a living, useful lesson to a whole crowd, a thousand people at one time and . . . shows us the absurdity of man's habits and vices or the sublimity of his virtues and lofty emotions."

He rejected the conventional comedy with its hackneyed plot, its artificial dialogue, its cardboard lovers, and its inevitable happy ending. Even Molière's plays, despite their author's great technical skill, seemed to him tedious, long-winded and too schematic. Modern drama, he believed, should reflect the problems of contemporary society and reveal its inner workings, 'the springs that keep it in motion'. "Nowadays," says the Second Art-lover in *Leaving the Theatre*, "a more potent theme for a drama plot is the striving to obtain a lucrative post, to display one's brilliance and eclipse the other man at all costs, to avenge oneself for being ignored or scoffed at. Are not rank, financial capital or an advantageous marriage more dynamic subjects now than love?"

He developed these ideas both in *Leaving the Theatre* and in his *Textbook of Literature for Russian Youth*, written in 1844–5 but not published until 1896. To the frivolous comedies prevalent in his time he opposed serious social comedy, designed to enlighten people as well as entertain them. The kernel of such a play is an idea or theme which gives it shape and unity. The theme must be relevant to contemporary life and its problems, and is best conveyed without explicit moralizing. The dramatist should therefore not employ mouthpieces or in any other way seek to foist his message upon the spectator, but must instead allow his play and its characters to speak for themselves. Nor should he impose artificially contrived situations upon his characters; the comic aspect of their behaviour, like all their actions, must spring from within themselves. The characters do not exist for the sake of the plot, but *vice versa*.

The humour of a satirical play is both instructive and destructive, for it enables us to see the truth by attacking those things that degrade man's finer instincts and disfigure him spiritually. As the Young Lady in *Leaving the Theatre* observes: "There are some of us who are prepared to laugh whole-heartedly at a person's crooked nose but have not the courage to laugh at a person's crooked soul." The purpose of social comedy is to show us our crooked souls and induce us to make them straight. To be convincing the playwright must draw on real life for his plot and characters, yet he should not slavishly imitate reality in every detail. The serious comedy-writer gives an objective picture of society, but he is not content to be 'a mere recorder of scenes taking place before his eyes, without using them to demonstrate something the world needs to know'. His dramas do not mirror surface appearances; they reflect the underlying nature of things. He selects some ordinary but revealing situation and presents us with what is essential and typical rather than a literal reproduction of life. In short, Gogol believed in artistic realism and rejected naturalism.

He consistently applied these dramatic principles in the plays that he wrote. *The Government Inspector*, unlike nearly all earlier Russian comedies, is based not on a love-plot but an important social problem, namely the corruption practised by the Tsar's administrators. The scenes in which Khlestakov woos the Governor's wife and daughter are pure parodies of the conventional love-plot, and there is no happy ending. Gogol dispensed with the stock figure of the *raisonneur*, whose function in traditional comedy was to act as the voice of morality: there are, however, some traces of the *raisonneur* in the character of Osip and even the Governor, as Gogol himself explains in his introductory observations.[64] He further shunned the dramatic cliché by rejecting the crude, unrealistic division of characters into good and bad, presenting instead a collection of petty knaves. And finally Khlestakov, unlike his counterpart in previous comedies of mistaken identity, is no true impostor but a rather dull-witted young man who assumes a false role without realizing it for a long time.

Nevertheless, Gogol did not depart entirely from the established dramatic canons; he retained, for example, the time-honoured conventions of the soliloquy and the aside. He also observed the classical unities of time, place

[64] Gogol was not the first Russian dramatist to exclude the *raisonneur*. This artificial, rather tedious personage had been abandoned at least thirty years earlier by Krylov and others.

and action, from which the play derives its compact structure and concentrated vigour. The events in the play, it is true, are spread over two days, but they move rapidly and could easily be encompassed within the space of twenty-four hours, as the rules of drama then required. The location is a district town situated in the very heart of Russia, and the scene shifts only between the Governor's house and the local inn. Lastly, the action itself is all of a piece, involving every character directly or indirectly, without the complication of any sub-plot or side issue. The play could well be described, in fact, as a broadly but not wholly realistic comedy with symbolic overtones, set in a neo-classical framework.

In his *Author's Confession* Gogol singles out *The Government Inspector* as a turning-point in his creative life, stating that it was the first work in which he had tried to exert a moral influence on society and in doing so became convinced that he had found his true vocation as a writer. In his early tales of Ukrainian life, he tells us, his humour had been gay and light-hearted. But then, under the influence of Pushkin, he came to take a more serious view of literature and decided to turn his comic gifts to satirical ends.[65] "I realized," he wrote, "that in my writings I had been laughing gratuitously, to no purpose, without knowing why myself. If one is going to laugh it is far better to have a good laugh, and at something that really deserves general ridicule. In *The Government Inspector* I decided to gather in one heap all the bad things I then knew to exist in Russia, all the injustices committed in places and cases where above all justice is required of man, and to ridicule everything at one go. But as we all know, this had a shattering effect. Behind the laughter, which had never before been so powerful in my writings, the reader could sense the sadness."[66]

Significantly, there is no suggestion here of the allegorical meaning Gogol had attached to his play only a year earlier in *The Denouement*. Instead he now claimed, with typical exaggeration, that his comedy contained an exposure of all the evils then abounding in Russia.[67] Yet the greatest social

[65] Gogol states that he turned to satirical humour in 1835, after publishing *Mirgorod*, but there were signs of this change at least two years earlier when he started his comedy *The Order of Vladimir, Third Class*. Moreover, he was influenced in this direction not only by Pushkin, but by Belinsky and other literary critics of the time, such as Polevoi. This is convincingly demonstrated by V. V. Gippius at the beginning of his essay *Проблематика и композиция «Ревизора»* (1936), an English translation of which is given in R. A. Maguire's *Gogol from the Twentieth Century* (1974), pp. 216–65.

[66] This last observation was probably inspired by the remark Nadezhdin made in his review about the sadness concealed beneath the surface of the play.

[67] Gogol made similar extravagant claims for his *Dead Souls*. In his letter to Pushkin of 7 October 1835 (where he asked for a drama plot) he wrote: "In this novel I want to show the

evil of the time, the system of serf-owning, is nowhere even mentioned in the play, much less exposed or ridiculed, as it had been previously, for example in two comic operas, Knyazhnin's *A Mishap with a Carriage* (1779) and Krylov's *The Coffee-grinder* (1783). The plain fact is that Gogol did not look upon serfdom as an outrage against human dignity. Moreover, as Chernyshevsky later observed, the satire on officialdom in *The Government Inspector* is comparatively mild.[68] Knowing that the censors would not allow him to tackle the really important bureaucrats of St. Petersburg, Gogol had to content himself with portraying a group of ordinary provincial officials who are dishonest and devious, but far from being black-hearted villains. He was much less bold and outspoken in his condemnation of bribery than I. Sokolov had been in his comedy *The Judge's Name-day* (1781) and V. Kapnist in his satirical verse drama *The Slanderer* (1798).

Bribery is the chief abuse that Gogol was attacking in his play, yet it is handled in a curiously ambiguous fashion, without any of the collusion one normally finds in such dealings. It is a peculiar, one-sided kind of bribery in which Khlestakov asks the town officials for financial assistance and takes their bribes on the understanding that these are loans, though it is very doubtful whether he seriously intends to repay them later. When the merchants press him to take a silver tray together with their 'loans' he accepts, but when they offer him sugar and wine he rejects these as bribes. It is the shrewd, practical Osip who snaps them up, for all is grist that comes to his mill.

Gogol's claim, in 1847, that he wrote *The Government Inspector* with the purpose of exerting a beneficial influence on Russian society by exposing its ills is a far cry from the statement he made eleven years earlier, in his letter to Pushkin, that he intended to write a comedy that would be 'funnier than the devil'. To be sure, the two aims are not necessarily incompatible, since the satirist relies on humour, the humour of ridicule, as the chief weapon in his armoury. It is clear, however, that when he began to write his play Gogol conceived it as a light comedy and had little or no thought of changing the hearts of his countrymen and bringing about a moral reform. Two years earlier, in 1833, he had abandoned his satirical comedy *The Order of Vladimir, Third Class*, rightly suspecting that it would run foul of the censor

whole of Russia, at least from one side." And a year later he wrote to Zhukovsky: "All of Russia will appear in it."

[68] The comment was made in a review of P. A. Kulish's edition of Gogol's works and letters (1857). See N. G. Chernyshevsky, *Полное собрание сочинений*, Moscow, Vol. 4 (1948), pp. 655–6.

since it touched the powerful bureaucracy of St. Petersburg. "There is nothing for it but to invent the most innocent plot that even a police-sergeant couldn't be offended by," he wrote to Pogodin at the time. "But what is a comedy," he added, "without truth and malice!" Accordingly he proceeded to write something totally innocuous, his improbable farce entitled *The Suitors*, but put it on one side, feeling that it was not yet ready for the stage.

In a similarly light-hearted mood he then embarked on *The Government Inspector*, producing in the first draft an amusing comedy full of farce, strong caricature and exuberant gaiety, something very similar in style to the vaudevilles then enjoying a great vogue in the Russian theatre. He continued working on the play for several months, during which time his conception changed into something altogether more ambitious and profound as he came to appreciate the full potentialities of his theme, one capable of demonstrating his firm conviction that works of art can influence men for good. In like manner *Dead Souls*, which he began in the same year as *The Government Inspector*, gradually evolved in the process of composition from a gay, picaresque novel, conceived without any moral purpose, into a grand epic 'poem' which, when completed, would lay bare the very soul of Russia and compare in scope with Dante's immortal trilogy.

By the time *The Government Inspector* was ready for stage presentation and publication it had been transmuted, in conformity with Gogol's new and deeper purpose, from a hastily written near-vaudeville into a well-made satirical comedy which bore only a few residual traces of farce. But despite Gogol's alterations and excisions the play was generally taken to be a farce and his moralistic intention, as we have seen, went almost wholly unnoticed. After seeing his comedy treated as a mere farce by so many people, and especially by most of the actors, Gogol was so disgusted that he put it aside for a few years. He later rewrote a good half of the play, paring down the farcical episodes even further and increasing its satirical content. Yet for all the artistic refinements he introduced into the work he in no way altered its essential character, which had already crystallized in the stage and published versions of 1836. He was thus substantially correct in stating that he had intended the play to be morally illuminating as well as diverting. This had not been his original aim, it is true, but it was soon to become the purpose inspiring it after the initial draft was completed. In this instance, at least, he was not seeking to impose on his play something which was never in his mind at any stage of its composition, as he had done previously in *The Denouement*.

In *Leaving the Theatre* and in the letter he wrote to Pogodin on 10 May 1836 Gogol claimed to be portraying officials whose illegal conduct was an exception to the general rule. This was plainly untrue, for he knew as well as everyone else that the vast majority of Russian officials practised bribery and corruption. Indeed, some years later he showed great interest in an honest official whom his mother had met in Kharkov.[69] In claiming to have presented exceptional cases he was evidently motivated by a deep feeling of alarm at the political construction put on his play. Most people regarded it as an attack on the Russian system of government, while for him it was no more than a denunciation of corrupt men.

In a letter to Zhukovsky, written at the end of 1847, he recalled the public reaction when his play first appeared. "People began to see in the comedy a desire to ridicule the legitimate order of things and governmental forms, whereas it was my intention to deride only arbitrary departures by some persons from the regular and lawful order. The performance of *The Government Inspector* made a painful impression on me. I was angry both with the spectators, who misunderstood me, and with myself, who was to blame for their failure to understand me." Gogol refers here to the malpractices of 'some persons', apparently still unwilling to acknowledge that corruption was the general rule among bureaucrats and not confined to a few individuals. He came nearer the truth in an essay on Russian poetry and drama which he included in his *Selected Passages*. Here he singled out Fonvizin's *The Minor* and Griboyedov's *Woe from Wit* as genuine social comedies which did not indulge in 'light-hearted mockery of the absurd aspects of society', but exposed its 'wounds and diseases, its grave internal abuses with the ruthless power of irony'. These comedy-writers, he stated further on, 'rose up not against an individual, but against a whole host of abuses, against the deviation of a whole society from the right path'. Although these remarks refer to Gogol's predecessors, they provide the key to his own purpose in *The Government Inspector*. At the time he wrote his play Gogol, like Fonvizin and Griboyedov, subscribed to the dictum *ridendo castigat mores*.

On reading *Selected Passages* the radicals and liberals among Gogol's admirers, such as Belinsky, Herzen and Turgenev, concluded that he had reneged on his former progressive views and become a political turncoat. This was a complete misconception on their part, however, for Gogol's political outlook, like his religious convictions, remained substantially the same throughout his life. The evidence of his close acquaintances and of his own writings, including his correspondence, leaves no doubt that politically

[69] In a letter dated August 1842 he asked his mother to tell the official that 'his nobility and honest poverty amidst those who grow rich by unlawful acts will find a response deep down in every noble heart'. In his *Parting Words* (Letter 30 of *Selected Passages*) he offered similar encouragement to an official who refused bribes.

he was always a conservative. Even as a schoolboy in 1827 he showed himself to be a legitimist and monarchist, and he expressed the same attitude towards political authority in the historical essays he published in *Arabesques* and in his dramatic fragment *Alfred*. He accepted the social order existing in Russia and believed in the strict observance of the country's laws. In his opinion the imperfections of the state machine were not the result of bad laws or of an unjust order but were due entirely to human failure.[70] This was exactly the view taken by the Russian moralists and satirists of the eighteenth century. In the words of Dobrov in Kapnist's *The Slanderer*: "The laws are sacred, but those who administer them are evil villains" (Законы святы, но исполнители – лихие супостаты).

Gogol's moral aim in writing *The Government Inspector* was to persuade state officials to behave with scrupulous honesty. The finale of the play was intended to show that dire consequences would befall those who disobeyed the law. It was meant to be seen as a triumph for the government, a victory for justice. But this was not how most of his contemporaries interpreted the ending. The whole logic of the play – and indeed the realities of Russian life – suggested to them that the officials, though temporarily stunned by the Gendarme's announcement, would soon recover and seek to suborn the real inspector. And if the latter ran true to type he would readily succumb to temptation and pocket their bribes. Hence Gogol's *deus ex machina* failed to retrieve the situation and the officials were seen to suffer the punishment not of the law but only of public ridicule and humiliation. Thus viewed, the comedy inevitably appeared to be an indictment of officialdom as such and by implication of the whole regime.

The widespread misunderstanding of Gogol's purpose was referred to by Prince Vyazemsky in a postscript which he added in 1876 to his article on *The Government Inspector*. "The comedy," he wrote, "was considered by many people to be a liberal declaration rather like Beaumarchais' comedy *The Barber of Seville*; it was seen as a kind of political fire-bomb that had been lobbed at society in the guise of a comedy. Some welcomed it and rejoiced in it as a bold, albeit disguised attack on the powers that be. In their view Gogol, though choosing a district town as his field of battle, was aiming higher ... Others, of course, looked upon the comedy as an attack on the state: they were alarmed and frightened by it and saw the unfortunate or fortunate comic writer almost as a dangerous rebel." Liberals and conservatives alike had seen in it an

[70] This opinion is most clearly articulated in his first written response to Belinsky's famous letter from Salzbrunn. Gogol's long reply, which he tore up, was later reconstituted from the fragments by his first biographer, P. A. Kulish.

attack on the system of government, but they were mistaken since 'there was nothing political in Gogol's conception'.

Gogol's optimistic moral view of *The Government Inspector* failed to carry conviction. His challenge to the conscience of his compatriots had fallen on deaf ears, and all his subsequent protestations and explanations were of no avail. The play now belonged to the public and it was the political significance attached to it, together with its outstanding artistic merits, that determined its historical place in Russian literature.

Structure, style and characterization

The excellence of *The Government Inspector* lies in its artistic unity, its vivid delineation of character, and its rich variety of style. In construction, characterization and dialogue it is a masterpiece of dramatic skill. With the Governor's terse opening announcement the spectator is plunged *in medias res*, his curiosity at once aroused. These few words set the tone for the whole play, bursting upon the assembled officials with explosive force and striking in their hearts a panic fear which provides the impetus for the ensuing events.

The pace of the action varies throughout the play. After the bombshell at the beginning the first act proceeds fairly slowly for a time, as the true state of affairs in the town is revealed by the instructions the Governor issues in order to pull the wool over the eyes of the visiting official by creating a façade of good order in the spirit of the famous 'Potemkin villages', erected fifty years earlier to deceive Catherine the Great. The action gathers momentum again after Bobchinsky and Dobchinsky report seeing Khlestakov at the inn and the Governor is galvanized into a flurry of activity. Acts II and III move at a leisurely tempo in their central scenes (II.8 and III.6) and more rapidly elsewhere. In Act IV a varied pace helps to avoid the monotony of repetition in the bribery scenes, then comes a swift development in the last part, leading to its culmination in Khlestakov's departure. After this the first seven scenes of Act V move slowly, to be followed by the Governor's sudden collapse in his very hour of triumph – a typically Gogolian *peripeteia* which strikes a note of genuine tragedy at the end.

Gogol, a master of stagecraft, paid the most scrupulous attention to the structure of his comedy and carefully composed the words and actions of all its characters. The play contains several unexpected turns, each of which propels the action forward until in the last act the plot moves inexorably to its climax and resolution, when the scales fall from the eyes of the townspeople. Thus interest is maintained as one comic situation succeeds another, with mounting tension, in a closely knit sequence. The development of the dramatic conflict, given the characters of the people involved, flows naturally and inevitably from the situation in which they find themselves, and there are no loose ends left untied at the finish. The play, with its remarkable compactness, forms an artistic whole, displaying both dramatic and psychological unity.

The comedy is founded on mutual fear and misunderstanding, and this is reflected in the very structure of the play, its exposition being divided between the protagonists. In the first exposition (Act I, Sc. 1–3) the Governor and his associates reveal a picture of their malfeasance in office. In the second exposition (Act II, Sc. 1–7) Khlestakov is presented, mainly through the wry observations of his manservant, following a procedure long established in comedy. Both expositions end on a note of tension; in the first the Governor learns of Khlestakov's sojourn at the inn and in the second Khlestakov is informed of the Governor's arrival on a 'courtesy call'. In each instance one misapprehends the reason for the other's presence.

There is an elegant symmetry in the design of the play. Its conclusion is as brief and dramatic as its opening; it closes, as it begins, with a group scene in which the arrival of an inspector is announced. The reading of a letter precipitates the denouement, just as the reading of a letter launches the action. Thus at the end of the comedy the dramatic wheel has turned full circle, as the officials are transfixed with horror in the face of a catastrophe that seems about to repeat itself.

The play presents, in Belinsky's words, 'a self-contained world', except for a brief time near the end, when Khlestakov's letter is read out aloud before the assembled company. Each official, on hearing the mocking description of himself, disclaims the likeness. The reading of the letter serves to hold up a mirror to each of the guilty men. Having lost face with their fellows on stage, the Postmaster, Zemlyanika and Khlopov in turn appeal to the spectators for sympathy. The Governor goes further, addressing the whole world, all Christendom, then, stepping outside the confines of the play, he rounds on the members of the audience and flings the laughter back in their faces. Metaphorically speaking, he holds the comedy up as a mirror and the spectators see themselves as the 'mugs' to which Gogol refers in his epigraph. At this, perhaps the most powerful moment of the play, the barrier falls between the stage and the audience, making them one, and though it rises again soon after, a significant symbolic act has been performed, whereby the spectators are compelled to look not outwards, but inside themselves. Laughter permeated with the shock of self-recognition has a cathartic effect.

The denouement of the play poses a difficult problem from the artistic point of view. The Gendarme's arrival, giving a final twist to the plot, is a brilliant *coup de théâtre*, but it fails to fulfil Gogol's avowed aim of showing the law triumphant in catching up with the offenders. The author's purpose could have been made unmistakably clear only if he had ended the play with the actual appearance of the real inspector and the dispensation of justice or with a speech in praise of the government or honesty – blatantly moralistic intrusions of the kind Russian audiences had come to expect, but which he wished to avoid at all costs. As it is, what Gogol describes as 'the electric shock' produced by the final words leaves the situation unresolved, for justice may in fact be done, but it is not seen to be done. The idea of retribution or nemesis does not take tangible shape, for the Gendarme's words may be taken to mean that the law will be upheld or equally be seen as heralding a recurrence of what has been enacted before. Thus everything remains as uncertain and menacing at the end as it was at the beginning. This ambiguity is regarded by some as highly effective, and by others as an artistic flaw. Both Belinsky and Nemirovich-Danchenko consider the Gendarme's appearance and pronouncement to be an essential part of the play, whereas the critic Khrapchenko treats it as an artificial contrivance since 'it is not dictated by the inner development of the action but embodies Gogol's belief in tsarist justice'.[71] Stepanov, another modern critic, agrees that the denouement reflects the author's loyalist outlook, but argues that it does not spoil the play because Gogol has brought about in his spectators a sense of the disparity between the ideal and the real and thus led them to draw the 'right' political conclusions.[72]

A different problem, one of a purely technical nature, is posed by the dumb scene, which represents the moment of truth, illuminating all that has gone before. This elaborately formal tableau, in which the play reaches the point of maximum tension and the effect of which should be shattering, according to Gogol, is notoriously difficult to stage effectively. With the best will in the world, few actors can stand for long like lifeless statues, frozen to the spot. The strain is altogether too great and in practice the curtain generally falls after about 10–15 seconds, although Gogol directed that the scene should last almost 1½ minutes, having already reduced it from 2–3 minutes after seeing the difficulty of sustaining it so long in production. One way of solving this problem is for the producer to modify the scene, as Meyerhold and Ilyinsky did, so that it may run the full length of time without losing its impact. Such a solution, though it violates the letter of Gogol's instructions, accords entirely with their spirit and serves to set a symbolic seal on the entire piece.

71 M. B. Khrapchenko, *Творчество Гоголя*, 1954, p. 170.
72 N. L. Stepanov, *Н. В. Гоголь. Творческий путь*, 1955, p. 361.

The Government Inspector is unrivalled by any other Russian play for its sheer comic power, sustained from beginning to end. In it the comic element, which is predominantly satirical, derives from three sources: situation, character and speech. Comic situations are the least important source of humour. The comic springs are chiefly in the characters themselves, though the play is not a comedy of character in the traditional sense, as applied to Molière's works, for example.

The nub of the plot is a case of mistaken identity which creates a situation of dramatic irony from the beginning of Act II almost to the very end of the play, when the truth comes out. The error opens up comic possibilities which are exploited to the full. The point of maximum comic intensity is attained in the very middle of the play, in Act III, Sc. 5, where the Governor and Zemlyanika vie with each other in self-praise, and Sc. 6, where Khlestakov holds the stage with a spontaneous outpouring of rodomontade. Other comic high points are Act II, Sc. 8, Act IV, Sc. 3–7, and Act V, Sc. 8. Comic confusion is at its best in Act II, Sc. 8, where the Governor first encounters Khlestakov. Much of the time the two protagonists talk at cross-purposes, and a humorously revealing contrast emerges between the words the Governor speaks out loud and his real thoughts, conveyed in asides. There is a piquant irony in the fact that he swallows Khlestakov's lies but disbelieves him when he tells the truth; the wily old fox is nonplussed by an innocent young puppy.

Physical comedy is used sparingly and for the most part with a purpose, not simply to serve a farcical turn; only in the wooing scenes of Act IV does the play verge on farce, and even then it is with the aim of parodying popular sentimental drama. Thus, when Dr. Hiebner babbles a few incoherent sounds we are given some inkling of the state of Russian medicine at that time, and when the Governor is about to don a hat-box instead of his hat he reveals his state of agitation. Even the antics of Bobchinsky and Dobchinsky are not mere buffoonery, but illustrate their curiosity or anxiety to please. These two droll dumplings are the most innocent people in the play and the only ones who are funny in themselves, yet even they no more strive to amuse than any of the others.

The comedy abounds in sparkling dialogue, punctuated by occasional flashes of wit. It is above all a play of verbal humour expressed in vigorous and varied language, with subtle overtones, many of them quite impossible to capture in English. The stylistic device used most frequently is repetition. This is sometimes employed for other than comic effects; in the opening scenes, for instance, the words 'inspector' and 'incognito' resound like sinister shots, and Khlestakov's repeated use of the patronizing remark

'Good' in the second half of Act IV betrays his growing arrogance. But generally the reverberations are humorous, as when Bobchinsky repeats the words with which Dobchinsky interrupts his rambling narrative, appropriating them to himself, or when the Postmaster twice repeats the unflattering description of the Governor given in Khlestakov's letter. A comic boomerang effect is produced by the phrase 'Oh, such goings-on!' (Ах, какой пассаж!) used first by Anna Andreyevna and then by her daughter when each discovers the other being wooed by Khlestakov. In the bribery scenes of Act IV each official uses the same form of words on entering ('I have the honour to introduce myself') and when taking his leave ('I will not presume to intrude on you further'), clasping his sword or bowing as he does so. The repetition of these stock formulae, and similar ones such as 'Quite so, sir' (так точно-с) and 'Not at all, sir' (никак нет-с) tends to diminish the humanity of the people who trot them out to the accompaniment of ritualized gestures, which fit perfectly Bergson's definition of the comic as 'something mechanical encrusted upon the living'. And a similar effect is achieved by Gogol's comparisons, in which human beings are demeaned by being likened to the denizens of the animal kingdom. In Khlestakov's eyes Zemlyanika is a perfect pig in a skull-cap and the Governor as stupid as a grey gelding. To the Governor the wispy Khlestakov in his tail-coat looks just like a fly with its wings clipped, and his description of Bobchinsky and Dobchinsky as bob-tailed magpies is equally apt.

Hyperbole, Gogol's most typical device, is effectively employed by three of the characters. Osip likens the rumblings in his stomach to the roar of a whole regiment of men sounding their bugles and declares that his hunger is so acute that he could devour 'the whole world'. The Governor indicates the remoteness of his provincial town by claiming that it is three years' gallop from any frontier, and later he reproaches the merchants with draining the contents of sixteen samovars a day, such is their addiction to tea. But Khlestakov's exaggerations are the boldest and most far-fetched of all, as befits his character. They reach a climax in the famous bragging scene (III,6), where he speaks of the sumptuous entertainment given at balls in St. Petersburg and cites by way of example a water-melon costing 700 roubles. He arrogates to himself the authorship of various dramatic, operatic and other works, adding casually that he tossed them all off in a single evening. Later he claims that when a temporary replacement was sought for the head of his department he was eventually seen as the only man for the job, whereupon no fewer than 35,000 couriers scoured the city streets in search of him.

Gogol further displays great inventive powers as a creator of verbal inconsequence and nonsense. A classic example of pseudo-explanation occurs early in the play when, in answer to the Governor's complaint that a certain court assessor always reeks of alochol, the Judge reports the unfortunate man as saying that as a child he was bruised by his nurse and there has been a whiff of vodka about him ever since. Illogicality shows itself again when the Director of Schools is reprimanded for allowing liberal ideas to be instilled into his pupils because one of the teachers pulled faces at them whilst the marshal of the nobility was on a visit. And Anna Andreyevna produces a noteworthy *non sequitur* when she indignantly protests that her eyes must be dark since she always tells her fortune by the queen of clubs.

Absurdity and ineptitude of speech are even commoner than illogicality. The Governor instructs the Postmaster to open other people's letters 'just a little' and read them. Khlestakov seeks to console Anna Andreyevna for living in the remote provinces by pointing out that the country, 'too', has its little hills and brooks. And later she reports him as threatening that if she did not requite his feelings he would put an end to his life 'by dying'. Zemlyanika, during his tête-à-tête with Khlestakov, is told that he appears a little taller than he did the previous day, and the complaisant official replies that it is very likely so, being only too ready to concede an overnight increase in stature in order to please his superior. In Act IV a typically Gogolian exchange takes place when Khlestakov, alone with Maria for the first time, enquires where she was intending to go, and she tells him she was going nowhere. When he demands to know why, her answer is that she thought her mother might be there, but he insists again on knowing why she was 'going nowhere'. Soon after this he proposes to her mother and pledges his instant undying love, but she demurs on the grounds that she is 'in a manner of speaking' already married. He brushes her objection aside and, striving to echo the literary sentimentalists, declaims rhapsodically: "We shall retreat to the shade of the waters . . ." – a precious piece of nonsense.

Gogol played a major part in breaking down the barriers between written and spoken Russian, thereby accomplishing the same kind of reform in prose that Pushkin had achieved in verse, and incidentally earning himself much opprobrium for flouting the literary canons of the time by using words and expressions that were not accepted in the beau monde. His dramatic dialogue is predominantly colloquial, but embraces many other styles, the formally polite, the high-flown romantic, the bureaucratic, the commonplace and the crude. Replete with the idioms and rhythms of spoken Russian, it incorporates anacolutha, pleonasms, solecisms, repetitions, hesitations and rhetorical questions – all features of everyday speech. The dialogue is thus natural, yet not naturalistic, for it is not a replica of authentic discourse, but ordinary speech concentrated and raised to the level of art. Gogol's mastery of language and verbal exuberance created dialogue such as had never been heard on the Russian stage before and has seldom been equalled since. His creative, poetic use of the vernacular has been noted by more than one commentator. In 1842 Stepan Shevyrev, a literary critic, wrote of the 'inexhaustible poetry of the play's comic style'[73] and later the famous producer Nemirovich-Danchenko said that he conceived of the play 'as if it were written in verse'. And indeed the work often attains the density of poetic diction, yielding many a pregnant and now proverbial phrase, such as the Governor's remarks "You take more than your rank allows!", "She (the N.C.O.'s wife) flogged herself", and Khlestakov's observation that the purpose of life is 'to pluck the flowers of pleasure' – his philosophy in a nutshell.

In the final text of the play, produced after much painstaking revision and refinement, every word and phrase counts and each remark, even the most inconsequential, throws some light on the character of the speaker. Each participant, while remaining faithful to the speech of the time and of his social class, possesses his own manner of speaking; here, in truth, the style proclaims the man. This difference in speech characteristics, largely an innovation in Russian drama,[74] is what brings the fictitious persons to life and stamps them with individuality. It is this gallery of memorable, sharply drawn characters, each with his or her own voice, that makes the comedy as fresh and alive today as when it was written.

The Governor, a petty bureaucratic tyrant and ambitious careerist of small education, is the sharpest and most rapacious as well as the most important of all the officials. He speaks with greater expressiveness and a wider range of tones than anyone else in the play, trimming his tongue to each person and situation he has to deal with. He now rants and bullies, now flatters and fawns. When addressing his colleagues he uses a familiar tone and exerts his authority with ironic politeness. With Khlestakov he is extremely deferential, couching his thoughts in dry officialese and assuming the mask of a loyal, upright guardian of order. With members of his family his speech is unbuttoned, sometimes even coarse and abusive, but he vents his ripest invective on the merchants, whom he believes to have betrayed him. His language is normally racy and colourful, seasoned with expletives, so strong at times that his wife chides him for it. It bespeaks a man of robust instinct,

[73] In 1836 Shevyrev, then the regular critic of the *Moscow Observer*, had refused to write a review of *The Government Inspector*, describing it, according to Belinsky, as 'a sordid comedy'. But Gogol and Shevyrev became close friends in 1839.

[74] Before Gogol only Fonvizin had individualized his dramatic characters through their speech, and then not fully.

one who professes religion only for reasons of respectability, referring hypocritically to God, sin and Christian duty, while at heart he is a fatalist. He is inclined to deliver himself of gnomic utterances, lapsing on occasion into rhetorical phrases of vacuous orotundity.

Second in importance among the town officials is the Judge, a pompous ass, fond of fornication and hare-coursing, who seeks to give the impression of being a liberal-minded sceptic who thinks for himself. He indulges in homespun philosophy and prides himself on his knowledge, though his reading is paltry and he is deplorably ignorant of the law, like most Russian magistrates at that time. He pontificates ponderously and in booming tones, using short, simple constructions for maximum effect, and although he occasionally resorts to a literary turn of phrase, his style is for the most part formal and undistinguished.

Most devious and sycophantic of the officials is Zemlyanika, a sneak and toady of aldermanic girth. He wheedles and ingratiates himself in unctuous, dulcet tones, posing as a zealous servant of the state and denouncing several of his colleagues behind their backs. It is he who, having suggested that they should bribe Khlestakov and see him individually, contrives to go in last of the officials so that he can tell tales against them without the risk of being informed on himself. His speech, now honeyed and now coarse, matches the duplicity of his character.

Very different is the Postmaster, who is no hypocrite but a simple soul with an insatiable curiosity about other people's doings, which he indulges by prying into the private correspondence that passes through his hands. The least articulate of the officials, he has difficulty in expressing his thoughts and feelings, easily gets tongue-tied or lost for words and speaks in short, broken phrases. His poverty of vocabulary reflects his poverty of spirit.

Khlopov is the official most lacking in personality. He is a timid, mouse-like creature, easily worried by the least thing and absolutely terrified at the prospect of his schools being inspected. He hardly dares to open his mouth for fear of putting his foot in it, and his speech is punctuated with expressions of anxiety and exclamations of alarm.

The fussy little pot-bellied squirelings Bobchinsky and Dobchinsky are figures that derive from the tradition of the *commedia dell'arte*. Yet though they are remarkably alike in appearance, these near-twins are nicely differentiated in character. Bobchinsky, a bachelor, is the sprightlier and more garrulous; Dobchinsky, the family man, is more staid and serious. They are extremely courteous to everyone they meet and share a passion for spreading tales about town. Both gesticulate a great deal and speak rapidly, fearful of being interrupted, liberally sprinkling their speech with particles and interjections. Their sentences are as shapeless and inelegant as they are themselves.

Osip, Khlestakov's manservant, is a dour, canny peasant who has seen much but says little. He is as economical with his tongue as with odd pieces of string or anything else and can sum up a situation in a few apt words. He speaks in an even tone and adopts an insolent, ironic manner towards his master, for whom he has scant respect. His language is that of a domestic serf who has lived long enough in St. Petersburg to acquire a superficial metropolitan veneer and a smattering of city speech. He makes abundant use of affective suffixes, comes out with pseudo-learned coinages such as заботность ('troublesomeness') and mispronounces words of foreign origin in the vernacular fashion, saying *keyatr* for *teatr* ('theatre') and *preshpekt* for *prospekt* ('avenue'). His monologue at the beginning of Act II, a gem of salty, idiomatic and at times ungrammatical Russian, is one of the finest pieces of writing in the whole play. The other servants, the policemen and the petitioners all speak a pure Russian of the people, and Gogol paid careful attention to reproducing the nuances of merchants' speech.

Anna Andreyevna and her daughter are typical women of the provincial gentry. The vain, snobbish mother fancies herself irresistible to men, yearns for life in high society and reveals her pretensions to gentility in her affected use of words and expressions derived from French; the one word амбре ('sweet scent') epitomizes her conception of bliss – a scent-laden boudoir, redolent of sensual pleasure. But when rebuking her husband or daughter she soon betrays her essential vulgarity and lapses into an earthier colloquial style. Maria is also flirtatious, but at the same time she is more modest and straightforward than her mother, who is plainly jealous of her. She is an artless, sentimental young lady, lacking in self-assurance. Her speech, bereft of individuality, is the most neutral language used by anyone in the play.

Khlestakov, the principal character, is one of Gogol's greatest creations, a figure worthy to be set beside Shakespeare's Falstaff and Rostand's Cyrano de Bergerac. A junior civil servant from a landowning family of modest means, he represents a new breed of bureaucrat, the young scion of the gentry who is attracted by the glitter of urban life and seeks to ape the grand style of the opulent, even to become a trend-setter. His dominant passion is to show off, to appear important and cultured, but besides being a poseur he is many other things: dandy, philanderer, sensualist, gambler, braggart, fantasist and empty windbag. He is a nullity, but a complex nullity. Whereas the Governor is a purposeful opportunist who actively exploits his position to the utmost, Khlestakov is an aimless opportunist who passively waits on people and events. The Governor's lies are those of a politician, directed towards self-preservation and self-advancement, while Khlestakov's lies are those of the romancer, aimed at self-gratification and self-aggrandizement. He lives wholly in the present, takes his pleasures where he can find them and acts entirely according to the whim of the moment. A shallow, irresponsible egotist, he is too weak to be a convincing villain and too stupid to be a scheming impostor.[75] He is genuinely surprised at the executive-style lunch with which he is regaled at the hospital, not realizing that it has been provided to soften him up. In his innocence he never suspects that the banknotes eagerly thrust into his hand by the officials are anything more than loans; he does not know how to take bribes because he is too lowly to have been offered them before. And it is a long time before it dawns on him that he has been taken for an important personage.

In contrast to the local officials, most of whom are ageing, portly and slow of speech, Khlestakov is youthful, slightly built and a rapid speaker. He is all quicksilver, mercurial, with swift changes of front, and his speech mirrors his fluid character. He gabbles jerkily, using disjointed and often unfinished phrases, as his grasshopper mind flits bewilderingly from one subject to another. His tone varies with his mood and his interlocutor. He can be pretentious and arrogant, or craven and conciliatory. Towards servants he is alternately wheedling and abusive; with others he can be polite or familiar, flippant or grave, now mincing, now grovelling, blustering and hectoring by turns and, when he is scared, yelling like a whipped whelp. His speech comprises many elements: colloquial and demotic vocabulary, civil service jargon, card players' slang, salon phrases and snatches of well-known verse. But his style is for the most part neutral and conventional. His comparisons are commonplace, his poetic rhetoric is banal, even his invective is trite. He is at his most inept when seeking to impress the ladies as a gallant by airing the little French he has and uttering phrases of exaggerated politeness, as for example when he enquires of Maria: "May I dare to be so happy as to offer you a chair?" He is at his best in the bragging scene, where in a state of verbal intoxication he vaunts himself with increasing extravagance in such megalomaniac flights of fancy that the officials, already frightened out of their wits, are stunned with awe. Here he is, revelling in the limelight, a Russian Munchausen who transforms lying into a creative art and imposes upon his

[75] D. Merezhkovsky, in his *Гоголь и черт*, Moscow, 1906, p. 10, describes Khlestakov as intelligent. He evidently misread the passage in *Extract from a Letter* (to Pushkin) where Gogol says that the leading role would have been better played if he had given it to one of the least talented actors and told him that the hero was 'cunning, perfectly proper, clever and perhaps even virtuous'. The truth is, of course, that Khlestakov is none of these things, but 'plain stupid', as Gogol states in his letter to Shchepkin of 10 May, 1836. Nor is Osip a fool, as Merezhkovsky says (p. 9), but a shrewd fellow, much sharper than Khlestakov.

listeners his own image of himself – commanding, magnificent, omnicompetent.

Various suggestions have been made as to the literary antecedents Gogol may have had in mind when he created his Khlestakov. Among these are famous liars of West European drama such as Dorante in Corneille's *Le Menteur* (1643), Mascarille in Molière's *Les Précieuses ridicules* (1659), Lelio in Goldoni's *Il Bugiardo* (1750), and similar figures in Russian comedy, including Verkholet in Knyazhnin's *The Braggart* (1786), Semyon in Krylov's *Lesson to the Daughters* (1807), Alnaskarov in Khmelnitsky's *Castles in the Air* (1818), and Pustolobov in Kvitka's *Visitor from the Capital* (written 1827). Similarities certainly exist between Khlestakov and these other stage liars, but there is a very important difference that marks him off from them. Gogol's hero is no deliberate deceiver; he lies without intending to delude other people, seeking only to impress them. In this respect he represents a significant transformation of the traditional figure of the impostor. To create a new, passive type of hero who stumbles into the role of a 'great man' was in fact a stroke of genius on Gogol's part.

There has been much conjecture, too, about possible prototypes of Khlestakov from among Gogol's contemporaries, understandably so since the Russian theatre, from the time of Catherine, had presented comedies with characters based on, and usually satirizing, living persons – the so-called комедии на лица.[76] Nikolai Sazonov, a prominent Russian emigré in Paris, confidently asserted in an anonymously published work that *The Government Inspector* was a political lampoon, the hero of which was none other than the Emperor himself, transformed into a petty official.[77] It is tempting to see Nicholas I, who frequently made tours of inspection in his empire, as a model for Khlestakov. However, quite apart from the total dissimiliarity in appearance and character between the two men, the claim is untenable in view of the deep reverence Gogol is known to have always had for the person of the Tsar. Satirist though he was, Gogol would have drawn the line at ridiculing the monarch, who for him was sacrosanct.

Much more plausible as Khlestakov's original is the journalist Pavel Svinyin, a notorious liar who figured in one of the anecdotes Pushkin is reported to have told Gogol and who is also known to have inspired Zarnitskin in Shakhovskoi's *Don't listen if you don't like it* (1818). Svinyin is probably also the true identity of a certain 'Radugin', the Muscovite notability who is shown in the literary supplement to *The Russian Invalid* (No. 83,

[76] See. D. J. Welsh, *Russian Comedy, 1765–1823*, The Hague, 1966, pp. 19–27.

[77] *La vérité sur l'empereur Nicolas*, Paris, 1854, p. 193.

1834) boasting to Saratov provincials of his high position and esteem in both capitals. Gogol attended at-homes given by the paper's editor A. Voyeikov and could well have met Svinyin at such gatherings.[78]

Tikhonravov, who produced the first scholarly edition of Gogol's works, saw a resemblance between Khlestakov and another contemporary journalist, Faddei Bulgarin. It is true that Bulgarin was an irrepressible braggart who laid claim to great literary talent and friendship with eminent writers, but Gogol clearly did not have him in mind when creating Khlestakov because in the first two versions of the play the hero actually boasts of dining with Bulgarin.[79]

Two scholars, V. Gippius and A. S. Dolinin, have proposed as Khlestakov's prototype Bulgarin's equally bumptious colleague Osip Senkovsky.[80] Gogol heartily disliked the indefatigable editor of *The Library for Reading*, whose brand of journalism he roundly condemned in an article of 1836, and he ridicules him in Act III, Sc. 6, where Khlestakov claims to be Baron Brambeus (a pseudonym used by Senkovsky), boasts of his fecundity as a writer and of his princely salary, adding that he corrects everyone's articles. It should be noted, however, that this forms only a small part of one scene, touching Khlestakov the would-be writer, and even then he claims the authorship of other works besides those of Senkovsky.

The evidence suggests that Gogol had Senkovsky in mind, partly at least, and possibly Svinyin too, when creating the character of Khlestakov, but he had a more immediate source of inspiration, namely himself. There seems no doubt that, consciously or unconsciously, he put a good deal of himself into his Khlestakov, for the resemblances are too striking to be ignored. Petty vanity, shameless mendacity, a desire to impress, even the habit of borrowing money – all these Khlestakovian traits were part of Gogol's complex makeup. Like his hero, Gogol was vain about his appearance, indeed the foppish tendency that was quite marked in him as a young man re-emerged occasionally even in his later years. Khlestakov's salient characteristic, as Gogol observed in a letter to Sosnitsky dated 2 November 1846, is his 'sincere desire to act the part of someone with a rank higher than his own'. Such was

[78] See L. V. Krestova, *Комментарий к комедии Н. В. Гоголя «Ревизор»*, Moscow, 1933, p. 100, and N. L. Brodsky, *Избранные труды*, Moscow, 1964, pp. 66–7.

[79] E. Voitolovskaya in her *Комментарий*, pp. 194–5, suggests that something of Bulgarin may have gone into the character of Zemlyanika, but there is no resemblance beyond the fact that both were informers (Bulgarin was exposed as such in Pushkin's squib *О записках Видока*, 1830).

[80] V. V. Gippius, 'Заметки о Гоголе. III. Вариант Хлестакова', *Ученые записки Ленинградского университета, серия филологических наук*, 1941, Vol. 76, No. 11, p. 10; A. S. Dolinin, 'Из истории борьбы Гоголя и Белинского за идейность в литературе', *Ученые записки Ленинградского гос. пед. института*, 1956, Vol. 18, No. 5, p. 40.

Gogol's own behaviour in 1832 when, according to Annenkov, he altered the rank in his travel document from collegiate registrar (14th grade) to collegiate assessor (8th grade) so that he should be mentioned in the *Moscow News*, which printed the names of all persons entering or leaving the city who possessed the eighth or a higher rank.

Gogol displayed a Khlestakov-like arrogance when he set out to conquer the academic world by proclaiming it his intention to write a history of the Ukraine in four to six volumes, a history of the Middle Ages in eight to nine volumes, and a history of the world in ten volumes, each of them, like the loans Khlestakov requests, larger than the one before. He accepted a post at St. Petersburg University and cast himself in the role of a great historian who, once armed with an extensive knowledge of the past, would be able to divine the future and even presume to advise the Tsar. And he revealed a breath-taking combination of presumptuousness and naivety, akin to Khlestakov's, in expecting *The Government Inspector* to bring about a magical revolution in the morals of his people, something no other Russian writer had ever dared to attempt.

In his later years Gogol's Khlestakovism took a spiritual turn as he became firmly convinced that he was a chosen instrument of God's will. His acts of philanthropy were performed ostentatiously, in flagrant contradiction to the humility he preached so earnestly. His letters to relatives and friends contained lofty moral advice expressed in an authoritative tone. He was bluntly rebuked by Sergei Aksakov for parading his piety and for his sermonizing, 'full of pride clothed in the ragged garb of humility'. The same priggish manner mars those letters in *Selected Passages* in which he sets himself up as a prophet and saviour of his generation, showing the light to his benighted countrymen. When abuse was heaped upon him for his pains he realized that he had gone too far, that his preacherly tone had been a mistake.

In a letter to Zhukovsky, written shortly after the book appeared, he described the effect it had produced as a slap in the face for the public, his friends, and most of all himself. "After its publication," he wrote, "I came to my senses, just as if I had come out of some dream, feeling, like a guilty schoolboy, that I had done more mischief than I intended. In my book I made an exhibition of myself in such a Khlestakovian fashion that I have not the courage to look at it ... How ashamed I am of myself ... Truly, there is something Khlestakovian about me." This confession amply confirmed the truth of his earlier observation, made in his *Extract from a Letter*, that there is something of Khlestakov in nearly all of us. "Your smart[81] Guards officer

[81] Gogol here uses the word ловкий in one of its Ukrainian, not Russian senses.

sometimes proves to be a Khlestakov;" he wrote, "your statesman sometimes proves a Khlestakov, and we literary men, sinners that we are, at times turn out to be Khlestakovs." Small wonder that when he suggested to Aksakov in 1839 that they should put on an amateur performance of *The Government Inspector* Gogol chose the part of Khlestakov for himself.

Khlestakov undoubtedly embodies some of his creator's character. Gogol endowed his hero with the frivolous, superficial aspect of his many-sided nature, just as he later transferred his own faults, real or imagined, to the fictional characters in his *Dead Souls*. If this was done consciously, and Gogol was a more conscious artist than many critics have supposed, then clearly, in part at least, he was indulging in an act of ironic self-mockery, and to that extent realizing the ideal he later proclaimed, at the end of his *Supplement to The Denouement*, that the noblest kind of laughter is directed at oneself. But Khlestakov should not be seen as a self-portrait on Gogol's part, for he resembles his creator only in certain respects and not at all in others.

It is a mistake, in fact, to look for a single prototype, since the assumption that there was one living original conflicts both with what Gogol wrote of Khlestakov in particular and with what he tells us of his method of creating character in general. In his *Extract from a Letter* he describes Khlestakov as a type that combines diverse features found in Russians of very different character. And what is true of Khlestakov applies to his other literary creations too. He reveals his method of character-drawing when he states in his *Confession*: "I have never *painted* a portrait in the sense of making a simple copy. I would *create* a portrait, but create it as a result of deliberation, not out of my imagination." In other words, his characters are not pure inventions but were drawn from reality, without being slavish copies of individuals. Like Turgenev's characters, they are composite figures, an amalgam of features taken from various living persons. And although they were not invented, they were nevertheless built up and worked upon by his creative imagination.

This raises the vexed question of verisimilitude. Does Gogol's method of creating character produce figures that are lifeless bundles of characteristics, distorted creatures with human attributes, or recognizably real people? Ever since the time when *The Government Inspector* first appeared critical opinion has been sharply divided on this issue. Nikolai Polevoi, writing in 1842, referred to Gogol's *dramatis personae* as 'ugly grotesques' and 'figures from a galanty show' (китайские тени).[82] On the other hand, Belinsky

[82] *Русский вестник*, 1842, Vol. 5, No. 1, p. 61.

described them a year later as 'people, not puppets', with characters that were 'drawn from the innermost recesses of Russian life'.[83] Over a century later critics still view his dramatic characters very differently. A. Anikst writes that the people in Gogol's comedies are 'not caricatures, not grotesque figures, but well-rounded characters taken from the heart of life'.[84] By contrast, D. Mirsky takes the view that Gogol's creatures are 'not realistic caricatures of the world without, but introspective caricatures of the fauna of his own mind', while allowing that those in *The Government Inspector* are 'more supple and human' and 'more ordinary, more average' than those in *Dead Souls*.[85] And for V. Erlich the world of *The Government Inspector* is 'populated by homunculi rather than by full-blown human beings, by puppets whose precariously contrived mode of existence is pointed up by their blatantly comic names'.[86]

This divergence of opinion is less perplexing than at first appears. The chief point of disagreement here is that some critics see Gogol's dramatic characters as human, and others see them as grotesque. And the fact is that there is some truth in both assessments. Belinsky was right in saying that the characters are not puppets, since they are no more marionettes than they are embodiments of a particular passion or idea, as were the characters of traditional comedy. But Belinsky was wrong in seeing them as absolutely real, flesh-and-blood people, for they are not fully rounded human characters such as one finds, for example, in Chekhov's plays or Tolstoy's novels. There is an element of caricature in Gogol's portrayal, as there must be in satire. He accentuates salient features in his characters, just as he magnifies their verbal idiosyncrasies. He uses the technique of intensification, of meticulously individualized caricature, to achieve his artistic purpose; only by a measure of exaggeration could his satirical point be made strongly enough to strike home with his audience. But his dramatic characters are not so overdrawn as to lose their credibility as human beings and become merely comic or grotesque masks. They are not the simple caricatures of farce, but still recognizable as people, though many are larger than life.

Gogol condemned the lay figures of melodrama and farce, and sought to create complex stage characters with varied and sometimes contradictory traits who were convincing as people. His belief that he had succeeded in this is expressed in *Leaving the Theatre* by one of his mouthpieces, the Second

[83] *Отечественные записки*, 1843. See V. G. Belinsky, *Полное собрание сочинений*, Moscow, Vol. 7 (1955), p. 85.

[84] A. Anikst, *Теория драмы в России от Пушкина до Чехова*, Moscow, 1972, p. 126.

[85] D. S. Mirsky, *A History of Russian Literature*, London, 1968, pp. 146, 154.

[86] V. Erlich, *Gogol*, New Haven and London, 1969, p. 103.

Spectator, who observes that the impression left by the play 'is all the stronger for the fact that none of the persons in it has lost his human image: the human is apparent everywhere'.

The characters of Gogol's comedy are moulded in the common clay of humanity. Even the least of them, who appear but briefly or not at all in the flesh – those fleeting figures on the fringes of the action – seem fully alive. They none of them resemble the grotesque creations of E. T. A. Hoffmann or Edgar Allan Poe. They are not monsters of ugliness or depravity; on the contrary, they are ordinary people and the officials, though rogues, are good-natured rogues with redeeming virtues. The degree of exaggeration in their portrayal is not such as to warrant speaking of them as grotesque, for the mark of the grotesque is that it grossly distorts nature, rendering it weird, alien and inhuman.[87]

There are genuine touches of verbal grotesque in *The Government Inspector*, but Gogol's caricature in the portrayal of the people in his play is not pushed to a grotesque extreme and does not destroy their essential humanity. His caricature is mild, just as his satire is gentle, even sympathetic, and not of the same order as the savage satire of a Swift or a Voltaire. Moreover, Gogol's figures are unmistakably human types and this would not be so if they were grotesquely drawn, since the grotesque is wholly individual and never typical. The names of many characters in the play have become bywords among Russians. And they are not only types belonging to their own class and period; they are universal types found in many kinds of society, in conditions quite different from those prevailing in the Russia of Gogol's time.

Just as the characters in *The Government Inspector* are often erroneously called grotesque, so is the town in which it is set sometimes described as queer and the whole world of the play as unreal, abnormal, even mad.[88] There is certainly some truth in these descriptions, but it is greatly exaggerated. The town, like its inhabitants, is not wholly real, but it is not so very different from real Russian towns of that time. Gogol made clear, again through the Second Spectator in *Leaving the Theatre*, that he was presenting a composite image of a typical provincial town, in the same way as he produced composite and typical characters to people it. His town differs from real ones only in that it is run by none but corrupt administrators; this was an exaggeration, but not a great exaggeration, at least in Russia under Nicholas I. Again, the words and

[87] There is no exaggeration at all in some of the portraits, for example those of Osip, Anna and Maria.

[88] See, for example, V. Bryusov, *Испепеленный*, Moscow, 1909, p. 14; S. Mashinsky, *Художественный мир Гоголя*, Moscow, 1971, pp. 253–4, p. 258; and W. Harrison's edition of the play, Bradda Books, Letchworth, 1964, pp. 9 and 12.

behaviour of the characters are odd and illogical, but only part of the time, only a little more often than one finds in real life; they are not to be compared with the ramblings and erratic acts of lunatics. The play would not have had the impact we know it had on Gogol's contemporaries if the town and its inhabitants had not been close enough to life to be recognized. The truth is that the world presented here is not far removed from reality. If it is 'abnormal' or 'mad', then its abnormality and madness are those of the ordinary world, not the world of pathology.[89]

Because much of Gogol's fiction takes us into the world of the grotesque, the fantastic and the absurd, it has been assumed, far too readily, that these are the dominant traits of everything he created. To be sure, there is an affinity between all his writings, but the hyperbolism inherent in Gogol's imagination manifests itself in very different degrees in his various works. *The Government Inspector* is not the same as *The Nose*, *Viy*, *The Memoirs of a Madman* or even *Dead Souls*, the work to which it stands closest. Nor, though it contains elements of the absurd, does it belong to the absurdist drama. While it deviates from literal truth to life, the play remains by and large 'realistic', though Gogol's literary manner cannot be adequately described by this or any other single term, however widely defined. No man, least of all a great artist, can be captured in one word.

Interpretation and significance

The Government Inspector is remarkable as a drama in uniting very different, seemingly incongruous elements and styles in one harmonious whole. It combines surface gaiety with hidden horror, ranging from farce at one extreme to tragedy at the other. It mingles laughter with tears, the literal with the symbolical, the trivial with the profound. It is at once absurdly frivolous and deeply serious. Its style ranges from the highly formal to the lowly informal. This unique blend of qualities makes it difficult to classify the play within any of the recognized dramatic genres. It may be best described, perhaps, as a satirical comedy of confusion and corruption.

The human problem on which Gogol focuses his attention in the play is that of bribery, a practice which had become institutionalized in Russia well before the age of Nicholas I. It had evolved an elaborate code, in which a

[89] V. Nabokov is mistaken in saying that the comedy has no connection with reality and calling it a 'dream play', whose characters are the kind of people one meets in a nightmare (*Nikolai Gogol*, Norfolk, Connecticut, 1944, pp. 41–2 and p. 54). Curiously enough, Nabokov and Belinsky, whose views of the play are in all other respects diametrically opposed, both failed to recognize it as a moral satire, being misled by the fact that it is not explicitly didactic.

distinction was made between 'innocent income' (безгрешные доходы), derived from private persons, and 'sinful income' (грешные доходы), acquired at the expense of the state. It was considered tactful to suborn indirectly and to avoid referring to the bribe as such, using instead various euphemisms, such as 'a lamb wrapped in paper' (барашек в бумажке). Gogol had observed bribery at first hand during his time in the civil service and came to deplore it as a grave social evil. At the time he wrote his play he believed that bribery could be banished, or at least diminished, by being ridiculed on the stage. Through his satire he was appealing to the conscience of Russian officials, reminding them of their duty to the state and urging them to mend their ways, but his plea fell on deaf ears. He overestimated the power of mockery and underestimated the force of habit. More conducive to probity in office are the payment of adequate salaries, open government and continual vigilance on the part of the authorities. But legislative and administrative mechanisms, helpful though they are, cannot of themselves ensure rectitude in the management of public affairs; in the last analysis this depends on the character of the officials and negotiators themselves. The truth of this is shown by the fact that no social system has succeeded in eliminating corruption from the conduct of administration or business, though the corruption is more rife in some countries, where it is sanctioned by custom, than in others, where it is condemned by public opinion. Gogol's play is thus as relevant to the world of the twentieth century as it was to its own time, and it points to a perennial evil of civilized societies.

Yet, when all is said and done, *The Government Inspector* is not simply, nor even primarily, an indictment of bribery or a satire on bureaucratic corruption and incompetence, any more than it is merely a comedy of mistaken identity. It has much wider implications, for there is always more in Gogol than meets the eye. At a deeper level it can be seen as an attack on all forms of moral depravity, of which bribery and corruption are but examples. Many other abuses are to be found in Gogol's town: beating, torture, lying, informing, misappropriation of funds, falsification of returns and interference with private mail. And besides these forms of bureaucratic oppression and injustice many vices are exhibited, among them hypocrisy, vanity, snobbery, acquisitiveness, place-seeking and love of power.

Particularly evident is that vice which in Russian goes by the name of *poshlost'*, a combination of smug vulgarity and pettiness of soul. It was Pushkin who first noted Gogol's exceptional flair for portraying the quality of *poshlost'* in people, and this gift is nowhere more vividly displayed than in *The Government Inspector*. What Gogol gives us here is a set of variations on the theme of *poshlost'*, with each of the characters shown as vulgar in his or her own way. Khlestakov himself is the embodiment of a particular kind of *poshlost'*, of a mental and spiritual vacuity allied to airy fantasizing about a life of fame and luxury. And he carries the others away on the troika of his imagination, inspiring them to indulge in similar fantasies. The Governor dreams of obtaining high rank and decorations; his wife fancies herself mistress of the finest house in all St. Petersburg; Dobchinsky conjures up a picture of the rich clothes Maria will wear there and the rare soups of which she will partake. The *poshlost'* assumes many guises, but always represents the commonplace core of corruption. In this way *The Government Inspector* demonstrates, as perhaps no other work of literature has done, the banality of evil and the evil of banality.

The real object of Gogol's wide-ranging satire is thus not any specific abuse, such as bribery, or particular vice, such as hypocrisy, but moral corruption as such, of which *poshlost'* is the most insidious and ubiquitous form. In Gogol's eyes most men were sunk in a morass of futile triviality, living lives of grey mediocrity in a state of spiritual sloth, prisoners of their own prejudices, passions and possessions. It was against this deadness of soul, this pervasive *poshlost'* that he wrestled constantly in his writings, for he had a horror of the void, especially the void inside man himself. He had perceived that the death in life is far more terrible than the death after life.

None of the characters in *The Government Inspector* gives anything more than a conventional nod in the direction of things of the mind or spirit. When Khlestakov expresses a wish for 'spiritual nourishment', he is merely aping those with lofty ideals and presenting a pathetic caricature of Gogol's own aspirations. And when he declares that his 'soul thirsts for culture' this turns out to be as much a travesty of real culture as his wooing is a parody of true romance. The Governor, a man ambitious for advancement, assures Khlestakov that he seeks no honours since 'beside virtue all else is dust and ashes', a remark that epitomizes his hypocrisy. The Judge, who is the would-be intellectual among the officials, alludes to what he mistakenly believes is a Masonic book, but this local Cicero is quite unable to make head or tail of court reports and is most at home discoursing on the merits of hunting-dogs. Khlopov, fearful lest the pupils in his schools should imbibe any subversive – that is to say, liberal – ideas, is too diffident to vouchsafe an opinion about anything. The Postmaster has not a single idea in his head and would be incapable of articulating it if he had. Anna exclaims to Khlestakov "How nice it must be to be a writer!" and Maria asks him to inscribe a verse or two in her autograph book, but most of their mental energy is expended in constant bickering about trivial matters, such as which dress each of them is going to wear. This being the intellectual and moral level of the participants, there is great symbolic truth in the final scene of the play, where the townspeople, struck dumb and motionless, reveal their state of living death in a moment of dramatic *rigor mortis*.

Thus, beneath all the humour and gaiety of the play lurks a disturbing sense of the malaise that afflicts all the people in it. They are funny and ridiculous, but they are also hollow, selfish creatures and the corruption in them, though petty, is frightening, the more so because they are such ordinary people. Gogol's view of life, though comic on the surface, is essentially pessimistic. He saw it, to quote his own words in *Dead Souls*, 'through the laughter visible to the world and the tears invisible and unknown to it'. The laughter from which *The Government Inspector* sprang was not a cruel laughter, born of malice, but a cleansing, liberating laughter mingled with tears of sadness and compassion for these morally underdeveloped people living such a mean, empty existence, heedless of all that gives life real meaning. There was at that time no rancour or venom in Gogol's satire. His laughter turned bitter and the iron entered his soul only later, while he was writing the first part of his great novel.[90]

Although the plot of *The Government Inspector* is based on the traditional theme of mistaken identity, Gogol, unlike previous dramatists who had used this device, exploited the error of judgement from which the action unfolds not simply or solely for comic effect, but to reveal a fundamental state of chaos in human life. He abhorred the disorder, especially the moral disorder, he perceived around him and considered the world to be out of joint. It is no accident that the plot of most of his works hinges on a deception, because for him deception was at the very heart of things. He saw human beings as enmeshed in a web of confusion and deceptions, misled not only by appearances but also by their own delusions and lies.

The problem of corruption afforded great scope for exploring in *The Government Inspector* his central theme of deception. The confusion and misunderstandings that abound in the play testify to the perils and pitfalls of speech, to the malignant power of rumour and gossip. The Governor's remark that 'words do no harm' is richly ironic in the context of a play which demonstrates with striking examples that words do indeed cause great mischief among men and can be their undoing. Words are not as innocent as they seem, just as nothing in the world is, to Gogol, what it seems. Words can conceal our thoughts as well as reveal them, a fact amply illustrated in the

[90] This is shown by A. Tertz (pen-name of Andrei Sinyavsky) in his *В тени Гоголя*, London, 1975, pp. 303–20. It is quite untrue to say of the play, as J. Lavrin does in his introduction to D. J. Campbell's translation, p. 9, that 'the laughter which permeates it is hardly less cruel and lashing than that in *Dead Souls*'.

play, whose dialogue becomes at times a series of juxtaposed monologues. Finally speech itself proves inadequate, being replaced by the silent language of frozen gestures. And although the mistake concerning the inspector is cleared up, nevertheless confusion still reigns at the end of the play. In purely dramatic terms a denouement is effected, but there is no real resolution, no true end. The situation is that of a vicious circle in which the action has returned to its starting-point.

Seeking an explanation for the error made by the officials, Zemlyanika lights on the devil. "How it came about, for the life of me I cannot explain," he says. "It is as though we were stupefied by some kind of fog, beguiled by the devil." It is naturally the devil that spreads the fog of cosmic confusion. Shortcomings soon find scapegoats, the most favoured of such goats being the devil and fate. But the true causes of the error and confusion in *The Government Inspector* are plain fear and stupidity, not supernatural forces. Fear, induced by bad consciences, fills the hearts of the officials throughout the play and motivates their behaviour. Gogol shows us what happens when fear dominates men's lives: fear breeds suspicion, deceit and, not least, self-deception. When taxed with having presented no positive characters in his play, Gogol pointed to laughter. In a similar way fear may be personified as a negative character in the work. The fear represents the serious, inner aspect of the play, just as the laughter expresses its external, comic aspect. The laughter and gaiety are on the outside, enjoyed by the spectator, not by the participants themselves; for them it is all deadly earnest since their situation is fraught with danger.

Fear is reinforced by stupidity. Khlestakov succeeds in his ephemeral role because he is too stupid to realize the dangerous situation he is in and because Bobchinsky and Dobchinsky, those virtuosos of topsy-turvy logic, insist that he is the inspector, deducing this from the fact that he had looked at the food on their plates at the inn. The Governor, who is by no means a fool, acts stupidly at a critical moment not only out of fear but because he is simply unable to believe that Khlestakov is really as stupid as he appears to be. The Governor is a victim of his own shrewdness, proving too clever by half and demonstrating the truth of his own dictum that 'in some cases a lot of brains is worse than none at all'. Sceptical of his adversary's claims and inclined at first to disbelieve his story, the Governor stills his own doubts with various more or less satisfactory explanations. He is prepared to accept that Khlestakov may have embroidered a little, for 'there is no speech without a little embroidering', but most of what the young visitor says must be true. Then, after the truth is known, the Governor in a passionate outburst reproaches himself with being blind and mad, but worst of all, stupid. And in the end he and his fellow-officials are not punished for their misdemeanours, but instead ridiculed for their folly. The essence of their folly is that they have taken a foolish nonentity for a clever person of importance. And Khlestakov, the nobody, is the victor since he escapes scot-free. Gogol dismayed and disoriented his contemporaries by going against the general rule of comedy whereby poetic justice should prevail, that is to say vice should be punished and virtue rewarded. Indeed, he had offended doubly by leaving out virtue and by failing to ensure that the miscreants are brought to book.

Thus it is not justice, much less virtue, that is seen to triumph in *The Government Inspector*, but rather human folly. The notion of justice is not given concrete shape, for the real inspector is a remote, insubstantial figure who remains behind the scenes, necessarily so, since his appearance on stage would have conflicted with the author's intention that the work should directly depict only what is negative or bad. Yet the real inspector was originally conceived by Gogol as the agent of retribution, the arm of secular justice, and subsequently re-interpreted, in *The Denouement*, as the symbol of divine justice. This later gloss may have been suggested by Belinsky's description of Khlestakov, in his assumed role, as a phantom or shadow of the Governor's bad conscience. To Belinsky the uneasy conscience of the Governor and his associates served simply to explain Khlestakov's easy success, but Gogol took this idea and extended it, transforming the false inspector into man's worldly conscience and the real inspector into man's true conscience, answerable only to God; by this means he linked it with the question of divine judgement. And in making the town symbolize the human soul he doubtless drew on his reading of works by churchmen, for the city-soul is an image found in medieval theology, most notably in St. Augustine's *De Civitate Dei*. The suggestion that the officials of the town represent various human passions was Gogol's own elaboration of the metaphor.

In essence, Gogol's allegorical exegesis propounds the view that man may be arraigned for his crimes by a human judge, but for his corruption or sins of the spirit he can be called to account only by the Supreme Judge. The play, seen in this light, is a salutary reminder of God's all-seeing eye and of the real sense in which we are all in this world on trial for our lives. Its author seems to be asking us, the spectators and readers, whether our lives could stand the test of an inspection, and reminding us that we are as much involved in the action of his play as the participants, because we are all capable of straying and likely to be deceived. We sit in judgement on those participants, but one that is higher than us sits in judgement on us in turn. The notion of God as a 'higher inspector' finds expression in a letter Gogol wrote to Alexandra Smirnova on 6 December 1849, where he says: "We find it hard, very hard, we who forget at every moment that our actions will be inspected not by some senator, but by Him who cannot be suborned."

As we know, this symbolic interpretation of *The Government Inspector* was imposed on the play retrospectively and formed no part of the original conception, in which justice was seen solely in secular terms. Gogol, in his mystical period, sought to allegorize his comedy in order to counteract the political meaning that most people had read into it. If his contemporaries could not understand it as the victory of secular justice that he had intended, then he would make them see it in terms of divine justice by removing it from the sphere of the literal altogether. Now it would be wrong to dismiss Gogol's religious symbolism out of hand. After all his play is, at the deepest level, a drama of corruption and judgement in which there reverberates the language of religion – 'miracle', 'faith', 'sin', 'God' and 'the devil'. And it is a challenge to the consciences of all who watch it. But the allegorical framework in which Gogol tried to fit it is too schematic and restrictive to be satisfactory, particularly when the play is given in the theatre. Shchepkin was right to object that Gogol's attempt to turn the town and the main characters into symbols drained most of the life out of a dramatic work that pulsated with vitality and human interest. It is neither a parable nor a morality play, but first and foremost a drama of real life and real people. Gogol had too great an understanding of the theatre and too much respect for Shchepkin not to see that the great actor was right. In the end, therefore, he decided not to insist on his revised interpretation and was content to place his play, as he did by implication in his *Selected Passages*, in the tradition of social comedy established by Fonvizin and Griboyedov. In building upon that tradition he had revolutionized the theatre in Russia, though he had failed in his purpose of revolutionizing Russian morals.

To conclude, *The Government Inspector* is a work of enormous scale, at one extreme an entertaining comedy of errors and, at the other, an illuminating drama of corruption. No single interpretation encompasses all its meaning; it may be understood and appreciated at several different levels – the anecdotal, the satirical, and the metaphysical. It is a play of great originality, that contains the inexhaustible riches of all great art. Its theme is universal and it speaks to the eternal human condition. Its laughter is directed at what is essential and permanent in man. It transcends its own time and people, belonging to all ages and all peoples. It has justly earned for itself the name of immortal comedy.

РЕВИЗОР

Комедия

в пяти действиях

На зе́ркало не́ча пеня́ть, ко́ли ро́жа крива́.
Наро́дная посло́вица.

ДЕЙСТВУЮЩИЕ ЛИЦА

Анто́н Анто́нович Сквозни́к-Дмухано́вский, городни́чий.

Анна Андре́евна, жена́ его́.

Ма́рья Анто́новна, дочь его́.

Лука́ Луки́ч Хлопов, смотри́тель учи́лищ.

Жена́ его́.

Аммо́с Фёдорович Ля́пкин-Тя́пкин, судья́.

Арте́мий Фили́ппович Земляни́ка, попечи́тель богоуго́дных заведе́ний.

Ива́н Кузьми́ч Шпе́кин, почтме́йстер.

Пётр Ива́нович До́бчинский
Пётр Ива́нович Бо́бчинский } городски́е поме́щики.

Ива́н Алекса́ндрович Хлестако́в, чино́вник из Петербу́рга.

Осип, слуга́ его́.

Христиа́н Ива́нович Ги́бнер, уе́здный ле́карь.

Фёдор Андре́евич Люлюко́в
Ива́н Ла́заревич Растако́вский
Степа́н Ива́нович Коро́бкин } отставны́е чино́вники, почётные ли́ца в го́роде.

Степа́н Ильи́ч Уховёртов, ча́стный при́став.

Свистуно́в
Пу́говицын
Держимо́рда } полице́йские.

Абду́лин, купе́ц.

Февро́нья Петро́вна Пошлёпкина, сле́сарша.

Жена́ у́нтер-офице́ра.

Ми́шка, слуга́ городни́чего.

Слуга́ тракти́рный.

Го́сти и го́стьи, купцы́, меща́не, проси́тели.

ХАРАКТЕРЫ И КОСТЮМЫ

ЗАМЕЧА́НИЯ ДЛЯ ГОСПО́Д АКТЁРОВ

Городни́чий, уже́ постаре́вший на слу́жбе и о́чень неглу́пый по-сво́ему челове́к. Хотя́ и взя́точник, но ведёт себя́ о́чень соли́дно; дово́льно сурьёзен; не́сколько да́же резонёр; говори́т ни гро́мко, ни ти́хо, ни мно́го, ни ма́ло. Его́ ка́ждое сло́во значи́тельно. Черты́ лица́ его́ гру́бы и жёстки, как у вся́кого, нача́вшего тяжёлую слу́жбу с ни́зших чино́в. Перехо́д от стра́ха к ра́дости, от ни́зости к высокоме́рию дово́льно быстр, как у челове́ка с гру́бо разви́тыми скло́нностями души́. Он оде́т, по обыкнове́нию, в своём мунди́ре с петли́цами и в ботфо́ртах со шпо́рами. Волоса́ на нём стри́женые, с про́седью.

Анна Андре́евна, жена́ его́, провинциа́льная коке́тка, ещё не совсе́м пожилы́х лет, воспи́танная вполови́ну на рома́нах и альбо́мах, вполови́ну на хло́потах в свое́й кладово́й и де́вичьей. Очень любопы́тна и при слу́чае выка́зывает тщесла́вие. Берёт иногда́ власть над му́жем потому́ то́лько, что тот не нахо́дится, что отвеча́ть ей; но власть э́та распространя́ется то́лько на ме́лочи и состои́т в вы́говорах и насме́шках. Она́ четы́ре ра́за переодева́ется в ра́зные пла́тья в продолже́ние пье́сы.

Хлестако́в, молодо́й челове́к лет двадцати́ трёх, то́ненький, ху́денький; не́сколько приглупова́т и, как говоря́т, без царя́ в голове́, — оди́н из тех люде́й, кото́рых в канцеля́риях называ́ют пусте́йшими. Говори́т и де́йствует без вся́кого соображе́ния. Он не в состоя́нии останови́ть постоя́нного внима́ния на како́й-нибудь мы́сли. Речь его́ отры́виста, и слова́ вылета́ют из уст его́ соверше́нно неожи́данно. Чем бо́лее исполня́ющий э́ту роль пока́жет чистосерде́чия и простоты́, тем бо́лее он вы́играет. Оде́т по мо́де.

Осип, слуга́, тако́в, как обыкнове́нно быва́ют слу́ги не́сколько пожилы́х лет. Говори́т сурьёзно, смо́трит не́сколько вниз, резонёр и лю́бит себе́ самому́ чита́ть нравоуче́ния для своего́ ба́рина. Го́лос его́ всегда́ почти́ ро́вен, в разгово́ре с ба́рином принима́ет суро́вое, отры́вистое и не́сколько да́же гру́бое выраже́ние. Он умне́е своего́ ба́рина и потому́ скоре́е дога́дывается, но не лю́бит мно́го говори́ть и мо́лча плут. Костю́м его́ — се́рый или си́ний поно́шенный сюрту́к.

Бо́бчинский и До́бчинский, о́ба ни́зенькие, коро́тенькие, о́чень любопы́тные; чрезвыча́йно похо́жи друг на дру́га; о́ба с небольши́ми брюшка́ми; о́ба говоря́т скороговоркою и чрезвыча́йно мно́го помога́ют же́стами и рука́ми. До́бчинский немно́жко вы́ше и сурьёзнее Бо́бчинского, но Бо́бчинский развя́знее и живе́е До́бчинского.

Ля́пкин-Тя́пкин, судья́, челове́к, прочита́вший пять и́ли шесть книг, и потому́ не́сколько вольноду́мен. Охо́тник большо́й на дога́дки, и потому́ ка́ждому сло́ву своему́ даёт вес. Представля́ющий его́ до́лжен всегда́ сохраня́ть в лице́ своём значи́тельную ми́ну. Говори́т ба́сом с продолгова́той растя́жкой, хри́пом и са́пом — как стари́нные часы́, кото́рые пре́жде шипя́т, а пото́м уже́ бьют.

Земляни́ка, попечи́тель богоуго́дных заведе́ний, о́чень то́лстый, неповоро́тливый и неуклю́жий челове́к, но при всём том проны́ра и плут. Очень услу́жлив и суетли́в.

Почтме́йстер, простоду́шный до наи́вности челове́к.

Про́чие ро́ли не тре́буют осо́бых изъясне́ний. Оригина́лы их всегда́ почти́ нахо́дятся пред глаза́ми.

Господа́ актёры осо́бенно должны́ обрати́ть внима́ние на после́днюю сце́ну. После́днее произнесённое сло́во должно́ произве́сть электри́ческое потрясе́ние на всех ра́зом, вдруг. Вся гру́ппа должна́ переме́нить положе́ние в оди́н миг о́ка. Звук изумле́ния до́лжен вы́рваться у всех же́нщин ра́зом, как бу́дто из одно́й груди́. От несоблюде́ния сих замеча́ний мо́жет исче́знуть весь эффе́кт.

ДЕЙСТВИЕ ПЕРВОЕ

Ко́мната в до́ме городни́чего

ЯВЛЕ́НИЕ I

Городни́чий, попечи́тель богоуго́дных заведе́ний, смотри́тель учи́лищ, судья́, ча́стный при́став, ле́карь, два кварта́льных.

Городни́чий. Я пригласи́л вас, господа́, с тем что́бы сообщи́ть вам пренеприя́тное изве́стие: к нам е́дет ревизо́р.

Аммо́с Фёдорович. Как ревизо́р?

Арте́мий Фили́ппович. Как ревизо́р?

Городни́чий. Ревизо́р из Петербу́рга, инко́гнито. И ещё с секре́тным предписа́ньем.

Аммо́с Фёдорович. Вот те на!

Арте́мий Фили́ппович. Вот не́ было забо́ты, так пода́й!

Лука́ Луки́ч. Го́споди бо́же! ещё и с секре́тным предписа́ньем!

Городни́чий. Я как бу́дто предчу́вствовал: сего́дня мне всю ночь сни́лись каки́е-то две необыкнове́нные кры́сы. Пра́во, э́таких я никогда́ не ви́дывал: чёрные, неесте́ственной величины́! пришли́, поню́хали — и пошли́ прочь. Вот я вам прочту́ письмо́, кото́рое получи́л я от Андре́я Ива́новича Чмы́хова, кото́рого вы, Арте́мий Фили́ппович, зна́ете. Вот что он пи́шет: «Любе́зный друг, кум и благоде́тель *(бормо́чет вполго́лоса, пробега́я ско́ро глаза́ми)*... и уве́домить тебя́». А! вот: «Спешу́, ме́жду про́чим, уве́домить тебя́, что прие́хал чино́вник с предписа́нием осмотре́ть всю губе́рнию и осо́бенно наш уе́зд (*значи́тельно поднима́ет па́лец вверх*). Я узна́л э́то от са́мых достове́рных люде́й, хотя́ он представля́ет себя́ ча́стным лицо́м. Так как я зна́ю, что за тобо́ю, как за вся́ким, во́дятся грешки́, потому́ что ты челове́к у́мный и не лю́бишь пропуска́ть того́, что плывёт в ру́ки...» (*остановя́сь*), ну, здесь свои́... «то сове́тую тебе́ взять предосторо́жность, и́бо он мо́жет прие́хать во вся́кий час, е́сли то́лько уже́ не прие́хал и не живёт где́-нибудь инко́гнито... Вчера́шнего дни я...» Ну, тут уж пошли́ дела́ семе́йные: «...сестра́ Анна Кири́ловна прие́хала к нам со свои́м му́жем; Ива́н Кири́лович о́чень потолсте́л и всё игра́ет на скры́пке...» — и про́чее, и про́чее. Так вот како́е обстоя́тельство!

Аммо́с Фёдорович. Да, обстоя́тельство тако́е... необыкнове́нно, про́сто необыкнове́нно. Что́-нибудь неда́ром.

Лука́ Луки́ч. Заче́м же, Анто́н Анто́нович, отчего́ э́то? Заче́м к нам ревизо́р?

Городни́чий. Заче́м! Так уж, ви́дно, судьба́! (*Вздохну́в.*) До сих пор, благодаре́ние бо́гу, подбира́лись к други́м города́м; тепе́рь пришла́ о́чередь к на́шему.

Аммо́с Фёдорович. Я ду́маю, Анто́н Анто́нович, что здесь то́нкая и бо́льше полити́ческая причи́на. Это зна́чит вот что: Росси́я... да... хо́чет вести́ войну́, и министе́рия-то, вот ви́дите, и подосла́ла чино́вника, что́бы узна́ть, нет ли где изме́ны.

Городни́чий. Эк куда́ хвати́ли! Ещё у́мный челове́к! В уе́здном го́роде изме́на! Что он, пограни́чный, что ли? Да отсю́да, хоть три го́да скачи́, ни до како́го госуда́рства не дое́дешь.

Аммо́с Фёдорович. Нет, я вам скажу́, вы не того́... вы не... Нача́льство име́ет то́нкие ви́ды: да́ром что далеко́, а оно́ себе́ мота́ет на ус.

Городни́чий. Мота́ет и́ли не мота́ет, а я вас, господа́, предуве́домил. Смотри́те, по свое́й ча́сти я ко́е-каки́е распоряже́нья сде́лал, сове́тую и вам. Осо́бенно вам, Арте́мий Фили́ппович! Без сомне́ния, проезжа́ющий чино́вник захо́чет пре́жде всего́ осмотре́ть подве́домственные вам богоуго́дные заведе́ния — и потому́ вы сде́лайте так, что́бы всё бы́ло прили́чно: колпаки́ бы́ли бы чи́стые, и больны́е не походи́ли бы на кузнецо́в, как обыкнове́нно они́ хо́дят по-дома́шнему.

Арте́мий Фили́ппович. Ну, э́то ещё ничего́. Колпаки́, пожа́луй, мо́жно наде́ть и чи́стые.

Городни́чий. Да, и то́же над ка́ждой крова́тью надписа́ть по-латы́ни и́ли на друго́м како́м языке́... э́то уж по ва́шей ча́сти, Христиа́н Ива́нович, — вся́кую боле́знь: когда́ кто заболе́л, кото́рого дня и числа́... Нехорошо́, что у вас больны́е тако́й кре́пкий таба́к ку́рят, что всегда́ расчиха́ешься, когда́ войдёшь. Да и лу́чше, е́сли б их бы́ло ме́ньше: то́тчас отнесу́т к дурно́му смотре́нию и́ли к неиску́сству врача́.

Арте́мий Фили́ппович. О! насчёт врачева́нья мы с Христиа́ном Ива́новичем взя́ли свои́ ме́ры: чем бли́же к нату́ре, тем лу́чше, — лека́рств дороги́х мы не употребля́ем. Челове́к просто́й: е́сли умрёт, то и так умрёт; е́сли вы́здоровеет, то и так вы́здоровеет. Да и Христиа́ну Ива́новичу затрудни́тельно бы́ло б с ни́ми изъясня́ться: он по-ру́сски ни сло́ва не зна́ет.

Христиа́н Ива́нович издаёт звук отча́сти похо́жий на бу́кву *и* и не́сколько на *е*.

Городни́чий. Вам то́же посове́товал бы, Аммо́с Фёдорович, обрати́ть внима́ние на прису́тственные места́. У вас там в пере́дней, куда́ обыкнове́нно явля́ются проси́тели, сторожа́ завели́ дома́шних гусе́й с ма́ленькими гусёнками, кото́рые так и шныря́ют под нога́ми. Оно́, коне́чно, дома́шним хозя́йством заводи́ться вся́кому похва́льно, и почему́ ж сто́рожу и не заве́сть его́? то́лько, зна́ете, в тако́м ме́сте неприли́чно... Я и пре́жде хоте́л вам э́то заме́тить, но всё ка́к-то позабыва́л.

Аммо́с Фёдорович. А вот я их сего́дня же велю́ всех забра́ть на ку́хню. Хоти́те, приходи́те обе́дать.

Городни́чий. Кро́ме того́, ду́рно, что у вас высу́шивается в само́м прису́тствии вся́кая дрянь и над са́мым шка́пом с бума́гами охо́тничий ара́пник. Я зна́ю, вы лю́бите охо́ту, но всё на вре́мя лу́чше его́ приня́ть, а там, как прое́дет ревизо́р, пожа́луй опя́ть его́ мо́жете пове́сить. Та́кже заседа́тель ваш... он, коне́чно, челове́к све́дущий, но от него́ тако́й за́пах, как бу́дто бы он сейча́с вы́шел из виноку́ренного заво́да, — э́то то́же нехорошо́. Я хоте́л давно́ об э́том сказа́ть вам, но был, не по́мню, че́м-то развлечён. Есть про́тив э́того сре́дства, е́сли уже́ э́то действи́тельно, как он говори́т, у него́ приро́дный за́пах: мо́жно ему́ посове́товать есть лук, и́ли чесно́к, и́ли что́-нибудь друго́е. В э́том слу́чае мо́жет помо́чь ра́зными медикаме́нтами Христиа́н Ива́нович.

Христиа́н Ива́нович издаёт тот же звук.

Аммо́с Фёдорович. Нет, э́того уже́ невозмо́жно вы́гнать: он говори́т, что в де́тстве ма́мка его́ уши́бла, и с тех пор от него́ отдаёт немно́го во́дкою.

Городни́чий. Да я так то́лько заме́тил вам. Насчёт же вну́треннего распоряже́ния и того́, что называ́ет в письме́ Андре́й Ива́нович грешка́ми, я ничего́ не могу́ сказа́ть. Да и стра́нно говори́ть: нет челове́ка, кото́рый бы за собо́ю не име́л каки́х-нибудь грехо́в. Это уже́ так сами́м бо́гом устро́ено, и волтериа́нцы напра́сно про́тив э́того говоря́т.

Аммо́с Фёдорович. Что ж вы полага́ете, Анто́н Анто́нович, грешка́ми? Грешки́ грешка́м — рознь. Я говорю́ всем откры́то, что беру́ взя́тки, но чем взя́тки? Борзы́ми щенка́ми. Это совсе́м ино́е де́ло.

Городни́чий. Ну, щенка́ми и́ли чем други́м — всё взя́тки.

Аммо́с Фёдорович. Ну, нет, Анто́н Анто́нович. А вот, наприме́р, е́сли у кого́-нибудь шу́ба сто́ит пятьсо́т рубле́й, да супру́ге шаль...

Городни́чий. Ну, а что из того́, что вы берёте взя́тки борзы́ми щенка́ми? Зато́ вы в бо́га не ве́руете; вы в це́рковь никогда́ не хо́дите; а я по кра́йней ме́ре в ве́ре твёрд и ка́ждое воскресе́нье быва́ю в це́ркви. А вы... О, я зна́ю вас: вы е́сли начнёте говори́ть о сотворе́нии ми́ра, про́сто во́лосы ды́бом поднима́ются.

Аммо́с Фёдорович. Да ведь сам собо́ю дошёл, со́бственным умо́м.

Городни́чий. Ну, в ино́м слу́чае мно́го ума́ ху́же, чем бы его́ совсе́м не́ было. Впро́чем, я так то́лько упомяну́л об уе́здном суде́; а по пра́вде сказа́ть, вряд ли кто когда́-нибудь загля́нет туда́: э́то уж тако́е зави́дное ме́сто, сам бог ему́ покрови́тельствует. А вот вам, Лука́ Луки́ч, так, как смотри́телю уче́бных заведе́ний, ну́жно позабо́титься осо́бенно насчёт учителе́й. Они́ лю́ди, коне́чно, учёные и воспи́тывались в ра́зных колле́гиях, но име́ют о́чень стра́нные посту́пки, натура́льно неразлу́чные с учёным зва́нием. Оди́н из них, наприме́р, вот э́тот, что име́ет то́лстое лицо́... не вспо́мню его́ фами́лии, ника́к не мо́жет обойти́сь без того́, что́бы, взоше́дши на ка́федру, не сде́лать грима́су, вот э́так *(де́лает грима́су)*, и пото́м начнёт руко́ю из-под га́лстука утю́жить свою́ бо́роду. Коне́чно, е́сли он ученику́ сде́лает таку́ю ро́жу, то оно́ ещё ничего́: мо́жет быть, оно́ там и ну́жно так, об э́том я не могу́ суди́ть; но вы посуди́те са́ми, е́сли он сде́лает э́то посети́телю, — э́то мо́жет быть о́чень ху́до: господи́н ревизо́р и́ли друго́й кто мо́жет приня́ть э́то на свой счёт. Из э́того чёрт зна́ет что мо́жет произойти́.

Лука́ Луки́ч. Что ж мне, пра́во, с ним де́лать? Я уж не́сколько раз ему́ говори́л. Вот ещё на днях, когда́ зашёл было в класс наш предводи́тель, он скрои́л таку́ю ро́жу, како́й я никогда́ ещё не ви́дывал. Он-то её сде́лал от до́брого се́рдца, а мне вы́говор: заче́м вольноду́мные мы́сли внуша́ются ю́ношеству.

Городни́чий. То же я до́лжен вам заме́тить и об учи́теле по истори́ческой ча́сти. Он учёная голова́ — э́то ви́дно, и све́дений нахвата́л тьму, но то́лько объясня́ет с таки́м жа́ром, что не по́мнит себя́. Я раз слу́шал его́: ну, пока́мест говори́л об ассири́янах и вавило́нянах — ещё ничего́, а как добра́лся до Алекса́ндра Македо́нского, то я не могу́ вам сказа́ть, что с ним сде́лалось. Я ду́мал, что пожа́р, ей-бо́гу! Сбежа́л с ка́федры и что си́лы есть хвать сту́лом о́б пол. Оно́, коне́чно, Алекса́ндр Македо́нский геро́й, но заче́м же сту́лья лома́ть? от э́того убы́ток казне́.

Лука́ Луки́ч. Да, он горя́ч! Я ему́ э́то не́сколько раз уже́ замеча́л... Говори́т: «Как хоти́те, для нау́ки я жи́зни не пощажу́».

Городни́чий. Да, тако́в уже́ неизъясни́мый зако́н суде́б: у́мный челове́к — и́ли пья́ница, и́ли ро́жу таку́ю состро́ит, что хоть святы́х выноси́.

Лука́ Луки́ч. Не приведи́ бог служи́ть по учёной ча́сти! Всего́ бои́шься: вся́кий меша́ется, вся́кому хо́чется показа́ть, что он то́же у́мный челове́к.

Городни́чий. Это бы ещё ничего́, — инко́гнито прокля́тое! Вдруг загля́нет: «А, вы здесь, голу́бчики! А кто, ска́жет, здесь судья́?» — «Ля́пкин-Тя́пкин». — «А пода́ть сюда́ Ля́пкина-Тя́пкина! А кто попечи́тель богоуго́дных заведе́ний?» — «Земляни́ка». — «А пода́ть сюда́ Земляни́ку!» — Вот что ху́до!

ЯВЛЕНИЕ II

Те же и почтме́йстер.

Почтме́йстер. Объясни́те, господа́, что, како́й чино́вник е́дет?

Городни́чий. А вы ра́зве не слы́шали?

Почтме́йстер. Слы́шал от Петра́ Ива́новича Бо́бчинского. Он то́лько что был у меня́ в почто́вой конто́ре.

Городни́чий. Ну что? Как вы ду́маете об э́том?

Почтме́йстер. А что ду́маю? война́ с ту́рками бу́дет.

Аммо́с Фёдорович. В одно́ сло́во! я сам то же ду́мал.

Городни́чий. Да, о́ба па́льцем в не́бо попа́ли!

Почтме́йстер. Пра́во, война́ с ту́рками. Это всё францу́з га́дит.

Городни́чий. Кака́я война́ с ту́рками! Про́сто нам пло́хо бу́дет, а не ту́ркам. Это уже́ изве́стно: у меня́ письмо́.

Почтме́йстер. А е́сли так, то не бу́дет войны́ с ту́рками.

Городни́чий. Ну что же, как вы, Ива́н Кузьми́ч?

Почтме́йстер. Да что я? Как вы, Анто́н Анто́нович?

Городни́чий. Да что я? Стра́ху-то нет, а так, немно́жко... Купе́чество да гражда́нство меня́ смуща́ет. Говоря́т; что я им со́лоно пришёлся, а я, вот ей-бо́гу, е́сли и взял с ино́го, то, пра́во, без вся́кой не́нависти. Я да́же ду́маю *(берёт его́ по́д руку и отво́дит в сто́рону)*, я да́же ду́маю, не́ было ли на меня́ како́го-нибудь доно́са. Заче́м же в са́мом де́ле к нам ревизо́р? Послу́шайте, Ива́н Кузьми́ч, нельзя́ ли вам, для о́бщей на́шей по́льзы, вся́кое письмо́, кото́рое прибыва́ет к вам в почто́вую конто́ру, входя́щее и исходя́щее, зна́ете, э́так немно́жко распеча́тать и прочита́ть: не соде́ржится ли в нём како́го-нибудь донесе́ния и́ли про́сто перепи́ски. Если же нет, то мо́жно опя́ть запеча́тать; впро́чем, мо́жно да́же и так отда́ть письмо́, распеча́танное.

Почтме́йстер. Зна́ю, зна́ю... Этому не учи́те, э́то я де́лаю не то чтоб из предосторо́жности, а бо́льше из любопы́тства: смерть люблю́ узна́ть, что есть но́вого на све́те. Я вам скажу́, что э́то преинтере́сное чте́ние. Ино́е письмо́ с наслажде́нием прочтёшь — так опи́сываются ра́зные пасса́жи... а назида́тельность кака́я... лу́чше, чем в «Моско́вских ве́домостях»!

Городни́чий. Ну что ж, скажи́те, ничего́ не начи́тывали о како́м-нибудь чино́внике из Петербу́рга?

Почтме́йстер. Нет, о петербу́ргском ничего́ нет, а о костромски́х и сара́товских мно́го говори́тся. Жаль, одна́ко ж, что вы не чита́ете пи́сем: есть прекра́сные места́. Вот неда́вно оди́н пору́чик пи́шет к прия́телю и описа́л бал в са́мом игри́вом... о́чень, о́чень хорошо́: «Жизнь моя́, ми́лый друг, течёт, говори́т, в эмпире́ях: ба́рышень мно́го, му́зыка игра́ет, штанда́рт ска́чет...» — с больши́м, с больши́м чу́вством описа́л. Я наро́чно оста́вил его́ у себя́. Хоти́те, прочту́?

Городни́чий. Ну, тепе́рь не до того́. Так сде́лайте ми́лость, Ива́н Кузьми́ч: е́сли на слу́чай попадётся жа́лоба и́ли донесе́ние, то без вся́ких рассужде́ний заде́рживайте.

Почтме́йстер. С больши́м удово́льствием.

Аммо́с Фёдорович. Смотри́те, доста́нется вам когда́-нибудь за э́то.

Почтме́йстер. Ах, ба́тюшки!

Городни́чий. Ничего́, ничего́. Друго́е де́ло, е́сли бы вы из э́того публи́чное что́-нибудь сде́лали, но ведь э́то де́ло семе́йственное.

Аммо́с Фёдорович. Да, нехоро́шее де́ло завари́лось! А я, признаю́сь, шёл было к вам, Анто́н Анто́нович, с тем, что́бы попо́тчевать вас собачо́нкою. Родна́я сестра́ тому́ кобелю́, кото́рого вы зна́ете. Ведь вы слы́шали, что Чепто́вич с Вархови́нским зате́яли тя́жбу, и тепе́рь мне ро́скошь: травлю́ за́йцев на зе́млях и у того́, и у друго́го.

Городни́чий. Ба́тюшка, не ми́лы мне тепе́рь ва́ши за́йцы: у меня́ инко́гнито прокля́тое сиди́т в голове́. Так и ждёшь, что вот отво́рится дверь и — шасть...

ЯВЛЕНИЕ III

Те же, Бо́бчинский и До́бчинский, о́ба вхо́дят запыха́вшись.

Бо́бчинский. Чрезвыча́йное происше́ствие!

До́бчинский. Неожи́данное изве́стие!

Все. Что, что тако́е?

До́бчинский. Непредви́денное де́ло: прихо́дим в гости́ницу...

Бо́бчинский (*перебива́я*). Прихо́дим с Петро́м Ива́новичем в гости́ницу...

До́бчинский (*перебива́я*). Э, позво́льте, Пётр Ива́нович, я расскажу́.

Бо́бчинский. Э, нет, позво́льте уж я... позво́льте, позво́льте... вы уж и сло́га тако́го не име́ете...

До́бчинский. А вы собьётесь и не припо́мните всего́.

Бо́бчинский. Припо́мню, ей-бо́гу припо́мню. Уж не меша́йте, пусть я расскажу́, не меша́йте! Скажи́те, господа́, сде́лайте ми́лость, чтоб Пётр Ива́нович не меша́л.

Городни́чий. Да говори́те, ра́ди бо́га, что тако́е? У меня́ се́рдце не на ме́сте. Сади́тесь, господа́! Возьми́те сту́лья! Пётр Ива́нович, вот вам стул!

Все уса́живаются вокру́г обо́их Петро́в Ива́новичей.

Ну, что, что тако́е?

Бо́бчинский. Позво́льте, позво́льте: я всё по поря́дку. Как то́лько име́л я удово́льствие вы́йти от вас по́сле того́, как вы изво́лили смути́ться полу́ченным письмо́м, да-с, — так я тогда́ же забежа́л... уж, пожа́луйста, не перебива́йте, Пётр Ива́нович! Я уж всё, всё, всё зна́ю-с. Так я, вот изво́лите ви́деть, забежа́л к Коро́бкину. А не заста́вши Коро́бкина-то до́ма, завороти́л к Растако́вскому, а не заста́вши Растако́вского, зашёл вот к Ива́ну Кузьмичу́, что́бы сообщи́ть ему́ полу́ченную ва́ми но́вость, да, и́дучи отту́да, встре́тился с Петро́м Ива́новичем...

До́бчинский (*перебива́я*). Во́зле бу́дки, где продаю́тся пироги́.

Бо́бчинский. Во́зле бу́дки, где продаю́тся пироги́. Да, встре́тившись с Петро́м Ива́новичем, и говорю́ ему́: «Слы́шали ли вы о но́вости-та, кото́рую получи́л Анто́н Анто́нович из достове́рного письма́?» А Пётр Ива́нович уж услыха́ли об э́том от клю́чницы ва́шей Авдо́тьи, кото́рая, не зна́ю, за че́м-то была́ посла́на к Фили́ппу Анто́новичу Почечу́еву.

До́бчинский (*перебива́я*). За бочо́нком для францу́зской во́дки.

Бо́бчинский (*отводя́ его́ ру́ки*). За бочо́нком для францу́зской во́дки. Вот мы пошли́ с Петро́м-то Ива́новичем к Почечу́еву... Уж вы, Пётр Ива́нович... э́нтого...

не перебива́йте, пожа́луйста, не перебива́йте!.. Пошли́ к Почечу́еву, да на доро́ге Пётр Ива́нович говори́т: «Зайдём, говори́т, в тракти́р. В желу́дке-то у меня́... с утра́ я ничего́ не ел, так желу́дочное трясе́ние...» да-с, в желу́дке-то у Петра́ Ива́новича... «А в тракти́р, говори́т, привезли́ тепе́рь све́жей сёмги, так мы заку́сим». То́лько что мы в гости́ницу, как вдруг молодо́й челове́к...

До́бчинский (*перебива́я*). Недурно́й нару́жности, в партикуля́рном пла́тье...

Бо́бчинский. Недурно́й нару́жности, в партикуля́рном пла́тье, хо́дит э́так по ко́мнате, и в лице́ э́такое рассужде́ние... физионо́мия... посту́пки, и здесь (*ве́ртит руко́ю о́коло лба*) мно́го, мно́го всего́. Я бу́дто предчу́вствовал и говорю́ Петру́ Ива́новичу: «Здесь что́-нибудь неспроста́-с». Да. А Пётр-то Ива́нович уж мигну́л па́льцем и подозва́ли тракти́рщика-с, тракти́рщика Вла́са: у него́ жена́ три неде́ли наза́д тому́ родила́, и тако́й пребо́йкий ма́льчик, бу́дет так же, как и отец́, содержа́ть тракти́р. Подозва́вши Вла́са, Пётр Ива́нович и спроси́ его́ потихо́ньку: «Кто, говори́т, э́тот молодо́й челове́к?», а Влас и отвеча́й на э́то: «Это», — говори́т... Э, не перебива́йте, Пётр Ива́нович, пожа́луйста не перебива́йте; вы не расска́жете, ей-бо́гу не расска́жете: вы пришепётываете; у вас, я зна́ю, оди́н зуб во рту со сви́стом... «Это, говори́т, молодо́й челове́к, чино́вник, — да-с, — е́дущий из Петербу́рга, а по фами́лии, говори́т, Ива́н Алекса́ндрович Хлестако́в-с, а е́дет, говори́т, в Сара́товскую губе́рнию и, говори́т, престра́нно себя́ аттесту́ет: другу́ю уж неде́лю живёт, из тракти́ра не е́дет, забира́ет всё на счёт и ни копе́йки не хо́чет плати́ть». Как сказа́л он мне э́то, а меня́ так вот свы́ше и вразуми́ло. «Э!» — говорю́ я Петру́ Ива́новичу...

До́бчинский. Нет, Пётр Ива́нович, э́то я сказа́л: «Э!»

Бо́бчинский. Снача́ла вы сказа́ли, а пото́м и я сказа́л. «Э! — сказа́ли мы с Петро́м Ива́новичем. — А с како́й ста́ти сиде́ть ему́ здесь, когда́ доро́га ему́ лежи́т в Сара́товскую губе́рнию?» Да-с! А вот он-то и есть э́тот чино́вник.

Городни́чий. Кто, како́й чино́вник?

Бо́бчинский. Чино́вник-та, о кото́ром изво́лили получи́ть нoти́цию, — ревизо́р.

Городни́чий *(в стра́хе)*. Что вы, госпо́дь с ва́ми! э́то не он.

До́бчинский. Он! и де́нег не пла́тит и не е́дет. Кому́ же б быть, как не ему́? И подоро́жная пропи́сана в Сара́тов.

Бо́бчинский. Он, он, ей-бо́гу он... Тако́й наблюда́тельный: всё обсмотре́л. Уви́дел, что мы с Петро́м-то Ива́новичем е́ли сёмгу, — бо́льше потому́, что Пётр Ива́нович насчёт своего́ желу́дка... да, так он и в таре́лки к нам загляну́л. Меня́ так и про́няло стра́хом.

Городни́чий. Го́споди, поми́луй нас гре́шных! Где же он там живёт?

До́бчинский. В пя́том но́мере, под ле́стницей.

Бо́бчинский В том са́мом но́мере, где про́шлого го́да подрали́сь прое́зжие офице́ры.

Городни́чий. И давно́ он здесь?

До́бчинский. А неде́ли две уж. Прие́хал на Васи́лья Египтя́нина.

Городни́чий. Две неде́ли! *(В сто́рону.)* Ба́тюшки, сва́тушки! Выноси́те, святы́е уго́дники! В э́ти две неде́ли вы́сечена у́нтер-офице́рская жена́! Ареста́нтам не выдава́ли прови́зии! На у́лицах каба́к, нечистота́! Позо́р! поноше́нье! *(Хвата́ется за́ голову.)*

Арте́мий Фили́ппович. Что ж, Анто́н Анто́нович? — е́хать пара́дом в гости́ницу.

Аммо́с Фёдорович. Нет, нет! Вперёд пусти́ть голову́, духове́нство, купе́чество; вот и в кни́ге «Дея́ния Иоа́нна Масо́на»...

Городни́чий. Нет, нет; позво́льте уж мне самому́. Быва́ли тру́дные слу́чаи в жи́зни, сходи́ли, ещё да́же и спаси́бо получа́л. Аво́сь бог вы́несет и тепе́рь. *(Обраща́ясь к Бо́бчинскому.)* Вы говори́те, он молодо́й челове́к?

Бо́бчинский. Молодо́й, лет двадцати́ трёх и́ли четырёх с небольши́м.

Городни́чий. Тем лу́чше: молодо́го скоре́е проню́хаешь. Беда́, е́сли ста́рый чёрт, а молодо́й весь наверху́. Вы, господа́, приготовля́йтесь по свое́й ча́сти, а я отпра́влюсь сам, и́ли вот хоть с Петро́м Ива́новичем, прива́тно, для прогу́лки, наве́даться, не те́рпят ли проезжа́ющие неприя́тностей. Эй, Свистуно́в!

Свистуно́в. Что уго́дно?

Городни́чий. Ступа́й сейча́с за ча́стным приста-вом; и́ли нет, ты мне ну́жен. Скажи́ там кому́-нибудь, что́бы как мо́жно поскоре́е ко мне ча́стного при́става, и приходи́ сюда́.

Кварта́льный бежи́т впопыха́х.

Арте́мий Фили́ппович. Идём, идём, Аммо́с Фёдорович! В са́мом де́ле мо́жет случи́ться беда́.

Аммо́с Фёдорович. Да вам чего́ боя́ться? Колпаки́ чи́стые наде́л на больны́х, да и концы́ в во́ду.

Арте́мий Фили́ппович. Како́е колпаки́! Больны́м ве́лено габерсу́п дава́ть, а у меня́ по всем коридо́рам несёт така́я капу́ста, что береги́ то́лько нос.

Аммо́с Фёдорович. А я на э́тот счёт поко́ен. В са́мом де́ле, кто зайдёт в уе́здный суд? А е́сли и загля́нет в каку́ю-нибудь бума́гу, так он жи́зни не бу́дет рад. Я вот уж пятна́дцать лет сижу́ на суде́йском сту́ле, а как загляну́ в докладну́ю запи́ску — а! то́лько руко́й махну́. Сам Соломо́н не разреши́т, что в не́й пра́вда и что непра́вда.

Судья́, попечи́тель богоуго́дных заведе́ний, смотри́тель учи́лищ и почтме́йстер ухо́дят и в двеня́х ста́лкиваются с возвраща́ющимся кварта́льным.

ЯВЛЕНИЕ IV

Городни́чий, Бо́бчинский, До́бчинский и кварта́льный.

Городни́чий. Что, дро́жки там стоя́т?

Кварта́льный. Стоя́т.

Городни́чий. Ступа́й на у́лицу... и́ли нет, посто́й! Ступа́й принеси́... Да други́е-то где? неуже́ли ты то́лько оди́н? Ведь я прика́зывал, что́бы и Про́хоров был здесь. Где Про́хоров?

Кварта́льный. Про́хоров в ча́стном до́ме, да то́лько к де́лу не мо́жет быть употреблён.

Городни́чий. Как так?

Кварта́льный. Да так: привезли́ его́ поутру́ мертве́цки. Вот уже́ два уша́та воды́ вы́лили, до сих пор не протрезви́лся.

Городни́чий *(хвата́ясь за́ голову)*. Ах, бо́же мой, бо́же мой! Ступа́й скоре́е на у́лицу, и́ли нет — беги́ пре́жде в ко́мнату, слышь! и принеси́ отту́да шпа́гу и но́вую шля́пу. Ну, Пётр Ива́нович, пое́дем!

Бо́бчинский. И я, и я... позво́льте и мне, Анто́н Анто́нович!

Городни́чий. Нет, нет, Пётр Ива́нович, нельзя́, нельзя́! Нело́вко, да и на дро́жках не поме́стимся.

Бо́бчинский. Ничего́, ничего́, я так: петушко́м, петушко́м побегу́ за дро́жками. Мне бы то́лько немно́жко в щёлочку-та, в дверь э́так посмотре́ть, как у него́ э́ти посту́пки...

Городни́чий (*принима́я шпа́гу, к кварта́льному*). Беги́ сейча́с, возьми́ деся́тских, да пусть ка́ждый из них возьмёт... Эк шпа́га как исцара́палась! Прокля́тый купчи́шка Абду́лин — ви́дит, что у городни́чего ста́рая шпа́га, не присла́л но́вой. О, лука́вый наро́д! А так, моше́нники, я ду́маю, там уж про́сьбы из-под полы́ и гото́вят. Пусть ка́ждый возьмёт в ру́ки по у́лице... чёрт возьми́, по у́лице — по метле́! и вы́мели бы всю у́лицу, что идёт к тракти́ру, и вы́мели бы чи́сто... Слы́шишь! Да смотри́: ты! ты! я зна́ю тебя́: ты там кума́ешься да крадёшь в ботфо́рты сере́бряные ло́жечки, — смотри́, у меня́ у́хо востро́!.. Что ты сде́лал с купцо́м Черня́евым — а? Он тебе́ на мунди́р дал два арши́на сукна́, а ты стяну́л всю шту́ку. Смотри́! не по чи́ну берёшь! Ступа́й!

ЯВЛЕНИЕ V

Те же и ча́стный при́став.

Городни́чий. А, Степа́н Ильи́ч! Скажи́те, ра́ди бо́га: куда́ вы запропасти́лись? На что э́то похо́же?

Ча́стный при́став. Я был тут сейча́с за воро́тами.

Городни́чий. Ну, слу́шайте же, Степа́н Ильи́ч! Чино́вник-то из Петербу́рга прие́хал. Как вы там распоряди́лись?

Ча́стный при́став. Да так, как вы прика́зывали. Кварта́льного Пу́говицына я посла́л с деся́тскими подчища́ть тротуа́р.

Городни́чий. А Держимо́рда где?

Ча́стный при́став. Держимо́рда пое́хал на пожа́рной трубе́.

Городни́чий. А Про́хоров пьян?

Ча́стный при́став. Пьян.

Городни́чий. Как же вы э́то так допусти́ли?

Ча́стный при́став. Да бог его́ зна́ет. Вчера́шнего дня случи́лась за го́родом дра́ка, — пое́хал туда́ для поря́дка, а возврати́лся пьян.

Городни́чий. Послу́шайте ж, вы сде́лайте вот что: кварта́льный Пу́говицын... он высо́кого ро́ста, так пусть стои́т для благоустро́йства на мосту́. Да размета́ть на́скоро ста́рый забо́р, что во́зле сапо́жника, и поста́вить соло́менную ве́ху, чтоб бы́ло похо́же на планиро́вку. Оно́ чем бо́льше ло́мки, тем бо́льше означа́ет де́ятельности градоправи́теля. Ах, бо́же мой! я и позабы́л, что во́зле того́ забо́ра нава́лено на́ сорок теле́г вся́кого со́ру. Что э́то за скве́рный го́род! то́лько где́-нибудь поста́вь како́й-нибудь па́мятник и́ли про́сто забо́р — чёрт их зна́ет отку́дова и нанесу́т вся́кой дря́ни! *(Вздыха́ет.)* Да е́сли прие́зжий чино́вник бу́дет спра́шивать слу́жбу: дово́льны ли? — что́бы говори́ли: «Всем дово́льны, ва́ше благоро́дие»; а кото́рый бу́дет недово́лен, то ему́ по́сле дам тако́го неудово́льствия... О, ох, хо, хо, х! гре́шен, во мно́гом гре́шен. *(Берёт вме́сто шля́пы футля́р.)* Дай то́лько, бо́же, что́бы сошло́ с рук поскоре́е, а та́м-то я поста́влю уж таку́ю свечу́, како́й ещё никто́ не ста́вил: на ка́ждую бе́стию купца́ наложу́ доста́вить по́ три пу́да во́ску. О бо́же мой, бо́же мой! Едем, Пётр Ива́нович! *(Вме́сто шля́пы хо́чет наде́ть бума́жный футля́р.)*

Ча́стный при́став. Анто́н Анто́нович, э́то коро́бка, а не шля́па.

Городни́чий *(броса́я коро́бку)*. Коро́бка так коро́бка. Чёрт с ней! Да е́сли спро́сят, отчего́ не вы́строена це́рковь при богоуго́дном заведе́нии, на кото́рую наза́д тому́ пять лет была́ ассигно́вана су́мма, то не позабы́ть сказа́ть, что начала́ стро́иться, но сгоре́ла. Я об э́том и ра́порт представля́л. А то, пожа́луй, кто́-нибудь, позабы́вшись, сду́ру ска́жет, что она́ и не начина́лась. Да сказа́ть Держимо́рде, что́бы не сли́шком дава́л во́ли кулака́м свои́м; он, для поря́дка, всем ста́вит фонари́ под глаза́ми — и пра́вому и винова́тому. Едем, е́дем, Пётр Ива́нович! *(Ухо́дит и возвраща́ется.)* Да не выпуска́ть солда́т на у́лицу безо всего́: э́та дрянна́я гарниза́ наде́нет то́лько сверх руба́шки мунди́р, а внизу́ ничего́ нет.

Все ухо́дят.

ЯВЛЕНИЕ VI

Анна Андре́евна и Ма́рья Анто́новна вбега́ют на сце́ну.

Анна Андре́евна. Где ж, где ж они́? Ах, бо́же мой!.. (*Отворя́я дверь.*) Муж! Анто́ша! Анто́н! (*Говори́т ско́ро.*) А всё ты, а всё за тобо́й. И пошла́ копа́ться: «Я була́вочку, я косы́нку». (*Подбега́ет к окну́ и кричи́т.*) Анто́н, куда́, куда́? Что, прие́хал? ревизо́р? с уса́ми! с каки́ми уса́ми?

Го́лос городни́чего. По́сле, по́сле, ма́тушка!

Анна Андре́евна. По́сле? Вот но́вости — по́сле! Я не хочу́ по́сле... Мне то́лько одно́ сло́во: что он, полко́вник? А? (*С пренебреже́нием.*) Уе́хал! Я тебе́ вспо́мню э́то! А всё э́та: «Ма́менька, ма́менька, погоди́те, зашпи́лю сза́ди косы́нку; я сейча́с». Вот тебе́ и сейча́с! Вот тебе́ ничего́ и не узна́ли! А всё прокля́тое коке́тство; услы́шала, что почтме́йстер здесь, и дава́й пред зе́ркалом жема́ниться: и с той стороны́, и с э́той стороны́ подойдёт. Вообража́ет, что он за ней воло́чится, а он про́сто тебе́ де́лает грима́су, когда́ ты отвернёшься.

Ма́рья Анто́новна. Да что ж де́лать, ма́менька? Всё равно́ чрез два часа́ мы всё узна́ем.

Анна Андре́евна. Чрез два часа́! поко́рнейше благодарю́. Вот одолжи́ла отве́том! Как ты не догада́лась сказа́ть, что чрез ме́сяц ещё лу́чше мо́жно узна́ть! (*Све́шивается в окно́.*) Эй, Авдо́тья! А? Что, Авдо́тья, ты слы́шала, там прие́хал кто́-то?.. Не слы́шала? Глу́пая кака́я! Ма́шет рука́ми? Пусть ма́шет, а ты всё бы таки его́ расспроси́ла. Не могла́ э́того узна́ть! В голове́ чепуха́, всё женихи́ сидя́т. А? Ско́ро уе́хали! да ты бы побежа́ла за дро́жками. Ступа́й, ступа́й сейча́с! Слы́шишь, побеги́ расспроси́, куда́ пое́хали; да расспроси́ хороше́нько: что за прие́зжий, како́в он, — слы́шишь? Подсмотри́ в щёлку и узна́й всё, и глаза́ каки́е: чёрные и́ли нет, и сию́ же мину́ту возвраща́йся наза́д, слы́шишь? Скоре́е, скоре́е, скоре́е, скоре́е! (*Кричи́т до тех пор, пока́ не опуска́ется за́навес. Так за́навес и закрыва́ет их обе́их, стоя́щих у окна́.*)

ДЕЙСТВИЕ ВТОРОЕ

Ма́ленькая ко́мната в гости́нице. Посте́ль, стол, чемода́н, пуста́я буты́лка, сапоги́, платяна́я щётка и про́чее

ЯВЛЕНИЕ I

Осип лежи́т на ба́рской посте́ле.

Чёрт побери́, есть так хо́чется и в животе́ трескотня́ така́я, как бу́дто бы це́лый полк затруби́л в тру́бы. Вот не дое́дем, да и то́лько, домо́й! Что ты прика́жешь де́лать? Второ́й ме́сяц пошёл, как уже́ из Пи́тера! Профинти́л доро́гою де́нежки, голу́бчик, тепе́рь сиди́т и хвост подверну́л, и не горячи́тся. А ста́ло бы, и о́чень бы ста́ло на прого́ны; нет, вишь ты, ну́жно в ка́ждом го́роде показа́ть себя́! *(Дра́знит его́.)* «Эй, Осип, ступа́й посмотри́ ко́мнату, лу́чшую, да обе́д спроси́ са́мый лу́чший: я не могу́ есть дурно́го обе́да, мне ну́жен лу́чший обе́д». Добро́ бы бы́ло в са́мом де́ле что́-нибудь пу́тное, а то ведь елистра́тишка просто́й! С проезжа́ющим знако́мится, а пото́м в карти́шки — вот тебе́ и доигра́лся! Эх, надое́ла така́я жизнь! Пра́во, на дере́вне лу́чше: оно́ хоть нет публи́чности, да и забо́тности ме́ньше; возьмёшь себе́ ба́бу, да и лежи́ весь век на пола́тях да ешь пироги́. Ну, кто ж спо́рит: коне́чно, е́сли пойдёт на пра́вду, так житьё в Пи́тере лу́чше всего́. Де́ньги бы то́лько бы́ли, а жизнь то́нкая и полити́чная: кея́тры, соба́ки тебе́ танцу́ют, и всё, что хо́чешь. Разгова́ривает всё на то́нкой делика́тности, что ра́зве то́лько дворя́нству усту́пит; пойдёшь на Щу́кин — купцы́ тебе́ крича́т: «Почте́нный!»; на перево́зе в ло́дке с чино́вником ся́дешь; компа́нии захоте́л — ступа́й в ла́вочку: там тебе́ кавале́р расска́жет про ла́гери и объя́вит, что вся́кая звезда́ зна́чит на не́бе, так вот как на ладо́ни всё ви́дишь. Стару́ха офице́рша забредёт; го́рничная ино́й раз загля́нет така́я... фу, фу, фу! *(Усмеха́ется и трясёт голово́ю.)* Галантере́йное, чёрт возьми́, обхожде́ние! Неве́жливого сло́ва никогда́ не услы́шишь, вся́кой тебе́ говори́т «вы». Наску́чило идти́ — берёшь изво́зчика и сиди́шь себе, как ба́рин, а не хо́чешь заплати́ть ему́ — изво́ль: у ка́ждого до́ма есть сквозны́е воро́та, и ты так шмыгнёшь, что тебя́ никако́й дья́вол не сы́щет. Одно́ пло́хо: ино́й раз сла́вно нае́шься, а в друго́й чуть не ло́пнешь с го́лоду, как тепе́рь, наприме́р. А всё он винова́т. Что с ним сде́лаешь? Ба́тюшка пришлёт де́нежки, чем бы их попридержа́ть — и куды́!.. пошёл кути́ть: е́здит на изво́зчике, ка́ждый день ты достава́й в кея́тр биле́т, а там че́рез неде́лю, глядь — и посыла́ет на толку́чий продава́ть но́вый фрак. Ино́й раз всё до после́дней руба́шки спу́стит, так что на нём всего́ оста́нется сертучи́шка да шине́лишка... Ей-бо́гу, пра́вда! И сукно́ тако́е ва́жное, а́глицкое! рублёв полтора́ста ему́ оди́н фрак ста́нет, а на ры́нке спу́стит рубле́й за два́дцать; а о брю́ках и говори́ть не́чего — нипочём иду́т. А отчего́? — оттого́, что де́лом не занима́ется: вме́сто того́ что́бы в до́лжность, а он идёт гуля́ть по прешпе́кту, в карти́шки игра́ет. Эх, е́сли б узна́л э́то ста́рый ба́рин! Он не посмотре́л бы на то, что ты чино́вник, а, подня́вши рубашо́нку, таки́х бы засы́пал тебе́, что дня б четы́ре ты почёсывался. Ко́ли служи́ть, так служи́. Вот тепе́рь тракти́рщик сказа́л, что не дам вам есть, пока́ не запла́тите за пре́жнее; ну, а ко́ли не запла́тим? *(Со вздо́хом.)* Ах, бо́же ты мой, хоть бы каки́е-нибудь щи! Кажи́сь, так бы тепе́рь весь свет съел. Стучи́тся; ве́рно, э́то он идёт. *(Поспе́шно схва́тывается с посте́ли.)*

ЯВЛЕНИЕ II

Осип и Хлестако́в.

Хлестако́в. На, прими́ э́то. *(Отдаёт фура́жку и тро́сточку.)* А, опя́ть валя́лся на крова́ти?

Осип. Да заче́м же бы мне валя́ться? Не вида́л я ра́зве крова́ти, что ли?

Хлестако́в. Врёшь, валя́лся; ви́дишь, вся скло́чена.

Осип. Да на что мне она́? Не зна́ю я ра́зве, что тако́е крова́ть? У меня́ есть но́ги; я и постою́. Заче́м мне ва́ша крова́ть?

Хлестако́в *(хо́дит по ко́мнате)*. Посмотри́, там в картузе́ табаку́ нет?

Осип. Да где ж ему́ быть, табаку́? Вы четвёртого дня после́днее вы́курили.

Хлестако́в *(хо́дит и разнообра́зно сжима́ет свои́ гу́бы; наконе́ц говори́т гро́мким и реши́тельным го́лосом)*. Послу́шай... эй, Осип!

Осип. Чего́ изво́лите?

Хлестако́в *(гро́мким, но не столь реши́тельным го́лосом)*. Ты ступа́й туда́.

Осип. Куда́?

Хлестако́в *(го́лосом во́все не реши́тельным и не гро́мким, о́чень бли́зким к про́сьбе)*. Вниз, в буфе́т... Там скажи́... что́бы мне да́ли пообе́дать.

Осип. Да нет, я и ходи́ть не хочу́.

Хлестако́в. Как ты сме́ешь, дура́к?

Осип. Да так; всё равно́, хоть и пойду́, ничего́ из э́того не бу́дет. Хозя́ин сказа́л, что бо́льше не даст обе́дать.

Хлестако́в. Как он сме́ет не дать? Вот ещё вздор!

Осип. «Ещё, говори́т, и к городни́чему пойду́; тре́тью неде́лю ба́рин де́нег не пло́тит. Вы́-де с ба́рином, говори́т, моше́нники, и ба́рин твой — плут. Мы́-де, говори́т, э́таких широмы́жников и подлецо́в вида́ли».

Хлестако́в. А ты уж и рад, скоти́на, сейча́с переска́зывать мне всё э́то.

Осип. Говори́т: «Этак вся́кий прие́дет, обживётся, задолжа́ется, по́сле и вы́гнать нельзя́. Я, говори́т, шути́ть не бу́ду, я пря́мо с жа́лобою, чтоб на съе́зжую да в тюрьму́».

Хлестако́в. Ну, ну, дура́к, по́лно! Ступа́й, ступа́й скажи́ ему́. Тако́е гру́бое живо́тное!

Осип. Да лу́чше я самого́ хозя́ина позову́ к вам.

Хлестако́в. На что ж хозя́ина? Ты поди́ сам скажи́.

Осип. Да, пра́во, су́дарь...

Хлестако́в. Ну, ступа́й, чёрт с тобо́й! позови́ хозя́ина.

Осип ухо́дит.

ЯВЛЕНИЕ III

Хлестако́в оди́н.

Ужа́сно как хо́чется есть! Так немно́жко прошёлся, ду́мал, не пройдёт ли аппети́т, — нет, чёрт возьми́, не прохо́дит. Да, е́сли б в Пе́нзе я не покути́л, ста́ло бы де́нег дое́хать домо́й. Пехо́тный капита́н си́льно подде́л меня́: што́сы удиви́тельно, бе́стия, сре́зывает. Всего́ каки́х-нибудь че́тверть часа́ посиде́л — и всё обобра́л. А при всём том страх хоте́лось бы с ним ещё раз срази́ться. Слу́чай то́лько не привёл. Како́й скве́рный городи́шка! В ово́шенных ла́вках ничего́ не даю́т в долг. Это уж про́сто по́дло. *(Насви́стывает снача́ла из «Ро́берта», пото́м «Не шей ты мне, ма́тушка», а наконе́ц ни се́ ни то.)* Никто́ не хо́чет идти́.

ЯВЛЕНИЕ IV

Хлестако́в, Осип и тракти́рный слуга́.

Слуга́. Хозя́ин приказа́л спроси́ть, что вам уго́дно.

Хлестако́в. Здра́вствуй, бра́тец! Ну, что ты, здоро́в?

Слуга́. Сла́ва бо́гу.

Хлестако́в. Ну что, как у вас в гости́нице? хорошо́ ли всё идёт?

Слуга́. Да, сла́ва бо́гу, всё хорошо́.

Хлестако́в. Мно́го проезжа́ющих?

Слуга́. Да, доста́точно.

Хлестако́в. Послу́шай, любе́зный, там мне до сих пор обе́да не прино́сят, так, пожа́луйста, поторопи́, чтоб поскоре́е, — ви́дишь, мне сейча́с по́сле обе́да ну́жно ко́е-че́м заня́ться.

Слуга́. Да хозя́ин сказа́л, что не бу́дет бо́льше отпуска́ть. Он, ника́к, хоте́л идти́ сего́дня жа́ловаться городни́чему.

Хлестако́в. Да что ж жа́ловаться? Посуди́ сам, любе́зный, как же? ведь мне ну́жно есть. Этак могу́ я совсе́м отоща́ть. Мне о́чень есть хо́чется; я не шутя́ э́то говорю́.

Слуга́. Так-с. Он говори́л: «Я ему́ обе́дать не дам, пока́мест он не запла́тит мне за пре́жнее». Тако́в уж отве́т его́ был.

Хлестако́в. Да ты урезо́нь, уговори́ его́.

Слуга́. Да что ж ему́ тако́е говори́ть?

Хлестако́в. Ты растолку́й ему́ сурьёзно, что мне ну́жно есть. Де́ньги са́ми собо́ю... Он ду́мает, что, как ему́, мужику́, ничего́, е́сли не пое́сть день, так и други́м то́же. Вот но́вости!

Слуга́. Пожа́луй, я скажу́.

ЯВЛЕНИЕ V

Хлестако́в оди́н.

Это скве́рно, одна́ко ж, е́сли он совсе́м ничего́ не даст есть. Так хо́чется, как ещё никогда́ не хоте́лось. Ра́зве из пла́тья что́-нибудь пусти́ть в оборо́т? Штаны́, что ли, прода́ть? Нет, уж лу́чше поголода́ть, да прие́хать домо́й в петербу́ргском костю́ме. Жаль, что Иохи́м не дал напрока́т каре́ты, а хорошо́ бы, чёрт побери́, прие́хать домо́й в каре́те, подкати́ть э́таким чёртом к како́му-нибудь сосе́ду-поме́щику под крыльцо́, с фонаря́ми, а Осипа сза́ди, оде́ть в livре́ю. Как бы, я вообража́ю, все переполоши́лись: «Кто тако́й, что тако́е?» А лаке́й вхо́дит (*вытя́гиваясь и представля́я лаке́я*): «Ива́н Алекса́ндрович Хлестако́в из Петербу́рга, прика́жете приня́ть?» Они́, пе́нтюхи, и не зна́ют, что тако́е зна́чит «прика́жете приня́ть». К ним е́сли прие́дет како́й-нибудь гусь поме́щик, так и вали́т, медве́дь, пря́мо в гости́ную. К до́чечке како́й-нибудь хоро́шенькой подойдёшь: «Суда́рыня, как я...» (*потира́ет ру́ки и подша́ркивает но́жкой*). Тьфу! (*плюёт*) да́же тошни́т, так есть хо́чется.

ЯВЛЕНИЕ VI

Хлестако́в, Осип, пото́м слуга́.

Хлестако́в. А что?

Осип. Несу́т обе́д.

Хлестако́в (*прихло́пывает в ладо́ши и слегка́ подпры́гивает на сту́ле*). Несу́т! несу́т! несу́т!

Слуга́ (*с таре́лками и салфе́ткой*). Хозя́ин в после́дний раз уж даёт.

Хлестако́в. Ну, хозя́ин, хозя́ин... Я плева́ть на твоего́ хозя́ина! Что там тако́е?

Слуга́. Суп и жарко́е.

Хлестако́в. Как, то́лько два блю́да?

Слуга́. То́лько-с.

Хлестако́в. Вот вздор како́й! я э́того не принима́ю. Ты скажи́ ему́: что э́то в са́мом де́ле тако́е!.. Этого ма́ло.

Слуга́. Нет, хозя́ин говори́т, что ещё мно́го.

Хлестако́в. А со́уса почему́ нет?

Слуга́. Со́уса нет.

Хлестако́в. Отчего́ же нет? Я ви́дел сам, проходя́ ми́мо ку́хни, там мно́го гото́вилось. И в столо́вой сего́дня поутру́ дво́е каки́х-то коро́теньких челове́ка е́ли сёмгу и ещё мно́го кой-чего́.

Слуга́. Да оно́-то есть, пожа́луй, да нет.

Хлестако́в. Как нет?

Слуга́. Да уж нет.

Хлестако́в. А сёмга, а ры́ба, а котле́ты?

Слуга́. Да э́то для тех, кото́рые почи́ще-с.

Хлестако́в. Ах ты, дура́к!

Слуга́. Да-с.

Хлестако́в. Поросёнок ты скве́рный... Как же они́ едя́т, а я не ем? Отчего́ же я, чёрт возьми́, не могу́ так же? Ра́зве они́ не таки́е же проезжа́ющие, как и я?

Слуга́. Да уж изве́стно, что не таки́е.

Хлестако́в. Каки́е же?

Слуга́. Обнакове́нно каки́е! они́ уж изве́стно: они́ де́ньги пла́тят.

Хлестако́в. Я с тобо́ю, дура́к, не хочу́ рассужда́ть. *(Налива́ет суп и ест.)* Что э́то за суп? Ты про́сто воды́ на́лил в ча́шку: никако́го вку́су нет, то́лько воня́ет. Я не хочу́ э́того су́пу, дай мне друго́го.

Слуга́. Мы при́мем-с. Хозя́ин сказа́л: ко́ли не хоти́те, то и не ну́жно.

Хлестако́в *(защища́я руко́ю ку́шанье)*. Ну, ну, ну... оста́вь, дура́к! Ты привы́к там обраща́ться с други́ми: я, брат, не тако́го ро́да! со мной не сове́тую... *(Ест.)* Бо́же мой, како́й суп! *(Продолжа́ет есть.)* Я ду́маю, ещё ни оди́н челове́к в ми́ре не еда́л тако́го су́пу: каки́е-то пе́рья пла́вают вме́сто ма́сла. *(Ре́жет ку́рицу.)* Ай, ай, ай, кака́я ку́рица! Дай жарко́е! Там су́пу немно́го оста́лось, Осип, возьми́ себе́. *(Ре́жет жарко́е.)* Что э́то за жарко́е? Это не жарко́е.

Слуга́. Да что ж тако́е?

Хлестако́в. Чёрт его́ зна́ет, что тако́е, то́лько не жарко́е. Это топо́р, зажа́ренный вме́сто говя́дины. *(Ест.)*

Моше́нники, кана́льи, чем они́ ко́рмят! И че́люсти заболя́т, е́сли съешь оди́н тако́й кусо́к. *(Ковыря́ет па́льцем в зуба́х.)* Подлецы́! Соверше́нно как деревя́нная кора́, ниче́м вы́тащить нельзя́; и зу́бы почерне́ют по́сле э́тих блюд. Моше́нники! *(Вытира́ет рот салфе́ткой.)* Бо́льше ничего́ нет?

Слуга́. Нет.

Хлестако́в. Кана́льи! подлецы́! и да́же хотя́ бы како́й-нибудь со́ус и́ли пиро́жное. Безде́льники! деру́т то́лько с проезжа́ющих.

Слуга́ убира́ет и уно́сит таре́лки вме́сте с Осипом.

ЯВЛЕНИЕ VII

Хлестако́в, пото́м Осип.

Хлестако́в. Пра́во, как бу́дто и не ел; то́лько что разохо́тился. Если бы ме́лочь, посла́ть бы на ры́нок и купи́ть хоть са́йку.

Осип *(вхо́дит)*. Там заче́м-то городни́чий прие́хал, осведомля́ется и спра́шивает о вас.

Хлестако́в *(испуга́вшись)*. Вот тебе́ на! Эка бе́стия тракти́рщик, успе́л уже́ пожа́ловаться! Что, е́сли в са́мом де́ле он пота́щит меня́ в тюрьму́? Что ж, е́сли благоро́дным о́бразом, я, пожа́луй... нет, нет, не хочу́! Там в го́роде таска́ются офице́ры и наро́д, а я, как наро́чно, за́дал то́ну и перемигну́лся с одно́й купе́ческой до́чкой... Нет, не хочу́... Да что он, как он сме́ет в са́мом де́ле? Что я ему́, ра́зве купе́ц и́ли реме́сленник? *(Бодри́тся и выпря́мливается.)* Да я ему́ пря́мо скажу́: «Как вы сме́ете, как вы...» *(У двере́й ве́ртится ру́чка; Хлестако́в бледне́ет и съёживается.)*

ЯВЛЕНИЕ VIII

Хлестако́в, городни́чий и До́бчинский. Городни́чий, воше́д, остана́вливается. Оба в испу́ге смо́трят не́сколько мину́т оди́н на друго́го, вы́пучив глаза́.

Городни́чий *(немно́го опра́вившись и протяну́в ру́ки по швам)*. Жела́ю здра́вствовать!

Хлестако́в *(кла́няется)*. Моё почте́ние...

Городни́чий. Извини́те.

Хлестако́в. Ничего́...

Городни́чий. Обя́занность моя́, как градонача́льника зде́шнего го́рода, забо́титься о том, что́бы проезжа́ющим и всем благоро́дным лю́дям никаки́х притесне́ний...

Хлестако́в *(снача́ла немно́го заика́ется, но к концу́ ре́чи говори́т гро́мко)*. Да что ж де́лать?.. Я не винова́т... Я, пра́во, заплачу́... Мне пришлю́т из дере́вни.

Бо́бчинский выгля́дывает из двере́й.

Он бо́льше винова́т: говя́дину мне подаёт таку́ю твёрдую, как бревно́; а суп — он чёрт зна́ет чего́ плесну́л туда́, я до́лжен был вы́бросить его́ за окно́. Он меня́ мори́л го́лодом по це́лым дням... Чай тако́й стра́нный: воня́ет ры́бой, а не ча́ем. За что ж я... Вот но́вость!

Городни́чий *(робе́я)*. Извини́те, я, пра́во, не винова́т. На ры́нке у меня́ говя́дина всегда́ хоро́шая. Приво́зят холмого́рские купцы́, лю́ди тре́звые и поведе́ния хоро́шего. Я уж не зна́ю, отку́да он берёт таку́ю. А е́сли что не так, то... Позво́льте мне предложи́ть вам перее́хать со мно́ю на другу́ю кварти́ру.

Хлестако́в. Нет, не хочу́! Я зна́ю, что зна́чит на другу́ю кварти́ру: то есть — в тюрьму́. Да како́е вы име́ете пра́во? Да как вы сме́ете?.. Да вот я... Я служу́ в Петербу́рге. *(Бодри́тся.)* Я, я, я...

Городни́чий *(в сто́рону)*. О го́споди ты бо́же, како́й серди́тый! Всё узна́л, всё рассказа́ли прокля́тые купцы́!

Хлестако́в *(храбря́сь)*. Да вот вы хоть тут со всей свое́й кома́ндой — не пойду́! Я пря́мо к мини́стру! *(Стучи́т кулако́м по́ столу.)* Что вы? что вы?

Городни́чий *(вы́тянувшись и дрожа́ всем те́лом)*. Поми́луйте, не погуби́те! Жена́, де́ти ма́ленькие... не сде́лайте несча́стным челове́ка.

Хлестако́в. Нет, я не хочу́! Вот ещё! мне како́е де́ло? Оттого́, что у вас жена́ и де́ти, я до́лжен идти́ в тюрьму́, вот прекра́сно!

Бо́бчинский выгля́дывает в дверь и в испу́ге пря́чется.

Нет, благодарю́ поко́рно, не хочу́.

Городни́чий *(дрожа́)*. По нео́пытности, ей-бо́гу по нео́пытности. Недоста́точность состоя́ния... Са́ми изво́льте посуди́ть: казённого жа́лованья не хвата́ет да́же на чай и са́хар. Если ж и бы́ли каки́е взя́тки, то са́мая ма́лость: к столу́ что́-нибудь да на па́ру пла́тья. Что же до у́нтер-офице́рской вдовы́, занима́ющейся купе́чеством, кото́рую я бу́дто бы вы́сек, то э́то клевета́, ей-бо́гу клевета́. Это вы́думали злоде́и мои́; э́то тако́й наро́д, что на жизнь мою́ гото́вы покуси́ться.

Хлестако́в. Да что? мне нет никако́го де́ла до них. *(В размышле́нии.)* Я не зна́ю, одна́ко ж, заче́м вы говори́те о злоде́ях и́ли о како́й-то у́нтер-офице́рской вдове́... Унтер-офице́рская жена́ совсе́м друго́е, а меня́ вы не сме́ете вы́сечь, до э́того вам далеко́... Вот ещё! смотри́ ты како́й!.. Я заплачу́, заплачу́ де́ньги, но у меня́ тепе́рь нет. Я потому́ и сижу́ здесь, что у меня́ нет ни копе́йки.

Городни́чий *(в сто́рону)*. О, то́нкая шту́ка! Эк куда́ метну́л! Како́го тума́ну напусти́л! разбери́ кто хо́чет. Не зна́ешь, с кото́рой стороны́ и приня́ться. Ну, да уж попро́бовать не куды́ пошло́! Что бу́дет, то бу́дет, попро́бовать на аво́сь. *(Вслух.)* Если вы то́чно име́ете нужду́ в де́ньгах и́ли в чём друго́м, то я гото́в служи́ть сию́ мину́ту. Моя́ обя́занность помога́ть проезжа́ющим.

Хлестако́в. Да́йте, да́йте мне взаймы́! Я сейча́с же расплачу́сь с тракти́рщиком. Мне бы то́лько рубле́й две́сти и́ли хоть да́же и ме́ньше.

Городни́чий *(поднося́ бума́жки)*. Ро́вно две́сти рубле́й, хоть и не труди́тесь счита́ть.

Хлестако́в *(принима́я де́ньги)*. Поко́рнейше благодарю́. Я вам то́тчас пришлю́ их из дере́вни... у меня́ э́то вдруг... Я ви́жу, вы благоро́дный челове́к. Тепе́рь друго́е де́ло.

Городни́чий *(в сто́рону)*. Ну, сла́ва бо́гу! де́ньги взял. Де́ло, ка́жется, пойдёт тепе́рь на лад. Я таки ему́ вме́сто двухсо́т четы́реста вверну́л.

Хлестако́в. Эй, Оси́п!

Осип вхо́дит.

Позови́ сюда́ тракти́рного слугу́! *(К городни́чему и До́бчинскому.)* А что ж вы стои́те? Сде́лайте ми́лость, сади́тесь. *(До́бчинскому.)* Сади́тесь, прошу́ поко́рнейше.

Городни́чий. Ничего́, мы и так постои́м.

Хлестако́в. Сде́лайте ми́лость, сади́тесь. Я тепе́рь ви́жу соверше́нно открове́нность ва́шего нра́ва и раду́шие, а то, признаю́сь, я уж ду́мал, что вы пришли́ с тем, что́бы меня́... *(До́бчинскому.)* Сади́тесь.

Городни́чий и До́бчинский садя́тся. Бо́бчинский выгля́дывает в дверь и прислу́шивается.

Городни́чий *(в сто́рону)*. Ну́жно быть посмеле́е. Он хо́чет, что́бы счита́ли его́ инко́гнитом. Хорошо́, подпу́стим и мы туру́сы: прики́немся, как бу́дто совсе́м и не зна́ем, что он за челове́к. *(Вслух.)* Мы, проха́живаясь по дела́м до́лжности, вот с Петро́м Ива́новичем До́бчинским, зде́шним поме́щиком, зашли́ наро́чно в гости́ницу, что́бы осве́домиться, хорошо́ ли соде́ржатся проезжа́ющие, потому́ что я не так, как ино́й городни́чий, кото́рому ни до чего́ де́ла нет; но я, я, кро́ме до́лжности, ещё по христиа́нскому человеколю́бию хочу́, чтоб вся́кому сме́ртному ока́зывался хоро́ший приём, — и вот, как бу́дто в награ́ду, слу́чай доста́вил тако́е прия́тное знако́мство.

Хлестако́в. Я то́же сам о́чень рад. Без вас я, признаю́сь, до́лго бы просиде́л здесь: совсе́м не знал, чем заплати́ть.

Городни́чий *(в сто́рону)*. Да, расска́зывай, не знал, чем заплати́ть! *(Вслух.)* Осме́люсь ли спроси́ть: куда́ и в каки́е места́ е́хать изво́лите?

Хлестако́в. Я е́ду в Сара́товскую губе́рнию, в со́бственную дере́вню.

Городни́чий *(в сто́рону, с лицо́м, принима́ющим ирони́ческое выраже́ние)*. В Сара́товскую губе́рнию! А? и не покрасне́ет! О, да с ним ну́жно у́хо востро́. *(Вслух.)* Благо́е де́ло изво́лили предприня́ть. Ведь вот относи́тельно доро́ги: говоря́т, с одно́й стороны́, неприя́тности насчёт заде́ржки лошаде́й, а ведь, с друго́й стороны́, развлече́нье для ума́. Ведь вы, чай, бо́льше для со́бственного удово́льствия е́дете?

Хлестако́в. Нет, ба́тюшка меня́ тре́бует. Рассерди́лся стари́к, что до сих пор ничего́ не вы́служил в Петербу́рге. Он ду́мает, что так вот прие́хал да сейча́с тебе́ Влади́мира в петли́цу и даду́т. Нет, я бы посла́л его́ само́го потолка́ться в канцеля́рию.

Городни́чий *(в сто́рону)*. Прошу́ посмотре́ть, каки́е пу́ли отлива́ет! и старика́ отца́ приплёл! *(Вслух.)* И на до́лгое вре́мя изво́лите е́хать?

Хлестако́в. Пра́во, не зна́ю. Ведь мой оте́ц упря́м и глуп, ста́рый хрен, как бревно́. Я ему́ пря́мо скажу́: как хоти́те, я не могу́ жить без Петербу́рга. За что ж, в са́мом де́ле, я до́лжен погуби́ть жизнь с мужика́ми? Тепе́рь не те потре́бности; душа́ моя́ жа́ждет просвеще́ния.

Городни́чий (*в сто́рону*). Сла́вно завяза́л узело́к! Врёт, врёт — и нигде́ не оборвётся! А ведь како́й невзра́чный, ни́зенький, ка́жется но́гтем бы придави́л его́. Ну, да посто́й, ты у меня́ проговори́шься. Я тебя́ уж заста́влю побо́льше рассказа́ть! (*Вслух.*) Справедли́во изво́лили заме́тить. Что мо́жно сде́лать в глуши́? Ведь вот хоть бы здесь: ночь не спишь, стара́ешься для оте́чества, не жале́ешь ничего́, а награ́да неизве́стно ещё когда́ бу́дет. (*Оки́дывает глаза́ми ко́мнату.*) Ка́жется, э́та ко́мната не́сколько сыра́?

Хлестако́в. Скве́рная ко́мната, и клопы́ таки́е, каки́х я нигде́ не ви́дывал: как соба́ки куса́ют.

Городни́чий. Скажи́те! тако́й просвещённый гость, и те́рпит — от кого́ же? — от каки́х-нибудь него́дных клопо́в, кото́рым бы и на свет не сле́довало роди́ться. Ника́к, да́же темно́ в э́той ко́мнате?

Хлестако́в. Да, совсе́м темно́. Хозя́ин завёл обыкнове́ние не отпуска́ть свече́й. Иногда́ что́-нибудь хо́чется сде́лать, почита́ть, и́ли придёт фанта́зия сочини́ть что́-нибудь — не могу́: темно́, темно́.

Городни́чий. Осме́люсь ли проси́ть вас... но нет, я недосто́ин.

Хлестако́в. А что?

Городни́чий. Нет, нет, недосто́ин, недосто́ин!

Хлестако́в. Да что ж тако́е?

Городни́чий. Я бы дерзну́л... У меня́ в до́ме есть прекра́сная для вас ко́мната, све́тлая, поко́йная... Но нет, чу́вствую сам, э́то уж сли́шком больша́я честь... Не рассерди́тесь — ей-бо́гу от простоты́ души́ предложи́л.

Хлестако́в. Напро́тив, изво́льте, я с удово́льствием. Мне гора́здо прия́тнее в прива́тном до́ме, чем в э́том кабаке́.

Городни́чий. А уж я так бу́ду рад! А уж как жена́ обра́дуется! У меня́ уже́ тако́й нрав: гостеприи́мство с са́мого де́тства, особли́во е́сли гость просвещённый челове́к. Не поду́майте, что́бы я говори́л э́то из ле́сти.

Нет, не име́ю э́того поро́ка, от полноты́ души́ выража́юсь.

Хлестако́в. Поко́рно благодарю́. Я сам то́же — я не люблю́ люде́й двули́чных. Мне о́чень нра́вится ва́ша открове́нность и раду́шие, и я бы, признаю́сь, бо́льше бы ничего́ и не тре́бовал, как то́лько ока́зывай мне пре́данность и уваже́нье, уваже́нье и пре́данность.

ЯВЛЕНИЕ IX

Те же и тракти́рный слуга́, сопровожда́емый Осипом. Бо́бчинский выгля́дывает в дверь.

Слуга́. Изво́лили спра́шивать?

Хлестако́в. Да; пода́й счёт.

Слуга́. Я уж да́веча по́дал вам друго́й счёт.

Хлестако́в. Я уж не по́мню твои́х глу́пых счето́в. Говори́, ско́лько там?

Слуга́. Вы изво́лили в пе́рвый день спроси́ть обе́д, а на друго́й день то́лько закуси́ли сёмги и пото́м пошли́ всё в долг брать.

Хлестако́в. Дура́к! ещё на́чал высчи́тывать. Всего́ ско́лько сле́дует?

Городни́чий. Да вы не изво́льте беспоко́иться, он подождёт. *(Слуге́.)* Пошёл вон, тебе́ пришлю́т.

Хлестако́в. В са́мом де́ле, и то пра́вда. *(Пря́чет де́ньги.)*

Слуга́ ухо́дит. В дверь выгля́дывает Бо́бчинский.

ЯВЛЕНИЕ X

Городни́чий, Хлестако́в, До́бчинский.

Городни́чий. Не уго́дно ли бу́дет вам осмотре́ть тепе́рь не́которые заведе́ния в на́шем го́роде, ка́к-то — богоуго́дные и други́е?

Хлестако́в. А что там тако́е?

Городни́чий. А так, посмотри́те, како́е у нас тече́ние дел... поря́док како́й...

Хлестако́в. С больши́м удово́льствием, я гото́в.

Бо́бчинский выставля́ет го́лову в дверь.

Городни́чий. Та́кже, е́сли бу́дет ва́ше жела́ние, отту́да в уе́здное учи́лище, осмотре́ть поря́док, в како́м преподаю́тся у нас нау́ки.

Хлестако́в. Изво́льте, изво́льте.

Городни́чий. Пото́м, е́сли пожела́ете посети́ть остро́г и городски́е тю́рьмы — рассмо́трите, как у нас соде́ржатся престу́пники.

Хлестако́в. Да заче́м же тю́рьмы? Уж лу́чше мы обсмо́трим богоуго́дные заведе́ния.

Городни́чий. Как вам уго́дно. Как вы наме́рены: в своём экипа́же и́ли вме́сте со мно́ю на дро́жках?

Хлестако́в. Да, я лу́чше с ва́ми на дро́жках пое́ду.

Городни́чий *(До́бчинскому)*. Ну, Пётр Ива́нович, вам тепе́рь нет ме́ста.

До́бчинский. Ничего́, я так.

Городни́чий *(ти́хо До́бчинскому)*. Слу́шайте: вы побеги́те, да бего́м, во все лопа́тки, и снеси́те две запи́ски: одну́ в богоуго́дное заведе́ние Земляни́ке, а другу́ю жене́. *(Хлестако́ву.)* Осме́люсь ли я попроси́ть позволе́ния написа́ть в ва́шем прису́тствии одну́ стро́чку к жене́, чтоб она́ пригото́вилась к приня́тию почте́нного го́стя?

Хлестако́в. Да заче́м же?.. А впро́чем, тут и черни́ла, то́лько бума́ги — не зна́ю... Ра́зве на э́том счёте?

Городни́чий. Я здесь напишу́. *(Пи́шет и в то же вре́мя говори́т про себя́.)* А вот посмо́трим, как пойдёт де́ло по́сле фри́штика да буты́лки-толстобрю́шки! Да есть у нас губе́рнская маде́ра: некази́ста на вид, а слона́ пова́лит с ног. То́лько бы мне узна́ть, что он тако́е и в како́й ме́ре ну́жно его́ опаса́ться. *(Написа́вши, отдаёт До́бчинскому, кото́рый подхо́дит к две́ри, но в э́то вре́мя дверь обрыва́ется и подслу́шивавший с друго́й стороны́ Бо́бчинский лети́т вме́сте с не́ю на сце́ну. Все издаю́т восклица́ния. Бо́бчинский подыма́ется.)*

Хлестако́в. Что? не ушибли́сь ли вы где́-нибудь?

Бо́бчинский. Ничего́, ничего́-с, без вся́кого-с помеша́тельства, то́лько сверх но́са небольша́я нашлёпка. Я забегу́ к Христиа́ну Ива́новичу: у него́-с есть пла́стырь тако́й, так вот оно́ и пройдёт.

Городни́чий *(де́лая Бо́бчинскому укори́тельный знак, Хлестако́ву)*. Э́то-с ничего́. Прошу́ поко́рнейше, пожа́луйте! А слуге́ ва́шему я скажу́, что́бы перенёс чемода́н. *(Осипу.)* Любе́знейший, ты перенеси́ всё ко мне, к городни́чему, — тебе́ вся́кий пока́жет. Прошу́ поко́рнейше! *(Пропуска́ет вперёд Хлестако́ва и сле́дует за ним, но, обороти́вшись, говори́т с укори́зной Бо́бчинскому.)* Уж и вы! не нашли́ друго́го ме́ста упа́сть! И растяну́лся, как чёрт зна́ет что тако́е. *(Ухо́дит; за ним Бо́бчинский.)*

За́навес опуска́ется.

ДЕЙСТВИЕ ТРЕТЬЕ

Ко́мната пе́рвого де́йствия

ЯВЛЕНИЕ I

Анна Андре́евна, Ма́рья Анто́новна стоя́т у окна́ в тех же са́мых положе́ниях.

Анна Андре́евна. Ну вот, уж це́лый час дожида́емся, а всё ты с свои́м глу́пым жема́нством: соверше́нно оде́лась, нет, ещё ну́жно копа́ться... Бы́ло бы не слу́шать её во́все. Экая доса́да! как наро́чно, ни души́! как бу́дто бы вы́мерло всё.

Ма́рья Анто́новна. Да, пра́во, ма́менька, чрез мину́ты две всё узна́ем. Уж ско́ро Авдо́тья должна́ прийти́. *(Всма́тривается в окно́ и вскри́кивает.)* Ах, ма́менька, ма́менька! кто́-то идёт, вон в конце́ у́лицы.

Анна Андре́евна. Где идёт? У тебя́ ве́чно каки́е-нибудь фанта́зии. Ну да, идёт. Кто же э́то идёт? Небольшо́го ро́ста... во фра́ке... Кто ж э́то? а? Это, одна́ко ж, доса́дно! Кто ж бы э́то тако́й был?

Ма́рья Анто́новна. Это До́бчинский, ма́менька.

Анна Андре́евна. Како́й До́бчинский! Тебе́ всегда́ вдруг вообрази́тся э́такое... Совсе́м не До́бчинский. *(Ма́шет платко́м.)* Эй, вы, ступа́йте сюда́! скоре́е!

Ма́рья Анто́новна. Пра́во, ма́менька, До́бчинский.

Анна Андре́евна. Ну вот, наро́чно, что́бы то́лько поспо́рить. Говоря́т тебе́ — не До́бчинский.

Ма́рья Анто́новна. А что? а что, ма́менька? Ви́дите, что До́бчинский.

Анна Андре́евна. Ну да, До́бчинский, тепе́рь я ви́жу, — из чего́ же ты спо́ришь? *(Кричи́т в окно́.)* Скоре́й, скоре́й! вы ти́хо идёте. Ну что, где они́? А? Да говори́те же отту́да — всё равно́. Что? о́чень стро́гий? А? А муж, муж? *(Немно́го отступя́ от окна́, с доса́дою.)* Тако́й глу́пый: до тех пор, пока́ не войдёт в ко́мнату, ничего́ не расска́жет!

ЯВЛЕНИЕ II

Те же и До́бчинский.

Анна Андре́евна. Ну, скажи́те, пожа́луйста: ну, не со́вестно ли вам? Я на вас одни́х полага́лась, как на поря́дочного челове́ка: все вдруг вы́бежали, и вы туда́ ж за ни́ми! и я вот ни от кого́ до сих пор то́лку не доберу́сь. Не сты́дно ли вам? Я у вас крести́ла ва́шего Ва́нечку и Ли́заньку, а вы вот как со мно́ю поступи́ли!

До́бчинский. Ей-бо́гу, ку́мушка, так бежа́л засвиде́тельствовать почте́ние, что не могу́ ду́ху переве́сть. Моё почте́ние, Ма́рья Анто́новна!

Ма́рья Анто́новна. Здра́вствуйте, Пётр Ива́нович!

Анна Андре́евна. Ну что? Ну, расска́зывайте: что и как там?

До́бчинский. Анто́н Анто́нович присла́л вам запи́сочку.

Анна Андре́евна. Ну, да кто он тако́й? генера́л?

До́бчинский. Нет, не генера́л, а не усту́пит генера́лу: тако́е образова́ние и ва́жные посту́пки-с,

Анна Андре́евна. А! так э́то тот са́мый, о кото́ром бы́ло пи́сано му́жу.

До́бчинский. Настоя́щий. Я э́то пе́рвый откры́л вме́сте с Петро́м Ива́новичем.

Анна Андре́евна. Ну, расскажи́те: что и как?

До́бчинский. Да, сла́ва бо́гу, всё благополу́чно. Снача́ла он при́нял бы́ло Анто́на Анто́новича немно́го суро́во, да-с; серди́лся и говори́л, что и в гости́нице всё нехорошо́, и к нему́ не пое́дет, и что он не хо́чет сиде́ть за него́ в тюрьме́; но пото́м, как узна́л неви́нность Анто́на Анто́новича и как покоро́че разговори́лся с ним, то́тчас перемени́л мы́сли, и, сла́ва бо́гу, всё пошло́ хорошо́. Они́ тепе́рь пое́хали осма́тривать богоуго́дные заведе́ния... А то, признаю́сь, уже́ Анто́н Анто́нович думали, не́ было ли та́йного доно́са; я сам то́же перетрухну́л немно́жко.

Анна Андре́евна. Да ва́м-то чего́ боя́ться? ведь вы не слу́жите.

До́бчинский. Да так, зна́ете, когда́ вельмо́жа говори́т, чу́вствуешь страх.

Анна Андре́евна. Ну, что ж... э́то всё, одна́ко ж, вздор. Расскажи́те, како́в он собо́ю? что, стар и́ли мо́лод?

До́бчинский. Молодо́й, молодо́й челове́к, лет двадцати́ трёх; а говори́т совсе́м так, как стари́к: «Изво́льте, говори́т, я пое́ду и туда́, и туда́...» *(разма́хивает рука́ми)* так э́то всё сла́вно. «Я, говори́т, и написа́ть и почита́ть люблю́, но меша́ет, что в ко́мнате, говори́т, немно́жко темно́».

Анна Андре́евна. А собо́й како́в он: брюне́т и́ли блонди́н?

До́бчинский. Нет, бо́льше шантре́т, и глаза́ таки́е бы́стрые, как зверьки́, так в смуще́нье да́же приво́дят.

Анна Андре́евна. Что тут пи́шет он мне в запи́ске? *(Чита́ет.)* «Спешу́ тебя́ уве́домить, ду́шенька, что состоя́ние моё было весьма́ печа́льное, но, упова́я на милосе́рдие бо́жие, за два солёные огурца́ осо́бенно и полпо́рции икры́ рубль два́дцать пять копе́ек...» *(остана́вливается)* Я ничего́ не понима́ю: к чему́ же тут солёные огурцы́ и икра́?

До́бчинский. А, э́то Анто́н Анто́нович писа́ли на черново́й бума́ге по ско́рости: там како́й-то счёт был напи́сан.

Анна Андре́евна. А, да, то́чно. *(Продолжа́ет чита́ть.)* «Но, упова́я на милосе́рдие бо́жие, ка́жется, всё бу́дет к хоро́шему концу́. Пригото́вь поскоре́е ко́мнату для ва́жного го́стя, ту, что вы́клеена жёлтыми бума́жками; к обе́ду прибавля́ть не труди́сь, потому́ что заку́сим в богоуго́дном заведе́нии у Арте́мия Фили́пповича, а вина́ вели́ побо́льше; скажи́ купцу́ Абду́лину, что́бы присла́л са́мого лу́чшего, а не то я переро́ю весь его́ по́греб. Целу́я, ду́шенька, твою́ ру́чку, остаю́сь твой: Анто́н Сквозни́к-Дмухано́вский...» Ах, бо́же мой! Это, одна́ко ж, ну́жно поскоре́й! Эй, кто там? Ми́шка!

До́бчинский *(бежи́т и кричи́т в дверь)*. Ми́шка! Ми́шка! Ми́шка!

Ми́шка вхо́дит.

Анна Андре́евна. Послу́шай: беги́ к купцу́ Абду́лину... посто́й, я дам тебе́ запи́сочку. *(Сади́тся к столу́, пи́шет записку и ме́жду тем говори́т.)* Эту запи́ску ты отда́й ку́черу Си́дору, чтоб он побежа́л с не́ю к купцу́ Абду́лину и принёс отту́да вина́. А сам поди́ сейча́с прибери́ хороше́нько э́ту ко́мнату для го́стя. Там поста́вить крова́ть, рукомо́йник и про́чее...

До́бчинский. Ну, Анна Андре́евна, я побегу́ тепе́рь поскоре́е посмотре́ть, как там он обозрева́ет.

Анна Андре́евна. Ступа́йте, ступа́йте! Я не держу́ вас.

ЯВЛЕНИЕ III

Анна Андре́евна и Ма́рья Анто́новна.

Анна Андре́евна. Ну, Ма́шенька, нам ну́жно тепе́рь заня́ться туале́том. Он столи́чная шту́чка: бо́же сохрани́, что́бы чего́-нибудь не осмея́л. Тебе́ прили́чнее всего́ наде́ть твоё голубо́е пла́тье с ме́лкими обо́рками.

Ма́рья Анто́новна. Фи, ма́менька, голубо́е! Мне совсе́м не нра́вится: и Ля́пкина-Тя́пкина хо́дит в голубо́м, и дочь Земляни́ки то́же в голубо́м. Нет, лу́чше я наде́ну цветно́е.

Анна Андре́евна. Цветно́е!.. Пра́во, говори́шь — лишь бы то́лько напереко́р. Оно́ тебе́ бу́дет гора́здо лу́чше, потому́ что я хочу́ наде́ть па́левое; я о́чень люблю́ па́левое.

Ма́рья Анто́новна. Ах, ма́менька, вам нейдёт па́левое!

Анна Андре́евна. Мне па́левое нейдёт?

Ма́рья Анто́новна. Нейдёт, я что уго́дно даю́, нейдёт: для э́того ну́жно, что́бы глаза́ бы́ли совсе́м тёмные.

Анна Андре́евна. Вот хорошо́! а у меня́ глаза́ ра́зве не тёмные? са́мые тёмные. Како́й вздор говори́т! Как же не тёмные, когда́ я и гада́ю про себя́ всегда́ на тре́фовую да́му?

Ма́рья Анто́новна. Ах, ма́менька! вы бо́льше черво́нная да́ма.

Анна Андре́евна. Пустяки́, соверше́нные пустяки́! Я никогда́ не была́ черво́нная да́ма. *(Поспе́шно уходит вместе с Марьей Антоновной и говорит за сценою.)* Этакое вдруг вообразится! червонная дама! Бог знает что такое!

По уходе их отворяются двери и Мишка выбрасывает из них сор. Из других дверей выходит Осип с чемоданом на голове.

ЯВЛЕНИЕ IV

Мишка и Осип.

Осип. Куда тут?

Мишка. Сюда, дядюшка, сюда!

Осип. Постой, прежде дай отдохнуть. Ах ты горемычное житьё! На пустое брюхо всякая ноша кажется тяжела.

Мишка. Что, дядюшка, скажите: скоро будет генерал?

Осип. Какой генерал?

Мишка. Да барин ваш.

Осип. Барин? Да какой он генерал?

Мишка. А разве не генерал?

Осип. Генерал, да только с другой стороны.

Мишка. Что ж, это больше или меньше настоящего генерала?

Осип. Больше.

Мишка. Вишь ты как! то-то у нас сумятицу подняли.

Осип. Послушай, малый: ты, я вижу, проворный парень; приготовь-ка там что-нибудь поесть.

Мишка. Да для вас, дядюшка, ещё ничего не готово. Простова блюда вы не будете кушать, а вот как барин ваш сядет за стол, так и вам того же кушанья отпустят.

Осип. Ну, а простова-то что у вас есть?

Мишка. Щи, каша да пироги.

Осип. Давай их, щи, кашу и пироги! Ничего, всё будем есть. Ну, понесём чемодан! Что, там другой выход есть?

Мишка. Есть.

Оба несут чемодан в боковую комнату.

ЯВЛЕНИЕ V

Кварта́льные отворя́ют о́бе полови́нки двере́й. Вхо́дит Хлестако́в; за ним городни́чий, да́лее попечи́тель богоуго́дных заведе́ний, смотри́тель учи́лищ, До́бчинский и Бо́бчинский с пла́стырем на носу́. Городни́чий ука́зывает кварта́льным на полу́ бума́жку — они́ бегу́т и снима́ют её, толка́я друг дру́га впопыха́х.

Хлестако́в. Хоро́шие заведе́ния. Мне нра́вится, что у вас пока́зывают проезжа́ющим всё в го́роде. В други́х города́х мне ничего́ не пока́зывали.

Городни́чий. В други́х города́х, осме́люсь доложи́ть вам, градоправи́тели и чино́вники бо́льше забо́тятся о свое́й, то есть, по́льзе. А здесь, мо́жно сказа́ть, нет друго́го помышле́ния, кро́ме того́, что́бы благочи́нием и бди́тельностию заслужи́ть внима́ние нача́льства.

Хлестако́в. За́втрак был о́чень хоро́ш; я совсе́м объе́лся. Что, у вас ка́ждый день быва́ет тако́й?

Городни́чий. Наро́чно для тако́го прия́тного го́стя.

Хлестако́в. Я люблю́ пое́сть. Ведь на то живёшь, что́бы срыва́ть цветы́ удово́льствия. Как называ́лась э́та ры́ба?

Арте́мий Фили́ппович (*подбега́я*). Лабарда́н-с.

Хлестако́в. Очень вку́сная. Где э́то мы за́втракали? в больни́це, что ли?

Арте́мий Фили́ппович. Так то́чно-с, в богоуго́дном заведе́нии.

Хлестако́в. По́мню, по́мню, там стоя́ли крова́ти. А больны́е вы́здоровели? там их, ка́жется, немно́го.

Арте́мий Фили́ппович. Челове́к де́сять оста́лось, не бо́льше; а про́чие все вы́здоровели. Это уж так устро́ено, тако́й поря́док. С тех пор как я при́нял нача́льство, — мо́жет быть, вам пока́жется да́же невероя́тным, — все как му́хи выздора́вливают. Больно́й не успе́ет войти́ в лазаре́т, как уже́ здоро́в; и не сто́лько медикаме́нтами, ско́лько че́стностью и поря́дком.

Городни́чий. Уж на что, осме́люсь доложи́ть вам, головоло́мна обя́занность градонача́льника! Сто́лько лежи́т вся́ких дел, относи́тельно одно́й чистоты́, почи́нки, попра́вки... сло́вом, наиумне́йший челове́к пришёл бы в затрудне́ние, но, благодаре́ние бо́гу, всё идёт благополу́чно. Ино́й городни́чий, коне́чно, раде́л бы о свои́х вы́годах; но, ве́рите ли, что, да́же когда́ ложи́шься спать, всё ду́маешь: «Го́споди бо́же ты мой, как бы так устро́ить, что́бы нача́льство уви́дело мою́ ре́вность и бы́ло дово́льно?..» Награди́т ли оно́, и́ли нет — коне́чно, в его́ во́ле; по кра́йней ме́ре я бу́ду споко́ен в се́рдце. Когда́ в го́роде во всём поря́док, у́лицы вы́метены, ареста́нты хорошо́ соде́ржатся, пья́ниц ма́ло... то чего́ ж мне бо́льше? Ей-е́й, и по́честей никаки́х не хочу́. Оно́, коне́чно, зама́нчиво, но пред доброде́телью всё прах и суета́.

Арте́мий Фили́ппович (*в сто́рону*). Эка, безде́льник, как распи́сывает! Дал же бог тако́й дар!

Хлестако́в. Это пра́вда. Я, признаю́сь, сам люблю́ иногда́ зау́мствоваться: ино́й раз про́зой, а в друго́й и стишки́ вы́кинутся.

Бо́бчинский (*До́бчинскому*). Справедли́во, всё справедли́во, Пётр Ива́нович! Замеча́ния таки́е... ви́дно, что нау́кам учи́лся.

Хлестако́в. Скажи́те, пожа́луйста, нет ли у вас каки́х-нибудь развлече́ний, о́бществ, где бы мо́жно бы́ло, наприме́р, поигра́ть в ка́рты?

Городни́чий (*в сто́рону*). Эге́, зна́ем, голу́бчик, в чей огоро́д ка́мешки броса́ют! (*Вслух.*) Бо́же сохрани́! здесь и слу́ху нет о таки́х о́бществах. Я карт и в ру́ки никогда́ не брал; да́же не зна́ю, как игра́ть в э́ти ка́рты. Смотре́ть никогда́ не мог на них равноду́шно; и е́сли случи́тся уви́деть э́так како́го-нибудь бубно́вого короля́ и́ли что́-нибудь друго́е, то тако́е омерзе́ние нападёт, что про́сто плю́нешь. Раз ка́к-то случи́лось, забавля́я дете́й, вы́строил бу́дку из карт, да по́сле того́ всю ночь сни́лись прокля́тые. Бог с ни́ми! Как мо́жно, что́бы тако́е драгоце́нное вре́мя убива́ть на них?

Лука́ Луки́ч (*в сто́рону*). А у меня́, подле́ц, вы́понтировал вчера́ сто рубле́й.

Городни́чий. Лу́чше ж я употреблю́ э́то вре́мя на по́льзу госуда́рственную.

Хлестако́в. Ну нет, вы напра́сно, одна́ко же... Всё зави́сит от той стороны́, с кото́рой кто смо́трит на вещь. Если, наприме́р, забасту́ешь тогда́, как ну́жно гнуть от трёх угло́в... ну, тогда́ коне́чно... Нет, не говори́те, иногда́ о́чень зама́нчиво поигра́ть.

ЯВЛЕНИЕ VI

Те же, Анна Андре́евна и Ма́рья Анто́новна.

Городни́чий. Осме́люсь предста́вить семе́йство моё: жена́ и дочь.

Хлестако́в *(раскла́ниваясь)*. Как я сча́стлив, суда́рыня, что име́ю в своём ро́де удово́льствие вас ви́деть.

Анна Андре́евна. Нам ещё бо́лее прия́тно ви́деть таку́ю осо́бу.

Хлестако́в *(рису́ясь)*. Поми́луйте, суда́рыня, соверше́нно напро́тив: мне ещё прия́тнее.

Анна Андре́евна. Как мо́жно-с! Вы э́то так изво́лите говори́ть для комплиме́нта. Прошу́ поко́рно сади́ться.

Хлестако́в. Во́зле вас стоя́ть уже́ есть сча́стие; впро́чем, е́сли вы так уже́ непре́менно хоти́те, я ся́ду. Как я сча́стлив, что наконе́ц сижу́ во́зле вас.

Анна Андре́евна. Поми́луйте, я ника́к не сме́ю приня́ть на свой счёт... Я ду́маю, вам по́сле столи́цы вояжиро́вка показа́лась о́чень неприя́тною.

Хлестако́в. Чрезвыча́йно неприя́тна. Привы́кши жить, comprenez-vous, в све́те, и вдруг очути́ться в доро́ге: гря́зные тракти́ры, мрак неве́жества... Если б, призна́юсь, не тако́й слу́чай, кото́рый меня́... *(посма́тривает на Анну Андре́евну и рису́ется пе́ред ней)* так вознагради́л за всё...

Анна Андре́евна. В са́мом де́ле, как вам должно́ быть неприя́тно.

Хлестако́в. Впро́чем, суда́рыня, в э́ту мину́ту мне о́чень прия́тно.

Анна Андре́евна. Как мо́жно-с! Вы де́лаете мно́го че́сти. Я э́того не заслу́живаю.

Хлестако́в. Отчего́ же не заслу́живаете? Вы, суда́рыня, заслу́живаете.

Анна Андре́евна. Я живу́ в дере́вне...

Хлестако́в. Да, дере́вня, впро́чем, то́же име́ет свои́ приго́рки, ручейки́... Ну, коне́чно, кто же сравни́т с Петербу́ргом! Эх, Петербу́рг! что за жизнь, пра́во! Вы, мо́жет быть, ду́маете, что я то́лько перепи́сываю; нет, нача́льник отделе́ния со мной на дру́жеской ноге́. Этак уда́рит по плечу́: «Приходи́, бра́тец, обе́дать!» Я то́лько на две мину́ты захожу́ в департа́мент, с тем то́лько, что́бы сказа́ть: «Это вот так, э́то вот так!» А там уж чино́вник для письма́, э́такая кры́са, перо́м то́лько — тр, тр... пошёл писа́ть. Хоте́ли было да́же меня́ колле́жским асе́ссором сде́лать, да, ду́маю, заче́м. И сто́рож лети́т ещё на ле́стнице за мно́ю со щёткою: «Позво́льте, Ива́н Алекса́ндрович, я вам, говори́т, сапоги́ почи́щу». *(Городни́чему.)* Что вы, господа́, стои́те? Пожа́луйста, сади́тесь!

Вместе:
Городни́чий. Чин тако́й, что ещё мо́жно постоя́ть.
Арте́мий Фили́ппович. Мы постои́м.
Лука́ Луки́ч. Не изво́льте беспоко́иться!

Хлестако́в. Без чино́в, прошу́ сади́ться.

Городни́чий и все садя́тся.

Я не люблю́ церемо́нии. Напро́тив, я да́же стара́юсь всегда́ проскользну́ть незаме́тно. Но ника́к нельзя́ скры́ться, ника́к нельзя́! То́лько вы́йду куда́-нибудь, уж и говоря́т: «Вон, говоря́т, Ива́н Алекса́ндрович идёт!» А оди́н раз меня́ при́няли да́же за главнокома́ндующего: солда́ты вы́скочили из гауптва́хты и сде́лали ружьём. По́сле уже́ офице́р, кото́рый мне о́чень знако́м, говори́т мне: «Ну, бра́тец, мы тебя́ соверше́нно при́няли за главнокома́ндующего».

Анна Андре́евна. Скажи́те как!

Хлестако́в. С хоро́шенькими актри́сами знако́м. Я ведь то́же ра́зные водеви́льчики... Литера́торов ча́сто ви́жу. С Пу́шкиным на дру́жеской ноге́. Быва́ло, ча́сто говорю́ ему́: «Ну что, брат Пу́шкин?» — «Да так, брат, — отвеча́ет, быва́ло, — так ка́к-то всё...» Большо́й оригина́л.

Анна Андре́евна. Так вы и пи́шете? Как э́то должно́ быть прия́тно сочини́телю! Вы, ве́рно, и в журна́лы помеща́ете?

Хлестако́в. Да, и в журна́лы помеща́ю. Мои́х, впро́чем, мно́го есть сочине́ний: «Жени́тьба Фигаро́», «Ро́берт Дья́вол», «Но́рма». Уж и назва́ний да́же не по́мню. И всё слу́чаем: я не хоте́л писа́ть, но театра́льная дире́кция говори́т: «Пожа́луйста, бра́тец, напиши́ что́-нибудь». Ду́маю себе́: «Пожа́луй, изво́ль, бра́тец!» И тут же в оди́н ве́чер, ка́жется, всё написа́л, всех изуми́л. У меня́ лёгкость необыкнове́нная в мы́слях. Всё э́то, что бы́ло под и́менем баро́на Брамбе́уса, «Фрега́т Наде́жды» и «Моско́вский телегра́ф»... всё э́то я написа́л.

Анна Андре́евна. Скажи́те, так э́то вы бы́ли Брамбе́ус?

Хлестако́в. Как же, я им всем поправля́ю статьи́. Мне Смирди́н даёт за э́то со́рок ты́сяч.

Анна Андре́евна. Так, ве́рно, и «Юрий Милосла́вский» ва́ше сочине́ние?

Хлестако́в. Да, э́то моё сочине́ние.

Анна Андре́евна. Я сейча́с догада́лась.

Ма́рья Анто́новна. Ах, ма́менька, там напи́сано, что э́то господи́на Заго́скина сочине́ние.

Анна Андре́евна. Ну вот: я и зна́ла, что да́же здесь бу́дешь спо́рить.

Хлестако́в. Ах да, э́то пра́вда: э́то то́чно Заго́скина; а есть друго́й «Юрий Милосла́вский», так тот уж мой.

Анна Андре́евна. Ну, э́то, ве́рно, я ваш чита́ла. Как хорошо́ напи́сано!

Хлестако́в. Я, признаю́сь, литерату́рой существу́ю. У меня́ дом пе́рвый в Петербу́рге. Так уж и изве́стен: дом Ива́на Алекса́ндровича. *(Обраща́ясь ко всем.)* Сде́лайте ми́лость, господа́, е́сли бу́дете в Петербу́рге, прошу́, прошу́ ко мне. Я ведь то́же балы́ даю́.

Анна Андре́евна. Я ду́маю, с каки́м там вку́сом и великоле́пием даю́тся балы́!

Хлестако́в. Про́сто не говори́те. На столе́, наприме́р, арбу́з — в семьсо́т рубле́й арбу́з. Суп в кастрю́льке пря́мо на парохо́де прие́хал из Пари́жа; откро́ют кры́шку—пар, кото́рому подо́бного нельзя́ отыска́ть в приро́де. Я вся́кий день на бала́х. Там у нас и вист свой соста́вился: мини́стр иностра́нных дел, францу́зский посла́нник, англи́йский, неме́цкий посла́нник и я. И уж так умори́шься игра́я, что про́сто ни на что не похо́же. Как взбежи́шь по ле́стнице к себе́ на четвёртый эта́ж — ска́жешь то́лько куха́рке: «На, Мавру́шка, шине́ль...» Что ж я вру — я и позабы́л, что живу́ в бельэта́же. У меня́ одна́ ле́стница сто́ит... А любопы́тно взгляну́ть ко мне в пере́днюю, когда́ я ещё не просну́лся: гра́фы и князья́ толку́тся и жужжа́т там, как шмели́, то́лько и слы́шно: ж... ж... ж... Ино́й раз и мини́стр...

Городни́чий и про́чие с ро́бостью встаю́т с свои́х сту́льев.

Мне да́же на паке́тах пи́шут: «Ва́ше превосходи́тельство». Оди́н раз я да́же управля́л департа́ментом.

И стра́нно: дире́ктор уе́хал, — куда́ уе́хал, неизве́стно. Ну, натура́льно, пошли́ то́лки: как, что, кому́ заня́ть ме́сто? Мно́гие из генера́лов находи́лись охо́тники и брали́сь, но подойду́т, быва́ло, — нет, мудрено́. Ка́жется и легко́ на вид, а рассмо́тришь — про́сто чёрт возьми́! По́сле ви́дят, не́чего де́лать, — ко мне. И в ту же мину́ту по у́лицам курье́ры, курье́ры, курье́ры... мо́жете предста́вить себе́, три́дцать пять ты́сяч одни́х курье́ров! Каково́ положе́ние? — я спра́шиваю. «Ива́н Алекса́ндрович, ступа́йте департа́ментом управля́ть!» Я, признаю́сь, немно́го смути́лся, вы́шел в хала́те; хоте́л отказа́ться, но ду́маю: дойдёт до госуда́ря, ну да и послужно́й спи́сок то́же... «Изво́льте, господа́, я принима́ю до́лжность, я принима́ю, говорю́, так и быть, говорю́, я принима́ю, то́лько уж у меня́: ни, ни, ни!.. Уж у меня́ у́хо востро́! уж я...» И то́чно: быва́ло, как прохожу́ че́рез департа́мент, — про́сто землетрясе́нье, всё дрожи́т и трясётся, как лист.

Городни́чий и про́чие трясу́тся от стра́ха. Хлестако́в горячи́тся сильне́е.

О! я шути́ть не люблю́. Я им всем за́дал остра́стку. Меня́ сам госуда́рственный сове́т бои́тся. Да что в са́мом де́ле? Я такой! я не посмотрю́ ни на кого́... я говорю́ всем: «Я сам себя́ зна́ю, сам». Я везде́, везде́. Во дворе́ц вся́кий день е́зжу. Меня́ за́втра же произведу́т сейча́с в фельдма́рш... *(Поска́льзывается и чуть-чу́ть не шлёпается на́ пол, но с почте́нием подде́рживается чино́вниками.)*

Городни́чий *(подходя́ и трясясь всем те́лом, си́лится вы́говорить)*. А ва-ва-ва... ва...

Хлестако́в *(бы́стрым, отры́вистым го́лосом)*. Что тако́е?

Городни́чий. А ва-ва-ва... ва...

Хлестако́в *(таки́м же го́лосом)*. Не разберу́ ничего́, всё вздор.

Городни́чий. Ва-ва-ва... шество, превосходи́тельство, не прика́жете ли отдохну́ть?.. вот и ко́мната и всё, что ну́жно.

Хлестако́в. Вздор — отдохну́ть. Изво́льте, я гото́в отдохну́ть. За́втрак у вас, господа́, хоро́ш... Я дово́лен, я дово́лен. *(С деклама́цией.)* Лабарда́н! лабарда́н! *(Вхо́дит в боковую ко́мнату, за ним городни́чий.)*

ЯВЛЕНИЕ VII

Те же, кро́ме Хлестако́ва и городни́чего.

Бо́бчинский *(До́бчинскому)*. Вот э́то, Пётр Ива́нович, челове́к-то! Вот оно́, что зна́чит челове́к! В жисть не́ был в прису́тствии тако́й ва́жной персо́ны, чуть не у́мер со стра́ху. Как вы ду́маете, Пётр Ива́нович, кто он тако́й в рассужде́нии чи́на?

До́бчинский. Я ду́маю, чуть ли не генера́л.

Бо́бчинский. А я так ду́маю, что генера́л-то ему́ и в подмётки не ста́нет! а когда́ генера́л, то уж ра́зве сам генерали́ссимус. Слы́шали: госуда́рственный-то сове́т как прижа́л? Пойдём расска́жем поскоре́е Аммо́су Фёдоровичу и Коро́бкину. Проща́йте, Анна Андре́евна!

До́бчинский. Проща́йте, ку́мушка!

Оба ухо́дят.

Арте́мий Фили́ппович *(Луке́ Луки́чу)*. Стра́шно про́сто. А отчего́, и сам не зна́ешь. А мы да́же и не в мунди́рах. Ну что, как проспи́тся да в Петербу́рг махнёт донесе́ние? *(Ухо́дит в заду́мчивости вме́сте с смотри́телем учи́лищ, произнеся́:)* Проща́йте, суда́рыня!

ЯВЛЕНИЕ VIII

Анна Андре́евна и Ма́рья Анто́новна.

Анна Андре́евна. Ах, како́й прия́тный!

Ма́рья Анто́новна. Ах, мила́шка!

Анна Андре́евна. Но то́лько како́е то́нкое обраще́ние! сейча́с мо́жно уви́деть столи́чную шту́чку. Приёмы и всё э́то тако́е... Ах, как хорошо́! Я страх люблю́ таки́х молоды́х люде́й! я про́сто без па́мяти. Я, одна́ко ж, ему́ о́чень понра́вилась: я заме́тила — всё на меня́ погля́дывал.

Ма́рья Анто́новна. Ах, ма́менька, он на меня́ гляде́л.

Анна Андре́евна. Пожа́луйста, с свои́м вздо́ром пода́льше! Это здесь во́все неуме́стно.

Ма́рья Анто́новна. Нет, ма́менька, пра́во!

Анна Андре́евна. Ну вот! Бо́же сохрани́, что́бы не поспо́рить! нельзя́, да и по́лно! Где ему́ смотре́ть на тебя́? И с како́й ста́ти ему́ смотре́ть на тебя́?

Ма́рья Анто́новна. Пра́во, ма́менька, всё смотре́л. И как на́чал говори́ть о литерату́ре, то взгляну́л на меня́, и пото́м, когда́ расска́зывал, как игра́л в вист с посла́нниками, и тогда́ посмотре́л на меня́.

Анна Андре́евна. Ну, мо́жет быть, оди́н како́й-нибудь раз, да и то так уж, лишь бы то́лько. «А, — говори́т себе́, — дай уж посмотрю́ на неё!»

ЯВЛЕНИЕ IX

Те же и городни́чий.

Городни́чий *(вхо́дит на цы́почках)*. Чш... ш...

Анна Андре́евна. Что?

Городни́чий. И не рад, что напои́л. Ну что, е́сли хоть одна́ полови́на из того́, что он говори́л, пра́вда? *(Заду́мывается.)* Да как же и не быть пра́вде? Подгуля́вши, челове́к всё несёт нару́жу: что на се́рдце, то и на языке́. Коне́чно, прилгну́л немно́го; да ведь не прилгну́вши не говори́тся никака́я речь. С мини́страми игра́ет и во дворе́ц е́здит... Так вот, пра́во, чем бо́льше ду́маешь... чёрт его́ зна́ет, не зна́ешь, что и де́лается в голове́; про́сто как бу́дто и́ли стои́шь на како́й-нибудь колоко́льне, и́ли тебя́ хотя́т пове́сить.

Анна Андре́евна. А я никако́й соверше́нно не ощути́ла ро́бости; я про́сто ви́дела в нём образо́ванного, све́тского, вы́сшего то́на челове́ка, а о чина́х его́ мне и ну́жды нет.

Городни́чий. Ну, уж вы — же́нщины! Всё ко́нчено, одного́ э́того сло́ва доста́точно! Вам всё — финтирлю́шки! Вдруг бря́кнут ни из того́ ни из друго́го словцо́. Вас посеку́т, да и то́лько, а му́жа и помина́й как зва́ли. Ты, душа́ моя́, обраща́лась с ним так свобо́дно, как бу́дто с каки́м-нибудь До́бчинским.

Анна Андре́евна. Об э́том я уж сове́тую вам не беспоко́иться. Мы кой-что́ зна́ем тако́е... *(Посма́тривает на дочь.)*

Городни́чий *(оди́н)*. Ну, уж с ва́ми говори́ть!.. Эка в са́мом де́ле ока́зия! До сих пор не могу́ очну́ться от стра́ха. *(Отворя́ет дверь и говори́т в дверь.)* Ми́шка, позови́ кварта́льных Свистуно́ва и Держимо́рду: они́ тут недалеко́ где́-нибудь за воро́тами. *(По́сле небольшо́го молча́ния.)* Чудно́ всё завело́сь тепе́рь на све́те:

хоть бы наро́д-то уж был ви́дный, а то ху́денький, то́ненький — как его́ узна́ешь, кто он? Ещё вое́нный всё-таки ка́жет из себя́, а как наде́нет фрачи́шку — ну то́чно му́ха с подре́занными кры́льями. А ведь до́лго крепи́лся да́веча в тракти́ре, зала́мливал таки́е аллего́рии и екиво́ки, что, кажи́сь, век бы не доби́лся то́лку. А вот наконе́ц и подался́. Да ещё наговори́л бо́льше, чем ну́жно. Ви́дно, что челове́к молодо́й.

ЯВЛЕНИЕ X

Те же и Осип. Все бегу́т к нему́ навстре́чу, кива́я па́льцами.

Анна Андре́евна. Подойди́ сюда́, любе́зный!

Городни́чий. Чш!.. что? что? спит?

Осип. Нет ещё, немно́жко потя́гивается.

Анна Андре́евна. Послу́шай, как тебя́ зову́т?

Осип. Осип, суда́рыня.

Городни́чий (*жене́ и до́чери*). По́лно, по́лно вам! (*Осипу.*) Ну что, друг, тебя́ накорми́ли хорошо́?

Осип. Накорми́ли, поко́рнейше благодарю́; хорошо́ накорми́ли.

Анна Андре́евна. Ну что, скажи́: к твоему́ ба́рину сли́шком, я ду́маю, мно́го е́здит гра́фов и князе́й?

Осип (*в сто́рону*). А что говори́ть? Ко́ли тепе́рь накорми́ли хорошо́, зна́чит по́сле ещё лу́чше нако́рмят. (*Вслух.*) Да, быва́ют и гра́фы.

Ма́рья Анто́новна. Ду́шенька Осип, како́й твой ба́рин хоро́шенький!

Анна Андре́евна. А что, скажи́, пожа́луйста, Осип, как он...

Городни́чий. Да переста́ньте, пожа́луйста! Вы э́такими пусты́миреча́ми то́лько мне меша́ете. Ну что, друг?..

Анна Андре́евна. А чин како́й на твоём ба́рине?

Осип. Чин обыкнове́нно како́й.

Городни́чий. Ах, бо́же мой, вы всё с свои́ми глу́пыми расспро́сами! не дади́те ни сло́ва поговори́ть о де́ле. Ну что, друг, как твой ба́рин?.. строг? лю́бит э́так распека́ть и́ли нет?

Осип. Да, поря́док лю́бит. Уж ему́ что́бы всё бы́ло в испра́вности.

Городни́чий. А мне о́чень нра́вится твоё лицо́. Друг, ты до́лжен быть хоро́ший челове́к. Ну что...

А н н а А н д р е́ е в н а. Послу́шай, Осип, а как ба́рин твой там, в мунди́ре хо́дит, и́ли...

Г о р о д н и́ ч и й. По́лно вам, пра́во, трещо́тки каки́е! Здесь ну́жная вещь: де́ло идёт о жи́зни челове́ка... *(К Осипу.)* Ну что, друг, пра́во, мне ты о́чень нра́вишься. В доро́ге не меша́ет, зна́ешь, чайку́ вы́пить ли́шний стака́нчик, — оно́ тепе́рь холоднова́то. Так вот тебе́ па́ра целко́виков на чай.

О с и п *(принима́я де́ньги)*. А поко́рнейше благодарю́, су́дарь. Дай бог вам вся́кого здоро́вья! бе́дный челове́к, помогли́ ему́.

Г о р о д н и́ ч и й. Хорошо́, хорошо́, я и сам рад. А что, друг...

А н н а А н д р е́ е в н а. Послу́шай, Осип, а каки́е глаза́ бо́льше всего́ нра́вятся твоему́ ба́рину?

М а́ р ь я А н т о́ н о в н а. Осип, ду́шенька! како́й ми́ленький но́сик у твоего́ ба́рина!

Г о р о д н и́ ч и й. Да посто́йте, да́йте мне!.. *(К Осипу.)* А что, друг, скажи́, пожа́луйста: на что бо́льше ба́рин твой обраща́ет внима́ние, то есть что ему́ в доро́ге бо́льше нра́вится?

О с и п. Лю́бит он, по рассмотре́нию, что как придётся. Бо́льше всего́ лю́бит, что́бы его́ при́няли хорошо́, угоще́ние чтоб бы́ло хоро́шее.

Г о р о д н и́ ч и й. Хоро́шее?

О с и п. Да, хоро́шее. Вот уж на что я крепостно́й челове́к, но и то смо́трит, что́бы и мне бы́ло хорошо́. Ей-бо́гу! Быва́ло, зае́дем куда́-нибудь: «Что, Осип, хорошо́ тебя́ угости́ли?» — «Пло́хо, ва́ше высокоблагоро́дие!» — «Э, говори́т, э́то, Осип, нехоро́ший хозя́ин. Ты, говори́т, напо́мни мне, как прие́ду». — «А, — ду́маю себе́ *(махну́в руко́ю)*, — бог с ним! я челове́к просто́й».

Г о р о д н и́ ч и й. Хорошо́, хорошо́, и де́ло ты говори́шь. Там я тебе́ дал на чай, так вот ещё сверх того́ на бара́нки.

О с и п. За что жа́луете, ва́ше высокоблагоро́дие? *(Пря́чет де́ньги.)* Ра́зве уж вы́пью за ва́ше здоро́вье.

А н н а А н д р е́ е в н а. Приходи́, Осип, ко мне, то́же полу́чишь.

М а́ р ь я А н т о́ н о в н а. Осип, ду́шенька, поцелу́й своего́ ба́рина!

Слы́шен из друго́й ко́мнаты небольшо́й ка́шель Хлестако́ва.

Г о р о д н и́ ч и й. Чш! *(Поднима́ется на цы́почки; вся сце́на вполго́лоса.)* Бо́же вас сохрани́ шуме́ть! Иди́те себе! по́лно уж вам...

А н н а А н д р е́ е в н а. Пойдём, Ма́шенька! я тебе́ скажу́, что я заме́тила у го́стя тако́е, что нам вдвоём то́лько мо́жно сказа́ть.

Г о р о д н и́ ч и й. О, уж там наговоря́т! Я ду́маю, поди́ то́лько да послу́шай — и у́ши пото́м заткнёшь. *(Обраща́ясь к Осипу.)* Ну, друг...

ЯВЛЕНИЕ XI

Т е ж е, Д е р ж и м о́ р д а и С в и с т у н о́ в.

Г о р о д н и́ ч и й. Чш! э́кие косола́пые медве́ди — стуча́т сапога́ми! Так и ва́лится, как бу́дто со́рок пуд сбра́сывает кто́-нибудь с теле́ги! Где вас чёрт таска́ет?

Д е р ж и м о́ р д а. Был по приказа́нию...

Г о р о д н и́ ч и й. Чш! *(Закрыва́ет ему́ рот.)* Эк как ка́ркнула воро́на! *(Дра́знит его́.)* Был по приказа́нию! Как из бо́чки, так рычи́т. *(К Осипу.)* Ну, друг, ты ступа́й приготовля́й там, что ну́жно для ба́рина. Всё, что ни есть в до́ме, тре́буй.

Осип ухо́дит.

А вы — стоя́ть на крыльце́ и ни с ме́ста! И никого́ не впуска́ть в дом сторо́ннего, осо́бенно купцо́в! Если хоть одного́ из них впу́стите, то... То́лько уви́дите, что идёт кто́-нибудь с про́сьбою, а хоть и не с про́сьбою, да похо́ж на тако́го челове́ка, что хо́чет пода́ть на меня́ про́сьбу, вза́шей так пря́мо и толка́йте! так его́! хороше́нько! *(Пока́зывает ного́ю.)* Слы́шите? Чш... чш... *(Ухо́дит на цы́почках вслед за кварта́льными.)*

ДЕЙСТВИЕ ЧЕТВЕРТОЕ

Та же ко́мната в до́ме городни́чего

ЯВЛЕНИЕ I

Вхо́дят осторо́жно, почти́ на цы́почках: Аммо́с Фёдорович, Арте́мий Фили́ппович, почтме́йстер, Лука́ Луки́ч, До́бчинский и Бо́бчинский, в по́лном пара́де и мунди́рах. Вся сце́на происхо́дит вполго́лоса.

Аммо́с Фёдорович *(стро́ит всех полукру́жием)*. Ра́ди бо́га, господа́, скоре́е в кружо́к, да побо́льше поря́дку! Бог с ним: и во дворе́ц е́здит, и госуда́рственный сове́т распека́ет! Стро́йтесь на вое́нную но́гу, непреме́нно на вое́нную но́гу! Вы, Пётр Ива́нович, забеги́те с э́той стороны́, а вы, Пётр Ива́нович, ста́ньте вот тут.

Оба Петра́ Ива́новича забега́ют на цы́почках.

Арте́мий Фили́ппович. Во́ля ва́ша, Аммо́с Фёдорович, нам ну́жно бы ко́е-что́ предприня́ть.

Аммо́с Фёдорович. А что и́менно?

Арте́мий Фили́ппович. Ну, изве́стно что.

Аммо́с Фёдорович. Подсу́нуть?

Арте́мий Фили́ппович. Ну да, хоть и подсу́нуть.

Аммо́с Фёдорович. Опа́сно, чёрт возьми́! раскричи́тся: госуда́рственный челове́к. А ра́зве в ви́де приноше́нья со стороны́ дворя́нства на како́й-нибудь па́мятник?

Почтме́йстер. Или же: «вот, мол, пришли́ по по́чте де́ньги, неизве́стно кому́ принадлежа́щие».

Арте́мий Фили́ппович. Смотри́те, чтоб он вас по по́чте не отпра́вил куды́-нибудь пода́льше. Слу́шайте: э́ти дела́ не так де́лаются в благоустро́енном госуда́рстве. Заче́м нас здесь це́лый эскадро́н? Предста́виться ну́жно поодино́чке, да ме́жду четырёх глаз и того́... как там сле́дует — что́бы и у́ши не слыха́ли. Вот как в о́бществе благоустро́енном де́лается. Ну, вот вы, Аммо́с Фёдорович, пе́рвый и начни́те.

Аммо́с Фёдорович. Так лу́чше ж вы: в ва́шем заведе́нии высо́кий посети́тель вкуси́л хле́ба.

Арте́мий Фили́ппович. Так уж лу́чше Луке́ Лукичу́, как просвети́телю ю́ношества.

Лука́ Луки́ч. Не могу́, не могу́, господа́. Я, признаю́сь, так воспи́тан, что, заговори́ со мно́ю одни́м чи́ном кто́-нибудь повы́ше, у меня́ про́сто и души́ нет, и язы́к как в грязь завя́знул. Нет, господа́, уво́льте, пра́во, уво́льте!

Арте́мий Фили́ппович. Да, Аммо́с Фёдорович, кро́ме вас, не́кому. У вас что ни сло́во, то Цицеро́н с языка́ слете́л.

Аммо́с Фёдорович. Что вы! что вы: Цицеро́н! Смотри́те, что вы́думали! Что ино́й раз увлечёшься, говоря́ о дома́шней сво́ре и́ли го́нчей ище́йке...

Все *(пристаю́т к нему́)*. Нет, вы не то́лько о соба́ках, вы и о столпотворе́нии... Нет, Аммо́с Фёдорович, не оставля́йте нас, бу́дьте отцо́м на́шим!.. Нет, Аммо́с Фёдорович!

Аммо́с Фёдорович. Отвяжи́тесь, господа́!

В э́то вре́мя слы́шны шаги́ и отка́шливание в ко́мнате Хлестако́ва. Все спеша́т напереры́в к дверя́м, толпя́тся и стара́ются вы́йти, что происхо́дит не без того́, что́бы не прити́снули ко́е-кого́. Раздаю́тся вполго́лоса восклица́ния.

Го́лос Бо́бчинского. Ой, Пётр Ива́нович, Пётр Ива́нович! наступи́ли на́ ногу!

Го́лос Земляни́ки. Отпусти́те, господа́, хоть ду́шу на покая́ние — совсе́м прижа́ли!

Выхва́тываются не́сколько восклица́ний: «Ай! ай!», наконе́ц все выпира́ются, и ко́мната остаётся пуста́.

ЯВЛЕНИЕ II

Хлестако́в оди́н, выхо́дит с за́спанными глаза́ми.

Я, ка́жется, всхрапну́л поря́дком. Отку́да они́ набра́ли таки́х тюфяко́в и пери́н? да́же вспоте́л. Ка́жется, они́ вчера́ мне подсу́нули чего́-то за за́втраком: в голове́ до сих пор стучи́т. Здесь, как я ви́жу, мо́жно с прия́тностию проводи́ть вре́мя. Я люблю́ раду́шие, и мне, признаю́сь, бо́льше нра́вится, е́сли мне угожда́ют от чи́стого се́рдца, а не то что́бы из интере́са. А до́чка городни́чего о́чень недурна́, да и ма́тушка така́я, что ещё мо́жно бы... Нет, я не зна́ю, а мне, пра́во, нра́вится така́я жизнь.

ЯВЛЕНИЕ III

Хлестако́в и Аммо́с Фёдорович.

Аммо́с Фёдорович *(входя́ и остана́вливаясь, про себя́)*. Бо́же, бо́же! вы́неси благополу́чно; так вот коле́нки и лома́ет. *(Вслух, вы́тянувшись и приде́рживая руко́ю шпа́гу.)* Име́ю честь предста́виться: судья́ зде́шнего уе́здного суда́, колле́жский асе́ссор Ля́пкин-Тя́пкин.

Хлестако́в. Прошу́ сади́ться. Так вы здесь судья́?

Аммо́с Фёдорович. С восемьсо́т шестна́дцатого был и́збран на трёхле́тие по во́ле дворя́нства и продолжа́л до́лжность до сего́ вре́мени.

Хлестако́в. А вы́годно, одна́ко же, быть судьёю?

Аммо́с Фёдорович. За три трёхле́тия предста́влен к Влади́миру четвёртой сте́пени с одобре́ния со стороны́ нача́льства. *(В сто́рону.)* А де́ньги в кулаке́, да кула́к-то весь в огне́.

Хлестако́в. А мне нра́вится Влади́мир. Вот Анна тре́тьей сте́пени уже́ не так.

Аммо́с Фёдорович *(высо́вывая понемно́гу вперёд сжа́тый кула́к. В сто́рону)*. Го́споди бо́же! не зна́ю, где сижу́. То́чно горя́чие у́гли под тобо́ю.

Хлестако́в. Что э́то у вас в руке́?

Аммо́с Фёдорович *(потеря́вшись и роняя на́ пол ассигна́ции)*. Ничего́-с.

Хлестако́в. Как ничего́? Я ви́жу, де́ньги упа́ли.

Аммо́с Фёдорович *(дрожа́ всем те́лом)*. Ника́к нет-с. *(В сто́рону.)* О бо́же, вот уж я и под судо́м! и теле́жку подвезли́ схвати́ть меня́!

Хлестако́в (*подыма́я*). Да, э́то де́ньги.

Аммо́с Фёдорович (*в сто́рону*). Ну, все ко́нчено — пропа́л! пропа́л!

Хлестако́в. Зна́ете ли что? да́йте их мне взаймы́.

Аммо́с Фёдорович (*поспе́шно*). Как же-с, как же-с... с больши́м удово́льствием. (*В сто́рону.*) Ну, смеле́е, смеле́е! Вывози́, пресвята́я ма́терь!

Хлестако́в. Я, зна́ете, в доро́ге издержа́лся: то да сё... Впро́чем, я вам из дере́вни сейча́с их пришлю́.

Аммо́с Фёдорович. Поми́луйте, как мо́жно! и без того́ э́то така́я честь... Коне́чно, сла́быми мои́ми си́лами, рве́нием и усе́рдием к нача́льству... постара́юсь заслужи́ть... (*Приподыма́ется со сту́ла, вы́тянувшись и ру́ки по швам.*) Не сме́ю бо́лее беспоко́ить свои́м прису́тствием. Не бу́дет ли како́го приказа́нья?

Хлестако́в. Како́го приказа́нья?

Аммо́с Фёдорович. Я разуме́ю, не дади́те ли како́го приказа́нья зде́шнему уе́здному суду́?

Хлестако́в. Заче́м же? Ведь мне никако́й нет тепе́рь в нём на́добности.

Аммо́с Фёдорович (*раскла́ниваясь и уходя́, в сто́рону*). Ну, го́род наш!

Хлестако́в (*по ухо́де его́*). Судья́ — хоро́ший челове́к!

ЯВЛЕНИЕ IV

Хлестако́в и почтме́йстер, вхо́дит вы́тянувшись, в мунди́ре, приде́рживая шпа́гу.

Почтме́йстер. Име́ю честь предста́виться: почтме́йстер, надво́рный сове́тник Шпе́кин.

Хлестако́в. А, ми́лости про́сим! Я о́чень люблю́ прия́тное о́бщество. Сади́тесь. Ведь вы здесь всегда́ живёте?

Почтме́йстер. Так то́чно-с.

Хлестако́в. А мне нра́вится зде́шний городо́к. Коне́чно, не так многолю́дно — ну, что ж? Ведь э́то не столи́ца. Не пра́вда ли, ведь э́то не столи́ца?

Почтме́йстер. Соверше́нная пра́вда.

Хлестако́в. Ведь э́то то́лько в столи́це бонто́н и нет провинциа́льных гусе́й. Как ва́ше мне́ние, не так ли?

Почтме́йстер. Так то́чно-с. (*В сто́рону.*) А он, одна́ко ж, ничу́ть не горд; обо всём расспра́шивает.

Хлестако́в. А ведь, одна́ко ж, призна́йтесь, ведь и в ма́леньком городке́ мо́жно прожи́ть сча́стливо?

Почтме́йстер. Так то́чно-с.

Хлестако́в. По моему́ мне́нию, что ну́жно? Ну́жно то́лько, что́бы тебя́ уважа́ли, люби́ли и́скренно, — не пра́вда ли?

Почтме́йстер. Соверше́нно справедли́во.

Хлестако́в. Я, признаю́сь, рад, что вы одного́ мне́ния со мно́ю. Меня́, коне́чно, назову́т стра́нным, но уж у меня́ тако́й хара́ктер. *(Гля́дя в глаза́ ему́, говори́т про себя́.)* А попрошу́-ка я у э́того почтме́йстера взаймы́! *(Вслух.)* Како́й стра́нный со мно́ю слу́чай: в доро́ге соверше́нно издержа́лся. Не мо́жете ли вы мне дать три́ста рубле́й взаймы́?

Почтме́йстер. Почему́ же? почту́ за велича́йшее сча́стие. Вот-с, изво́льте. От души́ гото́в служи́ть.

Хлестако́в. Очень благода́рен. А я, признаю́сь, смерть не люблю́ отка́зывать себе́ в доро́ге, да и к чему́? Не так ли?

Почтме́йстер. Так то́чно-с. *(Встаёт, вытя́гивается и приде́рживает шпа́гу.)* Не сме́я до́лее беспоко́ить свои́м прису́тствием... Не бу́дет ли како́го замеча́ния по ча́сти почто́вого управле́ния?

Хлестако́в. Нет, ничего́.

Почтме́йстер раскла́нивается и ухо́дит.

(Раску́ривая сига́рку.) Почтме́йстер, мне ка́жется, то́же о́чень хоро́ший челове́к. По кра́йней ме́ре услу́жлив. Я люблю́ таки́х люде́й.

ЯВЛЕНИЕ V

Хлестако́в и Лука́ Луки́ч, кото́рый почти́ выта́лкивается из двере́й. Сза́ди его́ слы́шен го́лос почти́ вслух: «Чего́ робе́ешь?»

Лука́ Луки́ч *(вытя́гиваясь не без тре́пета и приде́рживая шпа́гу)*. Име́ю честь предста́виться: смотри́тель учи́лищ, титуля́рный сове́тник Хло́пов.

Хлестако́в. А, ми́лости про́сим! Сади́тесь, сади́тесь. Не хоти́те ли сига́рку? *(Подаёт ему́ сига́ру.)*

Лука́ Луки́ч *(про себя́, в нереши́мости)*. Вот тебе́ раз! Уж э́того ника́к не предполага́л. Брать и́ли не брать?

Хлестако́в. Возьми́те, возьми́те; э́то поря́дочная сига́рка. Коне́чно, не то, что в Петербу́рге. Там, ба́тюшка, я ку́ривал сига́рочки по двадцати́ пяти́ рубле́й со́тенка, про́сто ру́чки пото́м себе́ поцелу́ешь, как вы́куришь. Вот ого́нь, закури́те. *(Подаёт ему́ свечу́.)*

Лука́ Луки́ч про́бует закури́ть и весь дрожи́т.

Да не с того́ конца́!

Лука́ Луки́ч *(от испу́га вы́ронил сига́ру, плю́нул и, махну́в руко́ю, про себя́).* Чёрт побери́ всё! сгуби́ла прокля́тая ро́бость!

Хлестако́в. Вы, как я ви́жу, не охо́тник до сига́рок. А я признаю́сь: э́то моя́ сла́бость. Вот ещё насчёт же́нского по́лу, ника́к не могу́ быть равноду́шен. Как вы? Каки́е вам бо́льше нра́вятся — брюне́тки и́ли блонди́нки?

Лука́ Луки́ч нахо́дится в соверше́нном недоуме́нии, что сказа́ть.

Нет, скажи́те открове́нно: брюне́тки и́ли блонди́нки?

Лука́ Луки́ч. Не сме́ю знать.

Хлестако́в. Нет, нет, не отгова́ривайтесь! Мне хо́чется узна́ть непреме́нно ваш вкус.

Лука́ Луки́ч. Осме́люсь доложи́ть... *(В сто́рону.)* Ну, и сам не зна́ю, что говорю́.

Хлестако́в. А! а! не хоти́те сказа́ть. Ве́рно, уж кака́я-нибудь брюне́тка сде́лала вам ма́ленькую загво́здочку. Призна́йтесь, сде́лала?

Лука́ Луки́ч молчи́т.

А! а! покрасне́ли! Ви́дите! ви́дите! Отчего́ ж вы не говори́те?

Лука́ Луки́ч. Оробе́л, ва́ше бла... преос... сия́т... *(В сто́рону.)* Про́дал прокля́тый язы́к, про́дал!

Хлестако́в. Оробе́ли? А в мои́х глаза́х то́чно есть что́-то тако́е, что внуша́ет ро́бость. По кра́йней ме́ре я зна́ю, что ни одна́ же́нщина не мо́жет их вы́держать, не так ли?

Лука́ Луки́ч. Так то́чно-с.

Хлестако́в. Вот со мной престра́нный слу́чай: в доро́ге совсе́м издержа́лся. Не мо́жете ли вы мне дать три́ста рубле́й взаймы́?

Лука́ Луки́ч (*хвата́ясь за карма́ны, про себя́*). Вот те шту́ка, е́сли нет! Есть, есть. (*Вынима́ет и подаёт, дрожа́, ассигна́ции.*)

Хлестако́в. Поко́рнейше благодарю́.

Лука́ Луки́ч (*вытя́гиваясь и приде́рживая шпа́гу*). Не сме́ю до́лее беспоко́ить прису́тствием.

Хлестако́в. Проща́йте.

Лука́ Луки́ч (*лети́т вон почти́ бего́м и говори́т в сто́рону*). Ну, сла́ва бо́гу! аво́сь не загля́нет в кла́ссы.

ЯВЛЕНИЕ VI

Хлестако́в и Арте́мий Фили́ппович, вы́тянувшись и приде́рживая шпа́гу.

Арте́мий Фили́ппович. Име́ю честь предста́виться: попечи́тель богоуго́дных заведе́ний, надво́рный сове́тник Земляни́ка.

Хлестако́в. Здра́вствуйте, прошу́ поко́рно сади́ться.

Арте́мий Фили́ппович. Име́л честь сопровожда́ть вас и принима́ть ли́чно во вве́ренных моему́ смотре́нию богоуго́дных заведе́ниях.

Хлестако́в. А, да! по́мню. Вы о́чень хорошо́ угости́ли за́втраком.

Арте́мий Фили́ппович. Рад стара́ться на слу́жбу оте́честву.

Хлестако́в. Я — признаю́сь, э́то моя́ сла́бость, — люблю́ хоро́шую ку́хню. Скажи́те, пожа́луйста, мне ка́жется, как бу́дто бы вчера́ вы бы́ли немно́жко ни́же ро́стом, не пра́вда ли?

Арте́мий Фили́ппович. Очень мо́жет быть. (*Помолча́в.*) Могу́ сказа́ть, что не жале́ю ничего́ и ре́вностно исполня́ю слу́жбу. (*Придвига́ется бли́же с свои́м сту́лом и говори́т вполго́лоса.*) Вот зде́шний почтме́йстер соверше́нно ничего́ не де́лает: все дела́ в большо́м запуще́нии, посы́лки заде́рживаются... изво́льте са́ми наро́чно разыска́ть. Судья́ то́же, кото́рый то́лько что был пред мои́м прихо́дом, е́здит то́лько за за́йцами, в прису́тственных места́х де́ржит соба́к и поведе́ния, е́сли призна́ться пред ва́ми, — коне́чно, для по́льзы оте́чества я до́лжен э́то сде́лать, хотя́ он мне родня́ и прия́тель, — поведе́ния са́мого предосуди́тельного. Здесь есть оди́н поме́щик, До́бчинский, кото́рого вы изво́лили ви́деть; и как то́лько э́тот До́бчинский куда́-нибудь вы́йдет и́з дому, то он там уж и сиди́т у жены́ его́, я присягну́ть гото́в... И наро́чно посмотри́те на дете́й: ни одно́ из них не похо́же на До́бчинского, но все, да́же де́вочка ма́ленькая, как вы́литый судья́.

Хлестако́в. Скажи́те пожа́луйста! а я ника́к э́того не ду́мал.

Арте́мий Фили́ппович. Вот и смотри́тель зде́шнего учи́лища... Я не зна́ю, как могло́ нача́льство пове́рить ему́ таку́ю до́лжность: он ху́же, чем якоби́нец, и таки́е внуша́ет ю́ношеству неблагонаме́ренные пра́вила, что да́же вы́разить тру́дно. Не прика́жете ли, я всё э́то изложу́ лу́чше на бума́ге?

Хлестако́в. Хорошо́, хоть на бума́ге. Мне о́чень бу́дет прия́тно. Я, зна́ете, э́так люблю́ в ску́чное вре́мя проче́сть что́-нибудь заба́вное... Как ва́ша фами́лия? я всё позабыва́ю.

Арте́мий Фили́ппович. Земляни́ка.

Хлестако́в. А, да! Земляни́ка. И что ж, скажи́те, пожа́луйста, есть у вас де́тки?

Арте́мий Фили́ппович. Как же-с, пя́теро; дво́е уже́ взро́слых.

Хлестако́в. Скажи́те, взро́слых! А как они́... как они́ того́?..

Арте́мий Фили́ппович. То есть, не изво́лите ли вы спра́шивать, как их зову́т?

Хлестако́в. Да, как их зову́т?

Арте́мий Фили́ппович. Никола́й, Ива́н, Елизаве́та, Ма́рья и Перепету́я.

Хлестако́в. Это хорошо́.

Арте́мий Фили́ппович. Не сме́я беспоко́ить свои́м прису́тствием, отнима́ть вре́мени, определённого на свяще́нные обя́занности... *(Раскла́нивается с тем, что́бы уйти́.)*

Хлестако́в *(провожа́я)*. Нет, ничего́. Это всё о́чень смешно́, что вы говори́ли. Пожа́луйста, и в друго́е то́же вре́мя... Я э́то о́чень люблю́. *(Возвраща́ется и, отвори́вши дверь, кричи́т вслед ему́.)* Эй, вы! как вас? я всё позабыва́ю, как ва́ше и́мя и о́тчество.

Арте́мий Фили́ппович. Арте́мий Фили́ппович.

Хлестако́в. Сде́лайте ми́лость, Арте́мий Фили́ппович, со мной стра́нный слу́чай: в доро́ге соверше́нно издержа́лся. Нет ли у вас де́нег взаймы́ — рубле́й четы́реста?

Арте́мий Фили́ппович. Есть.

Хлестако́в. Скажи́те, как кста́ти. Поко́рнейше вас благодарю́.

ЯВЛЕНИЕ VII

Хлестако́в, Бо́бчинский и До́бчинский.

Бо́бчинский. Име́ю честь предста́виться: жи́тель зде́шнего го́рода, Пётр Ива́нов сын Бо́бчинский.

До́бчинский. Поме́щик Пётр Ива́нов сын До́бчинский.

Хлестако́в. А, да я уж вас ви́дел. Вы, ка́жется, тогда́ упа́ли? Что, как ваш нос?

Бо́бчинский. Сла́ва бо́гу! не изво́льте беспоко́иться: присо́х, тепе́рь совсе́м присо́х.

Хлестако́в. Хорошо́, что присо́х. Я рад... (*Вдруг и отры́висто.*) Де́нег нет у вас?

Бо́бчинский. Де́нег? как де́нег?

Хлестако́в (*гро́мко и ско́ро*). Взаймы́ рубле́й ты́сячу.

Бо́бчинский. Тако́й су́ммы, ей-бо́гу, нет. А нет ли у вас, Пётр Ива́нович?

До́бчинский. При мне-с не име́ется, потому́ что де́ньги мои́, е́сли изво́лите знать, поло́жены в прика́з обще́ственного призре́ния.

Хлестако́в. Да, ну е́сли ты́сячи нет, так рубле́й сто.

Бо́бчинский (*ша́ря в карма́нах*). У вас, Пётр Ива́нович, нет ста рубле́й? У меня́ всего́ со́рок ассигна́циями.

До́бчинский (*смотря́ в бума́жник*). Два́дцать пять рубле́й всего́.

Бо́бчинский. Да вы поищи́те-то полу́чше, Пётр Ива́нович! У вас там, я зна́ю, в карма́не-то с пра́вой стороны́ проре́ха, так в проре́ху-то, ве́рно, ка́к-нибудь запа́ли.

До́бчинский. Нет, пра́во, и в проре́хе нет.

Хлестако́в. Ну, всё равно́. Я ведь то́лько так. Хорошо́, пусть бу́дет шестьдеся́т пять рубле́й. Это всё равно́. (*Принима́ет де́ньги.*)

До́бчинский. Я осме́ливаюсь попроси́ть вас относи́тельно одного́ о́чень то́нкого обстоя́тельства.

Хлестако́в. А что э́то?

До́бчинский. Де́ло о́чень то́нкого сво́йства-с: ста́рший-то сын мой, изво́лите ви́деть, рождён мно́ю ещё до бра́ка.

Хлестако́в. Да?

До́бчинский. То есть, оно́ так то́лько говори́тся, а он рождён мно́ю так соверше́нно, как бы и в бра́ке, и всё э́то, как сле́дует, я заверши́л пото́м зако́нными-с у́зами супру́жества-с. Так я, изво́лите ви́деть, хочу́, чтоб он тепе́рь уже́ был совсе́м, то есть, зако́нным мои́м сы́ном-с и называ́лся бы так, как я: До́бчинский-с.

Хлестако́в. Хорошо́, пусть называ́ется! Это мо́жно.

До́бчинский. Я бы и не беспоко́ил вас, да жаль насчёт спосо́бностей. Мальчи́шка-то э́такой... больши́е наде́жды подаёт: наизу́сть стихи́ ра́зные расска́жет и, е́сли где попадёт но́жик, сейча́с сде́лает ма́ленькие дро́жечки так иску́сно, как фо́кусник-с. Вот и Пётр Ива́нович зна́ет.

Бо́бчинский. Да, больши́е спосо́бности име́ет.

Хлестако́в. Хорошо́, хорошо́. Я об э́том постара́юсь, я бу́ду говори́ть... я наде́юсь... всё э́то бу́дет сде́лано, да, да... *(Обраща́ясь к Бо́бчинскому.)* Не име́ете ли и вы чего́-нибудь сказа́ть мне?

Бо́бчинский. Как же, име́ю о́чень нижа́йшую про́сьбу.

Хлестако́в. А что, о чём?

Бо́бчинский. Я прошу́ вас поко́рнейше, как пое́дете в Петербу́рг, скажи́те всем там вельмо́жам ра́зным: сена́торам и адмира́лам, что вот, ва́ше сия́тельство, и́ли превосходи́тельство, живёт в тако́м-то го́роде Пётр Ива́нович Бо́бчинский. Так и скажи́те: живёт Пётр Ива́нович Бо́бчинский.

Хлестако́в. Очень хорошо́.

Бо́бчинский. Да е́сли э́так и госуда́рю придётся, то скажи́те и госуда́рю, что вот, мол, ва́ше императо́рское вели́чество, в тако́м-то го́роде живёт Пётр Ива́нович Бо́бчинский.

Хлестако́в. Очень хорошо́.

До́бчинский. Извини́те, что так утруди́ли вас свои́м прису́тствием.

Бо́бчинский. Извини́те, что так утруди́ли вас свои́м прису́тствием.

Хлестако́в. Ничего́, ничего́. Мне о́чень прия́тно. *(Выпровожа́ет их.)*

ЯВЛЕНИЕ VIII

Хлестако́в оди́н.

Здесь мно́го чино́вников. Мне ка́жется, одна́ко ж, они́ меня́ принима́ют за госуда́рственного челове́ка. Ве́рно, я вчера́ им подпусти́л пы́ли. Экое дурачьё! Напишу́-ка я обо всём в Петербу́рг к Тряпи́чкину: он попи́сывает стате́йки — пу́сть-ка он их общёлкает хороше́нько. Эй, Осип, пода́й мне бума́гу и черни́лы!

Осип вы́глянул из двере́й, произнёсши: «Сейча́с».

А уж Тряпи́чкину, то́чно, е́сли кто попадёт на зубо́к, — береги́сь: отца́ родно́го не пощади́т для словца́, и деньгу́ то́же лю́бит. Впро́чем, чино́вники э́ти до́брые лю́ди; э́то с их стороны́ хоро́шая черта́, что они́ мне да́ли взаймы́. Пересмотрю́ наро́чно, ско́лько у меня́ де́нег. Это от судьи́ три́ста; э́то от почтме́йстера три́ста, шестьсо́т, семьсо́т, восемьсо́т... Кака́я зама́сленная бума́жка! Восемьсо́т, девятьсо́т... Ого́! за ты́сячу перевали́ло... Ну́-ка, тепе́рь, капита́н, ну́-ка, попади́сь-ка ты мне тепе́рь! Посмо́трим, кто кого́!

ЯВЛЕНИЕ IX

Хлестако́в и Осип с черни́лами и бума́гою.

Хлестако́в. Ну что, ви́дишь, дура́к, как меня́ угоща́ют и принима́ют? *(Начина́ет писа́ть.)*

Осип. Да, сла́ва бо́гу! То́лько зна́ете что, Ива́н Алекса́ндрович?

Хлестако́в *(пи́шет)*. А что?

Осип. Уезжа́йте отсю́да. Ей-бо́гу, уже́ пора́.

Хлестако́в *(пи́шет)*. Вот вздор! Заче́м?

Осип. Да так. Бог с ни́ми со все́ми! Погуля́ли здесь два денька́ — ну и дово́льно. Что с ни́ми до́лго свя́зываться? Плю́ньте на них! не ровён час, како́й-нибудь друго́й нае́дет... Ей-бо́гу, Ива́н Алекса́ндрович! А ло́шади тут сла́вные — так бы закати́ли!..

Хлестако́в (*пи́шет*). Нет, мне ещё хо́чется пожи́ть здесь. Пусть за́втра.

Осип. Да что за́втра! Ей-бо́гу, пое́дем, Ива́н Алекса́ндрович! Оно́ хоть и больша́я честь вам, да всё, зна́ете, лу́чше уе́хать скоре́е: ведь вас, пра́во, за кого́-то друго́го при́няли... И ба́тюшка бу́дет гне́ваться, что так заме́шкались. Так бы, пра́во, закати́ли сла́вно! А лошаде́й бы ва́жных здесь да́ли.

Хлестако́в (*пи́шет*). Ну, хорошо́. Отнеси́ то́лько наперёд э́то письмо́; пожа́луй, вме́сте и подоро́жную возьми́. Да зато́, смотри́, чтоб ло́шади хоро́шие бы́ли. Ямщика́м скажи́, что я бу́ду дава́ть по целко́вому; что́бы так, как фельдъегеря́, кати́ли и пе́сни бы пе́ли!.. (*Продолжа́ет писа́ть.*) Вообража́ю, Тряпи́чкин умрёт со́ смеху...

Осип. Я, су́дарь, отпра́влю его́ с челове́ком зде́шним, а сам лу́чше бу́ду укла́дываться, чтоб не прошло́ понапра́сну вре́мя.

Хлестако́в (*пи́шет*). Хорошо́. Принеси́ то́лько свечу́.

Осип (*выхо́дит и говори́т за сце́ной*). Эй, послу́шай, брат! Отнесёшь письмо́ на по́чту, и скажи́ почтме́йстеру, чтоб он при́нял без де́нег; да скажи́, чтоб сейча́с привели́ к ба́рину са́мую лу́чшую тро́йку, курье́рскую; а прого́ну, скажи́, ба́рин не пло́тит: прого́н, мол, скажи́, казённый. Да чтоб всё живе́е, а не то, мол, ба́рин се́рдится. Стой, ещё письмо́ не гото́во.

Хлестако́в (*продолжа́ет писа́ть*). Любопы́тно знать, где он тепе́рь живёт — в Почта́мтской и́ли Горо́ховой? Он ведь то́же лю́бит ча́сто переезжа́ть с кварти́ры и недопла́чивать. Напишу́ наудалу́ю в Почта́мтскую. (*Свёртывает и надпи́сывает.*)

Осип прино́сит свечу́. Хлестако́в печа́тает. В э́то вре́мя слы́шен го́лос Держимо́рды: «Куда́ ле́зешь, борода́? Говоря́т тебе́, никого́ не ве́лено пуска́ть».

(*Даёт Осипу письмо́.*) На, отнеси́.

Голоса́ купцо́в. Допусти́те, ба́тюшка! Вы не мо́жете не допусти́ть: мы за де́лом пришли́.

Го́лос Держимо́рды. Пошёл, пошёл! Не принима́ет, спит.

Шум увели́чивается.

Хлестако́в. Что там тако́е, Осип? Посмотри́, что за шум.

Осип (*гля́дя в окно́*). Купцы́ каки́е-то хотя́т войти́, да не допуска́ет кварта́льный. Ма́шут бума́гами: ве́рно, вас хотя́т ви́деть.

Хлестако́в (*подходя́ к окну́*). А что вы, любе́зные?

Голоса́ купцо́в. К твое́й ми́лости прибега́ем. Прикажи́, госуда́рь, про́сьбу приня́ть.

Хлестако́в. Впусти́те их, впусти́те! пусть иду́т. Осип, скажи́ им: пусть иду́т.

Осип ухо́дит.

(*Принима́ет из окна́ про́сьбы, развёртывает одну́ из них и чита́ет:*) «Его́ Высокоблагоро́дному Све́тлости Господи́ну Фина́нсову от купца́ Абду́лина...» Чёрт зна́ет что: и чи́на тако́го нет!

ЯВЛЕНИЕ X

Хлестако́в и купцы́ с ку́зовом вина́ и са́харными голова́ми.

Хлестако́в. А что вы, любе́зные?

Купцы́. Чело́м бьём ва́шей ми́лости.

Хлестако́в. А что вам уго́дно?

Купцы́. Не погуби́, госуда́рь! Обижа́тельство те́рпим совсе́м понапра́сну.

Хлестако́в. От кого́?

Оди́н из купцо́в. Да всё от городни́чего зде́шнего. Тако́го городни́чего никогда́ ещё, госуда́рь, не́ было. Таки́е оби́ды чини́т, что описа́ть нельзя́. Посто́ем совсе́м замори́л, хоть в пе́тлю полеза́й. Не по посту́пкам поступа́ет. Схва́тит за́ бороду, говори́т: «Ах ты, тата́рин!» Ей-бо́гу! Если бы, то есть, че́м-нибудь не ува́жили его́, а то мы уж поря́док всегда́ исполня́ем: что сле́дует на пла́тья супру́жнице его́ и до́чке — мы про́тив э́того не стои́м. Нет, вишь ты, ему́ всего́ э́того ма́ло — ей-е́й! Придёт в ла́вку и, что ни попадёт, всё берёт. Сукна́ уви́дит шту́ку, говори́т: «Э, ми́лый, э́то хоро́шее суко́нце: снеси́-ка его́ ко мне». Ну и несёшь, а в шту́ке-то бу́дет без ма́ла арши́н пятьдеся́т.

Хлестако́в. Неуже́ли? Ах, како́й же он моше́нник!

Купцы́. Ей-бо́гу! тако́го никто́ не запо́мнит городни́чего. Так всё и припря́тываешь в ла́вке, когда́ его́ зави́дишь. То есть, не то уж говоря́, чтоб каку́ю делика́тность, вся́кую дрянь берёт: черносли́в тако́й, что лет уже́ по семи́ лежи́т в бо́чке, что у меня́ сиде́лец не бу́дет есть, а он це́лую горсть туда́ запу́стит. Имени́ны его́ быва́ют на Анто́на, и уж, кажи́сь, всего́ нанесёшь, ни в чём не нужда́ется. Нет, ему́ ещё подава́й: говори́т, и на Ону́фрия его́ имени́ны. Что де́лать? и на Ону́фрия несёшь.

Хлестако́в. Да э́то про́сто разбо́йник!

Купцы́. Ей-ей! А попро́буй прекосло́вить, наведёт к тебе́ в дом це́лый полк на посто́й. А е́сли что, вели́т запере́ть две́ри. «Я тебя́, говори́т, не бу́ду, говори́т, подверга́ть теле́сному наказа́нию и́ли пы́ткой пыта́ть — э́то, говори́т, запрещено́ зако́ном, а вот ты у меня́, любе́зный, пое́шь селёдки!»

Хлестако́в. Ах, како́й моше́нник! Да за э́то про́сто в Сиби́рь.

Купцы́. Да уж куда́ ми́лость твоя́ ни запрова́дит его́, всё бу́дет хорошо́, лишь бы, то есть, от нас пода́льше. Не побре́згай, оте́ц наш, хле́бом и со́лью: кла́няемся тебе́ сахарцо́м и кузовко́м вина́.

Хлестако́в. Нет, вы э́того не ду́майте: я не беру́ совсе́м никаки́х взя́ток. Вот е́сли бы вы, наприме́р, предложи́ли мне взаймы́ рубле́й три́ста — ну, тогда́ совсе́м де́ло друго́е: взаймы́ я могу́ взять.

Купцы́. Изво́ль, оте́ц наш! *(Вынима́ют де́ньги.)* Да что три́ста! Уж лу́чше пятьсо́т возьми́, помоги́ то́лько.

Хлестако́в. Изво́льте: взаймы́ — я ни сло́ва, я возьму́.

Купцы́ *(подно́сят ему́ на серебряном подно́се де́ньги)*. Уж, пожа́луйста, и подно́сик вме́сте возьми́те.

Хлестако́в. Ну, и подно́сик мо́жно.

Купцы́ *(кла́няясь)*. Так уж возьми́те за одни́м ра́зом и сахарцу́.

Хлестако́в. О нет, я взя́ток никаки́х...

Оси́п. Ва́ше высокоблагоро́дие! заче́м вы не берёте? Возьми́те! в доро́ге всё пригоди́тся. Дава́й сюда́ го́ловы и кулёк! Подава́й всё! всё пойдёт впрок. Что там? верёвочка? Дава́й и верёвочку, — и верёвочка в доро́ге пригоди́тся: теле́жка облома́ется и́ли что друго́е, подвяза́ть мо́жно.

Купцы́. Так уж сде́лайте таку́ю ми́лость, ва́ше сия́тельство. Если уже́ вы, то есть, не помо́жете в на́шей про́сьбе, то уж не зна́ем, как и быть: про́сто хоть в пе́тлю полеза́й.

Хлестако́в. Непреме́нно, непреме́нно! Я постара́юсь.

Купцы́ ухо́дят. Слы́шен го́лос же́нщины: «Нет, ты не сме́ешь не допусти́ть меня́! Я на тебя́ нажа́луюсь ему́ самому́. Ты не толка́йся так бо́льно!»

Кто там? *(Подхо́дит к окну́.)* А, что ты, ма́тушка?

Голоса́ двух же́нщин. Ми́лости твое́й, оте́ц, прошу́! Повели́, госуда́рь, вы́слушать!

Хлестако́в *(в окно́)*. Пропусти́ть её.

ЯВЛЕНИЕ XI

Хлестако́в, сле́сарша и у́нтер-офице́рша.

Сле́сарша *(кла́няясь в но́ги)*. Ми́лости прошу́...

Унтер-офице́рша. Ми́лости прошу́...

Хлестако́в. Да что вы за же́нщины?

Унтер-офице́рша. Унтер-офице́рская жена́ Ивано́ва.

Сле́сарша. Сле́сарша, зде́шняя меща́нка, Февро́нья Петро́ва Пошлёпкина, оте́ц мой...

Хлестако́в. Стой, говори́ пре́жде одна́. Что тебе́ ну́жно?

Сле́сарша. Ми́лости прошу́: на городни́чего чело́м бью! Пошли́ ему́ бог вся́кое зло! Чтоб ни де́тям его́, ни ему́, моше́ннику, ни дядья́м, ни тёткам его́ ни в чём никако́го прибы́тку не́ было!

Хлестако́в. А что?

Сле́сарша. Да му́жу-то моему́ приказа́л забри́ть лоб в солда́ты, и о́чередь-то на нас не припада́ла, моше́нник тако́й! да и по зако́ну нельзя́: он жена́тый.

Хлестако́в. Как же он мог э́то сде́лать?

Сле́сарша. Сде́лал, моше́нник, сде́лал — побе́й бог его́ и на том и на э́том све́те! Что́бы ему́, е́сли и тётка есть, то и тётке вся́кая па́кость, и оте́ц е́сли жив у него́, то чтоб и он, кана́лья, околе́л и́ли поперхну́лся наве́ки, моше́нник тако́й! Сле́довало взять сы́на портно́го, он же и пьяню́шка был, да роди́тели бога́тый пода́рок да́ли, так он и присы́кнулся к сы́ну купчи́хи Пантеле́евой, а Пантеле́ева то́же подосла́ла к супру́ге полотна́ три шту́ки; так он ко мне. «На что, говори́т, тебе́ муж? он уж тебе́ не годи́тся». Да я́-то зна́ю — годи́тся и́ли не годи́тся; э́то моё де́ло, моше́нник тако́й! «Он, говори́т, вор; хоть он тепе́рь и не укра́л, да всё равно́, говори́т, он украдёт, его́ и без того́ на сле́дующий год возьму́т в ре́круты». Да мне́-то каково́ без му́жа, моше́нник тако́й! Я сла́бый челове́к, подле́ц ты тако́й! Чтоб всей родне́ твое́й не довело́сь ви́деть све́та бо́жьего! А е́сли есть тёща, то чтоб и тёще...

Хлестако́в. Хорошо́, хорошо́. Ну, а ты? *(Выпровожа́ет стару́ху.)*

Сле́сарша *(уходя́)*. Не позабу́дь, оте́ц наш! будь ми́лостив!

Унтер-офице́рша. На городни́чего, ба́тюшка, пришла́...

Хлестако́в. Ну, да что, заче́м? говори́ в коро́тких слова́х.

Унтер-офице́рша. Вы́сек, ба́тюшка!

Хлестако́в. Как?

Унтер-офице́рша. По оши́бке, оте́ц мой. Ба́бы-то на́ши задрали́сь на ры́нке, а поли́ция не подоспе́ла, да и схвати́ меня́. Да так отрапортова́ли: два дни сиде́ть не могла́.

Хлестако́в. Так что ж тепе́рь де́лать?

Унтер-офице́рша. Да де́лать-то, коне́чно, не́чего. А за оши́бку-то повели́ ему́ заплати́ть штрафт. Мне от своего́ сча́стья не́ча отка́зываться, а де́ньги бы мне тепе́рь о́чень пригоди́лись.

Хлестако́в. Хорошо́, хорошо́. Ступа́йте, ступа́йте! я распоряжу́сь.

В окно́ высо́вываются ру́ки с про́сьбами.

Да кто там ещё? *(Подхо́дит к окну́.)* Не хочу́, не хочу́! Не ну́жно, не ну́жно! *(Отходя́.)* Надое́ли, чёрт возьми́! Не впуска́й, Осип!

Осип *(кричи́т в окно́)*. Пошли́, пошли́! Не вре́мя, за́втра приходи́те!

Дверь отворя́ется, и выставля́ется кака́я-то фигу́ра во фри́зовой шине́ли, с небри́тою бородо́ю, разду́тою губо́ю и перевя́занною щеко́ю; за не́ю в перспекти́ве пока́зывается не́сколько други́х.

Пошёл, пошёл! чего́ ле́зешь? *(Упира́ется пе́рвому рука́ми в брю́хо и выпира́ется вме́сте с ним в прихо́жую, захло́пнув за собо́ю дверь.)*

ЯВЛЕНИЕ XII

Хлестако́в и Ма́рья Анто́новна.

Ма́рья Анто́новна. Ах!

Хлестако́в. Отчего́ вы так испуга́лись, суда́рыня?

Ма́рья Анто́новна. Нет, я не испуга́лась.

Хлестако́в *(рису́ется)*. Поми́луйте, суда́рыня, мне о́чень прия́тно, что вы меня́ при́няли за тако́го челове́ка, кото́рый... Осме́люсь ли спроси́ть вас: куда́ вы наме́рены бы́ли идти́?

Ма́рья Анто́новна. Пра́во, я никуда́ не шла.

Хлестако́в. Отчего́ же, наприме́р, вы никуда́ не шли?

Ма́рья Анто́новна. Я ду́мала, не здесь ли ма́менька...

Хлестако́в. Нет, мне хоте́лось бы знать, отчего́ вы никуда́ не шли?

Ма́рья Анто́новна. Я вам помеша́ла. Вы занима́лись ва́жными дела́ми.

Хлестако́в *(рису́ется)*. А ва́ши глаза́ лу́чше, не́жели ва́жные дела́... Вы ника́к не мо́жете мне помеша́ть, никаки́м о́бразом не мо́жете; напро́тив того́, вы мо́жете прине́сть удово́льствие.

Ма́рья Анто́новна. Вы говори́те по-столи́чному.

Хлестако́в. Для тако́й прекра́сной осо́бы, как вы. Осме́люсь ли быть так сча́стлив, что́бы предложи́ть вам стул? Но нет, вам до́лжно не стул, а трон.

Ма́рья Анто́новна. Пра́во, я не зна́ю... мне так ну́жно бы́ло идти́. *(Се́ла.)*

Хлестако́в. Како́й у вас прекра́сный плато́чек!

Ма́рья Анто́новна. Вы насме́шники, лишь бы то́лько посмея́ться над провинциа́льными.

Хлестако́в. Как бы я жела́л, суда́рыня, быть ва́шим плато́чком, что́бы обнима́ть ва́шу лиле́йную ше́йку.

Ма́рья Анто́новна. Я совсе́м не понима́ю, о чём вы говори́те: како́й-то плато́чек... Сего́дня кака́я стра́нная пого́да!

Хлестако́в. А ва́ши гу́бки, суда́рыня, лу́чше, не́жели вся́кая пого́да.

Ма́рья Анто́новна. Вы всё э́дакое говори́те... Я бы вас попроси́ла, чтоб вы мне написа́ли лу́чше на па́мять каки́е-нибудь стишки́ в альбо́м. Вы, ве́рно, их зна́ете мно́го.

Хлестако́в. Для вас, суда́рыня, всё, что хоти́те. Тре́буйте, каки́е стихи́ вам?

Ма́рья Анто́новна. Каки́е-нибудь э́дакие — хоро́шие, но́вые.

Хлестако́в. Да что стихи́! я мно́го их зна́ю.

Ма́рья Анто́новна. Ну, скажи́те же, каки́е же вы мне напи́шете?

Хлестако́в. Да к чему́ же говори́ть? я и без того́ их зна́ю.

Ма́рья Анто́новна. Я о́чень люблю́ их...

Хлестако́в. Да у меня́ мно́го их вся́ких. Ну, пожа́луй, я вам хоть э́то: «О ты, что в го́рести напра́сно на бо́га ро́пщешь, челове́к!..» Ну и други́е... тепе́рь не могу́ припо́мнить; впро́чем, э́то всё ничего́. Я вам лу́чше вме́сто э́того предста́влю мою́ любо́вь, кото́рая от ва́шего взгля́да... *(Придвига́я стул.)*

Ма́рья Анто́новна. Любо́вь! Я не понима́ю любо́вь... я никогда́ и не зна́ла, что за любо́вь... *(Отдвига́ет стул.)*

Хлестако́в *(придвига́я стул)*. Отчего́ ж вы отдвига́ете свой стул? Нам лу́чше бу́дет сиде́ть бли́зко друг к дру́гу.

Ма́рья Анто́новна *(отдвига́ясь)*. Для чего́ ж бли́зко? всё равно́ и далеко́.

Хлестако́в *(придвига́ясь)*. Отчего́ ж далеко́? всё равно́ и бли́зко.

Ма́рья Анто́новна *(отдвига́ется)*. Да к чему́ ж э́то?

Хлестако́в *(придвига́ясь)*. Да ведь э́то вам ка́жется то́лько, что бли́зко; а вы вообрази́те себе́, что далеко́. Как бы я был сча́стлив, суда́рыня, е́сли б мог прижа́ть вас в свои́ объя́тия.

Ма́рья Анто́новна *(смо́трит в окно́)*. Что э́то там как бу́дто бы полете́ло? Соро́ка и́ли кака́я друга́я пти́ца?

Хлестако́в *(целу́ет её в плечо́ и смо́трит в окно́)*. Это соро́ка.

Ма́рья Анто́новна *(встаёт в негодова́нии)*. Нет, э́то уж сли́шком... На́глость така́я!..

Хлестако́в *(уде́рживая её)*. Прости́те, суда́рыня: я э́то сде́лал от любви́, то́чно от любви́.

Ма́рья Анто́новна. Вы почита́ете меня́ за таку́ю провинциа́лку... *(Си́лится уйти́.)*

Хлестако́в *(продолжа́я уде́рживать её).* Из любви́, пра́во из любви́. Я так то́лько, пошути́л, Ма́рья Анто́новна, не серди́тесь! Я гото́в на коле́нках у вас проси́ть проще́ния. *(Па́дает на коле́ни.)* Прости́те же, прости́те! Вы ви́дите, я на коле́нях.

ЯВЛЕНИЕ XIII

Те же и Анна Андре́евна.

Анна Андре́евна *(уви́дев Хлестако́ва на коле́нях).* Ах, како́й пасса́ж!

Хлестако́в *(встава́я).* А, чёрт возьми́!

Анна Андре́евна *(до́чери).* Это что зна́чит, суда́рыня? Это что за посту́пки таки́е?

Ма́рья Анто́новна. Я, ма́менька...

Анна Андре́евна. Поди́ прочь отсю́да! слы́шишь: прочь, прочь! И не сме́й пока́зываться на глаза́.

Ма́рья Анто́новна ухо́дит в слеза́х.

Извини́те, я, признаю́сь, приведена́ в тако́е изумле́ние...

Хлестако́в *(в сто́рону).* А она́ то́же о́чень аппети́тна, о́чень недурна́. *(Броса́ется на коле́ни.)* Суда́рыня, вы ви́дите, я сгора́ю от любви́.

Анна Андре́евна. Как, вы на коле́нях? Ах, вста́ньте, вста́ньте! здесь пол совсе́м нечи́ст.

Хлестако́в. Нет, на коле́нях, непреме́нно на коле́нях! Я хочу́ знать, что тако́е мне суждено́: жизнь и́ли смерть.

Анна Андре́евна. Но позво́льте, я ещё не понима́ю вполне́ значе́ния слов. Если не ошиба́юсь, вы де́лаете деклара́цию насчёт мое́й до́чери?

Хлестако́в. Нет, я влюблён в вас. Жизнь моя́ на волоске́. Если вы не увенча́ете постоя́нную любо́вь мою́, то я недосто́ин земно́го существова́ния. С пла́менем в груди́ прошу́ руки́ ва́шей.

Анна Андре́евна. Но позво́льте заме́тить: я в не́котором ро́де... я за́мужем.

Хлестако́в. Это ничего́! Для любви́ нет разли́чия; и Карамзи́н сказа́л: «Зако́ны осужда́ют». Мы удали́мся под сень струй... Руки́ ва́шей, руки́ прошу́!

ЯВЛЕНИЕ XIV

Те же и Ма́рья Анто́новна, вдруг вбега́ет.

Ма́рья Анто́новна. Ма́менька, па́пенька сказа́л, что́бы вы... *(Уви́дя Хлестако́ва на коле́нях, вскри́кивает.)* Ах, како́й пасса́ж!

Анна Андре́евна. Ну что ты? к чему́? заче́м? Что за ве́треность така́я! Вдруг вбежа́ла, как угоре́лая ко́шка. Ну что ты нашла́ тако́го удиви́тельного? Ну что тебе́ взду́малось? Пра́во, как дитя́ како́е-нибудь трёхле́тнее. Не похо́же, не похо́же, соверше́нно не похо́же на то, что́бы ей бы́ло восемна́дцать лет. Я не зна́ю, когда́ ты бу́дешь благоразу́мнее, когда́ ты бу́дешь вести́ себя́, как прили́чно благовоспи́танной деви́це; когда́ ты бу́дешь знать, что тако́е хоро́шие пра́вила и соли́дность в посту́пках.

Ма́рья Анто́новна *(сквозь слёзы)*. Я, пра́во, ма́менька, не зна́ла...

Анна Андре́евна. У тебя́ ве́чно како́й-то сквозно́й ве́тер разгу́ливает в голове́; ты берёшь приме́р с дочере́й Ля́пкина-Тя́пкина. Что тебе́ гляде́ть на них? не ну́жно тебе́ гляде́ть на них. Тебе́ есть приме́ры други́е — пе́ред тобо́ю мать твоя́. Вот каки́м приме́рам ты должна́ сле́довать.

Хлестако́в *(схва́тывая за́ руку дочь)*. Анна Андре́евна, не проти́вьтесь на́шему благополу́чию, благослови́те постоя́нную любо́вь!

Анна Андре́евна *(с изумле́нием)*. Так вы в неё?..

Хлестако́в. Реши́те: жизнь и́ли смерть?

Анна Андре́евна. Ну вот ви́дишь, ду́ра, ну вот ви́дишь: из-за тебя́, э́такой дря́ни, гость изво́лил стоя́ть на коле́нях; а ты вдруг вбежа́ла, как сумасше́дшая. Ну вот, пра́во, сто́ит, что́бы я наро́чно отказа́ла: ты недосто́йна тако́го сча́стия.

Ма́рья Анто́новна. Не бу́ду, ма́менька. Пра́во, вперёд не бу́ду.

ЯВЛЕНИЕ XV

Те же и городни́чий впопыха́х.

Городни́чий. Ва́ше превосходи́тельство! не погуби́те! не погуби́те!

Хлестако́в. Что с ва́ми?

Городни́чий. Там купцы́ жа́ловались ва́шему превосходи́тельству. Че́стью уверя́ю, и наполови́ну нет того́, что они́ говоря́т. Они́ са́ми обма́нывают и обме́ривают наро́д. Унтер-офице́рша налгала́ вам, бу́дто бы я её вы́сек; она́ врёт, ей-бо́гу врёт. Она́ сама́ себя́ вы́секла.

Хлестако́в. Провали́сь у́нтер-офице́рша — мне не до неё!

Городни́чий. Не ве́рьте, не ве́рьте! Это таки́е лгуны́... им вот э́дакой ребёнок не пове́рит. Они́ уж и по всему́ го́роду изве́стны за лгуно́в. А насчёт моше́нничества, осме́люсь доложи́ть: э́то таки́е моше́нники, каки́х свет не производи́л.

Анна Андре́евна. Зна́ешь ли ты, како́й че́сти удосто́ивает нас Ива́н Алекса́ндрович? Он про́сит руки́ на́шей до́чери.

Городни́чий. Куда́! куда́!.. Рехну́лась, ма́тушка! Не изво́льте гне́ваться, ва́ше превосходи́тельство: она́ немно́го с при́дурью, такова́ же была́ и мать её.

Хлестако́в. Да, я то́чно прошу́ руки́. Я влюблён.

Городни́чий. Не могу́ ве́рить, ва́ше превосходи́тельство!

Анна Андре́евна. Да когда́ говоря́т тебе́?

Хлестако́в. Я не шутя́ вам говорю́... Я могу́ от любви́ свихну́ть с ума́.

Городни́чий. Не сме́ю ве́рить, недосто́ин тако́й че́сти.

Хлестако́в. Да, е́сли вы не согласи́тесь отда́ть руки́ Ма́рьи Анто́новны, то я чёрт зна́ет что гото́в...

Городни́чий. Не могу́ ве́рить: изво́лите шути́ть, ва́ше превосходи́тельство!

Анна Андре́евна. Ах, како́й чурба́н в са́мом де́ле! Ну, когда́ тебе́ толку́ют?

Городни́чий. Не могу́ ве́рить.

Хлестако́в. Отда́йте, отда́йте! Я отча́янный челове́к, я решу́сь на всё: когда́ застрелю́сь, вас под суд отдаду́т.

Городни́чий. Ах, бо́же мой! Я, ей-е́й, не винова́т ни душо́ю, ни те́лом. Не изво́льте гне́ваться! Изво́льте поступа́ть так, как ва́шей ми́лости уго́дно! У меня́, пра́во, в голове́ тепе́рь... я и сам не зна́ю, что де́лается. Тако́й дура́к тепе́рь сде́лался, каки́м ещё никогда́ не быва́л.

Анна Андре́евна. Ну, благословля́й!

Хлестако́в подхо́дит с Ма́рьей Анто́новной.

Городни́чий. Да благослови́т вас бог, а я не винова́т.

Хлестако́в целу́ется с Ма́рьей Анто́новной. Городни́чий смо́трит на них.

Что за чёрт! в са́мом де́ле! *(Протира́ет глаза́.)* Целу́ются! Ах, ба́тюшки, целу́ются! То́чный жени́х! *(Вскри́кивает, подпры́гивая от ра́дости.)* Ай, Анто́н! Ай, Анто́н! Ай, городни́чий! Во́на, как де́ло-то пошло́!

ЯВЛЕНИЕ XVI

Те же и Осип.

Осип. Ло́шади гото́вы.

Хлестако́в. А, хорошо́... я сейча́с.

Городни́чий. Как-с? Изво́лите е́хать?

Хлестако́в. Да, е́ду.

Городни́чий. А когда́ же, то есть... вы изво́лили са́ми намекну́ть насчёт, ка́жется, сва́дьбы?

Хлестако́в. А э́то... На одну́ мину́ту то́лько... на оди́н день к дя́де — бога́тый стари́к; а за́втра же и наза́д.

Городни́чий. Не сме́ем ника́к уде́рживать, в наде́жде благополу́чного возвраще́ния.

Хлестако́в. Как же, как же, я вдруг. Проща́йте, любо́вь моя́... нет, про́сто не могу́ вы́разить. Проща́йте, ду́шенька! *(Целу́ет её ру́чку.)*

Городни́чий. Да не ну́жно ли вам в доро́гу чего́-нибудь? Вы изво́лили, ка́жется, нужда́ться в де́ньгах?

Хлестако́в. О нет, к чему́ э́то? *(Немно́го поду́мав.)* А впро́чем, пожа́луй.

Городни́чий. Ско́лько уго́дно вам?

Хлестако́в. Да вот тогда́ вы да́ли две́сти, то есть не две́сти, а четы́реста, — я не хочу́ воспо́льзоваться ва́шею оши́бкою, — так, пожа́луй, и тепе́рь сто́лько же, что́бы уже́ ро́вно бы́ло восемьсо́т.

Городни́чий. Сейча́с! *(Вынима́ет из бума́жника.)* Ещё, как наро́чно, са́мыми но́венькими бума́жками.

Хлестако́в. А, да! *(Берёт и рассма́тривает ассигна́ции.)* Это хорошо́. Ведь э́то, говоря́т, но́вое сча́стье, когда́ но́венькими бума́жками.

Городни́чий. Так то́чно-с.

Хлестако́в. Проща́йте, Анто́н Анто́нович! Очень обя́зан за ва́ше гостеприи́мство. Я признаю́сь от всего́ се́рдца: мне нигде́ не́ было тако́го хоро́шего приёма. Проща́йте, Анна Андре́евна! Проща́йте, моя́ ду́шенька, Ма́рья Анто́новна!

Выхо́дят.

За сце́ной:

Го́лос Хлестако́ва. Проща́йте, а́нгел души́ мое́й, Ма́рья Анто́новна!

Го́лос городни́чего. Как же э́то вы? пря́мо так на перекладно́й и е́дете?

Го́лос Хлестако́ва. Да, я привы́к уж так. У меня́ голова́ боли́т от рессо́р.

Го́лос ямщика́. Тпр...

Го́лос городни́чего. Так по кра́йней ме́ре че́м-нибудь застла́ть, хотя́ бы ко́вриком. Не прика́жете ли, я велю́ пода́ть ко́врик?

Го́лос Хлестако́ва. Нет, заче́м? э́то пусто́е; а впро́чем, пожа́луй, пусть даю́т ко́врик.

Го́лос городни́чего. Эй, Авдо́тья! ступа́й в кладову́ю, вынь ковёр са́мый лу́чший — что по голубо́му по́лю, перси́дский. Скоре́й!

Го́лос ямщика́. Тпр...

Го́лос городни́чего. Когда́ же прика́жете ожида́ть вас?

Го́лос Хлестако́ва. За́втра и́ли послеза́втра.

Го́лос Осипа. А, э́то ковёр? дава́й его́ сюда́, клади́ вот так! Тепе́рь дава́й-ка с э́той стороны́ се́на.

Го́лос ямщика́. Тпр...

Го́лос Осипа. Вот с э́той стороны́! сюда́! ещё! хорошо́. Сла́вно бу́дет! *(Бьёт руко́ю по ковру́.)* Тепе́рь сади́тесь, ва́ше благоро́дие!

Го́лос Хлестако́ва. Проща́йте, Анто́н Анто́нович!

Го́лос городни́чего. Проща́йте, ва́ше превосходи́тельство!

Же́нские голоса́. Проща́йте, Ива́н Алекса́ндрович!

Го́лос Хлестако́ва. Проща́йте, ма́менька!

Го́лос ямщика́. Эй вы, залётные!

Колоко́льчик звени́т. За́навес опуска́ется.

ДЕЙСТВИЕ ПЯТОЕ

Та же ко́мната

ЯВЛЕНИЕ I

Городни́чий, Анна Андре́евна и Ма́рья Анто́новна.

Городни́чий. Что, Анна Андре́евна? а? Ду́мала ли ты что́-нибудь об э́том? Экой бога́тый приз, кана́льство! Ну, призна́йся открове́нно: тебе́ и во сне не ви́делось — про́сто из како́й-нибудь городни́чихи и вдруг... фу ты, кана́льство!.. с каки́м дьяволом породни́лась!

Анна Андре́евна. Совсе́м нет; я давно́ э́то зна́ла. Это тебе́ в дико́винку, потому́ что ты просто́й челове́к, никогда́ не ви́дел поря́дочных люде́й.

Городни́чий. Я сам, ма́тушка, поря́дочный челове́к. Одна́ко ж, пра́во, как поду́маешь, Анна Андре́евна, каки́е мы с тобо́й тепе́рь пти́цы сде́лались! а, Анна Андре́евна? Высо́кого полёта, чёрт побери́! Посто́й же, тепе́рь же я зада́м пе́рцу всем э́тим охо́тникам подава́ть про́сьбы и доно́сы. Эй, кто там?

Вхо́дит кварта́льный.

А, э́то ты, Ива́н Ка́рпович! Призови́-ка сюда́, брат, купцо́в. Вот я их, кана́лий! Так жа́ловаться на меня́? Вишь ты, прокля́тый иуде́йский наро́д! Посто́йте ж, голу́бчики! Пре́жде я вас корми́л до усо́в то́лько, а тепе́рь накормлю́ до бороды́. Запиши́ всех, кто то́лько ходи́л бить чело́м на меня́, и вот э́тих бо́льше всего́ писа́к, писа́к, кото́рые закру́чивали им про́сьбы. Да объяви́ всем, чтоб зна́ли: что вот, де́скать, каку́ю честь бог посла́л городни́чему, — что выдаёт дочь свою́ не то что́бы за како́го-нибудь просто́го челове́ка, а за тако́го, что и на све́те ещё не́ было, что мо́жет всё сде́лать, всё, всё, всё! Всем объяви́, что́бы все зна́ли. Кричи́ во весь наро́д, валя́й в колокола́, чёрт возьми́! Уж когда́ торжество́, так торжество́!

Кварта́льный ухо́дит.

Так вот как, Анна Андре́евна, а? Как же мы тепе́рь, где бу́дем жить? здесь и́ли в Пи́тере?

Анна Андре́евна. Натура́льно в Петербу́рге. Как мо́жно здесь остава́ться!

Городни́чий. Ну, в Пи́тере так в Пи́тере; а оно́ хорошо́ бы и здесь. Что, ведь, я ду́маю, уже́ городни́чество тогда́ к чёрту, а, Анна Андре́евна?

Анна Андре́евна. Натура́льно, что за городни́чество!

Городни́чий. Ведь оно́, как ты ду́маешь, Анна Андре́евна, тепе́рь мо́жно большо́й чин зашиби́ть, потому́ что он запанибра́та со все́ми мини́страми и во дворе́ц е́здит, так поэ́тому мо́жет тако́е произво́дство сде́лать, что со вре́менем и в генера́лы вле́зешь. Как ты ду́маешь, Анна Андре́евна: мо́жно влезть в генера́лы?

Анна Андре́евна. Ещё бы! коне́чно, мо́жно.

Городни́чий. А, чёрт возьми́, сла́вно быть генера́лом! Кавале́рию пове́сят тебе́ че́рез плечо́. А каку́ю кавале́рию лу́чше, Анна Андре́евна: кра́сную и́ли голубу́ю?

Анна Андре́евна. Уж коне́чно, голубу́ю лу́чше.

Городни́чий. Э? вишь, чего́ захоте́ла! хорошо́ и кра́сную. Ведь почему́ хо́чется быть генера́лом? — потому́ что, случи́тся, пое́дешь куда́-нибудь — фельдъегеря́ и адъюта́нты поска́чут везде́ вперёд: «Лошаде́й!» И там на ста́нциях никому́ не даду́т, всё дожида́ется: все э́ти титуля́рные, капита́ны, городни́чие, а ты себе́ и в ус не ду́ешь. Обе́даешь где́-нибудь у губерна́тора, а там — стой, городни́чий! Хе, хе, хе! *(Залива́ется и помира́ет со́ смеху.)* Вот что, кана́льство, зама́нчиво!

Анна Андре́евна. Тебе́ всё тако́е гру́бое нра́вится. Ты до́лжен по́мнить, что жизнь ну́жно совсе́м перемени́ть, что твои́ знако́мые бу́дут не то что како́й-нибудь судья́-соба́чник, с кото́рым ты е́здишь трави́ть за́йцев, и́ли Земляни́ка; напро́тив, знако́мые твои́ бу́дут с са́мым то́нким обраще́нием: гра́фы и все све́тские... То́лько я, пра́во, бою́сь за тебя́: ты иногда́ вы́молвишь тако́е словцо́, како́го в хоро́шем о́бществе никогда́ не услы́шишь.

Городни́чий. Что ж? ведь сло́во не вреди́т.

Анна Андре́евна. Да хорошо́, когда́ ты был городни́чим. А там ведь жизнь соверше́нно друга́я.

Городни́чий. Да, там, говоря́т, есть две ры́бицы: ря́пушка и ко́рюшка, таки́е, что то́лько слю́нка потечёт, как начнёшь есть.

Анна Андре́евна. Ему́ всё бы то́лько ры́бки! Я не ина́че хочу́, чтоб наш дом был пе́рвый в столи́це и чтоб у меня́ в ко́мнате тако́е бы́ло амбре́, чтоб нельзя́ бы́ло войти́ и ну́жно бы то́лько э́так зажму́рить глаза́. *(Зажму́ривает глаза́ и ню́хает.)* Ах, как хорошо́!

ЯВЛЕНИЕ II

Те же и купцы́.

Городни́чий. А! Здоро́во, соко́лики!

Купцы́ *(кла́няясь)*. Здра́вия жела́ем, ба́тюшка!

Городни́чий. Что, голу́бчики, как пожива́ете? как това́р идёт ваш? Что, самова́рники, арши́нники, жа́ловаться? Архиплу́ты, протобе́стии, надува́лы мирски́е! жа́ловаться? Что, мно́го взя́ли? Вот, ду́мают, так в тюрьму́ его́ и заса́дят!.. Зна́ете ли вы, семь черте́й и одна́ ве́дьма вам в зу́бы, что...

Анна Андре́евна. Ах, бо́же мой, каки́е ты, Анто́ша, слова́ отпуска́ешь!

Городни́чий *(с неудово́льствием)*. А, не до слов тепе́рь! Зна́ете ли, что тот са́мый чино́вник, кото́рому вы жа́ловались, тепе́рь же́нится на мое́й до́чери? Что? а? что тепе́рь ска́жете? Тепе́рь я вас... у!.. Обма́нываете наро́д... Сде́лаешь подря́д с казно́ю, на́ сто ты́сяч наду́ешь её, поста́вивши гнило́го сукна́, да пото́м поже́ртвуешь два́дцать арши́н, да и дава́й тебе́ ещё награ́ду за э́то? Да е́сли б зна́ли, так бы тебе́... И брю́хо суёт вперёд: он купе́ц; его́ не тронь. «Мы, говори́т, и дворя́нам не усту́пим». Да дворяни́н... ах ты, ро́жа! — дворяни́н у́чится нау́кам: его́ хоть и секу́т в шко́ле, да за де́ло, чтоб он знал поле́зное. А ты что? — начина́ешь плу́тнями, тебя́ хозя́ин бьёт за то, что не уме́ешь обма́нывать. Ещё мальчи́шка, «Отче на́ша» не зна́ешь, а уж обме́риваешь; а как разопрёт тебе́ брю́хо да набьёшь себе́ карма́н, так и зава́жничал! Фу ты, кака́я не́видаль! Оттого́, что ты шестна́дцать самова́ров вы́дуешь в день, так оттого́ и ва́жничаешь? Да я плева́ть на твою́ го́лову и на твою́ ва́жность!

Купцы́ *(кла́няясь)*. Винова́ты, Анто́н Анто́нович!

Городни́чий. Жа́ловаться? А кто тебе́ помо́г сплутова́ть, когда́ ты стро́ил мост и написа́л де́рева на два́дцать ты́сяч, тогда́ как его́ и на́ сто рубле́й не́ было? Я помо́г тебе́, козли́ная борода́! Ты позабы́л э́то? Я, показа́вши э́то на тебя́, мог бы тебя́ та́кже спрова́дить в Сиби́рь. Что ска́жешь? а?

Оди́н из купцо́в. Бо́гу винова́ты, Анто́н Анто́нович! Лука́вый попу́тал. И зака́емся вперёд жа́ловаться. Уж како́е хошь удовлетворе́ние, не гневи́сь то́лько!

Городни́чий. Не гневи́сь! Вот ты тепе́рь валя́ешься у ног мои́х. Отчего́? — оттого́, что моё взяло́; а будь хоть немно́жко на твое́й стороне́, так ты бы меня́, кана́лья, втопта́л в са́мую грязь, ещё бы и бревно́м све́рху навали́л.

Купцы́ *(кла́няются в но́ги)*. Не погуби́, Анто́н Анто́нович!

Городни́чий. Не погуби́! Тепе́рь: не погуби́! а пре́жде что? Я бы вас... *(Махну́в руко́й.)* Ну, да бог прости́т! по́лно! Я не памятозло́бен; то́лько тепе́рь смотри́, держи́ у́хо востро́! Я выдаю до́чку не за како́го-нибудь просто́го дворяни́на: чтоб поздравле́ние бы́ло... понима́ешь? не то, чтоб отбоя́риться каки́м-нибудь балычко́м и́ли голово́ю са́хару... Ну, ступа́й с бо́гом!

Купцы́ ухо́дят.

ЯВЛЕНИЕ III

Те же, Аммо́с Фёдорович, Арте́мий Фили́ппович, пото́м Растако́вский.

Аммо́с Фёдорович *(ещё в дверя́х)*. Ве́рить ли слу́хам, Анто́н Анто́нович? к вам привали́ло необыкнове́нное сча́стие?

Арте́мий Фили́ппович. Име́ю честь поздра́вить с необыкнове́нным сча́стием. Я душе́вно обра́довался, когда́ услы́шал. *(Подхо́дит к ру́чке Анны Андре́евны.)* Анна Андре́евна! *(Подходя́ к ру́чке Ма́рьи Анто́новны.)* Ма́рья Анто́новна!

Растако́вский *(вхо́дит).* Анто́на Анто́новича поздравля́ю. Да продли́т бог жизнь ва́шу и но́вой четы́ и даст вам пото́мство многочи́сленное, внуча́т и правнуча́т! Анна Андре́евна! *(Подхо́дит к ру́чке Анны Андре́евны.)* Ма́рья Анто́новна! *(Подхо́дит к ру́чке Ма́рьи Анто́новны.)*

ЯВЛЕНИЕ IV

Те же, Коро́бкин с жено́ю, Люлюко́в.

Коро́бкин. Име́ю честь поздра́вить Анто́на Анто́новича! Анна Андре́евна! *(Подхо́дит к ру́чке Анны Андре́евны.)* Ма́рья Анто́новна! *(Подхо́дит к её ру́чке.)*

Жена́ Коро́бкина. Душе́вно поздравля́ю вас, Анна Андре́евна, с но́вым сча́стием.

Люлюко́в. Име́ю честь поздра́вить, Анна Андре́евна! *(Подхо́дит к ру́чке и пото́м, обрати́вшись к зри́телям, щёлкает языко́м с ви́дом удальства́.)* Ма́рья Анто́новна! Име́ю честь поздра́вить. *(Подхо́дит к её ру́чке и обраща́ется к зри́телям с тем же удальство́м.)*

ЯВЛЕНИЕ V

Мно́жество госте́й в сюртука́х и фра́ках подхо́дят снача́ла к ру́чке Анны Андре́евны, говоря́: «Анна Андре́евна!», пото́м к Ма́рье Анто́новне, говоря́: «Ма́рья Анто́новна!» Бо́бчинский и До́бчинский прота́лкиваются.

Бо́бчинский. Име́ю честь поздра́вить!

До́бчинский. Анто́н Анто́нович! име́ю честь поздра́вить!

Бо́бчинский. С благополу́чным происше́ствием!

До́бчинский. Анна Андре́евна!

Бо́бчинский. Анна Андре́евна!

Оба подхо́дят в одно́ вре́мя и ста́лкиваются лба́ми.

До́бчинский. Ма́рья Анто́новна! *(Подхо́дит к ру́чке.)* Честь име́ю поздра́вить. Вы бу́дете в большо́м, большо́м сча́стии, в золото́м пла́тье ходи́ть и делика́тные ра́зные супы́ ку́шать; о́чень заба́вно бу́дете проводи́ть вре́мя.

Бо́бчинский *(перебива́я)*. Ма́рья Анто́новна, име́ю честь поздра́вить! Дай бог вам вся́кого бога́тства, черво́нцев и сынка́-с э́такого ма́ленького, вон э́нтакого-с *(пока́зывает руко́ю)*, чтоб мо́жно бы́ло на ладо́нку посади́ть, да-с! Всё бу́дет мальчи́шка крича́ть: уа! уа! уа!..

ЯВЛЕНИЕ VI

Ещё не́сколько госте́й, подходя́щих к ру́чкам, Лука́ Луки́ч с жено́ю.

Лука́ Луки́ч. Име́ю честь...

Жена́ Луки́ Лукича́ *(бежи́т вперёд)*. Поздравля́ю вас, Анна Андре́евна!

Целу́ются.

А я так, пра́во, обра́довалась. Говоря́т мне: «Анна Андре́евна выдаёт до́чку». «Ах, бо́же мой!» — ду́маю себе́, и так обра́довалась, что говорю́ му́жу: «Послу́шай, Лука́нчик, вот како́е сча́стие Анне Андре́евне!» «Ну, — ду́маю себе́, — сла́ва бо́гу!» И говорю́ ему́: «Я так восхищена́, что сгора́ю нетерпе́нием изъяви́ть ли́чно Анне Андре́евне...» «Ах, бо́же мой! — ду́маю себе́, — Анна Андре́евна и́менно ожида́ла хоро́шей па́ртии для свое́й до́чери, а вот тепе́рь така́я судьба́: и́менно так сде́лалось, как она́ хоте́ла», и так, пра́во, обра́довалась, что не могла́ говори́ть. Пла́чу, пла́чу, вот про́сто рыда́ю. Уже́ Лука́ Луки́ч говори́т: «Отчего́ ты, На́стенька, рыда́ешь?» — «Лука́нчик, говорю́, я и сама́ не зна́ю, слёзы так вот реко́й и лью́тся».

Городни́чий. Поко́рнейше прошу́ сади́ться, господа́! Эй, Ми́шка, принеси́ сюда́ побо́льше сту́льев.

Го́сти садя́тся.

ЯВЛЕНИЕ VII

Те же, ча́стный при́став и кварта́льные.

Ча́стный при́став. Име́ю честь поздра́вить вас, ва́ше высокоблагоро́дие, и пожела́ть благоде́нствия на мно́гие ле́та.

Городни́чий. Спаси́бо, спаси́бо! Прошу́ сади́ться, господа́!

Го́сти уса́живаются.

Аммо́с Фёдорович. Но скажи́те, пожа́луйста, Анто́н Анто́нович, каки́м о́бразом всё э́то начало́сь, постепе́нный ход всего́, то есть, де́ла.

Городни́чий. Ход де́ла чрезвыча́йный: изво́лил собственноли́чно сде́лать предложе́ние.

Анна Андре́евна. Очень почти́тельным и са́мым то́нким о́бразом. Всё чрезвыча́йно хорошо́ говори́л. Говори́т: «Я, Анна Андре́евна, из одного́ то́лько уваже́ния к ва́шим досто́инствам...» И тако́й прекра́сный, воспи́танный челове́к, са́мых благоро́днейших пра́вил. «Мне, ве́рите ли, Анна Андре́евна, мне жизнь — копе́йка; я то́лько потому́, что уважа́ю ва́ши ре́дкие ка́чества».

Ма́рья Анто́новна. Ах, ма́менька! ведь э́то он мне говори́л.

Анна Андре́евна. Переста́нь, ты ничего́ не зна́ешь и не в своё де́ло не меша́йся! «Я, Анна Андре́евна, изумля́юсь...» В таки́х ле́стных рассыпа́лся слова́х... И когда́ я хоте́ла сказа́ть: «Мы ника́к не сме́ем наде́яться на таку́ю честь», он вдруг упа́л на коле́ни и таки́м са́мым благоро́днейшим о́бразом: «Анна Андре́евна, не сде́лайте меня́ несча́стнейшим! согласи́тесь отвеча́ть мои́м чу́вствам, не то я сме́ртью око́нчу жизнь свою́».

Ма́рья Анто́новна. Пра́во, ма́менька, он обо мне э́то говори́л.

Анна Андре́евна. Да, коне́чно... и об тебе́ бы́ло, я ничего́ э́того не отверга́ю.

Городни́чий. И так да́же напуга́л: говори́л, что застре́лится. «Застрелю́сь, застрелю́сь!» — говори́т.

Мно́гие из госте́й. Скажи́те пожа́луйста!

Аммо́с Фёдорович. Экая шту́ка!

Лука́ Луки́ч. Вот по́длинно, судьба́ уж так вела́.

Арте́мий Фили́ппович. Не судьба́, ба́тюшка, судьба́ — инде́йка: заслу́ги привели́ к тому́. *(В сто́рону.)* Этакой свинье́ ле́зет всегда́ в рот сча́стье!

Аммо́с Фёдорович. Я, пожа́луй, Анто́н Анто́нович, прода́м вам того́ кобелька́, кото́рого торгова́ли.

Городни́чий. Нет, мне тепе́рь не до кобелько́в.

Аммо́с Фёдорович. Ну, не хоти́те, на друго́й соба́ке сойдёмся.

Жена́ Коро́бкина. Ах, как, Анна Андре́евна, я ра́да ва́шему сча́стию! вы не мо́жете себе́ предста́вить.

Коро́бкин. Где же тепе́рь, позво́льте узна́ть, нахо́дится имени́тый гость? Я слы́шал, что он уе́хал заче́м-то.

Городни́чий. Да, он отпра́вился на оди́н день по весьма́ ва́жному де́лу.

Анна Андре́евна. К своему́ дя́де, чтоб испроси́ть благослове́ния.

Городни́чий. Испроси́ть благослове́ния; но за́втра же... *(Чиха́ет.)*

Поздравле́ния слива́ются в оди́н гул.

Мно́го благода́рен! Но за́втра же и наза́д... *(Чиха́ет.)*

Поздрави́тельный гул; слышне́е други́х голоса́:

Ча́стного при́става. Здра́вия жела́ем, ва́ше высокоблагоро́дие!

Бо́бчинского. Сто лет и куль черво́нцев!

До́бчинского. Продли́ бог на со́рок сороко́в!

Арте́мия Фили́пповича. Чтоб ты пропа́л!

Жены́ Коро́бкина. Чёрт тебя́ побери́!

Городни́чий. Поко́рнейше благодарю́! И вам того́ ж жела́ю.

Анна Андре́евна. Мы тепе́рь в Петербу́рге наме́рены жить. А здесь, признаю́сь, тако́й во́здух... дереве́нский уж сли́шком!.. признаю́сь, больша́я неприя́тность... Вот и муж мой... он там полу́чит генера́льский чин.

Городни́чий. Да, признаю́сь, господа́, я, чёрт возьми́, о́чень хочу́ быть генера́лом.

Лука́ Луки́ч. И дай бог получи́ть!

Растако́вский. От челове́ка невозмо́жно, а от бо́га всё возмо́жно.

Аммо́с Фёдорович. Большо́му кораблю́ — большо́е пла́ванье.

Арте́мий Фили́ппович. По заслу́гам и честь.

Аммо́с Фёдорович *(в сто́рону)*. Вот вы́кинет шту́ку, когда́ в са́мом де́ле сде́лается генера́лом! Вот уж кому́ приста́ло генера́льство, как коро́ве седло́! Ну, брат, нет, до э́того ещё далека́ пе́сня. Тут и почи́ще тебя́ есть, а до сих пор ещё не генера́лы.

Арте́мий Фили́ппович *(в сто́рону)*. Эка, чёрт возьми́, уж и в генера́лы ле́зет! Чего́ до́брого, мо́жет, и бу́дет генера́лом. Ведь у него́ ва́жности, лука́вый не́ взял бы его́, дово́льно. *(Обраща́ясь к нему́.)* Тогда́, Анто́н Анто́нович, и нас не позабу́дьте.

Аммо́с Фёдорович. И е́сли что случи́тся, наприме́р, кака́я-нибудь на́добность по дела́м, не оста́вьте покрови́тельством.

Коро́бкин. В сле́дующем году́ повезу́ сынка́ в столи́цу на по́льзу госуда́рства, так сде́лайте ми́лость, окажи́те ему́ ва́шу проте́кцию, ме́сто отца́ заступи́те сиро́тке.

Городни́чий. Я гото́в с свое́й стороны́, гото́в стара́ться.

Анна Андре́евна. Ты, Анто́ша, всегда́ гото́в обеща́ть. Во-пе́рвых, тебе́ не бу́дет вре́мени ду́мать об э́том. И как мо́жно, и с како́й ста́ти себя́ обременя́ть э́такими обеща́ниями?

Городни́чий. Почему́ ж, душа́ моя́? иногда́ мо́жно.

Анна Андре́евна. Мо́жно, коне́чно, да ведь не вся́кой же мелюзге́ ока́зывать покрови́тельство.

Жена́ Коро́бкина. Вы слы́шали, как она́ тракту́ет нас?

Го́стья. Да, она́ такова́ всегда́ была́; я её зна́ю: посади́ её за стол, она́ и но́ги свои́...

ЯВЛЕНИЕ VIII

Те же и почтме́йстер впопыха́х, с распеча́танным письмо́м в руке́.

Почтме́йстер. Удиви́тельное де́ло, господа́! Чино́вник, кото́рого мы при́няли за ревизо́ра, был не ревизо́р.

Все. Как не ревизо́р?

Почтме́йстер. Совсе́м не ревизо́р, — я узна́л э́то из письма́...

Городни́чий. Что вы? что вы? из како́го письма́?

Почтме́йстер. Да из со́бственного его́ письма́. Прино́сят ко мне на по́чту письмо́. Взгляну́л на а́дрес — ви́жу: «в Почта́мтскую у́лицу». Я так и обомле́л. «Ну, — ду́маю себе́, — ве́рно, нашёл беспоря́дки по почто́вой ча́сти и уведомля́ет нача́льство». Взял да и распеча́тал.

Городни́чий. Как же вы?..

Почтме́йстер. Сам не зна́ю; неесте́ственная си́ла побуди́ла. Призва́л было уже́ курье́ра, с тем что́бы отпра́вить его́ с эштафе́той, — но любопы́тство тако́е одоле́ло, како́го ещё никогда́ не чу́вствовал. Не могу́, не могу́! слы́шу, что не могу́! тя́нет, так вот и тя́нет! В одно́м у́хе так вот и слы́шу: «Эй, не распеча́тывай! пропадёшь, как ку́рица»; а в друго́м сло́вно бес како́й ше́пчет: «Распеча́тай, распеча́тай, распеча́тай!» И как придави́л сургу́ч — по жи́лам ого́нь, а распеча́тал — моро́з, ей-бо́гу моро́з. И ру́ки дрожа́т, и всё помути́лось.

Городни́чий. Да как же вы осме́лились распеча́тать письмо́ тако́й уполномо́ченной осо́бы?

Почтме́йстер. В то́м-то и шту́ка, что он не уполномо́ченный и не осо́ба!

Городни́чий. Что ж он, по-ва́шему, тако́е?

Почтме́йстер. Ни сё ни то; чёрт зна́ет что тако́е!

Городни́чий *(запа́льчиво)*. Как ни сё ни то? Как вы сме́ете называ́ть его́ ни тем ни сем, да ещё и чёрт зна́ет чем? Я вас под аре́ст...

Почтме́йстер. Кто? вы?

Городни́чий. Да, я!

Почтме́йстер. Коротки́ ру́ки!

Городни́чий. Зна́ете ли, что он же́нится на мое́й до́чери, что я сам бу́ду вельмо́жа, что я в са́мую Сиби́рь законопа́чу?

Почтме́йстер. Эх, Анто́н Анто́нович! что Сиби́рь? далеко́ Сиби́рь. Вот лу́чше я вам прочту́. Господа́! позво́льте прочита́ть письмо́?

Все. Чита́йте, чита́йте!

Почтме́йстер *(чита́ет)*. «Спешу́ уве́домить тебя́, душа́ Тряпи́чкин, каки́е со мной чудеса́. На доро́ге обчи́стил меня́ круго́м пехо́тный капита́н, так что трактирщик хоте́л уже́ было посади́ть в тюрьму́; как вдруг, по мое́й петербу́ргской физионо́мии и по костю́му, весь го́род при́нял меня́ за генера́л-губерна́тора. И я тепе́рь живу́ у городни́чего, жуи́рую, волочу́сь напропалу́ю за его́ жено́й и до́чкой; не реши́лся то́лько, с кото́рой нача́ть, — ду́маю, пре́жде с ма́тушки, потому́ что, ка́жется, гото́ва сейча́с на все услу́ги. По́мнишь, как мы с тобо́й бе́дствовали, обе́дали наширомы́жку и как оди́н раз было конди́тер схвати́л меня́ за воротни́к по по́воду съе́денных пирожко́в на счёт дохо́дов а́глицкого короля́? Тепе́рь совсе́м друго́й оборо́т. Все мне даю́т взаймы́ ско́лько уго́дно. Оригина́лы стра́шные. От сме́ху ты бы у́мер. Ты, я зна́ю, пи́шешь стате́йки: помести́ их в свою́ литерату́ру. Во-пе́рвых: городни́чий — глуп, как си́вый ме́рин...»

Городни́чий. Не мо́жет быть! Там нет э́того.

Почтме́йстер *(пока́зывает письмо́)*. Чита́йте са́ми.

Городни́чий *(чита́ет)*. «Как си́вый ме́рин». Не мо́жет быть! вы э́то са́ми написа́ли.

Почтме́йстер. Как же бы я стал писа́ть?

Арте́мий Фили́ппович. Чита́йте!

Лука́ Луки́ч. Чита́йте!

Почтме́йстер *(продолжа́я чита́ть)*. «Городни́чий — глуп, как си́вый ме́рин...»

Городни́чий. О, чёрт возьми́! ну́жно ещё повторя́ть! как бу́дто оно́ там и без того́ не стои́т.

Почтме́йстер *(продолжа́я чита́ть)*. Хм... хм... хм... хм... «си́вый ме́рин. Почтме́йстер то́же до́брый челове́к...» *(Оставля́я чита́ть.)* Ну, тут обо мне то́же он неприли́чно вы́разился.

Городни́чий. Нет, чита́йте!

Почтме́йстер. Да к чему́ ж?..

Городни́чий. Нет, чёрт возьми́, когда́ уж чита́ть, так чита́ть! Чита́йте всё!

Арте́мий Фили́ппович. Позво́льте, я прочита́ю. *(Надева́ет очки́ и чита́ет.)* «Почтме́йстер точь-в-то́чь департа́ментский сто́рож Михе́ев; должно́ быть, та́кже, подле́ц, пьёт го́рькую».

Почтме́йстер *(к зри́телям)*. Ну, скве́рный мальчи́шка, кото́рого на́до вы́сечь; бо́льше ничего́!

Арте́мий Фили́ппович *(продолжа́я чита́ть)*. «Надзира́тель над богоуго́дным заведе́... и... и... и...» *(Заика́ется.)*

Коро́бкин. А что ж вы останови́лись?

Арте́мий Фили́ппович. Да нечёткое перо́... впро́чем, ви́дно, что негодя́й.

Коро́бкин. Да́йте мне! Вот у меня́, я ду́маю, полу́чше глаза́. *(Берёт письмо́.)*

Арте́мий Фили́ппович *(не дава́я письма́)*. Нет, э́то ме́сто мо́жно пропусти́ть, а там да́льше разбо́рчиво.

Коро́бкин. Да позво́льте, уж я зна́ю.

Арте́мий Фили́ппович. Прочита́ть я и сам прочита́ю; да́лее, пра́во, всё разбо́рчиво.

Почтме́йстер. Нет, всё чита́йте! ведь пре́жде всё чи́тано.

Все. Отда́йте, Арте́мий Фили́ппович, отда́йте письмо́! *(Коро́бкину.)* Чита́йте!

Арте́мий Фили́ппович. Сейча́с. *(Отдаёт письмо́.)* Вот, позво́льте... *(Закрыва́ет па́льцем.)* Вот отсю́да чита́йте.

Все приступа́ют к нему́.

Почтме́йстер. Чита́йте, чита́йте! вздор, всё чита́йте!

Коро́бкин *(читая).* «Надзира́тель за богоуго́дным заведе́нием Земляни́ка — соверше́нная свинья́ в ермо́лке».

Арте́мий Фили́ппович *(к зри́телям).* И не остроу́мно! Свинья́ в ермо́лке! где ж свинья́ быва́ет в ермо́лке?

Коро́бкин *(продолжа́я чита́ть).* «Смотри́тель учи́лищ проту́хнул насквóзь лу́ком».

Лука́ Луки́ч *(к зри́телям).* Ей-бо́гу, и в рот никогда́ не брал лу́ку.

Аммо́с Фёдорович *(в сто́рону).* Сла́ва бо́гу, хоть по кра́йней ме́ре обо мне нет!

Коро́бкин *(чита́ет).* «Судья́...»

Аммо́с Фёдорович. Вот тебе́ на! *(Вслух.)* Господа́, я ду́маю, что письмо́ дли́нно. Да и чёрт ли в нём: дрянь э́такую чита́ть.

Лука́ Луки́ч. Нет!

Почтме́йстер. Нет, чита́йте!

Арте́мий Фили́ппович. Нет, уж чита́йте!

Коро́бкин *(продолжа́ет).* «Судья́ Ля́пкин-Тя́пкин в сильне́йшей сте́пени мовето́н...» *(Остана́вливается.)* Должно́ быть, францу́зское сло́во.

Аммо́с Фёдорович. А чёрт его́ зна́ет, что оно́ зна́чит! Ещё хорошо́, е́сли то́лько моше́нник, а мо́жет быть, и того́ ещё ху́же.

Коро́бкин *(продолжа́я чита́ть).* «А впро́чем, наро́д гостеприи́мный и доброду́шный. Проща́й, душа́ Тря́пичкин. Я сам, по приме́ру твоему́, хочу́ заня́ться литерату́рой. Ску́чно, брат, так жить; хо́чешь наконе́ц пи́щи для души́. Ви́жу: то́чно, ну́жно че́м-нибудь высо́ким заня́ться. Пиши́ ко мне в Сара́товскую губе́рнию, а отту́да в дере́вню Подкати́ловку. *(Перевора́чивает письмо́ и чита́ет а́дрес.)* Его́ благоро́дию, ми́лостивому госуда́рю, Ива́ну Васи́льевичу Тряпи́чкину, в Санктпетербу́рге, в Почта́мтскую у́лицу, в до́ме под ну́мером девяно́сто седьмы́м, поворотя́ на двор, в тре́тьем этаже́ напра́во».

Одна́ из дам. Како́й реприма́нд неожи́данный!

Городни́чий. Вот когда́ заре́зал, так заре́зал! Уби́т, уби́т, совсе́м уби́т! Ничего́ не ви́жу. Ви́жу каки́е-то свины́е ры́лы вме́сто лиц, а бо́льше ничего́... Вороти́ть, вороти́ть его́! *(Ма́шет руко́ю.)*

Почтме́йстер. Куды́ вороти́ть! Я, как наро́чно, приказа́л смотри́телю дать са́мую лу́чшую тро́йку; чёрт угора́здил дать и вперёд предписа́ние.

Жена́ Коро́бкина. Вот уж то́чно, вот бесприме́рная конфу́зия!

Аммо́с Фёдорович. Одна́ко ж, чёрт возьми́, господа́! он у меня́ взял три́ста рубле́й взаймы́.

Арте́мий Фили́ппович. У меня́ то́же три́ста рубле́й.

Почтме́йстер *(вздыха́ет)*. Ох! и у меня́ три́ста рубле́й.

Бо́бчинский. У нас с Петро́м Ива́новичем шестьдеся́т пять-с на ассигна́ции-с, да-с.

Аммо́с Фёдорович *(в недоуме́нии расставля́ет ру́ки)*. Как же э́то, господа́? Как э́то, в са́мом де́ле, мы так оплоша́ли?

Городни́чий *(бьёт себя́ по́ лбу)*. Как я — нет, как я, ста́рый дура́к? Вы́жил, глу́пый бара́н, из ума́!.. Три́дцать лет живу́ на слу́жбе; ни оди́н купе́ц, ни подря́дчик не мог провести́; моше́нников над моше́нниками обма́нывал, пройдо́х и плу́тов таки́х, что весь свет гото́вы обворова́ть, поддева́л на уду́. Трёх губерна́торов обману́л!.. Что губерна́торов! *(махну́в руко́й)* не́чего и говори́ть про губерна́торов...

Анна Андре́евна. Но э́то не мо́жет быть, Анто́ша: он обручи́лся с Ма́шенькой...

Городни́чий *(в сердца́х)*. Обручи́лся! Ку́киш с ма́слом — вот тебе́ обручи́лся! Ле́зет мне в глаза́ с обруче́ньем!.. *(В исступле́нии.)* Вот смотри́те, смотри́те, весь мир, всё христиа́нство, все смотри́те, как одура́чен городни́чий! Дурака́ ему́, дурака́, ста́рому подлецу́! *(Грози́т самому́ себе́ кулако́м.)* Эх ты, толстоно́сый! Сосу́льку, тря́пку при́нял за ва́жного челове́ка! Вон он тепе́рь по всей доро́ге залива́ет колоко́льчиком! Разнесёт по всему́ све́ту исто́рию. Ма́ло того́ что пойдёшь в посме́шище, — найдётся щелкопёр, бумагомара́ка, в коме́дию тебя́ вста́вит. Вот что оби́дно! Чи́на, зва́ния не пощади́т, и бу́дут все ска́лить зу́бы и бить в ладо́ши. Чему́ смеётесь? — Над собо́ю смеётесь!.. Эх вы!.. *(Стучи́т со зло́сти нога́ми о́б пол.)* Я бы всех э́тих бумагомара́к! У, щелкопёры, либера́лы прокля́тые! чёртово се́мя! Узло́м бы вас всех завяза́л, в муку́ бы стёр вас всех да чёрту в подкла́дку! в ша́пку туды́ ему́!.. *(Суёт кулако́м и бьёт каблуко́м в пол. По́сле не́которого молча́ния.)* До сих пор не могу́ прийти́ в себя́. Вот, по́длинно, е́сли бог хо́чет наказа́ть, так отни́мет пре́жде ра́зум. Ну что бы́ло в э́том вертопра́хе похо́жего на ревизо́ра? Ничего́ не́ было! Вот про́сто ни на полмизи́нца не́ было похо́жего — и вдруг все: ревизо́р! ревизо́р! Ну кто пе́рвый вы́пустил, что он ревизо́р? Отвеча́йте!

Арте́мий Фили́ппович *(расставля́я ру́ки)*. Уж как э́то случи́лось, хоть убе́й, не могу́ объясни́ть. То́чно тума́н како́й-то ошеломи́л, чёрт попу́тал.

Аммо́с Фёдорович. Да кто вы́пустил, — вот кто вы́пустил: э́ти молодцы́! *(Пока́зывает на До́бчинского и Бо́бчинского.)*

Бо́бчинский. Ей-е́й, не я! и не ду́мал...

До́бчинский. Я ничего́, совсе́м ничего́...

Арте́мий Фили́ппович. Коне́чно, вы.

Лука́ Луки́ч. Разуме́ется. Прибежа́ли, как сумасше́дшие, из тракти́ра: «Прие́хал, прие́хал и де́нег не пло́тит...» Нашли́ ва́жную пти́цу!

Городни́чий. Натура́льно, вы! спле́тники городски́е, лгуны́ прокля́тые!

Арте́мий Фили́ппович. Чтоб вас чёрт побра́л с ва́шим ревизо́ром и расска́зами!

Городни́чий. То́лько ры́скаете по го́роду да смуща́ете всех, трещо́тки прокля́тые! Спле́тни се́ете, соро́ки короткохво́стые!

Аммо́с Фёдорович. Пачкуны́ прокля́тые!

Лука́ Луки́ч. Колпаки́!

Арте́мий Фили́ппович. Сморчки́ короткобрю́хие!

Все обступа́ют их.

Бо́бчинский. Ей-бо́гу, э́то не я, э́то Пётр Ива́нович.

До́бчинский. Э, нет, Пётр Ива́нович, вы ведь пе́рвые того́...

Бо́бчинский. А вот и нет; пе́рвые-то бы́ли вы.

ЯВЛЕНИЕ ПОСЛЕДНЕЕ

Те же и жанда́рм.

Жанда́рм. Прие́хавший по именно́му повеле́нию из Петербу́рга чино́вник тре́бует вас сей же час к себе́. Он останови́лся в гости́нице.

Произнесённые слова́ поража́ют, как гро́мом, всех. Звук изумле́ния единоду́шно излета́ет из да́мских уст; вся гру́ппа, вдруг перемени́вши положе́ние, остаётся в окамене́нии.

НЕМАЯ СЦЕНА

Городни́чий посереди́не в ви́де столпа́, с распростёртыми рука́ми и заки́нутою наза́д голово́ю. По пра́вую сто́рону его́ жена́ и дочь с устреми́вшимся к нему́ движе́ньем всего́ те́ла; за ни́ми почтме́йстер, преврати́вшийся в вопроси́тельный знак, обращённый к зри́телям; за ним Лука́ Луки́ч, потеря́вшийся са́мым неви́нным о́бразом; за ним, у са́мого кра́я сце́ны, три да́мы, го́стьи, прислони́вшиеся одна́ к друго́й с са́мым сатири́ческим выраже́ньем лица́, относя́щимся пря́мо к семе́йству городни́чего. По ле́вую сто́рону городни́чего: Земляни́ка, наклони́вший го́лову не́сколько на́бок, как бу́дто к чему́-то прислу́шивающийся; за ним судья́ с растопы́ренными рука́ми, присе́вший почти́ до земли́ и сде́лавший движе́нье губа́ми, как бы хоте́л посвиста́ть и́ли произне́сть: «Вот тебе́, ба́бушка, и Юрьев день!» За ним Коро́бкин, обрати́вшийся к зри́телям с прищу́ренным гла́зом и е́дким намёком на городни́чего; за ним, у са́мого кра́я сце́ны, Бо́бчинский и До́бчинский с устреми́вшимися движе́ньями рук друг к дру́гу, рази́нутыми рта́ми и вы́пученными друг на дру́га глаза́ми. Про́чие го́сти остаю́тся про́сто столба́ми. Почти́ полторы́ мину́ты окамене́вшая гру́ппа сохраня́ет тако́е положе́ние. За́навес опуска́ется.

ABBREVIATIONS

acc.	accusative	impf.	imperfective
adj.	adjective	inf.	infinitive
adv.	adverb	instr.	instrumental
affect.	affectionate	interj.	interjection
arch.	archaic	interrog.	interrogative
attrib.	attributive	lit.	literally
cf.	compare	masc.	masculine
Ch.Sl.	Church Slavonic	mod.	modern
coll.	colloquial	neut.	neuter
comp.	comparative	nom.	nominative
conj.	conjunction	obs.	obsolete
corr.	corruption	part.	partitive
dat.	dative	pcle.	particle
derog.	derogatory	pers.	person
dial.	dialectal	pf.	perfective
dim.	diminutive	pl.	plural
Eng.	English	pop.	popular
esp.	especially	poss.	possessive
exc.	except	pot.	potential
f.,ff.	following	predic.	predicative
fam.	familiar	prep.	preposition
fem.	feminine	prepl.	prepositional
fig.	figurative	pres.	present
Fr.	French	pron.	pronoun
freq.	frequentative	p.t.	past tense
fut.	future	Russ.	Russian
G.	Gogol	sc.	scilicet
gen.	genitive	sing.	singular
Ger.	German	superl.	superlative
illit.	illiterate	Ukr.	Ukrainian
imp.	imperative	usu.	usually
impers.	impersonal	voc.	vocative

R	Revizor	R3	First edition (1836)
R1	First draft	R4	Second edition (1841)
R2	Stage text	R5	Third edition (1842)

Ozhegov S. I. Ozhegov *Словарь русского языка*, 4th ed. Moscow, 1960.

Shansky N. M. Shansky *Этимологический словарь русского языка*, Moscow, 1963–.

Ushakov D. N. Ushakov *Толковый словарь русского языка*, 4 vols. Moscow, 1935–40.

NOTES

Epigraph

На зеркало неча (= нечего) пенять, коли рожа крива, 'It's no use blaming the mirror if your mug is crooked'. G. added this proverb to the 1842 edition (R5) as a rejoinder to critics who had accused him of slandering all officials and presenting a false picture of Russia; he was saying in effect that he was holding up no distorting mirror to contemporary society. He may have been inspired here by the 18th-century poet Kantemir who in his first satire, attacking enemies of education, exhorted his readers to remember that 'Дурной лицом николи (= нисколько) зеркала не любит' ('The person with an ugly face dislikes a mirror').

Dramatis Personae

Like many a playwright before him, G. used descriptive or meaningful names. This simple but effective method of characterization was used by Roman dramatists, revived in France and England in the 17th century, and taken up by Russian comedy-writers in Catherine's time, first by V. Lukin, then by others. Unlike his 18th-century predecessors, G. did not generally stress the link between names and distinctive personal traits; his invented surnames mostly contain only an allusion, not a summary of character. Moreover, G., who was a great collector of names, often used real names in his works, esp. expressive or odd-sounding ones. Many of the surnames found in the play are in fact authentic, though rare in some cases. Those which G. coined himself are marked with an asterisk.

Сквозник-Дмухановский*: a pompous, quasi-aristocratic name suggesting 'a puff of wind', compounded from сквозник (dial. for сквозняк), 'draught' and Ukr. дмухати, 'to blow', which has obvious associations with надуть, 'to swindle' and продувной, 'crafty', 'roguish'.

Хлопов: a name derived from хлоп or холоп, 'bond slave', 'serf', that suggests servility and befits his humble, timid character. His first name Лука may be a reminder of лук, the onions of which he is said to reek (V.8.119).

Ляпкин-Тяпкин*: a comic rhyming name derived from the pop. expression ляп-тяп, said of something done in a brisk but crude fashion (cf. ляпать, 'to do anyhow' and тяпать, 'to hack'). This refers to his slapdash way of administering the law.

Земляника*: lit. 'Strawberry', not a real name, but a possible one, given the existence in Russian of such surnames as Ягода, 'Berry', Жук, 'Beetle', Пастернак, 'Parsnip', and others drawn from the animal and vegetable kingdoms. Probably chosen to suggest his soft, pliant nature as well as rubicundity and plumpness (he is the fattest of all the officials).

Шпекин*: probably from шпек, a variant of шпик, 'police spy', a reference to the Postmaster's practice of opening and reading private letters with police connivance.

Добчинский, Бобчинский*: believed to be derived from Ukr. surname Добко and dog's name Бобко. The close similarity of their names matches their physical resemblance to each other and is underlined by the fact that they share the same имя-отчество. They have a symbiotic relationship, though not related by blood, like Lewis Carroll's near-twins Tweedledum and Tweedledee.

Хлестаков*: from the root хлест- and its variants; хлестать, not with the meaning 'to lash' but in the coll. sense 'to spout', 'prattle', 'lie', for the hero is not so much a scourge as a mendacious windbag; cf. хлёст, 'brazen braggart', хлёсткий, 'pert', хлыст or хлыщ, 'frivolous coxcomb'. The whole complex of associations is captured splendidly by Nabokov, who writes that the name is a stroke of genius, conveying to the Russian reader 'an effect of lightness and rashness, a prattling tongue, the swish of a slim walking cane, the slapping sound of playing cards, the braggadocio of a nincompoop and the dashing ways of a lady-killer'. From the hero's name comes the word хлестаковщина, meaning 'shameless or frivolous boasting'.

Осип: coll. form of Иосиф, with loss of initial yot and substitution of п for ф (as in Степан for Stephen); the equivalent of 'Joe'.

Гибнер: the Ger. surname Hiebner, a variant of Hübner, puts Russians in mind of гибнуть, 'to perish', suggesting that this is the likely fate of the doctor's patients.

Люлюков*: from люлюкать, 'to rock in a cradle (люлька)'; the smallest speaking part in the play.

Растаковский*: from intensive prefix раз- and adj. таковский, 'very much of such a kind', i.e. an odd fellow. In R1 and 2 this retired military officer appeared in a separate scene with Khlestakov (as Hiebner did in R2), but his role was thereafter reduced to a very small part in Act V.

Коробкин: from коробка, 'box'; another very small speaking part.

Уховёртов*: from ухо, 'ear' and вертеть, 'to twist', 'turn'; cf. уховёртка, 'earwig'. The name suggests that the Police Superintendent handles people roughly, by the ears.

Свистунов, Пуговицын: real names, appropriate to police officers, from свистун, 'whistler', and пуговица, 'button', suggesting the whistle used by a policeman and the buttons on his uniform.

Держиморда*: from держи, 'hold' and морда, 'snout', 'mug', the same type of noun formation as вертихвостка, 'flirt' and скопидом, 'hoarder', 'miser'. It has obvious suggestions of police brutality, associated with the name ever since G. coined it.

Абдулин (also spelt, more correctly, Абдуллин): from Arabic *Abdullah* (lit. 'God's servant'), the name of Mohammed's father. The surname indicates that he is of Muslim Asian extraction (non-Russians predominated in the merchant class at that time); it could well have been chosen for its vocal associations with обдуть, 'to cheat'. Abdulin is the chief spokesman of the merchants, who appear as a group, forming a kind of chorus.

Пошлёпкина*: from пошлёпать, 'to shuffle', suggests the slow, shambling gait of an old woman, which she is.

Мишка: dim. of Миша, coll. short form of Михаил; the suffix -ка adds a touch of familiarity or disdain to the name. The Governor's servant is a young lad got up as a казачок ('young Cossack'), the usual attire of serf boys in service with the gentry. See III.2.76.

All other names occurring in the text, except Tryapichkin, are authentic.

Characters and Costumes

It was unusual at that time for dramatists to preface their plays with notes on the characters, but G. evidently felt it necessary to show the actors that they were to play real people, not the stereotypes of conventional comedy and vaudeville. Some details given in R3 concerning appearance and dress, supplied apparently by the theatrical supervisor Khrapovitsky, were cut out of R5.

1. Городничий: governor of a district town, an office created by Catherine II in 1775, though the word had been used since the 16th century to denote the warden of a town. The *gorodnichy* was an official, appointed by the Senate to perform the same judicial and administrative functions in a district town as were exercised in the provincial town by the губернатор. He had wide powers, being not only chief of police but also in charge of public works, prisons, the fire service and billeting of troops. In the 19th century, until the office was abolished in 1862, such governors were usually retired officials or retired army officers.

Many translators of the play give 'Mayor' for Городничий, but a mayor is an elected head whose powers are much more limited than were those of a governor. Cf. I.3.119.

на службе, 'in service', i.e. of the state. Members of the nobility or gentry (дворянство) normally made their careers in the military or civil service. Service for life was imposed by Peter the Great, an obligation reduced to 25 years in 1736 and abolished altogether in 1762, but most gentry continued to enter state service even after that.

3. сурьёзен: obs. = серьёзен; a folk-etymological change of pronunciation in a word of foreign origin (Fr. *sérieux*) under the influence of суровый, 'severe'. Cf. ll.28 & 38.

несколько... резонёр, 'something of a moralizer' or 'somewhat sententious'. The *raisonneur*, or mouthpiece of morality, was a stock figure in earlier comedies.

6. с низших чинов, 'from the lowest ranks'. Most officials in the tsarist civil service were graded according to the Table of Ranks (Табель о рангах), introduced by Peter the Great in 1722 and retained until the Revolution. There were fourteen grades, each with its equivalent commissioned rank in the army and navy, its own title and appropriate salary. Below these were several more junior grades of clerical post. Once an official was given a rank in the Table he became a life member of the gentry class, and the much-coveted status of hereditary membership was conferred on those who reached one of the top eight grades (this was restricted from 1845 to the top five and from 1856 to the top four grades).

8. одет... в своём мундире, 'dressed in his uniform' (today одетый в takes the acc.). Each official was provided with a set of equipment that enabled him to dress for various purposes in different outfits. The two most important of these were the undress uniform (вицмундир), worn when on duty, and the full-dress uniform (парадный мундир), used on formal occasions. The first consisted of a tail-coat with an open collar, two rows of six buttons on the chest and cuffs cut away at the back, a waistcoat, cravat, trousers (with footstraps) worn over boots, and a black top hat. The full-dress uniform differed from this in having a tail-coat with a stand-up collar and a row of nine buttons, a black cocked hat with silver tassels at each end and on the side a red tab surmounted by a black cockade, white gloves, sword-belt and sword. The uniform coat was dark green in all branches of the service except education, where it was dark blue. The waistcoat was the same colour as the coat or white (always white in full dress), likewise the trousers, which were white in summer, the season in which the play is set. The Governor, unlike the other officials, wears uniform at every appearance, being in full dress in Act II when he calls at the inn. Distinctive features of his uniform are a red stand-up collar and red cuffs with two buttons on each, gold tabs on collar and cuffs, and high boots into which his trousers are tucked. See notes below.

9. с петлицами, 'with tabs', i.e. coloured cloth patches embroidered with galloon and stitched to a uniform, in this case one at each side of the Governor's collar and two on each cuff.

в ботфортах: from Fr. *bottes fortes*, high boots which came above the knees at the front, as worn by cavalry in the Napoleonic wars; very similar to Wellingtons of the same period.

11f. ещё не совсем пожилых лет, 'still in her middle years'. In R1 (III.3) Anna claims to be only thirty-two, but is clearly indulging in feminine understatement about her age. She is nearer forty.

12f. на... альбомах. It was fashionable at that time for young ladies to keep albums or autograph books in which they and their friends inscribed verses or songs, mostly of a light or romantic kind. In IV.12 Maria requests some verses for her album from Khlestakov. Album verses are referred to in Pushkin's *Евгений Онегин*, IV.28:

> Конечно, вы не раз видали
> Уездной барышни альбом,
> Что все подружки измарали
> С конца, с начала и кругом.

Девичья [комната]: the room in a gentry household where the domestic serf women (дворовые девки) lived, worked and slept.

18. разные платья. Russian ladies of the period wore long dresses with a tight bodice reinforced with whalebone and usually laced at the back, an open neck and exposed shoulders, covered during the day-time with a scarf, a cape or a modesty-piece at the front, leg-of-mutton or puff sleeves, narrow waist and long flared skirt reaching to the ankles. Beneath the dress they wore a bone corset and several starched under-skirts, one of which was hooped. With these went flat shoes similar to dancing slippers, and as part of the morning attire a white mob-cap was worn. The head was generally adorned with a ribbon tied in a bow or with a hair-piece.

19f. тоненький, худенький, 'slender and slight of build'. A dim. suffix added to an adj. does not indicate a diminution of the quality denoted, but has a purely affective or stylistic value that attaches more to the noun than to the epithet itself. Cf. низенькие, коротенькие (ll.34f.).

20. приглуповат (obs.), 'on the stupid side'.

20f. без царя в голове, 'muddle-headed' or 'with a mind that runs to chaos'. Cf. saying: Свой ум — царь в голове, 'The mind is master of the head'.

26. Одет по моде. Khlestakov, as a young gentleman who dressed in the fashion of the time, would wear a tail-coat, probably black or dark blue, with plain or striped trousers of a different colour, waistcoat, shirt with jabot and frilly cuffs, cravat, white gloves, patent leather shoes and a top hat (though G. indicates a peaked cap at the beginning of II.2). His foppish streak might be displayed by wearing a brightly coloured waistcoat, such as G. himself sported at times.

33. молча плут, 'a silent rogue'. A rare example of an adv. used to qualify a noun and preceding it. The adv. usu. comes second, such constructions being elliptical, e.g. обед даром from обед, который получают даром.

серый или синий поношенный сюртук. A frock-coat, dark in colour, was the usual garb for a manservant. With it went a cravat, trousers and boots. Osip's coat is threadbare and grimy.

34ff. G. amplified this description of the two squires in his *Предуведомление*, where he states: "Both have round faces and are neatly dressed, with slicked hair. Dobchinsky even has a small bald patch in the middle of his crown; he is clearly no bachelor like Bobchinsky, but a married man. Yet for all that Bobchinsky, being the livelier, prevails over him and even dominates his mind to some degree." Writing to Shchepkin on 10 May 1836, G. observed that their little bellies should protrude like those of pregnant women. As regards their dress, he stated that the one with light hair (Dobchinsky) should wear a dark coat, and the dark-haired one (Bobchinsky) – a light coat. Both should have dark trousers.

40. судья. Lyapkin-Tyapkin is judge of the district court (уездный суд), an institution created by Catherine's reform of 1775 to deal with minor civil and criminal cases involving members of the gentry. He is the only elected official in the town and ranks second in importance after the Governor.

41. вольнодумен: obs. = свободомыслящий, 'freethinking'. This trait in the Judge recalls the masonic wiseacres (умники) satirized in Russian comedies of the early 19th century. See note on ум at I.1.142f.

41f. Охотник большой на догадки, 'A great one for conjectures'. Охотник ('lover of') is more usu. constructed with до + gen., as at IV.5.21f.

44. с продолговатой (= продолжительной) растяжкой, 'with prolonged lengthening', i.e. with great deliberation.

47. попечитель богоугодных заведений, 'director of charitable institutions'. In tsarist Russia such institutions (almshouses, orphanages, hospitals etc.) were not organized on a voluntary basis, as they were in England, but administered by various government organs, chiefly the приказ общественного призрения (see IV.7.18f). The only institution mentioned by name in the play is the local charity hospital, but there may have been others in the town too.

The mod. expression for charitable institution is благотворительное учреждение.

50. Почтмейстер. Shpekin is in charge of the postal service in the town and district. At that time this involved not only handling mail but also providing horses and chaises for travellers.

52. пред: Ch.Sl. form of перед. Cf. чрез for через (I.6.21).

54. Последнее произнесённое слово, i.e. the announcement by the Gendarme, who for some reason is omitted from the list of characters.

произвесть. In the first half of the 19th century most infinitives in -сти and -зти had alternative forms in -сть and -зть. The latter are now arch. and pop.

56. в один миг ока, 'in the twinkling of an eye'. A conflation of в один миг and в мгновение ока, a Slavonicism in which мгновение has its original meaning of 'winking' (мигание). Prokopovich, given a free hand to correct G.'s style for the edition of 1842, deleted the word ока and also changed сих on l.58 to этих, but G.'s wording has been restored in most recent editions.

58. сих, 'of these': gen. pl. of arch. pron. сей.

ACT I

Of the officials only the Governor and the Postmaster wear uniform in this act. The rest, including the district doctor, an official of the tenth grade, are dressed in civilian clothes.

Scene 1

2. смотритель училищ. From the beginning of the 19th century each district in Russia had a штатный смотритель ('permanent director of schools') who was head of the district school (уездное училище) for children of town-dwellers and who supervised the parish schools (приходские школы) for children of serfs, also a почётный смотритель училищ ('honorary superintendent of schools'), appointed from among the local gentry to oversee education as a whole. Khlopov is the permanent director. His uniform coat, unlike that of the other officials, is dark blue, with a collar of matching velvet.

частный пристав, 'police superintendent' in charge of a district or precinct (часть) in a town and its station-house (частный дом). He was responsible to the *gorodnichy* and his uniform was the same, except that he had silver, not gold tabs on his cuffs, dark green trousers, knee-boots, a sabre and only a cocked hat (carried under the left arm when not worn). Though included in the list of characters at the beginning of the act, Ukhovertov does not appear until Sc. 5.

3. Квартальный [надзиратель]: a non-commissioned police-officer in charge of a ward or sector (квартал), a sub-division of the часть (see above). This was then the lowest rank in the regular police, with a uniform the same as the superintendent's, except for having no collar tabs.

4ff. This succinct opening speech, which sets the tone for the whole play, was the result of careful pruning at each stage. In R1, where the names do not all coincide with those in later versions, it runs: Я пригласил вас, господа... Вот и Антона Антоновича, и Григория Петровича, и Христиана Ивановича, и всех вас [для] того, чтобы сообщить одно чрезвычайно важное известие, которое, признаюсь вам, чрезвычайно меня потревожило. И вдруг сегодня неожиданное известие. Меня уведомляют, что отправился из Петербурга чиновник с секретным предписанием обревизовать всё, относящееся по части управления, и именно в нашу губернию, что уже выехал 10 дней назад тому и с часу на час должен быть, если не действительно уже находится инкогнито в нашем [городе].

The following is the version found in R2, with the words excised for R3 given in italics: Я пригласил вас, господа... *вот и Артемия Филипповича, и Аммоса Фёдоровича, Луку Лукича и Христиана Ивановича* с тем, чтобы сообщить вам *одно* пренеприятное известие. Меня уведомляют, что отправился инкогнито из Петербурга чиновник с секретным предписанием обревизовать в нашей губернии всё, относящееся по части гражданского управления. In R5 the long second sentence was reduced to the brief words: к нам едет ревизор.

5. пренеприятное известие, 'a most unpleasant piece of news'. The prefix пре-, of Ch.Sl. origin, gives intensive force to an adj. or adv. and has an arch., coll. flavour. Other examples in this act are преинтересный (I.2.40), пребойкий and престранно (I.3.67 & 78).

6. ревизор, 'a government inspector'. Peter the Great introduced financial inspectors (фискалы) to uncover abuses and also appointed a chief inspector (обер-ревизор) to report to the Senate. Under Nicholas I administrative inspections were generally carried out by a high-ranking officer, sometimes by a senior official or a senator. Such visitations, which often lasted for several months, were made on an *ad hoc* basis, usually after the authorities in St. Petersburg had been apprised of irregularities in one of the provinces. The inspectors took so long to reach their destination that, despite the secrecy surrounding their activities, the local officials nearly always had prior warning of their arrival and were able to arrange a cover-up. Cf. Dostoyevsky, *Записки из мёртвого дома*: Едет из Петербурга ревизор... Слышно было, что все трусят, хлопочут, хотят товар лицом показать ('show things to advantage').

The common translation of ревизор as 'inspector-general' (i.e. head of an inspectorate) is quite wrong. P. Mérimée, the first French translator of the play, appears to have been responsible for this error, which others have perpetuated.

9. инкогнито. In the reign of Nicholas I inspectors frequently travelled in the guise of private persons.

11. Вот те на! 'Well, I never!' Here те is a coll. contracted and enclitic form of тебе, and на is an interj.

12f. Вот не было заботы, так подай! 'We hadn't a care, and now this!' i.e. our luck was too good to hold: a remark in the coll. idiom, close to the saying не было печали, так черти накачали. The expression не было заботы is now used only ironically to mean 'as if we hadn't enough trouble already'.

14. Господи боже! 'Good God!' lit. 'Lord God!' From господь and бог, these voc. forms, both borrowed from Ch.Sl., are the only ones in common use. Such exclamations, like their Eng. equivalents, have lost all religious associations and simply express surprise or shock.

16f. сегодня... всю ночь, 'all last night'. The phrase сегодня ночью (or в ночь) may mean 'tonight' or 'last night', according to context. Until the 18th century Eng. 'tonight' could also mean 'last night'.

17. The two rats, transparent symbols of the false and true inspectors, were large black dogs in R1 and 2.

18. видывал: freq. of видал. Frequentative forms derived from simple (i.e. unprefixed) verbs were very common in literary Russ. from the 17th century to the middle of the 19th, but came to be frowned on increasingly by educated speakers as patriarchal in flavour and their use declined thereafter, so that today they are purely coll. and mostly arch. They are used occasionally in the inf., otherwise only in the past tense, this latter form being described by Lomonosov and other grammarians as the давнопрошедшее время, a term used to denote either the pluperfect or, as here, the remote past. But this is a misnomer, since the habitual action expressed by such verbs relates to *any* long period of past time, not necessarily in the distant past. Thus я знавал means exactly the same as 'I used to know'. Cf. едал (II.6.46), куривал (IV.5.13).

19f. пришли, понюхали — и пошли прочь: an alliterative phrase that reminds one irresistibly of Caesar's famous words: *Veni, vidi, vici*. A suitable equivalent would be 'they sneaked in, sniffed about and sneaked out again'.

23. кум, 'godfather' (of my child or children)'. No single word exists for this in Eng. By the godchildren themselves the godfather is referred to as крёстный [отец].

24f. Спешу... уведомить тебя: a fairly common epistolary formula at that time, also found at the beginning of both the other letters quoted in the play (see III.2.54; V.8.45).

26. всю губернию и... наш уезд. In 1708 Peter the Great divided Russia into eight large administrative provinces (губернии), each under a governor (губернатор). After this the number of provinces gradually increased and they were further divided into smaller units. By Catherine's Statute on the Provinces of 1775 the empire was divided into forty provinces, each with a population of 300–400,000, and these were subdivided into districts (уезды), each having 20–30,000 souls. The chief town in each province was called the губернский город, and in each district – the уездный город. These administrative units survived with little alteration until 1929, when the term губерния was replaced by область and уезд by район.

28. достоверных людей. Incorrect use of достоверный ('trustworthy'), which properly applies to sources, documents etc., as at I.3.41. The Russ. for 'reliable' in reference to persons is надёжный, and верный can be used of a source or a person.

29f. за тобою... водятся грешки, 'you have your little sins'. The prep. за + instr. is used with быть and a few other verbs, such as водиться, заметить, знать, числиться, to ascribe some quality or habit to a person. Cf. Он знает за собой эту слабость, 'He is aware of this weakness in himself'.

The word грешки is here a euphemism for malfeasance in office, esp. the practice of taking bribes. 'What floats into your hands' (l.31) is similarly a euphemism for bribes.

30. ты человек умный. Note the placing of the attrib. adj. after the noun for emphasis. Cf. дела семейные (l.36) and *passim*.

32. остановясь: obs. = остановившись. Past gerunds in -я from pf. verbs in -ить were formerly in common use, but are now largely confined to a few adverbial expressions such as сломя голову, 'at breakneck speed' and немного погодя, 'a little later'.

ну, здесь свои... 'oh well, we're all friends here . . .' i.e. I can speak freely. As a noun свои means 'one's own people'; cf. свой человек, 'one of us'.

32f. взять предосторожность: obs. = принять (меры) предосторожности, 'to take precautions'.

35. дни = дня. This old gen. sing. of день was still used, though arch., in the 19th century. The ending -и was taken from Old Russ. masc. declension type гость, of which путь is the only surviving example, the other nouns of this class having been assimilated to type конь.

35f. тут уж пошли дела семейные, 'the rest is about family matters'. The pf. пойти is used here in the coll. sense 'to begin'. Cf. I.6.5; II.1.5 & 39; III.6.125.

36. сестра Анна Кириловна. Сестра is used loosely for 'cousin' (двоюродная сестра), as shown by the fact that the writer of the letter has a different patronymic. The spelling with one л derives from Кирила, a coll. form of Кирилл, 'Cyril'.

38. всё here = 'still', not 'continually' or 'keeps on'.

на скрыпке. In the first half of the 19th century the root скрип- was commonly spelt скрып-, reflecting the tendency to harden a soft 'r' in some dialects.

41f. Что-нибудь недаром, 'There's something behind all this' or 'There's more in this than meets the eye'.

44. Зачем к нам ревизор [едет]? Ellipse of verbs, esp. verbs of motion, is common in spoken Russ. Cf. куда [едешь]? (I.6.7).

45. Так уж, видно, судьба! 'It must be just fate!' The pcle. уж, not always translatable, here emphasizes так ('*such*, evidently, is fate!').

46. благодарение богу: obs. = слава богу, 'thank God'. Cf. III.5.41.

51. Россия... хочет вести войну, 'Russia is about to (*not* wants to) wage war'. This meaning of хотеть is also found in Ger. *wollen*.

51f. министерия-то. When added to nouns, the emphatic pcle. -то is sometimes equivalent to a definite article ('the ministry'). The obs. word министерия (from Fr. *ministère*) meant 'post of minister' (должность министра) or 'ministry' (министерство), but some commentators suggest that it is used, or rather misused here to mean 'the government', which makes better sense in the context.

53. нет ли где измены, 'whether there is treason anywhere'. In coll. Russ. the pcle. -нибудь is often dropped from an indefinite adv. or pron. Cf. I.73: на другом каком[-нибудь] языке, 'in some other language'.

54. Эк куда хватили! 'Whooh, what a far-fetched idea!' Here хватить has the coll. sense of 'going too far'. Very similar in meaning is Эк куда метнул! 'A likely story!' (II.8.63f.).

54f. Ещё умный человек! 'And you call yourself an intelligent man!' (A) ещё or ещё и always introduces a reproving and usu. sarcastic remark.

56. Да conveys an objection with a touch of scorn or irritation: 'Why (man) . . .'

56f. отсюда хоть три года скачи, ни до какого государства не доедешь, 'though you gallop from here for three years, you won't reach any state (i.e. foreign country)'. The imp. sing., which has several idiomatic uses, is concessive in sense when accompanied by conj. хоть. Cf. хоть убей, 'for the life of me', lit. 'though you kill me' (V.8.204).

Three years is a gross exaggeration; despite the vastness of the country and the difficulties of travelling at that time a rider on horseback could have reached Russia's western frontier from a central province in 7–10 days. The Governor's remark, in the modified form до них три года скачи, не доскачешь, is still used to describe a provincial backwater.

58. я вам скажу, 'I tell you'. In conversational Russ. many introductory phrases have the verb of locution in fut. tense, where Eng. uses the pres. Cf. доложу вам; попрошу вас.

58f. вы не того... 'you don't er . . .' The gen. form того is a pcle. commonly used as a verbal filler, like 'er' and 'um'. Cf. IV.1.29; IV.6.55.

59. виды, 'plans' or 'designs': a sense found only in pl.

60. оно себе мотает на ус. Idiom: 'they (the authorities) take good note of everything'. It was widely believed that the government in St. Petersburg had an all-seeing eye (всевидящее око) and fear of inspection was rife, for officials found guilty of jobbery could be demoted, dismissed or imprisoned. In fact, however, inspectors were not often sent to the provinces and the punishments they meted out were generally not severe.

63. советую и вам [sc. **так же поступить**].

66f. сделайте так, чтобы, 'see to it that'. The same sense is expressed by заботиться о том, чтобы (II.8.10).

67f. колпаки были бы чистые, 'make sure the nightcaps are clean'. The pcle. бы has the same force here as чтобы, i.e. it expresses an injunction.

73. надписать: inf. used as imp. to express a strong, often peremptory command. Most such commands in the play are, appropriately enough, spoken by the Governor, e.g. five times in Sc. 5.

по-латыни: coll. = по-латински, 'in Latin', from coll. noun латынь, a Russ. borrowing from Ukr., where it is a modified form of *Latine*. The hyphen has been introduced by analogy with adverbs of type по-гречески.

73f. это уж по вашей части, 'that's *your* province'. For уж as intensive pcle. see I.45.

75. когда кто заболел, 'when each one fell ill'. When used with an adv. or another pron., кто has a distributive sense, as in кто как мог, 'each as best he could' and кто что любит, 'different people like different things', i.e. 'tastes differ'.

77. расчихаешься, когда войдёшь, 'you have a fit of sneezing whenever you go inside'. The idiomatic use of fut. pf. to express habitual action (fut. pf. freq.) occurs *passim* and often combines, as here, with the 2nd pers. sing. denoting an indefinite 'you' (= 'one'). For further examples see Osip's opening speech in Act II.

Да и лучше [было бы]: a common ellipse with some impers. expressions. Cf. Eng. '(It would be) better to . . .'

78f. смотрение: obs. = присмотр, 'care' (of the patients).

79. неискусство: obs. = неискусность, 'lack of skill', 'incompetence'.

80–4. Concerning the state of medical care at that time the Marquis de Custine wrote: "In case of illness you must either prescribe for yourself or call in a foreign practitioner. If you send for the nearest doctor you are a dead man, for the art of medicine is in its infancy in Russia" (*Russia*, London, 1844, Vol. I, p. 187).

81. мы с Христианом Ивановичем, 'Christian Ivanovich and I'. Double subjects and objects denoting persons, esp. where one is expressed as a pron., are usu. joined by prep. с rather than conj. и. For other examples of the sociative instr. cf. I.2.70; I.3.8.

взяли. . . меры, 'have taken . . . measures'. In G.'s time both взять меры and принять меры were used, but the first is now obs. The Russ. and Eng. expressions are calques of Fr. *prendre des mesures*.

82. к натуре: obs. = к природе. Today натура can mean 'nature' in the sense of 'temperament', but not in the broad general sense.

83f. Человек простой: если умрёт, то и так умрёт, '(Your) ordinary man, if he dies, (then) he'll die anyway'. Note that простой is attrib., not predic., hence this is not an observation about mankind in general, as many translators have assumed, but a slighting remark about the so-called 'lower orders', chiefly the peasants.

86. он по-русски ни слова не знает: знать по-русски is loose coll. usage for знать русский язык. By making the doctor a dumb German (немой немец), G. was appealing to anti-German sentiment. In his time most doctors in Russia, like many other professional men, were Germans who often remained aloof and unrussified, thereby evoking much resentment in the native population.

87f. The doctor utters a sound described as a cross between *и* and *е*, presumably the Ger. vowel ö, which sounds most strange to a Russian ear.

90. присутственные места (obs.), 'government offices', here the district court-house, as is clear from l.144. Присутствие (l.101) has the same meaning.

91. У вас там в передней, 'In your ante-room there'. The construction у + gen. is a common idiomatic alternative to the poss. adj. Cf. I.2.6.

93. гусёнками = гусятами. Words with the suffix -ёнок/-онок superseded Old Russ. neut. forms in -я (pl. -ята) to denote young animals, e.g. телёнок replaced теля, 'calf'. For several centuries both pl. forms were used, the original -ята and the regular -ёнки, but the latter, frequently used by G., is now pop. or dial.

так и шныряют под ногами, 'keep poking about under (people's) feet'. Here так и modifies the verb in the same sense as всё, i.e. denotes a persistent action. Cf. I.2.73f.

оно, when used as the indefinite subject of an impers. expression, is a redundant coll. pcle. Its use is characteristic of the Governor's speech; cf. I.5.25; III.10.38; V.1.36f. & 41f.

94. домашним хозяйством заводиться, 'to take up housekeeping', meaning here 'to start keeping domestic animals'.

95. и почему ж сторожу и не завесть его? 'and why indeed should a porter not take it up?' Note that in questions the dat. and inf. construction is the normal Russ. equivalent of an Eng. verb used with a modal auxiliary. Cf. Что ж мне, право, с ним делать? 'But what can I do with him, I ask you?' (l.163).

97. всё как-то позабывал, 'I somehow kept forgetting'. In all his writings G. showed a marked preference for coll. позабыть over standard забыть. Cf. I.5.27 & 47 and elsewhere.

99. Хотите, приходите обедать, 'Come and dine (with me), if you like'. Asyndetic or paratactic (i.e. non-conjunctive) constructions are a feature of coll. Russ., often occurring in proverbs, e.g. За двумя зайцами погонишься — ни одного не поймаешь, 'Grab all, lose all', lit. 'If you chase two hares you won't catch either'. The omission of если is esp. common with хочешь, хотите; cf. хочешь не хочешь, 'willy-nilly' ('whether you wish it or no').

102. с бумагами: i.e. in which the court records are kept.

103. всё here = всё же or всё-таки, 'still', 'all the same'. Cf. l.129.

лучше его принять, 'best remove it'. Принять in the sense убрать is pop.

104. а там, как проедет ревизор, 'and then when the inspector has left (lit. passed through)'. For там in coll. sense 'after that', 'later', cf. I.5.37; II.1.40, and for как as coll. equivalent of когда cf. l.174.

пожалуй, 'if you like': an obs. sense.

105. заседатель here = заседатель уездного суда, 'district court assessor', elected by the local gentry for a three-year term of office, like the Judge. Each district court had two assessors, whose role was relatively unimportant.

106. от него [исходит] такой запах, как будто бы, 'he smells as if'.

109. развлечён: here in the obs. sense of отвлечён, 'distracted'.

110. если уже, 'if indeed'. Here уже = уж as intensive pcle.

116. мамка его ушибла, 'his nurse bruised him' (by banging him on the head). The word ушибла evokes associations with the coll. meaning of ушибленный, 'cracked in the head'.

117. с тех пор от него отдаёт немного водкою, 'there's been a whiff of vodka about him ever since'. Отдавать in the coll. sense 'to smell of' is always impf. and usu. impers., as here.

118. Да я так только заметил вам, 'Well, I just thought I'd mention it to you'. For this use of так (только), 'just in passing', 'for no particular reason', cf. I.143 and IV.7.32.

119. Насчёт же внутреннего распоряжения, 'But as regards our internal (i.e. local) arrangements', an oblique, formal way of saying 'the way we run the town's affairs'.

121. странно говорить, i.e. странно было бы об этом говорить, the equivalent of нечего (и) говорить, 'needless to say', 'it goes without saying'.

121f. Generic subjunctive (бы... имел), used when a negative antecedent in the main clause (нет человека) makes the following statement contrary to fact. Potebnya states that this construction spread in Russian under the influence of the Classical and later of West European languages.

123. волтерианцы (now spelt вольтерьянцы), 'Voltairians': properly followers of the famous French rationalist philosopher Voltaire (1694–1778), but commonly used by conservatives at that time to mean 'free-thinkers', i.e. sceptics, agnostics, even libertines. The Governor, arguing for original sin, is getting a dig in at the freethinking Judge.

126. Грешки грешкам — рознь, 'There are sins and sins' or 'All sins are not alike'. The word рознь, pop. in G.'s time but now standard, retains its original meaning of 'difference' only in this idiomatic construction.

127f. The expression брать борзыми щенками, 'to take bribes in the form of borzoi puppies', has come to mean 'take bribes in kind', being used of people who regard them as less 'sinful' than monetary bribes.

132f. если у кого-нибудь шуба стоит пятьсот рублей, 'if a person's fur coat costs 500 roubles', the person in question being the Governor.

да супруге [достаётся] шаль, 'and his wife comes by a shawl'. Clothes and lengths of cloth were often given as bribes. Cf. IV.10.14f., IV.11.27f.

138. вы если начнёте. Note the deferred conj., a coll. usage, of which other examples are как (III.7.11) and чтоб (III.10.55).

142f. много ума хуже, чем [если] бы его совсем не было, 'a lot of brains is worse than none at all'. The Governor's remark expresses more than distrust of intellect or cleverness. From the early 19th century the word ум was often used in a pejorative sense to denote dangerous freethinking (the derivatives умный and умник were similarly derog.). The woeful consequences of too much intellect, in this sense, are the theme of Griboyedov's *Горе от ума*.

149. в разных коллегиях. The institutions referred to are colleges of secondary (not higher) education then existing in a number of large towns such as Kiev, Kharkov and St. Petersburg. The mod. sense of коллегия is 'board of managers' or 'panel of judges'.

151f. вот этот, что имеет толстое лицо, 'the one with the fat face'. In coll. Russ. что is sometimes used for a nom. or acc. form of который, just as 'that' replaces 'who' or 'which' in Eng. Cf. I.4.34; I.5.24.

152. не вспомню его фамилии, 'I can't remember his name'. The idiomatic use of fut. pf. to express possibility or ability (fut. pf. pot.) is less common than the frequentative use (see l.77). Like the latter, it often combines with the indefinite 2nd pers. sing., e.g. пронюхаешь, 'you can nose out' (I.3.128f.).

153. взошедши: obs. = взойдя. Today compound verbs in -йти (also in -везти, -вести, -нести) have past gerunds in -я, formed from the pres./fut. stem.

153f. без того, чтобы... не сделать гримасу, 'without pulling a face'. The use of acc., instead of gen., for the direct object of a negated verb was then very coll. (cf. IV.12.60f. and IV.13.24). The tendency to use the acc., esp. with fem. sing., in such constructions has greatly increased since G.'s time.

Yu. Lotman suggests that this trait in the anonymous teacher may have been inspired by Prof. N. N. Sandunov of Moscow University, who in his lectures expressed disapproval of the law by gestures and grimaces, being unable to voice criticisms openly. G. could certainly have heard of this from Muscovite friends, but since there is no political innuendo here it seems likelier that he was drawing on memories of his own schooldays.

155. потом начнёт, 'then he'll begin'. The fut. pf. freq. (see l.77) can often be rendered by the Eng. fut., which has the same idiomatic sense.

157. может быть, оно там и нужно так, 'it *may* even be necessary to do that'. Here, as earlier on the same line, оно is coll. for это. The pcle. там conveys a hint of doubt or disdain.

160. господин ревизор, 'the inspecting gentleman'. The Eng. title 'Mr.' is excluded here, since it is used with common nouns only in direct address. The phrase господа актёры, at the beginning of *Characters and Costumes*, may be translated as 'the ladies and gentlemen of the theatre'.

164. Вот ещё на днях, 'Why, only the other day'.

165. зашёл было в класс, 'was just calling in (*or* about to enter) the classroom'. The pcle. было with a verb in the p.t. (usu. pf.) signifies an unfulfilled action, one that was intended or begun but abandoned or interrupted.

предводитель [дворянства], 'marshal of the nobility', a powerful figure in the locality, head of the landowning gentry in the district or province, elected to preside over their triennial assembly (дворянское собрание) and represent their interests in organs of local government.

165f. он скроил (= состроил) такую рожу, 'he pulled such a face'.

166f. Он-то её сделал от доброго сердца, а мне выговор [sc. **сделали**], 'It was done in all innocence on his part, but I got a wigging'. Note emphatic -то ('*he* did it') and ellipse of verb.

Teachers and educational administrators were not only reprimanded but sometimes lost their jobs for minor breaches of discipline by their pupils. Nicholas I, who visited schools from time to time in his beloved role of imperial inspector, once had a teacher dismissed for allowing a pupil to sit with his elbows on the desk, and on another occasion sacked a headmaster because some senior boys with unshaven faces had stared through a window at their sovereign.

167f. G.'s ludicrous example of 'freethinking' conceals a serious point. A number of freethinkers were removed from academic posts towards the end of Alexander I's reign and under Nicholas I the authorities, who saw the Decembrist Revolt as the political expression of liberal ideas received from Western Europe, sought to prevent the further spread of such subversive notions. G. had known the suppression of freethinking at his school in Nezhin, where N. G. Belousov and three colleagues were dismissed, on the personal orders of the Tsar, for 'having a harmful influence on young people'. For details of this affair see S. Mashinsky, *Гоголь и «дело о вольнодумстве»*, Moscow, 1959.

170. учитель по исторической части: a pompous, long-winded way of saying учитель истории.

171. сведений нахватал тьму, 'he's picked up heaps of knowledge'. A neat touch of unconscious irony: the Governor, an uneducated person himself, means his remark as a compliment to the learned teacher, but it has the opposite effect through his use of нахватать, synonymous here with нахвататься, 'to pick up in a random and superficial fashion'. Cf. Griboyedov, *Горе от ума*, II.3: И знаков тьму отличья нахватал; a similar phrase in which Famusov expresses admiration for the way Skalozub has 'acquired heaps of decorations'.

174f. как добрался до Александра Македонского, 'when he got to Alexander of Macedon', i.e. Alexander the Great, the famous conqueror of antiquity.

176f. что силы есть, 'with all his might'. In this and similar expressions, such as что есть духу and что было мочи, the pron. что has the force of сколько.

177. хвать стулом об пол, '(grabbed a chair and) went bang with the chair on the floor'. Cf. Krylov, *Пустынник и Медведь*: Что силы есть — хвать друга камнем в лоб! Verbal stems of the type хвать are used with dramatic exclamatory effect instead of a finite verb (here хватал). Most such forms, expressing a sudden movement or sharp sound, can also be used as verbal interjections, e.g. трах! 'bang!', хлоп! 'pop!' Some grammarians, such as Bulakhovsky, regard them as a variant of the 'impulsive' imp. (see I.3.69); others, like Potebnya, treat them as a separate category.

Yu. Lotman states that G. took this detail from the Russian translation, pub. in 1804, of a German book of theatrical anecdotes. The story, which concerns an English actor named Charles Hulet (1701–36), was undoubtedly taken from Vol. 3 of Thomas Davies, *Dramatic Miscellanies*, 1784. Hulet, apprenticed to Edmund Curl, a London bookseller, was once rehearsing on his own Lee's *The Rival Queens* (or *The Death of Alexander the Great*), in which he was to play Clytus. To quote Davies: "Charles, acting the part of Alexander in the kitchen, with an elbow-chair for his Clytus, in a fury, with a poker in his hand instead of a javelin, broke it to pieces with such noise and violence that Curl, in the parlour, called out to know what was the matter. 'Nothing, sir', said the apprentice, 'but Alexander has killed Clytus'." (pp.273–4).

Оно, конечно, 'Now, of course'. Here оно is an emphatic pcle.

177f. This remark is sometimes quoted or paraphrased in the sense: 'one must keep a sense of proportion'. Cf. Chekhov, *Скука жизни*: Александр Македонский великий человек, но стульев ломать не следует, так и русский народ — великий народ, но из этого не следует, что ему нельзя в лицо правду говорить.

178f. от этого убыток казне, 'it's a drain on public funds'.

181. Как хотите, 'Say what you will', not 'please yourself'. Cf. II.8.133.

185. что хоть святых выноси, 'that it's enough to shock the saints', an idiom meaning lit. 'you may as well take out the sacred images'. In pop. parlance святые ('saints') signifies 'icons', which depict holy men. Orthodox believers used to draw a curtain across the icon corner or remove the images altogether when there was unseemly behaviour or language, also during festivities.

186f. Не приведи бог служить по учёной части! 'Heaven help anyone that works in the educational line!' In expressions such as не приведи (or не дай) бог, 'God forbid', and чёрт побери, 'devil take it', the imp. sing., used with a 3rd pers. subject, has optative force.

189. Это [было] бы ещё ничего, 'That wouldn't matter'. The omission of p.t. of быть is common in бы constructions, esp. impersonal ones, presumably to avoid a clash of very similar words. Cf. Pushkin, *Борис Годунов*, 8: Рада бы сама спрятаться.

191f. А подать сюда Ляпкина-Тяпкина! 'I want to see (Mr.) Lyapkin-Tyapkin!' Inf. as imp. (see I.73). For this coll. sense of подать ('send along'), cf. F. A. Koni, *Принц с хохлом, бельмом и горбом*, I.7: Ушёл? Ну и чёрт с ним! Тем лучше; подавай другого!

194. Вот что худо! 'That's the nasty part!'

Scene 2

The Postmaster, being on duty, wears his uniform, which is green, like that of the Governor, but with a stand-up collar of black velvet and matching cuffs decorated with lace. His trousers and waistcoat are pale yellow.

8f. The deduction, from the fact that an official had been sent to the province, that war with the Turks was imminent, is absurd, of course, but the possibility of such a war at that time was real, for Russia and Turkey had fought numerous times during the previous two centuries, most recently in the conflict of 1828–9. However, there were no further hostilities between Russia and 'the sick man of Europe', as Nicholas I called the Ottoman Empire, until fighting broke out in 1853, leading to the Crimean War.

10. В одно слово! 'You've taken the words out of my mouth!'

13f. Это всё француз гадит, 'It's the French up to their usual dirty tricks'. For всё = 'continually' cf. I.1.97.

In several of their many conflicts with Russia the Turks had been supported by France, whom the Russians long regarded as their most dangerous rival. In the latter part of the 19th century, when England came to be cast in that role, an expression commonly heard was англичанка нагадила, – the Englishwoman being Queen Victoria.

20. как вы [думаете]. . .? 'What do *you* think?' The same verb is omitted on 11.21, 23. Cf. I.1.44.

23. Страху-то нет [у меня], 'It isn't that I'm afraid'. The masc. gen. sing. in -у, a relic of an Old Russ. declension, was more widely used in the 19th century than today, esp. in part. expressions. Of the numerous examples in the play the following are now obs.: вкусу (II.6.38), полу (IV.5.23), порядку (IV.1.6f.), прибытку (IV.11.14), супу (II.6.39 & 46), тону (II.7.12).

23f. а так, немножко. . . 'but, well a little . . . (sc. uneasy)': R2 and 3 have а так как-то неловко.

24. гражданство: like граждане, originally meant simply 'townspeople' (горажане), but in the official language of the 18th and 19th centuries it denoted urban dwellers of the upper and middle classes, i.e. excluding the мещане. It now signifies 'citizenship'.

24ff. G. had a battle with the censor over this sentence. The version he first submitted ran thus: **Я, признаться сказать, уж слишком подстриг здешнее купечество и гражданство, так что вряд ли и ножницы такие в свете найдутся, которые бы могли ещё что-нибудь захватить, на меня-то они все теперь. . . так вот бы съели, попадись я только им.** When this was forbidden he substituted for the middle part: **вряд ли теперь и цирюльник такой сыщется, который бы мог что-нибудь захватить с них.** This, too, was rejected and the following appeared in R3: **Я, признаться сказать, им немножко солоно пришёлся. Они на меня как коршуны. . . так бы всего и растрепали, только перья полетят во все стороны.** In R5 there is no reference to the rapacity of the merchants and the Governor presents himself as an almost benign oppressor who extorts without any personal animosity, but despite the softer wording he still emerges as a harsh, venal administrator.

25. я им солоно пришёлся, 'I've given them a rough time' or 'I've squeezed them hard'.

28f. Informing had been officially encouraged in Russia since the Code of 1649 made denunciation of plotters against the crown mandatory under pain of death. Successive tsarist governments came to rely on private citizens for information about seditious or illegal activities. Under Nicholas I the Third Section had many informers on its pay-roll.

29. Зачем же. . . ? 'Why else . . .?' For же = 'else' cf. I.3.96.

30. нельзя ли вам. . .? 'd'you think you could . . .?' Interrog. constructions containing a negated verb or a negative impersonal followed by ли express a polite question or tentative suggestion. Cf. II.10.2 & 46; IV.Sc.3–5.

The Governor has no power to *order* the Postmaster, since agencies of the postal system were almost entirely independent of all other local authorities. The Postmaster, be it noted, has least to fear of all the officials because his job offered little scope for unscrupulous or politically dangerous activities.

33f. не содержится ли в нём какого-нибудь донесения, '(to see) whether it contains a report of any kind'. Intransitive verbs which approximate in meaning to быть follow its impers. construction in the negative, with the object expressed in the gen.

37ff. The perusal of private letters, known as перлюстрация, was widely practised in Russia at that time by both postmasters and agents of the Third Section. Letters of suspect persons, including most writers, were regularly intercepted, as well as the greater part of those sent from abroad. In his famous letter to G., written in Silesia, Belinsky complained about the inspection of correspondence, saying: Живя в России, я не мог бы этого сделать (i.e. write freely), ибо тамошние Шпекины распечатывают чужие письма не из одного личного удовольствия, но и по долгу службы, ради доносов. Similarly J. Buchanan, American envoy to St. Petersburg from 1831–3, wrote to Gen. A. Jackson: "To put my letters in the post-office here would be most certainly to expose them to the Russian government; indeed they scarcely think it necessary to do up the seals decently of those which I receive" (Letter of 1/13 October, 1832).

38. не то чтоб, 'not so much' or 'not just'. Cf. IV.2.8 and V.1.25.

39. смерть люблю, 'I'm terribly fond of'. Besides смерть a few other nouns (беда, страх, ужас), sometimes followed by как, are used adverbially in coll. Russ. to mean 'awfully', 'terribly'. Cf. II.3.8; III.8.6; IV.4.34.

39f. что есть нового на свете, 'what is going on (lit. what is new) in the world'. Note the part. gen.

42. In *Мёртвые души*, at the end of Ch. I, G. refers to пассаж (from Fr. *passage*) as a word then used by provincial gentry in the sense of предприятие, 'enterprise', 'venture', but 'happening' (esp. strange or unexpected) is a closer equivalent.

43. The newspaper *Московские ведомости*, founded by Moscow University, was published from 1756 until the Revolution. A serious official organ, it expressed a liberal outlook until the end of the 18th century, but thereafter became more and more conservative.

47. Kostroma and Saratov: important trading centres on the Volga, each the main town in its province.

49. пишет к приятелю. In the 19th century писать took an indirect object either with or, less often, without к, whereas today the prep. is never used, but the alternative constructions are still found in письмо (к) + dat.

Note also the historic pres., which occurs *passim*, being much more widely used in Russ. than in Eng.

50. в самом игривом... [sc. **виде**], 'in the most whimsical (way)'.

51. жизнь моя... течёт... в эмпиреях, 'I live a life of idyllic bliss', lit. 'my life is passed in the empyrean'. The latter is the name given by the ancient Greeks to the highest region of heaven, hence, in early Christian cosmology, the abode of God and the angels.

говорит: in its parenthetic use generally pronounced in a rapid, slurred manner as грит.

52. штандарт скачет: a good example of metonymy, a trope that G. was fond of using. By штандарт is meant штандарт-юнкер, 'standard-bearer'. An exact parallel exists in the Eng. word ensign, meaning 'flag' or 'banner' and, by extension, 'the junior officer that carried the regimental colours'.

54. Хотите, прочту (= чтобы я прочёл его)? 'Would you like me to read it?' Note the omission of pronouns and the paratactic construction (cf. I.1.99).

55. [мне] не до того. Idiom: 'I've no time for that' or 'I've other things on my mind'. Like nom. subjects, 'logical' dat. and acc. subjects of impers. constructions are often dropped. Cf. если [вам]... попадётся жалоба, 'if you come across a complaint' (1.56f.).

56. на случай: obs. = случайно, 'by chance'.

65. это дело семейственное, 'this is a family matter', i.e. something to be kept among ourselves. Here семейственный, which now means 'family-loving' or 'arranged by private dealing', is used in obs. sense of семейный.

66f. нехорошее дело заварилось! 'there's trouble brewing!' A pf. verb expressing a resultant state often corresponds to an Eng. pres. tense. Cf. (я) пропал! 'I am undone!' (IV.3.30) and (ты) рехнулась, 'you are out of your mind' (IV.15.21).

67. я... шёл было к вам, 'I was going to come and see you'. Here было indicates an unfulfilled intention. Cf. I.1.165.

68. попотчевать вас собачонкою, 'to make you a present of a little dog'. Though the suffix -онка usu. expresses contempt, собачонка is not derog. here, but affect., with a touch of coarseness.

68f. Родная сестра тому кобелю, 'A sister of that dog'. The qualifier родной is sometimes used to distinguish a brother or sister from a cousin (двоюродный); cf. I.1.36. The dat. of relationship has been replaced in the case of nouns by the gen. or a poss. adj., but is still used with a pron., as in он мне родня и приятель, 'he's a relative and friend of mine' (IV.6.29).

70f. мне роскошь, 'I'm in clover', lit. 'to me (there is) luxury'. The noun serves here as an impers. subject.

71. травлю зайцев. A subtle satirical point was being made in showing the Judge to be fond of hare-coursing; a phrase commonly used by law officials anxious to get rid of inconvenient persons and cases was гони зайца дальше, 'chase the hare away'. The connection between the law and hares would not be lost on 19th-century audiences. G. took his cue here from Kapnist, who makes the association explicit when referring to a law-court member in *Ябеда*, I.1:

> Товарищ же его до травли русаков
> Охотник страстной: с ним со сворой добрых псов
> И сшедшую с неба доехать правду можно.

72. Батюшка, 'My dear fellow'. Some editions have pl. Батюшки ('Good heavens!'), this being what G. actually wrote in his printed copy of R3 when preparing the final text, but it was probably a *lapsus calami*. The sing. makes better sense. Cf. I.3.111f.

72f. не милы мне теперь ваши зайцы, 'I have no liking for (i.e. I don't want to hear about) your hares just now'.

73. у меня инкогнито проклятое сидит в голове, 'this damned incognito is preying on my mind'.

73f. Так и ждёшь, 'You keep expecting'. Cf. I.1.93.

74. The end of the Governor's speech was given much greater dramatic impact by G.'s stylistic changes. R1: и входит ревизор is explicit, unemotional; R2: и войдёт он сам avoids the dreaded word ревизор; R3: и войдёт... suppresses the subject; R5: и — шасть replaces the neutral verb 'to enter' with the vigorous, highly coll. шасть. The latter, a verb form of the same type as хвать (I.1.17), signifies the sudden appearance or arrival of a person in the past, but here the p.t. is used expressively for the fut., as in я пошёл, 'I'm off'.

Scene 3

5. что такое? 'what is it?' (Irish Eng. 'what is it at all?'). When used with another pron., такой imparts to it a slight emphasis. Thus Куда такое он пошёл? 'Where ever has he gone?' Cf. II.4.26; III.9.25; V.1.62.

13. вы уж и слога такого не имеете, 'you just haven't the right sort of style'. In this use такой contrasts with не такой, 'the wrong sort of'.

14. вы собьётесь [sc. **с толку**], 'you'll get muddled up' or 'you'll lose the thread'.

16f. Уж не мешайте, 'Just don't interfere'. The emphatic pcle. уж here expresses irritation.

17. пусть (= дайте) я расскажу, 'let me tell it'. The use of пусть with a 1st pers. subject, to express a desire, is rare. Cf. Pushkin, *Каменный гость*, 3: О пусть умру сейчас у ваших ног. . .

18. сделайте милость, 'be so kind (as to)': a formal expression much less used nowadays than in the 19th century, but not obs., *pace* Ozhegov.

21. У меня сердце не на месте, 'My heart is in my mouth'.

25f. я всё по порядку [sc. **расскажу**], 'I'll tell it all from the beginning (lit. in order)'.

27. Изволить served as an auxiliary of respect, imparting a note of deference to the main verb, like the Eng. 'to deign' or 'be pleased'. Sometimes it is best rendered by using 'graciously' or 'pray' or 'sir'. Nowadays it is used with ironic disapproval or for comic effect.

28. The pcle. -с, known as словоер, is an abbreviation of сударь, 'sir', or сударыня, 'madam', that was much used by the gentry, officials and esp. servants, when addressing superiors. Its use declined in the latter part of the 19th century and today it is employed only in a mocking or facetious fashion, like изволить. The excessively polite Bobchinsky makes liberal use of it.

так, like то and тогда, is used as a correlative conj. to introduce a main clause following a subordinate one. Eng. has either 'then' or, more often, no correlative.

31. заставши. In the first half of the 19th century past gerunds in -вши were as common as those in -в, but thereafter the shorter suffix gained ascendancy and is now accounted the standard literary form, -вши being considered coll. In G.'s works the -вши form preponderates, whereas Pushkin used the -в form almost exclusively.

34. идучи: now arch. and pop. for идя, but in G.'s time this and several other pres. gerunds in -учи, such as живучи and гуляючи, were used in literary Russ. without any of the folksiness associated today with all such forms, exc. будучи.

40. -та is an obs. and dial. form of the pcle., or article suffix, -то. Cf. чиновник-та (I.91).

42. услыхали. The old-fashioned pl. of respect arose in the 18th century when, under the influence of Fr. *vous*, вы came to be widely used as a polite sing. By analogy with this, peasants began to use они for он or она and a pl. verb with a sing. subject when referring to their social superiors, a practice which spread even among some of the gentry. In the play this pl. is used only by Bobchinsky (cf. I.66) and Dobchinsky (III.2.33f. & 60). Nowadays its use is rare and facetious.

Авдотья, a common peasant woman's name before the Revolution, is a coll. form of Евдокия, 'Eudoxia'.

44. Почечуев: a real surname, derived from pop. почечуй, 'piles', 'haemorrhoids'.

48f. с Петром-то Ивановичем. Observe the coll. use of enclave, i.e. the insertion of a pcle. or other word in a normally inseparable word combination, such as the имя-отчество. Cf. государственный-то совет (III.7.10f.).

49. энтого: pop. = этого, here used in the sense of filler того (see I.1.59). Cf. энтакий for такой (V.5.19).

52. трактир (obs.) is used here, and elsewhere in the play, in the sense of 'inn' or 'hostelry', without the pejorative connotation of a cheap, low-class establishment it later acquired.

53. желудочное трясение, 'stomach rumbling (lit. quaking)' or 'collywobbles', for which the usual Russ. is урчание в желудке.

55f. только что мы [вошли] в гостинипу. Cf. I.1.44.

58. недурной наружности, 'of passable appearance'. G. gives the same general description of his other chief hero, Chichikov, at the beginning of *Мёртвые души*, thus likening him and Khlestakov in their exterior ordinariness.

59. в партикулярном платье (obs.), 'in civilian clothes'.

62. рассуждение here has the obs. meaning of рассудительность, 'good sense', 'sound judgement'.

64f. здесь что-нибудь неспроста, 'there's something here not all it seems': much the same meaning as что-нибудь недаром (I.1.41f.). In the context of the play an apt translation would be 'I smell a rat', esp. since the Governor's account of his dream about rats in Sc. 1 is preceded by the identical words: 'I had a kind of foreboding'.

65. мигнул пальцем, 'winked a finger': a humorous hybrid of кивнул пальцем, 'beckoned', and мигнул глазом, 'winked'. Cf. G.'s use of моргнуть усом, 'to wink (i.e. twitch) one's moustache' in *Шинель* and other tales.

69. спроси. The imp. sing. is used idiomatically to express a sudden or impulsive action in the past. But here, as V. Gofman points out, спроси and отвечай on l.71 are merely provincial speech mannerisms and mean no more than спросил, отвечал. An example of an authentic impulsive imp. is схвати (IV.11.49).

73. вы пришепётываете, 'you have a slight lisp'. The verb does not signify an Eng. lisp ('th' for 's' or 'z'), but a tendency to шепелявить, i.e. to pronounce с and з as, or very like, ш and ж respectively. The reverse speech defect or affectation is denoted by the verb сюсюкать.

76. фамилия, 'surname': a comic error for имя. Cf. *Иван Фёдорович*

Шпонька и его тётушка, II: фамилия моя Григорий Григорьевич Сторченко.

78. себя аттестует (obs.), 'commends himself'. By taking this to mean 'behaves', previous editors and translators have missed the ironic humour.

78f. другую уж неделю живёт, 'he's been living (here) for over a week now', lit. 'lives the second week'. This sense of другой is found in на другой день, 'on the next (sc. after the first) day'.

79. на счёт (obs.), 'on credit' or 'on tick'.

81. а меня так вот свыше и вразумило, 'all of a sudden it just came to me out of the blue', lit. 'I was made to understand from above'. The conj. 'a' here has the force of вдруг, and так is to be taken with и, i.e. as так и, in the emphatic sense of 'just', 'simply' (cf. I.102), not to be confused with так и, 'continually' (cf. I.1.93).

83ff. By arguing as to who said 'Ah!' before whom, Bobchinksy and Dobchinsky are vying for the honour of having first discerned in Khlestakov the expected inspector. Their dispute has given rise to the expression Кто раньше сказал «Э!», used to describe an argument over some trivial point.

87. А с какой стати сидеть ему здесь. . . ? 'Now what reason could he have for staying here . . .?' Cf. I.1.95.

87f. дорога ему лежит в Саратовскую губернию, 'he is bound for Saratov province'.

92. Нотиция: obs. = извещение, 'notification', 'notice'.

93. Что вы! 'What are you saying!' A very common exclamation of shocked surprise or disbelief.

господь с вами! 'bless your life!' i.e. you must be mistaken. The phrase expresses a friendly protest or gentle correction.

96. Кому же б быть, как не ему? 'Who else could it be but him?' Cf. I.1.95.

подорожная [грамота]. This was an official travel document issued in Russia from the 15th century and was required by law for journeys by post-chaise. The document bore the stamp of the imperial eagle and stated the bearer's name, rank and destination, also whether he was travelling in a private or official capacity. It entitled the holder to request a coach and driver and a specified number of horses, depending on his rank, and indicated which kind, ordinary post-horses (почтовые) or express (курьерские). See IV.9.37f.

102. к нам serves as a coll. equivalent of наши, qualifying a noun in the acc. after в, just as у + gen. does duty for a poss. adj. when the noun stands in the prepl. after в. Cf. I.1.91.

Меня так и проняло страхом, 'I was absolutely petrified with fear'. In some editions this is preceded by the words Такой осмотрительный, the adj. meaning here not 'circumspect', but 'observant'. It may have been removed as incorrect usage.

106f. прошлого года: obs. = в прошлом году, 'last year'. The gen. of time was more widely used in older Russ. than in the language of today, where it is confined to expressions of date and a few adverbial forms such as третьего дня, 'the day before yesterday', and сегодня, 'today', lit. 'of this day'.

109f. Приехал на [день святого] Василья Египтянина, 'He arrived on the feast of St. Basil the Egyptian'. Feast-days, denoted simply by the name of the saint they honoured, were then a common way of referring to the time of some event. The saint alluded to here, however, is rather obscure. No Basil the Egyptian is found in the Orthodox Church calendar, but feasts of other saints belonging to the universal church were sometimes celebrated in Russia. Of all the Basils in the church canon only one appears to fit the description 'Egyptian', namely the St. Basil who was martyred at Alexandria under Septimius Severus in 202 A.D., together with the better-known St. Leonides. The two saints share the same feast-day, 22 April, according to the Gregorian calendar, i.e. 4 May by the older Julian calendar used in Russia until the Revolution.

111f. Батюшки, сватушки! 'Ye godfathers and godmothers!' or 'Saints alive!' Батюшки, lit. '(Holy) fathers', a common expression of surprise, is here expanded into a rhyming exclamation by adding the pl. of сватушка, a dim. of сват, 'father of one's son- or daughter-in-law'.

112. Выносите, 'Deliver (us)': obs. sense. Cf. I.123 and IV.3.3.

угодники [божьи] = угодные богу, 'those pleasing to God', i.e. 'holy men', 'saints'. The adj. богоугодный, 'charitable', has the same origin.

114. На улицах кабак, нечистота! 'The streets are a pigsty, filth (everywhere)!' Кабак ('tavern', 'pot-house') derives its fig. sense from the fact that such establishments were often dirty and disorderly.

114f. поношенье (obs.), 'disgrace', 'ignominy'.

117. парадом: not 'in a body', 'all together', as some have taken it to mean, but 'with full ceremony', 'in full-dress uniform', i.e. в полном параде (cf. IV.1.3). This is borne out by R2 and 3, where Zemlyanika says: нам теперь поскорей одеться в мундиры и сей же час ехать к нему в гостиницу.

119. Голова: 'mayor', chief elected representative of the town's merchants, manufacturers etc. Catherine's Charter of 1785 had introduced a measure of local self-government, whereby town-dwellers elected a mayor and council every three years. But the councils proved ineffectual bodies; real power lay with the governor and his fellow-officials.

119f. «Деяния Иоанна Масона». This refers to *Self-Knowledge, a Treatise*, by John Mason, an English nonconformist preacher. Published in 1745, the book had an instant success and was soon translated into other European languages. A Russian translation was published in 1783 by the Novikov Press at Moscow University. No doubt the fact that it was translated by I. P. Turgenev, a prominent freemason and friend of Novikov, and that its author's name could be read as 'John the Mason', led G. to assume that it was some manual of masonic rites, while in reality it consists of moralistic essays thickly interspersed with didactic utterances of ancient and medieval writers.

In R2 and 3 the Judge's reference to the clergy is made clearer in the words: Недурно бы тоже и священство. Это имеет глубокое и тайное значение.

121. позвольте уж мне самому [**это обделать**, as in R2 and 3], 'let me handle this', or 'just leave it to me'.

122. сходили [sc. **благополучно**], 'they passed off all right'.

123. Авось бог вынесет [**меня**], 'Perhaps (with any luck) God will deliver me'. The word авось expresses the optimistic side of the fatalism that was long regarded as part of the Russian national character. The Governor is a typical fatalist. Cf. II.8.66f.

128f. The Governor is aware that there was emerging a new breed of highly-placed young officials, including some inspectors, but being young they could be easily duped. Saltykov-Shchedrin later dubbed them государственные младенцы ('babes of the state'). See V. Shklovsky, *Заметки о прозе русских классиков*, 1953, pp. 123–4, and *Повести о прозе*, Vol. 2, 1966, pp. 118–20.

129f. весь наверху, 'all on the surface', i.e. easily seen through, an open book. An idiosyncratic usage; the normal Russ. for this is весь наружу or весь виден.

130. приготовляйтесь по своей части, 'make things ready in your own department'.

131. хоть here means 'if you like', 'perhaps'.

134. Что [**вам**] **угодно?** 'What can I do for you?' lit. 'What is pleasing to you?' A common formula.

135. Ступай, 'Off you go'. This imp. of dismissal, used mainly to subordinates, is generally more familiar and categorical than иди. Only the impf. has this meaning.

137. чтобы как можно поскорее ко мне [**прислали**], 'to send me as quickly as possible'. The illit. mixture of поскорее and как можно скорее, which both have the same meaning, is characteristic of the Governor's racy coll. style.

140. Идём, 'Let us go'. With verbs of going the 1st pers. pl. pres., as well as fut. pf., is used to express the imp. Cf. едем I.5.40 & 53).

143. надел, '(once you've) put on'. In Eng. the imp. would be more appropriate here.

да и концы в воду, 'and none will be the wiser'. This expression is said to have arisen in the time of Ivan the Terrible, when citizens of Novgorod suspected of treason were thrown into the R. Volkhov with a stone tied round their necks so that their remains (концы) were hidden or buried in the water. Hence also спрятать (or хоронить) концы в воду, 'to cover one's tracks'.

144. Какое колпаки! 'Nightcaps indeed!' Какое, as a coll. adv., expresses indignant rejection of what has just been said, like Eng. '. . . my foot (*or* my eye)!' Какой is similarly used, as at III.1.17.

145. габерсуп: from *Habersuppe*, a dial. form of Ger. *Hafersuppe*, 'oatmeal soup', a kind of gruel given to invalids.

146. несёт такая капуста, 'there's such a smell of cabbage'. Loose coll. usage; in this impers. use нести properly takes the instr. Cf. I.1.117.

G's distaste for the smell of cooked cabbage is expressed elsewhere, e.g. *Записки сумасшедшего*: Я терпеть не люблю капусты, запах которой валит из всех мелочных лавок в Мещанской.

что береги только нос, 'that you just have to hold (lit. look after) your nose'. The imp. sing. is used idiomatically to express an action one is constrained to perform.

150f. на судейском стуле, 'on the bench': an old-fashioned expression.

151f. только рукой махну, 'I just throw up my hands (in despair)', lit. 'I just wave my hand': fut. pf. freq. This gesture of resignation or dismissal is a downward sweep of the right hand away from the body, accompanied by a slight leftward movement of the head.

Most judges in Russia at that time knew little of the law, having had no legal training, and merely signed the papers prepared for them by the clerk of the court. Indeed, Lyapkin-Tyapkin is among the minority of judges in being actually literate.

152. Solomon, king of Israel in the 10th century B.C., was noted for his wisdom and judgement.

154f. G. omitted Dr. Hiebner from the list of those who leave at the end of this scene.

Scene 4

3. дрожки: a low, four-wheeled open carriage used in summer. It was drawn by one horse and carried two passengers, who sat on a long narrow bench, their feet resting on lateral bars. The word also denotes a hackney carriage or cab, and since this is the sense attached to the anglicized form 'droshky', the latter is not appropriate here.

10. только is here a pcle. that emphasizes да.

12f. мертвецки [пьян], 'dead drunk'.

When an actor named Prokhorov was missing at a rehearsal for the first production of the play, Sosnitsky (the *gorodnichy*), upon enquiring where he had got to, was told that he was having one of his drinking bouts. After that G. replaced Knut, the original name of his drunken policeman, with that of the actor, who thereby achieved a modest measure of immortality.

16. скорее, 'quickly', lit. 'more quickly'. The comp. adv. occasionally corresponds to an Eng. positive adv. When used with imp. force it is best rendered by a verb, e.g. скорее! 'hurry!' (I.6.35), or sometimes a noun, e.g. смелее! 'courage!' (IV.3.33f.).

17. слышь! 'd'you hear!' A pop. allegro form, i.e. contraction in rapid speech, of слышишь.

23. я так, 'I'll manage' or 'I'll be all right'. Cf. II.10.25.

петушком, lit. 'like a cockerel': Bobchinsky means to say пешком, 'on foot'. From this *lapsus linguae* петушком, used with a verb of motion, has acquired the meaning 'meekly', 'subserviently', e.g. Saltykov-Shchedrin, *Помпадуры и помпадурши*: В первый раз в жизни я шёл «рядом» с начальником, а не следом за ним «петушком». But where this influence is not present петушком means the opposite, i.e. 'swaggering' or 'strutting', cock-like.

24f. Мне бы только... посмотреть, 'I'd just like to take a look'. The бы construction is here optative.

28. Десятские: guards or constables chosen by the men of ten households in a town to be responsible to the local police for order there. In the countryside peasant десятские were responsible to сотские, who looked after a hundred houses. Both names date from pre-Petrine times.

29f. купчишка (coll. derog. dim. of купец), 'miserable merchant' or 'dog of a merchant'.

31. народ: here in the coll. sense of 'lot', 'bunch' (of people). Cf. II.8.53; V.1.19; V.8.137f.

34. вымели бы = чтобы вымели, 'they are to sweep'. Cf. I.1.67f.

There was a statutory obligation on local authorities to have the streets swept every Saturday, a duty apparently more honoured in the breach than the observance, since Russian provincial towns were generally very dirty and littered with rubbish.

36. кумаешься = кумишься [sc. **с купцами**], 'you get friendly (with merchants)'. The verb, from meaning 'to become related by compaternity, i.e. by standing godfather (кум) or godmother (кума) to one's child', developed the sense 'to establish close relations through sponsorship' and hence 'to get on friendly terms with'. The form used here comes from Ukr. куматися, where Russ. has кумиться, – an error surprisingly not corrected by Prokopovich.

36f. крадёшь в ботфорты, 'you steal (by slipping things) into your boots'.

37f. у меня ухо востро! 'I have sharp eyes (lit. a sharp ear)!' Вострый is an arch. form of острый, with prosthetic в- (cf. восемь and obs. осемь).

38. Что ты сделал с купцом Черняевым — а? 'What was that trick you played on the merchant Chernyayev – eh?'

40. не по чину берёшь! 'you take more than your rank allows!' These words, probably the most famous in the play, have become proverbial, though they are usually associated with bribe-taking, whereas in context they plainly refer to straightforward appropriation. Sometimes they are quoted humorously in a more general sense to mean: 'you are getting above yourself!'. The philosopher H. Bergson cites them in his classic work *Le Rire* (1900) as revealing 'une organisation morale de l'immoralité'.

Scene 5

3. Note that the Governor addresses the superintendent as вы, but uses the familiar ты to the police sergeants.

На что это похоже? 'What sort of way is that to behave?'

13f. Пожарная труба (obs.), 'fire-engine'. At that time the police also served as firemen.

18. бог его знает, 'God knows'. In this and similar expressions, such as чёрт его (or их) знает, the pron. object stands for 'it' or anticipates the subject to follow. Cf. II.30f. and II.6.52.

20. возвратился пьян. In the first half of the 19th century an adj. serving as a complement to a verb stood in the short form, whereas today it is put in the long form, nom. or instr.

23. для благоустройства, 'for (i.e. to give an appearance of) good order' (obs. sense of noun).

разметать, '(pull down and) scatter the pieces about'. This verb, then in coll. use to describe the dismantling of a fence or hut (i.e. a plank structure), was substituted by G. for the earlier развалить. A similar verb of double action is перебрать, 'to dismantle and rebuild'.

25. соломенную веху: not a straw marker, but a wooden stake with a wisp of straw attached at the top, used as a landmark. Cf. *Повесть о том, как поссорился Иван Иванович с Иваном Никифоровичем*, VII: везде стояли шесты с привязанным вверху пуком соломы: производилась какая-то планировка!

26. ломки, '(of) breaking', i.e. demolitions.

28. навалено на сорок телег всякого сору, 'there's forty cart-loads of all kinds of rubbish piled up', lit. 'rubbish (enough) for forty carts'. The number 40 is purely conventional, as in many Russ. folk sayings, e.g. Мороз — сорок пудов на воз (i.e. there's a very heavy frost).

28f. Что это за скверный город! 'What a rotten town this is!' The construction что за, a calque of Ger. *was für*, is a coll. equivalent of какой.

29. только... поставь = стоит (только) поставить, 'you have only to put up'. This modality of the imp. sing. expresses sufficient cause for some consequence to follow.

31. откудова: pop. = откуда, 'where . . . from'.

32. Служба. In Muscovy the word was used in a collective sense to mean 'servitors', hence in later military parlance 'soldiers', and in the civilian sphere 'the police', as here.

33. Всем довольны, 'No complaints'. Privates in the Russian army were trained at that time to reply in unison with these words when an inspecting officer enquired about their welfare. So mechanical were their responses that when a general with a sense of humour once asked some soldiers: "Do your commanders feed you on sugar cakes?" the men promptly chorused: "They do, your Excellency". See M. O. Gershenzon, *Эпоха Николая I*, 1910, p. 94.

33f. ваше благородие, 'your Honour', a translation of *Euer Wohlgeboren*; all terms of address in the tsarist civil service were modelled on Ger. originals. G. erred here in putting the title used to address officers and officials of the 9th and lower grades, since an inspector would have the rank of general and be called 'your Excellency' (see quotation above).

36f. Дай только, боже, чтобы сошло [мне] с рук, 'God grant (*or* Please God) I come through this safely' or 'get away with this', lit. 'get it off my hands'.

37f. а там-то я поставлю уж такую свечу, '*then* I'll put up *such* a candle'. The pcles. -то and уж emphasize там and такую respectively.

The Governor speaks of setting up a candle in church before an image of his patron saint Antony, in thanksgiving for a safe deliverance. Some of the candles used were indeed gigantic, "thick enough to be placed as pillars in the façade of a temple", according to J. G. Kohl, *Russia*, 1844, p. 58.

39. бестию купца, 'rogue of a merchant' or 'rascally merchant'. Appositional compound nouns, much commoner in Russ. than in Eng., are usu. rendered by expressing the second noun as a dependent poss., e.g. гусь помещик, 'ass of a landowner' (II.5.16), or by making one noun into an adj., e.g. сосед-помещик, 'neighbouring landowner' (II.5.9), старик отец, 'old father' (II.8.129).

41. бумажный футляр [от шляпы]: obs. = картонка для шляпы, 'hat-box'. In making the Governor almost don the box G. introduced a comic touch very similar to one used earlier in *Сорочинская ярмарка*, VIII: А Черевик, как будто облитый горячим кипятком, схвативши на голову горшок вместо шапки, бросился к дверям. . .

44f. Коробка так коробка, 'The box so it is'. Так, as a conj. of consequence, is used between two occurrences of the same word or phrase to express a strong affirmation.

45–8. The reference to the hospital chapel that never got built through misappropriation of the funds provided for it no doubt put G.'s contemporaries in mind of the scandal over the unfinished Church of Christ the Saviour in Moscow. The building of this enormous edifice, designed to commemorate Russia's victory over Napoleon, was abandoned in 1832 after the discovery of abuses which cost the treasury an estimated 580,000 roubles. The members of the building commission were dismissed and the architect, A. L. Vitberg, unjustly charged with embezzlement, was exiled. This affair is alluded to in *Мёртвые души*, XI.

51–3. Derzhimorda's method of keeping public order is a perfect illustration of кулачная расправа ('fist-law').

55. безо всего, 'without everything', i.e. 'with nothing on', a military type of exaggeration for 'improperly dressed'.

гарниза = гарнизонщина, 'scurvy garrison troops'. The word гарнизон, from Fr. *garnison*, was used from the beginning of the 18th century and the derivative гарниза, according to earlier dictionaries stressed on the last syllable, may have arisen under the influence of collective nouns of the type беднота ('the poor') or may have been a slang 'hellenized' variant used by seminarists and others acquainted with Greek.

55–7. To keep cool while working in hot weather Russian peasants often wore a knee-length shirt and boots, but no trousers. Soldiers followed the same practice, but were required to wear full uniform when appearing in public. This reference to the soldiers going about trouserless makes clear, incidentally, that the play is set in late spring or summer. Other indications are the Governor's use of his дрожки (see I.4.3) and the fact that in Sc. 6 Anna leans out of a window, which would not be possible in winter when windows in Russia are fitted with an extra frame and kept firmly shut.

Scene 6

4. Антоша: affect. dim. of Антон.

5. всё ты [виновата], 'it's all your fault'. This pregnant use of всё, arising from an ellipse, occurs also at I.15.

за тобой: obs. = из-за тебя, 'because of you'. This use of за in a causal sense is now confined to a few stock phrases such as за старостью лет, 'through old age'.

пошла копаться, '(you) started to rummage about'.

6. Я булавочку, я косынку [хочу or **достану]**, 'I want (*or* I'm going to get) a pin, a scarf'.

7. с усами! Despite the punctuation, a question, as indicated in R2. Anna wishes to know whether the visitor is a military man, since 'anything martial or military, it is well known, greatly appeals to women' (*Мёртвые души*, VIII). Only army officers, acting or retired, were then allowed to wear moustaches, and from 1837 were actually ordered to do so. Civilian officials, by contrast, were required to be clean-shaven and were sometimes referred to as безусые ('the moustacheless ones').

9. матушка, 'my dear', lit. 'mother dear'. Like мать (моя), this dim. form was formerly used as a fam. term of address, just as батюшка ('father') was used to a man, without signifying blood relationship (cf. I.2.72). Many kinship terms (бабушка, брат, дед, дядя, тётя) are still used to address people other than relatives.

10. Вот новости! 'What next!' or 'Did you ever?' A common expression of surprise and displeasure, like Вот ещё! (II.8.41).

12f. Я тебе вспомню это! 'You won't forget this!' The usual verb in this expression is припомню.

13. А всё эта [говорит], 'And this one keeps on saying'.

Маменька. In G.'s time маменька and папенька were used by children of the gentry as affect., respectful terms of address to their parents. Nowadays the usual affect. forms of мама and папа are мамочка, папочка and мамаша, папаша.

14. Вот тебе и сейчас! 'So much for your straight away!' The formula вот тебе и... expresses strong displeasure at some turn of events, esp. the failure of something to happen.

16f. и давай пред зеркалом жеманиться, 'and started mincing before the looking-glass'. Colloquially, давай + inf. expresses the inception of an action in the past.

17f. Note the disparaging use of 3rd instead of 2nd pers. forms in addressing or referring to someone who is present (Maria).

22f. покорнейше благодарю, 'thank you very much', lit. 'I most humbly thank you': a common formula, here used ironically. Cf. благодарю покорно (II.8.45).

23. Вот одолжила ответом! 'That's a fine answer to give!'

26f. Глупая какая! 'The stupid girl!' The long form of the adj. often has the force of a noun. Cf. Какой приятный! 'What a nice man!' (III.8.2).

27. Машет руками? All translators take this to mean that the Governor is waving Avdotya aside or good-bye, but this cannot be so since he has already driven off (see l.12). The sense is made clear in R1–2, where the housekeeper herself says she has approached a police officer to question him, but 'all he does is flail his arms about like a mad thing' (руками только машет, как угорелый).

27f. ты всё бы таки его расспросила, 'you should still have questioned him', i.e. the police officer. The pcle. бы here gives the verb a sense of hypothetical or 'retrospective' advice (as on l.29) and всё should be taken with таки, i.e. as всё-таки, 'all the same'.

28f. В голове [у неё] чепуха, всё женихи сидят, 'Her head is full of nonsense, – all she thinks of is men', i.e. prospective husbands. For сидеть в голове, 'to preoccupy one's mind', cf. I.2.73.

34. сию же минуту, 'this very instant', 'instantly'.

возвращайся назад. The adv., though redundant, is often used with this verb.

ACT II

Scene 1

1. постеле: from постеля, an obs. and pop. form of постель.

4. да и только: a coll. parenthesis, here with the intensifying sense 'for sure', whereas at III.9.21 it has its primary, restrictive sense, synonymous with только и всего, 'and that's all'.

4f. Что ты прикажешь делать? 'What can you do?' lit. 'What will you have me do?' The 2nd pers. forms of приказать often express a wish, rather than a command.

5. Второй месяц пошёл, как уже [уехали], 'It's over a month now since we left'. For пойти in the coll. sense 'to begin' cf. I.1.35f.

Питер is coll. for 'Petersburg', being an abbreviation of (Санкт) Питербурх, the original form of the name.

5f. Профинтил (pop.), 'He's squandered' or 'frittered away'.

7. хвост подвернул, fig. 'he has drawn in his horns', lit. 'tucked in his tail'.

стало бы [денег], 'there'd have been enough (money)'. Стать is used here impersonally in the coll. and arch. sense 'to suffice'. Cf. II.3.4.

8. прогоны = прогонные [деньги], obs. for 'fare (paid for a journey by post-chaise)', from прогон, 'post-stage'. The sing. is used in the same sense at IV.9.38.

вишь ты, 'look you' or 'you see'. It is not certain whether the coll. form вишь is a contraction of видишь or comes from Old Russ. imp. sing. вижь, 'see'.

9. дразнит: here coll. for передразнивает, 'mimics'. Cf. III.11.7.

10. обед спроси самый лучший. Observe the word order, with the separation of the modifier from its noun, a device common in coll. Russ. Cf. I.28.

12. Добро бы было в самом деле что-нибудь путное, 'It would be all right if he really was somebody'. Here путный means 'amounting to something', 'of some merit'.

а то, 'but the fact is' or 'as it is', i.e. contrary to what has just been said.

13. елистратишка: a corr. of [коллежский] регистратор, 'collegiate registrar', the lowest (14th) grade in the Table of Ranks. This masterly derisive coinage, possibly suggested by the first name Елистрат, combines metathesis of 'r' and its replacement by 'l', both features of illit. Russ. speech, with the affective suffix -ишка.

14. картишки: usu. an affect. dim. of карты, but here derog. The effect of the contemptuous suffixes -ишка and -онка, which Osip is fond of using, can be conveyed in Eng. often only by tone of voice.

вот тебе и доигрался! 'now look where it's landed him!' i.e. he has lost all his money. Cf. I.6.14.

15. на деревне has a pop. flavour compared with standard в деревне.

16. публичности . . . заботности. Публичность is a high-flown way of saying 'the public', 'people', and заботность ('troublesomeness') is a pseudo-learned word meaning no more than заботы, 'worries'. Their use is characteristic of Osip, a peasant who has seen something of city life and tries to imitate the speech of educated people and their servants.

17. лежи. . . да ешь: imp. sing. forms used with modal force ('you can lie . . . and eat').

Полати (pl.): a broad plank bed placed high up in a peasant's hut between the stove and the adjacent wall.

18. если пойдёт на правду: pop. = если сказать правду, 'if the truth be told'.

19. Деньги бы только были, 'So long as you have money'. For the optative force of бы in the construction только бы ('if only') cf. I.4.24f.

20. политичная, 'polite': an obs., illit. usage.

кеятры: a pop. corr. of театры.

20f. собаки тебе танцуют. Performing dogs were a popular form of entertainment at fairs.

21. всё: neut. sing. in collective sense ('everyone').

23. Щукин [двор] was an open-air market situated next to the Большая Садовая. In 1862 it was destroyed by fire, together with the adjacent Apraksin Dvor. On this site now stands a large department store bearing the name of the latter market.

Почтенный! 'Honourable sir!' This obs. mode of address was polite in G.'s time, but later acquired a ring of familiarity in pop. speech.

24. на перевозе в лодке. The Neva was crossed at that time by ferry-boats and, in summer, by pontoon bridges. The first permanent bridge across the river was opened in 1850.

24f. [ты] компании захотел, '(if) it's company you want'. The pf. past is sometimes used colloquially instead of the pf. fut. in the first part of general statements, the construction of which is often paratactic, as here. Cf. Наскучило [тебе] идти — берёшь извозчика, 'if you're fed up with walking, you take a cab' (ll.31f.).

25. кавалер, lit. 'chevalier', 'knight of an order', hence 'a soldier awarded a decoration', and in obs. pop. speech just a polite term for 'soldier', as here.

26. лагери = лагеря, '(military) camps'. The pl. form in -и now has a fig. sense only.

объявит: illit. for объяснит, 'will explain'.

27f. офицерша, 'officer's wife'. Wives were referred to colloquially by the noun denoting their husband's profession, with the addition of -ша. Such titles are little used today, exc. facetiously, since the suffix -ша now forms nouns denoting a woman by her own profession.

28. горничная... такая. It is common practice to detach такой and какой from the noun they qualify. Cf. какое... право (II.8.29f.); такие... правила (IV.6.42).

29f. Галантерейное...обхождение! 'Gallantivanting (i.e. gallant) manners!' In coll. speech the adj. галантерейный, relating to галантерея, 'fancy goods', 'haberdashery', had earlier been misused for галантный, 'gallant', but this was the first time it had been employed with irony.

чёрт возьми. Note the enclave (cf. I.3.48).

31. всякой = всякий, 'anyone': a common spelling at that time, reflecting the older pronunciation of masc. nom. sing. endings (as -əj) still widely used then in pop. speech.

тебе говорят «вы». Osip, accustomed as a serf to being called ты, is flattered to be addressed in the polite pl. form.

32. берёшь извозчика, 'you take a cab (lit. cabby)'. Licensed cabmen, wearing numbered discs around their necks, had droshkies or, in winter, sledges for hire. Before taking one, it was necessary to make a bargain, as fares were not regulated by the authorities.

сидишь себе, 'you sit at your ease'. The pron. form себе, used as a coll. pcle., conveys a sense of 'pleasing oneself', 'blithely unconcerned'. Cf. Pushkin, *Сказка о рыбаке и рыбке*:

> Ступай себе в синее море,
> Гуляй там себе в просторе.

34. сквозные ворота, 'gates of a communicating courtyard (сквозной двор)', i.e. one leading to the next street. Such yards, a notable feature of the apartment blocks in St. Petersburg, provided a convenient means of escaping from the cabman without paying one's fare. In R1 & 2 Osip says that his master cheats the cabmen (извозчиков надувает).

Шмыгнуть is the *mot juste* here, since it means 'to nip' or 'to slip' in a very precise sense, viz. in order to escape notice.

36. чуть не лопнешь с голоду, 'you nearly burst with hunger (fut. pf. freq.). Cf. Fr. *crever de faim*.

38. чем бы их попридержать, 'instead of hanging on to it (the money) for a bit'. The addition of по- ('for a little time') to already prefixed verbs is characteristic of coll. Russ. Cf. позаняться, 'to busy oneself for a while'.

39. и куды (obs. pop. = **куда**)**!** 'not on your life!' or 'not him!' In coll. Russ. куда and где are used in an exclamatory way to dismiss an idea as unlikely or absurd. They are constructed with the dat. and inf., e.g. Куда (or где) ему понять! 'How could he (be expected to) understand!'

пошёл кутить, 'off he goes (lit. he started) having a gay old time'. Here кутить does not mean 'to go on the spree', but refers to the fact that Khlestakov spent the money he was sent on riding around in cabs and visiting theatres.

40. ты доставай, 'you have to get'. For the imp. sing. of arbitrarily imposed action cf. береги (I.3.146).

41. глядь, 'lo and behold': a coll. shortened form of imp. гляди used as an interj.

толкучий [рынок], 'second-hand market' or 'flea-market', so called because of the jostling crowd there (cf. толкать, 'to shove' and толкотня, 'crush').

42. Спустить here means not 'to gamble away' (проиграть в азартные игры), as given in Ushakov's dictionary, but 'to sell off' (распродать), as on l.45.

43. сертучишка: derog. dim. of сертук, an obs. pop. variant of сюртук, 'frock-coat'. Today the spelling of this suffix is -ишко where the parent noun is masc. and inanimate, but -ишка where it is animate. In G.'s time the latter form was used in both cases.

шинелишка (derog. dim. of шинель), 'wretched overcoat'. See III.6.115f.

44. И сукно такое важное, аглицкое! 'And the cloth is such fine stuff – English!' This pop. sense of важный ('of good quality') occurs also at IV.9.21. The form áглицкий (cf. V.8.57) is an arch. variant of английский, also then stressed on the first syllable. It is now used only in a disparaging sense.

English cloth, which had the reputation of being the best in the world, was imported into Russia in considerable quantities at that time.

рублёв: obs. and coll. gen. pl.; cf. normal рублей (l.46).

45. ему... станет, 'will cost him'. The use of стать (в) + acc. in the sense 'to cost' is coll. and arch., surviving in only a few expressions, e.g. это мне станет в копеечку, 'it will cost me a pretty penny'; во что бы ни стало, 'at all costs'.

47. нипочём идут, 'they go for a song (lit. for nothing)'. Cf. почём (coll.), 'how much each or per standard unit of sale'.

Khlestakov's habit of selling his clothes to raise money was no doubt based on G.'s own experience of St. Petersburg, where the cost of living was high. In a letter to his mother, dated 1 September 1830, he wrote: Часто большие неудобства встречаются иногда от замедления [sc. денег], и тогда принуждён я бываю продавать за бесценок самонужнейшие вещи...

48. вместо того чтобы [идти] в должность, а он идёт гулять, 'instead of going to the office he goes for a stroll'. Note the illit. confusion of two constructions. To be correct, the sentence requires the deletion of the conj. 'а' or the replacement of the first part by some such words as ему следует в должность.

49. Прешпект is an obs. pop. corr. of проспект, 'avenue'. The с was changed to ш under Polish influence, as in пашпорт for паспорт; cf. эштафета (V.8.18). The avenue Osip refers to is evidently the famous

Nevsky Prospekt, since G. writes in his *Предуведомление*: Обрываемый и обрезываемый доселе во всём, даже и в замашке пройтись козырём по Невскому проспекту, он [Хлестаков] почувствовал простор...

50. Он не посмотрел бы на то, что... 'He wouldn't be put off by the fact that ...' This sense of the construction не посмотреть на, 'to disregard', is also found in the prep. несмотря на, 'regardless of', 'despite'.

51. таких бы [sc. **розог**] **засыпал тебе**, 'he would lay into you so hard', lit. 'with such strokes (of the birch)'.

52. б... ты почёсывался, 'you'd be rubbing yourself (every so often)', i.e. on the backside.

This part of Osip's speech, as V. Gippius points out, must have given offence to many contemporary spectators, who were accustomed to polite society comedies.

52f. Коли служить, так служи, 'If you've got a job to do, then do it', lit. 'if you are to serve, then serve' (the verb служить covers both military and civilian service). Osip is not speaking for himself, but quoting the words he imagines Khlestakov's father might use as he administers a thrashing.

53. теперь: here in the coll. sense 'just now (= a short while ago)', a meaning not given in Ushakov or the 17-vol. Academy Dictionary. Cf. III.10.13.

53f. сказал, что не дам (for **даст**) **вам есть.** The confusion of indirect with direct speech by the uneducated is a survival of earlier syntax. The substitution of 3rd for 1st pers. forms in indirect speech, not found in Old Russ., became normal only after the middle of the 18th century, under the influence of Latin and German.

54. за прежнее, 'for what you've had before'. The neut. form of the adj. is commonly substantivized, as in главное, 'the main thing'. Cf. другое, 'another matter' (II.8.58); пустое, 'a trifling matter' (IV.16.47); полезное, 'something useful' (V.2.23).

55f. хоть бы какие-нибудь щи! 'oh for some cabbage soup!' For the optative force of бы in хоть бы, 'if only', 'how I wish', cf. I.4.24f.

56. кажись: old imp. sing. used in pop. and dial. speech for кажется, 'it seems'. Cf. III.9.38; IV.10.29.

так бы... съел, 'I could eat'. Так бы expresses a strong desire to do something, так reinforcing the optative бы.

Scene 2

It was traditional for the hero of a comedy to make his entrance in the second act, as Khlestakov does here.

2. на: coll. interj., 'here, (take this)', used when handing something to a person. Cf. III.6.115.

On stage Khlestakov is often given not a фуражка ('peaked cap'), as indicated here, but a top hat, which he should have to be in fashion. See note on *Characters and Costumes*, l.26.

5. что ли? This question tag, here used rhetorically, expresses uncertainty or (mock) surprise, having much the same sense as разве, 'perhaps', 'is that so?'

6. склочена: incorrect for смята or искомкана, 'crumpled', an error (possibly deliberate), pointed out by F. Bulgarin, a contemporary critic. The verb склочить is a pop. variant of всклочить, 'to tousle', 'dishevel', i.e. it strictly applies to hair only.

7. Да на что мне она [sc. **нужна**]**?** 'What would I want with it now?' На что in the sense of зачем, 'for what purpose', is coll. Cf. На что ж хозяина [позвать]? 'What d'you want to call the landlord for?' (l.44).

11. Картуз, 'paper bag': obs. sense.

12. Да где ж ему быть, табаку? 'Now how could there be – tobacco?' For this use of где see II.1.39, and for the dat. with быть cf. I.3.96.

12f. четвёртого дня (obs.), 'three days ago': like the still current третьего дня, a relic of the old gen. of time (see. I.3.106f.).

17. Чего изволите? 'Yes, sir?' lit. 'What do you wish?' This phrase, used mainly by servants, is a little more ingratiating than Что угодно? (cf. I.3.134).

23. чтобы мне дали пообедать, 'to give me some lunch'. Note that a verb, rather than a noun, is often used in reference to meals. Cf. Ему принесли завтракать, 'His breakfast was brought'.

24. Да нет, 'Oh, no'. Да is here emphatic.

26. Да так, 'Well, I do (dare)', i.e. I just won't go.

26f. ничего из этого не будет, 'nothing will come of it' or 'it won't do any good'.

29f. Вот ещё вздор! 'What nonsense!' Here ещё is an intensive pcle. The word вздор, like дурак, is frequently on Khlestakov's lips.

32. The landlord is quoted here as saying that Khlestakov was staying at the inn 'for the third week' (третью неделю), but at I.3.78f. as saying 'for the second week' (другую неделю), a discrepancy G. overlooked when making textual changes.

пло́тит (for пла́тит): a common pronunciation of the Moscow region, arising from аканье, by analogy with verbs which have a stress shift in the pres. tense from the ending in the 1st pers. sing. to the stem vowel 'o' in the other forms, e.g. ношу́ (pronounced нашу́), но́сит. Cf. IV.9.38; V.8.214.

Вы-де. The pop. enclitic pcle. де, a contracted form of дѣет, 3rd pers. sing. of Old Russ. дѣяти, 'to say', is used to indicate that the speaker is quoting someone else's words. The other pcles. of citation are дескать and мол.

34. Широмыжник is a variant of шаромыжник = шаромыга, 'sponger', 'cheat'. In pop. etymology the word was derived from the phrase *cher ami*, used by French soldiers begging for food and shelter during the retreat from Moscow in 1812 (hence the spellings шерамыга, широмыга). In fact it was formed by adding the suffix -ыга to шаром, taken from the obs. expression шаром-даром, 'at another's expense'.

35. А ты уж и рад, 'And you are only too glad'. The pcle. уж conveys the speaker's annoyance here. Cf. I.3.16f.

37f. приедет, обживётся, задолжается: fut. pf. pot. Cf. I.1.152.

38. Я шутить не буду, 'I won't be trifled with' or 'I won't stand any nonsense'. Cf. III.6.144.

39f. Note the highly elliptical construction: я прямо [пойду к городничему] с жалобою, чтобы [увели вас] на съезжую, да [посадили] в тюрьму.

Съезжая [изба], lit. 'assembly hut', in the Muscovite period denoted 'the office of the town governor (воевода)', and in the 18th century 'a police-station', but in G.'s time it signified 'lock-up' or 'cells'.

44. поди: coll. = пойди, 'go'. Cf. III.2.81; III.10.81; IV.13.8.

47. чёрт с тобой! here expresses grudging consent mingled with annoyance: 'very well then, damn you!'

Scene 3

2. ужасно как хочется [мне] есть! 'I'm awfully hungry!' The word как, pronounced without stress, is used with the adv. ужасно in the same way as with the adverbialized nouns ужас, смерть. Cf. I.2.39.

2ff. Note the play on the verb пройти(сь): прошёлся... пройдёт... не проходит.

4. Penza: a provincial capital some 380 m. south-east of Moscow.

Although G. does not name the town which forms the setting of the play, intending it to be seen as a fictional place, typical of provincial Russia, there are nevertheless clues to its location. Veresayev asserts that the play is set in Kursk, since this is the only town in Russia proper that the playwright had then observed at first hand, having been delayed there for a week in 1832 when his carriage broke down (see V. Veresayev, *Как работал Гоголь*, 1934, pp. 62–3). Kursk, however, was not a district town but a provincial capital, and it lies not on Khlestakov's route as given in the later versions, but on that given in R1, viz. from St. Petersburg via Tula to the area of Yekaterinoslav (now Dnepropetrovsk).

A. S. Dolinin notes that the original route corresponded to that taken by P. Svinyin (one of Khlestakov's possible prototypes) in the 1820s when he visited Bessarabia and posed there as an important official from the capital. Khlestakov's route was altered, Dolinin surmises, to tally with that taken by Pushkin when he journeyed to Pugachev country in 1833 and was suspected of being an inspector in disguise. It should be pointed out, however, that Pushkin travelled via Saratov and Penza only on his return journey.

In R2–5 Khlestakov's destination is given as Saratov province, whither he travels via Penza. The town where he is staying thus lies between Penza and Saratov, probably in Penza province, but is clearly off the main highway, since Bobchinsky asks why their visitor has stopped there when he is bound for Saratov province (see I.3.87f.). The district town which best fits this description is Chembar, now called Belinsky after the famous critic who lived there for many years. By a curious irony of history it was in Chembar that Russia's indefatigable chief inspector, Tsar Nicholas I, was laid up for a fortnight after breaking his collarbone when his coach overturned in the autumn of 1836, only a few months after he had attended the premiere of the play. He too had travelled from Penza.

5f. сильно поддел меня, 'took me in properly'.

6. штосы удивительно, бестия, срезывает, 'wins (lit. cuts the cards) amazingly at stoss, the rogue'. Штос (from Ger. *Stoss*) was a variation of faro, a card game fashionable among European upper classes in the 18th and 19th centuries.

6f. каких-нибудь четверть часа, 'only about a quarter of an hour'. The indefinite pron. какой-нибудь, when used with numerals, expresses approximation with an added sense of 'no more than'.

8. страх хотелось бы [мне], 'I'd have dearly loved'. For this use of страх see I.2.39.

9. Случай только не привёл [sc. **меня ещё с ним встретиться**], 'I just did not have the opportunity (to meet him again)'. Some editions have here: . . . не привёл встретиться — на всё нужно случай. This variant, not given in the Academy edition, may have crept in by error: it appears to be a corruption of the R3 wording (Впрочем, как же встретиться, на это всё нужно случай).

10. городишка, 'God-forsaken little town'. For the mod. spelling (-ишко) cf. II.1.43.

Овошенная лавка, generally taken to mean овощная лавка, 'green-grocer's shop', occurs in all versions of the text. G. sems to have used the form овошенный (possibly a dial. variant of овощной) deliberately; cf. his use of normal овощная лавка in *Мёртвые души*, VI. However, judging from Khlestakov's remark in R1 that he had done the rounds of such shops and sampled their sturgeon fillets and cheese (пробовал балыки и сыр), perhaps they should be understood as grocers' (бакалейные лавки), rather than greengrocers'.

11f. из «Роберта». The opera *Robert le Diable*, composed by Giacomo Meyerbeer, had its premiere in Paris in 1831 and was first performed in St. Petersburg in December 1834. A great success throughout Europe, it was much 'in the air' of the Russian capital at that time; cf. *Петербургские записки 1836 года*: До сих пор не прошёл тот энтузиазм, с каким бросился весь Петербург на... дикую, проникнутую адским наслаждением музыку «Роберта». Khlestakov, who is here whistling a tune from the opera, later claims to be its composer (see III.6.74).

12. «Не шей ты мне, матушка»: the first line of *Красный сарафан*, written by N. G. Tsyganov and set to music by A. E. Varlamov. Published in 1833, it soon became one of the most popular Russian songs of the day.

12f. ни сё ни то, 'neither one thing nor the other', i.e. something betwixt and between. Сё is the neut. sing. of the Old Russ. demonstrative pron. ('this'), whose original forms сь, ся, се were later lengthened to сей, сия, сие.

Scene 4

3. братец: like брат, in commoner use then than today as a friendly way of addressing a man, i.e. the equivalent of 'my friend' (to a stranger) or 'old man' (to an acquaintance). Cf. Khlestakov's use of both forms in III.6.61–77.

что ты...? 'how are you?' For this coll. use of что cf. III.6.67.

5. Слава богу, 'Quite well' or 'Can't complain'. This use of the common expression слава богу ('thank goodness', lit. 'glory to God') arises from the ellipse of здоров. Cf. IV.7.8.

11. любезный, 'my (good) man': an obs. familiar or patronizing mode of address to a social inferior. Cf. I.19; III.10.2; IV.9.60f.; IV.10.2.

12f. чтоб поскорее [sc. **мне принесли обед**]. For the absolute comp. ('as soon as possible') cf. I.3.137.

18. Да что ж жаловаться? 'But why on earth (should he) complain?'

19. как же [sc. **мне быть без обеда**, as in R2]**?**

27. сурьёзно: obs. = серьёзно. Cf. *Characters and Costumes*, I.3.

28. Деньги сами собой, 'The money is a separate matter', i.e. I must eat, money apart. Khlestakov is not promising to pay the landlord for his food, but asserting his right as a барин to be fed, whether he can pay or not.

29. ему... ничего, если не поесть день, 'he thinks nothing of missing food for a day'. Note the use of ничего as an impers. expression ('it does not matter').

31. Пожалуй, 'All right' or 'Very well' (expressing reluctant consent). Cf. I.1.104.

Scene 5

4. пустить в оборот, 'put on the market', lit. 'put into circulation'.

5. что ли...? 'or something?' Cf. II.2.5.

уж лучше, 'much better'. For уж as emphatic pcle. see I.1.45.

6. Иохим (or **Иоахим**): Russ. form of Ger. *Joachim*. Johann-Albert Joachim (1762–1834) was a coach-builder well known in St. Petersburg at that time. G. lived on the top floor of Joachim's house on the Большая Мещанская for a few months in 1829. There is a story that one day, when his landlord was dunning him for the rent, G., who was entertaining some fellow-writers at the time, got rid of him by saying: "Leave me alone, or I'll put you into a comedy". Significantly perhaps, one variant of R1 here reads проклятый Иохим.

7. хорошо бы, 'it would be nice'. The ellipse of было is common with impers. expressions used conditionally. Cf. I.1.189.

8. этаким чёртом, 'in grand style', lit. 'like such a devil'. In coll. Russ. чёртом is used as an adv. meaning 'dashingly', 'in a devil-may-care fashion'.

9f. с фонарями, 'with coach-lamps' – probably lit, even in daytime, in order to show off.

10. There is rich irony in the contrast between Khlestakov's fantasy and reality. He wishes to give the impression of being a rich gentleman who owns his own coach (in fact he uses a post-chaise) and with his manservant dressed in resplendent livery (whereas Osip actually wears a grimy frock-coat).

12. лакей, i.e. Osip. In the Academy edition, but in few others, this is followed by the phrase золотая ливрея, presumably a later addition.

14. прикажете принять? 'shall I show him in?' lit. 'do you wish to receive him?' For the use of приказать in this obs. formula cf. II.1.4f.

16f. так и валит... в гостиную, 'just barges . . . into the drawing-room'. Here валит = валится (as given in R2 and 3), i.e. 'goes tumbling or crashing'. Cf. III.11.3.

Khlestakov happily mixes his zoological metaphors, calling the typical country landowner first a гусь ('goose', fig. 'ass') and then a медведь ('bear', i.e. 'boor', 'oaf').

17. Дочечка, 'daughter dear', a second-stage dim. of дочь (via дочка).

Khlestakov's use of dim. forms in reference to women and their apparel is most evident in Act IV, Sc. 12.

18f. подшаркивает ножкой, 'scrapes his foot slightly' (at the thought of making up to a pretty daughter of some landowner).

19. Тьфу! An onomatopoeic interj. of disgust, imitating the sound of spitting. Its nearest Eng. equivalents are 'Pah!' and 'Ugh!'

Scene 6

2. А что? 'Well?' The same phrase also means 'What is it?', as at II.8.159.

4f. Note the force of the prefixes при-, expressing 'accompaniment' (прихлопывает, 'claps his hands as he speaks') and под-, denoting 'to a small degree' (подпрыгивает, 'bobs up and down').

8f. Я плевать на твоего хозяина! 'I don't give a damn about (lit. spit upon) your landlord!' The use of the nom., instead of the normal dat. subject with the inf., is quite common in this expression and gives it greater force. Cf. V.2.29f.

14. Этого мало, 'That's not enough'.

15. ещё много, 'it's too *much*'. Here ещё is an emphatic pcle., as in оно (= это) ещё ничего, 'it's no matter' (I.1.157). Cf. II.2.29f.

20. двое... человека: incorrect for два человека or двое мужчин. The two men in question are, of course, Bobchinsky and Dobchinsky (see I.3.99–102).

21. и ещё много кой-чего, 'and a great deal more besides'. Кой-что: pop. = кое-что, 'something' or 'some things'.

24. Да уж нет, 'There just *isn't*'.

26. для тех, которые почище-с, 'for the better class of customer, sir'. This meaning of почище derives from чистый in the obs. sense of 'socially superior', 'best' (of people).

34. Обнаковенно какие! 'The usual kind!' Обнаковенно is an illit. corr. of обыкновенно. Cf. III.10.23.

38. The critic Bulgarin, fastidiously objecting to G.'s use of the verb вонять ('to stink'), remarked that any self-respecting manservant would say (дурно) пахнуть instead. As Vyazemsky pointed out, however, it is not Osip but Khlestakov who uses вонять, a word no gentleman would hesitate to employ, even in the presence of ladies. Perhaps it was this exchange that prompted G. to observe, in *Мёртвые души*, VIII, that the provincial society ladies he satirizes there would never dream of saying этот стакан... воняет, but use some such euphemism as этот стакан нехорошо ведёт себя.

39. другого, 'some other (soup)': part. gen.

40. Мы примем-с, 'We'll take it away, sir'. For принять in this sense cf. I.1.103.

44. брат, 'my friend': here ironic. Cf. II.4.3.

со мной не советую [тебе шуток делать, as in R2], 'I advise you not to (try to be funny) with me'.

46. едал: from едать, coll. freq. form of есть, 'to eat'. Cf. I.1.18.

47. It is common practice in Russia for a portion of chicken or meat to be put in a serving of soup. Khlestakov is thus cutting at a piece of chicken in his soup, hence the feathers he complains of finding there.

61f. и даже хотя бы какой-нибудь соус или пирожное, 'and not even a fish course or dessert'. In this scene соус does not denote 'sauce' or 'gravy', as translators have rendered it, but is used in the obs. coll. meaning of 'entrée', a sense derived from the fact that the fish or meat in such a dish was served with a sauce (i.e. *pars pro toto*). This is borne out by Khlestakov's surprise at being offered only two courses (see l.11).

Scene 7

2f. только что разохотился, 'it's merely whetted my appetite', lit. 'I have only acquired a keen desire (for it)'. Usu. только что means 'only a moment ago', but here что, which is not translated, serves to focus только on the following word.

3. Если бы [у меня была] мелочь, 'If I had some change'.

послать бы, in which the inf. has pot. force, is equivalent to (я) мог бы послать, 'I could send'.

7f. Эка бестия трактирщик, 'That good-for-nothing innkeeper'. Here, and at III.9.28, эка is the fem. short form of the pop. pron. экий (= какой), used in exclamations of surprise, annoyance and ridicule. At III.5.53 and V.7.86 эка is a variant of the interj. эк! ('whooh!', 'my goodness!').

10. благородным образом, 'in a dignified (lit. honourable) manner', i.e. like a gentleman.

12. Задать тон (in the part. gen. form тону) here means not 'to set the tone or fashion', but has the obs. sense 'to give oneself airs', 'try to cut a dash'.

Scene 8

This scene, in which the two main characters confront each other for the first time, is pure comedy of error, based on the old dramatic device of mistaken identity. Among critics there is disagreement about the likelihood of the Governor taking Khlestakov for an inspector.

Bulgarin considered the error to be quite implausible. A shrewd, experienced official like the Governor would not be taken in by a scapegrace like Khlestakov for one moment. He would at once demand to see the visitor's papers (travel documents and identity card), if only to give the appearance of being efficient.

In reply to this, Vyazemsky claimed that the Governor's blunder is perfectly understandable if one remembered the saying that 'fear has big eyes' (у страха глаза велики). The news that a stranger is staying at the inn comes to the Governor and his associates in a critical moment of panic fear, after the reading of Chmykhov's letter. Furthermore, there is no reason why the Governor should not suspect that Khlestakov has *two* sets of documents, one false and one genuine.

Belinsky, too, argued that the Governor's mistake is soundly motivated. He has a letter warning him to expect an inspector in disguise. Only the previous night he had dreamt of two rats, and the dream now assumes in his mind a sinister, prophetic significance, bringing forebodings of trouble. His uneasy conscience over the wrongs he has done evokes in him fear, a fear reinforced by superstition and suspicion. The news of the stranger at the inn only increases his apprehension. In this state of mind it is natural that he should mistake Khlestakov for the dreaded inspector and imagine his innocent, quite truthful remarks to be subtle wiles.

Dobrolyubov, in his diary entry of 3 January 1857, wrote that it seemed unnatural that the Governor, without prompting, should speak about taking bribes and the flogging of the N.C.O.'s wife (see ll.49–53). He has no reason to put ideas into his interlocutor's head; a person with a bad conscience is more likely to keep quiet about his misdeeds. Dobrolyubov failed to see that the Governor, believing that Khlestakov had been told everything by the merchants (ll.33–4), mentions these crimes in an attempt to exonerate himself before being accused.

2. вошед: obs. = войдя. Cf. I.1.153.

4. The verb оправиться may mean either 'to recover oneself' or 'to adjust one's dress'. The latter seems more appropriate here, as a superfluous nervous action the Governor performs before 'stretching his arms along his seams' (протянув руки по швам), i.e. coming to attention.

5. Желаю здравствовать! 'My greetings to you!' lit. 'I wish you to be well'. This more formal variant of здравствуйте is now used mainly in a jocular way.

9f. Here, and at III.5.38, Skvoznik-Dmukhanovsky, the governor of an unimportant district town, calls himself a градоначальник, a title that properly pertained to the governor of a large town and the surrounding territory that were administratively independent of the province. He describes himself correctly as a градоправитель ('town governor') at I.5.27.

10ff. чтобы проезжающим... никаких притеснений [sc. **не делалось**], 'that travellers . . . should not suffer any ill-treatment (lit. oppression)'.

13. заикается here does not mean 'stutters', as at V.8.90, but 'hesitates', 'falters (in speaking)'.

21. За что ж я... [sc. **должен отвечать?**]

24. холмогорские купцы, 'merchants from Kholmogory', a town situated some 50 m. south-east of Archangel. The Kholmogory area was famous for the fine quality of beef produced by its dairy cattle, a breed developed by crossing native stock with animals brought from Western Europe.

25. Я уж не знаю, 'I just don't know'.

26. что = что-нибудь. Cf. I.1.53.

не так, 'not as it should be' or 'not right'. Cf. note on (не) такой at I.3.13.

29f. Да какое вы имеете право? After this, in R1–4, Khlestakov offered to produce his travel document (подорожная), showing him to be an official travelling to his father's estate.

30. Да вот я... [sc. **буду жаловаться на вас**].

Я служу, 'I am in the service (of the state)', i.e. a government official. Cf. III.2.37.

35f. At this point in R2 and 3 (a little earlier in R1) Khlestakov, instead of banging his fist on the table and threatening to go to his minister, declared that he would not give himself up and, seizing a bottle, prepared to offer physical resistance. Yu. Mann's opinion that G. changed this because it was not in keeping with the character of Khlestakov, who never premeditates his actions, is unconvincing. By grabbing a bottle to defend himself, Khlestakov was acting impulsively, on the spur of the moment. Shenrok is probably right in concluding that the gesture smacked too much of farce, which G. was concerned to reduce to a minimum when working on R5.

38. вытянувшись [во фронт or **в струнку]**, 'standing to attention'.

39. Помилуйте, 'Have pity'. This older, 'liturgical' sense of the word contrasts with its more usual meaning at III.6.8.

дети маленькие. The Governor, who has no small children, but only his 17-year-old daughter Maria, resorts to the conventional plea used by those seeking for mercy. Similarly, in the last extant chapter of *Мёртвые души*, Part 2, the unmarried Chichikov beseeches mercy for the sake of his non-existent wife and children.

41. Вот ещё! 'The very idea!'

41f. мне какое дело [до этого]? 'What do I care (about that)?' Cf. мне нет никакого дела до них, 'I don't care in the least about them' (ll.55f.).

48f. Though the Governor exaggerates in saying that his salary is insufficient to cover the cost of tea and sugar, it is certainly true that civil servants, except those in the top posts, were poorly paid. In Muscovite Russia administrators subsisted on 'feeding' (кормление), i.e. payments in money and kind from the local population. Officials were first given regular salaries by Peter the Great and these were increased in 1763, under Catherine, in order to encourage efficiency and reduce corruption. Even so, their salaries were inadequate for most of them to live on, since they were paid in paper money (see IV.3.23), which rapidly depreciated in relation to silver coinage during the early part of the 19th century. Consequently bribe-taking flourished among officials as a means of supplementing their meagre incomes.

49f. самая малость, 'the merest trifle'. The pron. самый, used with certain nouns denoting a quantity (usu. small), intensifies them to the extreme limit.

50. Пара платья: an obs. term for 'a suit of clothes', the jacket and trousers making a 'pair'. Today пара alone is used in the same sense.

51. According to V. Filippov, in his edition of *Ревизор* (1963, p. 157), not long before the play was written a decree had been issued whereby it was strictly forbidden to inflict corporal punishment on N.C.O.'s wives. The Governor thus seeks to mitigate his offence by referring to the woman as a *widow*.

занимающейся купечеством, 'who is engaged in trade', i.e. keeps a stall at market. Купечество is a collective noun for 'merchants', 'tradesmen' (as at I.3.119); the sense of 'trading' clearly intended here is obs. and rare, not given in Russ. dictionaries.

52. высек, here, as at IV.11.45, means not 'flogged', but 'had flogged' by someone else (i.e. велел высечь). Verbs of arresting, punishing and the like are commonly used in the sense of having something done on one's orders. Cf. посадить [меня] в тюрьму, 'to have me thrown in prison' (V.8.48).

53. злодеи, 'enemies': obs. sense.

59. до этого вам далеко, 'that's beyond your power', lit. 'you are a long way from that', a phrase meaning the same as коротки руки (V.8.37).

Khlestakov is correct in saying that the Governor has no power to have him flogged, since officials of all grades were legally exempt from corporal punishment.

60. Смотри ты какой! 'Well, really!' An expression of indignation addressed to a generalized ты, not a warning to the Governor.

63. О, тонкая штука! 'Oh, the crafty devil!' The noun штука (from Ger. *Stück*), 'piece', has the coll. meanings of 'thing', or 'person' (as here), and 'trick'.

63f. Эк куда метнул! See I.1.54. This pop. expression, coined by G., is now used to mean 'what high-falutin' nonsense!'

64. Какого туману напустил! 'What a dust he's raised!' lit. 'what a fog he's let loose!' This is a common expression for 'obscuring the truth'.

64f. разбери кто хочет, 'make of it what you can', lit. 'let who will sort it out'. The imp. sing. разбери is here equivalent to a 3rd pers. imp. (пусть разберёт), though with attenuated force, akin to a subjunctive. Cf. спасайся кто может, the Russ. rendering of *sauve qui peut*.

66. да уж попробовать, 'but I'll have a try'. The use of the inf. instead of the fut. renders the expression more forceful.

не куды пошло: pop. = куда ни шло, 'come what may', 'whatever befall'.

67. на авось, 'on the off-chance' or 'at a venture (hoping for the best)'. For the optimistic connotation of авось see I.3.123.

71f. Мне бы только рублей двести, 'I'd only want about 200 roubles'. The бы with dat. construction, arising probably from the ellipse of хотелось, is commonly used when borrowing money or ordering food. Cf. Мне бы вина, 'I'd like some wine'.

74. хоть и не трудитесь, 'you needn't (lit. don't you) even trouble'.

76. из деревни, 'from the estate (lit. village)', i.e. of my father.

76f. у меня это вдруг, *not* (with случилось understood) 'it happened to me suddenly', i.e. losing all my money, as most translators interpret the phrase, but (with сделается understood) 'I'll do it promptly', i.e. repay you. Вдруг in this sense ('immediately', 'very soon') is obs.

80. таки, 'however', 'though', not 'after all'.

81. ввернул here = подсунул, 'slipped' or 'passed (on the sly)'; an unusual sense of ввернуть, which usu. means 'to put in a word or remark'.

87. и так, 'as we are'.

90. а то has several meanings, the commonest of which is 'or else', 'otherwise' (e.g. at I.5.49). Here, and at III.2.33, it means 'but then (= whereas earlier)', i.e. contrary to what I know now, and is best rendered as 'before'. See also II.1.12.

95. инкогнитом illustrates the tendency in coll. speech to decline foreign borrowings in -o, which are indeclinable in literary Russ.

95f. подпустим и мы турусы, 'we'll try some bluff too' or – picking up the dust raised by Khlestakov (l.64) – 'we'll throw some dust in his eyes too'. This idiom is believed to come from the medieval siege-towers (турусы), brought up to assault a beleaguered town when the battering-rams failed to breach its walls. Tales about these engines of war were considered so far-fetched that турусы на колёсах came to mean 'a cock-and-bull story'.

102. которому ни до чего дела нет, 'who doesn't care about anything'. Cf. II.41f.

105. в награду, 'as a reward'. For this use of в + acc. cf. в наказание, 'as a punishment' and в подарок, 'as a present'.

110. Да, рассказывай! 'Oh yes, tell me another!' or 'Oh, that's a good one!'

111. Осмелюсь, 'I shall venture', was formerly used as a polite auxiliary with such verbs as сказать, спросить, доложить, when addressing a superior. The corresponding Eng. formula is usu. couched in the conditional: 'If I may be so bold as to . . .' Cf. II.10.29.

117. и не покраснеет! 'and not even a blush!' lit. 'he cannot even blush!' (fut. pf. pot.).

с ним нужно ухо востро [sc. **держать**], 'you have to keep a sharp lookout with this one'. Cf. I.4.37.

120. насчёт задержки лошадей. Travellers were often delayed at post-houses because high-ranking persons were given priority in the providing of horses. See also V.1.55f.

121. чай, 'I expect' or 'I daresay'. This arch. and coll. parenthetic word is an apocopated form of чаю, from чаять, 'to expect'.

124. ничего не выслужил, 'I have obtained no advancement'. Promotion in the tsarist civil service depended on length of service (выслуга) or merit (заслуга). Some officials gained rapid promotion by displaying outstanding ability and devotion to duty or through patronage. The majority were promoted automatically, after so many years of service, but few ever reached the 8th grade, which brought with it the coveted status of hereditary membership of the gentry. Cf. *Characters and Costumes*, 1.6.

126. тебе Владимира в петлицу и дадут, 'they'll give you the (Order of) Vladimir, 4th class'. The Order of St. Vladimir, founded in 1782, had four classes, the badge of the lowest being a cross suspended from a ribbon and worn in a bottonhole (в петлице) on the breast of the uniform coat. The point of Khlestakov's remark is that this decoration, which conferred hereditary membership of the gentry on its recipient, was awarded for long service or outstanding merit and that an official, to receive *any* decoration, had to be in at least the 9th grade of the service.

127. потолкаться (coll.), 'to knock about for a while' (i.e. in a government office) is aptly chosen, for in the time of Nicholas I the duties of most officials, esp. in the lower grades, were far from onerous. Even during the short hours they worked they were often left with much time on their hands.

128. прошу посмотреть, 'will you just listen', lit. 'I ask you to look'. For this idiomatic use of прошу, whereby the speaker addresses the world at large, cf. Griboyedov, *Горе от ума*, I.13: Прошу служить у барышни влюблённой!

128f. какие пули отливает! 'what yarns he spins!' This idiom, which G. was fond of using, arose in the first half of the 18th century. It was an old superstitious practice among Russians to spread some improbable tale or rumour whenever a church bell was being cast, a custom which gave rise to the saying Колокола отливают, так вести распускают. The same custom was later adopted with the casting of cannon and, by extension, the moulding of bullets. Hence отливать пули acquired the meaning 'to tell tall stories'.

132. глуп... как бревно, 'as stupid as a donkey (lit. log)'. The usual expression today is глуп как пробка ('as a cork').

старый хрен, 'the old buffer'. In this coll. phrase хрен ('horse-raddish') is substituted for хрыч, a term of abuse for an old man, just as 'buffer' and 'buzzard' are used euphemistically for 'bugger'.

135. Теперь [у меня] не те потребности, 'Now my needs are different'. Не тот means either 'wrong' or 'other'.

The kind of needs Khlestakov has in mind and the culture or 'enlightenment' his soul thirsts for («душа моя жаждет просвещения») are those so vehemently denounced by Kostanzhoglo in *Мёртвые души*, 2, III, i.e. the appurtenances of fashionable city life – fine clothes, society balls, clubs, card-parties, coffee-houses, light theatrical entertainments and the like.

137. Славно завязал узелок! 'What a tangled web he weaves!' lit. 'He's tied the knot splendidly!' i.e. so that no one can undo it.

138. и нигде не оборвётся! 'and never dries up (*or* gets stuck)!' lit. 'and will not break off anywhere!' Fut. pf. freq.

140. ты у меня проговоришься, 'I'll get the truth out of you'. Observe the use of the ethic gen. in this and similar statements, e.g. Он у меня работает, 'I make him work' (sc. lazy though he is)'.

142f. Ведь хоть бы здесь, 'Why now, take this place for instance'. Here хоть бы = хоть in the coll. sense of 'for example'. Cf. its optative sense at II.1.55.

143f. стараешься для отечества, 'you do your best to serve your country'. Cf. IV.6.13f.

147f. Russian hotels at that time were notoriously infested with bugs, fleas, cockroaches and other vermin. At the beginning of *Игроки* the inn servant tells Ikharev: Если блоха или клоп укусит, уж это наша ответственность.

148. как собаки кусают: note the alliteration, which can be matched by rendering the phrase as 'the brutes bite like bulldogs'.

149. Скажите! 'Good gracious!' or 'Bless my soul!' Скажите, sometimes followed by как (III.6.63) or пожалуйста (IV.6.37), is a common exclamation of amazement or shocked surprise.

150. от кого же? 'and from what?' The pron. кто, unlike Eng. 'who', may be applied to animals as well as humans.

155. [мне] придёт фантазия, 'the fancy takes me': fut. pf. freq.

156. темно, 'it's too dark'. The impers. adv., like the predic. adj., may signify an excess of the quality denoted. Cf. V.8.37.

165. от простоты души, 'in all innocence'.

172. особливо: obs. = особенно, 'especially'.

174f. от полноты души выражаюсь, 'I speak with a full heart'. In most fig. expressions душа is rendered as 'heart', rather than 'soul'.

177f. нравится ваша откровенность и радушие. It is normal Russ. practice to make the verb agree in the sing. with a following compound subject, i.e. with the first noun only. Cf. V.8.218.

179. Note the redundant second бы, which is commonly introduced, for reinforcement, into clauses already containing a бы or чтобы. Cf. чтобы. . . назывался бы (IV.7.45–7).

179f. как только оказывай мне, 'except only that one (*or* people) should show me'. Here the imp. sing. expresses obligation.

Scene 9

5. давеча (pop.), 'not long since'.

11f. Всего сколько [вам] следует [с меня]? 'How much do I owe you altogether?'

14. Пошёл вон, 'Off with you' or 'Clear off'. The idiomatic use of the past pf. to express an imp. is found with one or two other verbs, e.g. встал(и), 'get up', and начал(и), 'get started'. Cf. Пошёл (IV.9.52) and пошли (IV.11.62).

15. и то правда, 'that's right'.

Scene 10

2. Не угодно ли будет вам. . .? 'Would you care to . . .?' Cf. I.2.30.

6f. какое у нас течение дел, 'how things proceed here' (a stilted way of saying как у нас идут дела).

15. острог: originally a stockade surrounding a medieval stronghold, then a wooden fortress, and finally, in the 18th and 19th centuries, a convict prison. Contrary to what is indicated here, however, there would have been no convict prison for Khlestakov to inspect in the district town, since such prisons were invariably located in or near large towns, usu. provincial capitals. It seems more likely that G. was simply ignorant of this fact than that he was stretching the truth in order to underline the importance of the police in the Russian state at that time, as suggested by V. Filippov in his edition of the play (1963, p. 156).

18. обсмотрим: coll. = осмотрим, 'we shall look round'.

27f. две записки. In fact the Governor writes only one note, to his wife. The note he intended writing to Zemlyanika, which he mentions for the first time in R5, is promptly forgotten – whether by accident or design on G.'s part is uncertain.

33. Да зачем же [**беспокоиться**, as in R1–4]**?**

впрочем here means 'oh, still', i.e. expresses a sudden change of mind, a habit highly characteristic of Khlestakov. Cf. IV.16.18 & 48.

38. фриштик, from Ger. *Frühstück*, 'breakfast', was formerly used as a coll. equivalent of завтрак. Here it clearly means 'lunch', since Khlestakov has already eaten at the inn. This is the first recorded use of the word in Russian.

39. губернская мадера: Madeira wine of the best quality, obtainable only in county towns, or provincial capitals (губернские города), and evidently sold in squat or 'fat-bellied' bottles (бутылки-толстобрюшки).

40. Только бы мне узнать, что он такое, 'If only I could find out what he is'. Cf. II.1.19.

In this aside (ll.37–41), added in R5, the Governor, not yet sure whom he is dealing with, displays his calculating character in scheming to loosen Khlestakov's tongue with drink. Ironically, this has the effect not of revealing the truth, as the Governor believes, but of producing a sustained flow of fanciful lies.

47f. без всякого-с помешательства, 'no damage at all, sir'. The word помешательство has an obs. sense of помеха, 'hindrance', but here signifies rather повреждение, 'harm', 'injury'. Its other, still current sense of 'insanity' lends the phrase a touch of absurdity.

48. сверх носа небольшая нашлёпка, 'a small lump on top of the nose'. A comic effect is gained here by the fact that сверх means 'on top of' in both the literal and the fig. sense. (i.e. 'in addition to'), the latter being reinforced by the word нашлёпка, which denotes 'lump' in pop. parlance, but has the primary meaning of 'something slapped on'.

51. укорительный: obs. = укоризненный, 'reproachful'.

53. пожалуйте! 'kindly step this way!' The imp. pl. of пожаловать, 'to bestow the favour of', 'be so gracious as to', is used as a polite invitation to come or go somewhere.

54. Любезнейший: an obs. substantivized superl. with the same meaning as любезный, 'my good man'. Cf. II.4.11.

58. Уж и вы! 'Ooh you!' Cf. I.3.16f.

ACT III

Scene 1

1–4. That Anna and Maria should have stood by the window in the same positions, i.e. without moving, for a whole hour is plainly an exaggeration, typical of G., who often describes actions as lasting for an unbelievably long time; e.g. Оба... смотрят несколько минут один на другого (II.8.2–3). On the other hand, an hour is manifestly too short a time to encompass all that happens between the end of Act I and the beginning of this act: the meeting and conversation between the Governor and Khlestakov, followed by their tour of the hospital and a copious lunch there.

4. всё ты: see I.6.5.

5f. Было бы [лучше] не слушать её вовсе, 'I ought not to have listened to her at all'.

6. Экая досада! 'What a nuisance!' or 'How vexing!'

ни души [sc. **не видно**]**!** 'not a soul (in sight)!'

7. как будто бы вымерло всё, 'you'd think everyone was dead (lit. had died out)'. For всё as neut. sing. collective cf. II.1.21.

8f. чрез минуты две, 'in a couple of minutes'. When the numeral follows the noun, to express approximation, a governing prep. is usu. placed in the middle.

17. Какой Добчинский! 'Dobchinsky indeed!' See I.3.144.

17f. Тебе всегда вдруг вообразится этакое... 'You're always suddenly imagining such (strange) things ...' The coll. pron. этакий is stronger and more expressive than такой, being used to convey surprise, admiration or contempt (the initial э is by origin exclamatory).

23. Говорят тебе, 'I tell you'. In coll. Russ. verbs of locution are used in the 3rd pers. pl., instead of the 1st pers. sing., when the speaker repeats with emphasis some assertion, command or request. Cf. Тебя просят молчать, 'I'm asking you to be quiet'.

24f. Видите: it was normal then for children to use the вы form to their parents.

27. из чего: obs. = отчего, 'for what reason', 'why'.

28. скорей = скорее. The comp. suffix -ей is an apocopated form of -ее, used in coll. speech and poetry.

30. отступя, 'after stepping back'. This past gerund form in -я is still used. Cf. I.1.32.

Scene 2

3. Я на вас одних полагалась, 'I was counting solely on you (lit. on you alone)'. In the 18th century and the first half of the 19th it was normal to use the pl. of a noun or pron. predicated of вы, where this referred to a single person. Today одного would be used here.

5f. и я вот ни от кого до сих пор толку не доберусь, 'and all this time I haven't been able to get a word of sense out of anyone'. Не доберусь is loose pop. usage for не добьюсь, 'I cannot obtain' (fut. pf. pot.). The correct construction, не добиться толку, occurs at III.9.38.

6f. вашего Ванечку и Лизаньку, 'your Vanechka and Lizanka'; affect. dim. forms of Ваня (from Иван) and Лиза (from Елизавета). Observe that the adj. in Russ. usu. agrees only with the first of two nouns, though qualifying both.

8. кумушка: here, and at III.7.13, Dobchinsky uses this as an affect. form of кума in the literal sense of 'godmother', rather than as a friendly term of address ('dear lady'), applicable to any woman of mature years.

9. не могу духу перевесть, 'I cannot get my breath back'. For the arch. inf. form see *Characters and Costumes*, 1.54.

14. что и как там? 'what happened – how did things go there?' (Расскажите) что и как is a common expression meaning 'Tell us all about it'.

15f. Записочка: a dim. of записка, 'note', 'message'.

18f. Here Dobchinsky gives it as his opinion that Khlestakov is not a general, though not inferior to one in education and demeanour, presumably on the grounds that the visitor is too young to have attained such high rank. After hearing Khlestakov vaunt himself, however, he is prepared to say the young man is 'very likely a general' (III.7.7).

19. важные поступки, 'grand (*or* impressive) ways'.

21. было писано: the passive voice formed with an impf. verb is nowadays rare, with a coll. or arch. flavour.

22. Настоящий, 'The same', lit. 'the real one'.

26f. Сначала он принял было Антона Антоновича немного сурово, 'At first he received Anton Antonovich a little harshly' (a considerable understatement). Here было indicates an action or attitude that is later reversed (ll.29–32). Cf. I.1.165.

30. покороче, 'in a more friendly way'; comp. of короткий in the fig. sense 'friendly', 'intimate', with the softening prefix по- ('a little').

34f. перетрухнул (coll.), 'got the wind up'.

38. Да так, 'But – well'. Так is used when the speaker is unable or unwilling to give a reason. Cf. I.1.118.

41. каков он собою? 'what does he look like?' The instr. собой, used after an adj. or noun, means 'in one's person'. Cf. Он хорош собой, 'He is good-looking'.

46. так это всё славно, 'all so splendid it is'; так, qualifying славно, heads the clause for emphasis. Dobchinsky is lost in admiration at Khlestakov's 'fine' manner of speaking.

51. шантрет (arch.): a blend of шатен (from Fr. *châtain*), 'person with (chestnut) brown hair' and брюнет, 'man with dark hair'. A suitable equivalent would be 'aubrown'.

51f. глаза такие быстрые, как зверки, '(his) eyes dart about like ferrets', lit. 'are as quick as little beasts'.

54–7. G.'s interlarding of the Governor's letter with phrases from the hotel bill on which it was written cannot have been suggested by a similiar episode in Paul de Kock's *Sans cravate, ou les Commissionnaires*, as P. Stolpyansky thought, since this novel was published not at the beginning of the 1830s, as he states, but in 1844.

56. божие: Ch.Sl. spelling of божье, 'God's' (neut. sing.).

два солёные огурца: today an adj. placed immediately before a masc. or neut. noun governed by the numeral 2, 3, or 4 stands in the gen. pl., whereas in the 19th century the nom.-acc. ending was equally common (with an adj. qualifying a fem. noun the latter was standard, but now both endings are found here).

особенно here has the obs. sense of особо, 'separately', 'as an item on its own'.

58f. к чему же тут... икра? 'what ever is all this about . . . caviare?'

61. по скорости, 'in haste', 'to save time'. This is an obs. coll. meaning of скорость (= спешность).

66f. Бумажки here means обои, 'wallpaper', an obs., pop. usage not given in Russ. dictionaries. The sing. бумажка means 'piece of paper' at III.5.5 and 'bank-note' (coll.) at IV.8.15.

69. вина вели побольше [sc. **прислать**].

70. а не то = а то in the sense 'or else' (cf. II.8.90). The Governor's threat to ransack Abdulin's cellar was excised by the censor from R2 and 3.

72f. Это... нужно поскорей [sc. **сделать**]**!** 'There's not a moment to lose!' Here, as elsewhere in the play, поскорей (-ее) means 'as quickly as possible'. Cf. II.4.12f.

76. Mishka, as a казачок (see note in *Dramatis personae*), wears a казакин (a kind of caftan with gathers at the back) or a черкеска (a long collarless coat with a narrow waist).

80. Сидор: coll. form of the first name Исидор.

87. держу is here coll. for задерживаю, 'I detain'.

Scene 3

This scene was much shortened and modified. In R1 Anna spoke at length of the admiration her eyes evoked, told how one military officer nearly blew his brains out for her *beaux yeux* and another secreted himself in a huge bag of quails in order to gain access to her room. This last anecdote was omitted from R2, and the rest of Anna's boasting from R3. What remains is a brief exchange which reveals the essential vanity and pettiness of the mother and daughter in their bickering about the colour of dresses and eyes. Anna's sole concern is to be more fashionably dressed than her daughter, in order to impress the young man from the capital.

2. Машенька: affect. dim. of Маша, a fam. form of Марья.

3. столичная штучка. Most translators render this as 'a dandy from the capital', 'a Petersburg dandy' etc., but штучка, dim. of штука, means no more than 'person' (see II.8.63). For Anna to describe Khlestakov here as a dandy would be both illogical and inaccurate, because she knows nothing yet of the way he dresses and, though he has a dash of the dandy about him, he is in fact far from being a fully-fledged fop. A closer equivalent, keeping some of the alliterative quality of the phrase, is 'a proper Petersburger'.

4. боже сохрани, 'God forbid (lit. preserve)'. The nom. бог and voc. боже are both used in this and similar expressions. Cf. I.1.186.

чтобы... не осмеял: the expletive не (i.e. without negative force) is used with the subjunctive when expressing fear lest something might happen. Cf. Я боюсь, чтобы (or как бы) он не утонул, 'I'm afraid he might drown'.

5. приличнее всего, 'it is most becoming': this sense of приличный ('fitting', 'appropriate') is obs.

5f. The colour blue, which for the Romantics symbolized pure love, is here used ironically, to represent a romanticism that has degenerated into a banal bourgeois taste. Anna may well suggest that Maria wears her blue dress with little frills (с мелкими оборками) because this style had by then become unfashionable. Cf. *Мёртвые души*, IX: Да, поздравляю вас: оборок более не носят.

10. цветное here = разноцветное, 'with mixed colours'.

12. лишь бы только наперекор, 'just to be contrary'. The conj. лишь бы только means either 'just in order to' or 'just so long as'. Cf. III.8.23.

13. Палевый, 'pale yellow' (from Fr. *paille*, 'straw'). This colour was in vogue among ladies of the capital at that time, as readers were informed by the fashion section of *Библиотека для чтения* (June 1835). Anna could well have been one of the many provincial readers of this magazine (see III.6.80).

15. вам нейдёт: arch. and coll. = не идёт, 'does not suit you'.

18. я что угодно даю, 'I'll wager anything', lit. 'I give anything (you like)'.

21. Вот хорошо! 'I like that!' A similar ironic use is made of хороший in its short forms, e.g. Ты тоже хорош! 'You're a fine one, to be sure!'

22. самые тёмные, 'as dark as can be'.

23f. гадаю про себя... на трефовую даму, 'I tell my fortune by the queen of clubs', i.e. a dark lady. In games of patience the king of hearts and queen of clubs were believed to foretell the marriage of a man and a woman respectively. Cf. Goncharov, *Обломов*: Раскладывают гран-пасьянс, гадают на червонного короля да на трефовую даму, предсказывая марьяж.

30f. Бог знает что такое! 'What a thing to say!' lit. 'God knows what!'

Scene 4

2. Куда тут [идти]? 'Which way?'

3. дядюшка: affect. dim. of дядя, 'uncle', colloquially used to address a grown-up or an older man. Cf. I.6.9.

4f. горемычное житьё (coll.), 'wretched life' or 'dog's life'.

5f. кажется тяжела. Nowadays the predic. instr. (тяжёлой) would be used here, as it is at III.5.33 and III.6.18. Use of the nom. in the predicate was much commoner in the 19th century than today.

13. Генерал, да только с другой стороны, 'A general, only the other way round (*or* bottom side up)': Osip's cryptic way of saying that his master, who is at the bottom of the bureaucratic ladder, would be a general if the order of ranks were reversed.

17. Вишь ты как! 'Ooh, fancy that!' Cf. II.1.8.

17f. то-то у нас сумятицу подняли, 'so that's why there's been (lit. they raised) a commotion at our place'. Here то-то = вот почему.

20. приготовь-ка, 'just prepare (*or* make)'. The coll. pcle. -ка attached to the imp. has a hortatory force, turning the command into a friendly request, rather like the addition in English of some such phrase as 'there's a good fellow'.

22. простова (= простого) блюда, 'plain fare (lit. dish)'. The masc. and neut. gen. sing. ending of an adj. was sometimes spelt phonetically in the 19th century, mostly to produce a visual rhyme in verse.

28f. The point of Osip's enquiry is to ascertain whether there is an 'emergency' exit by which he and his master may escape if need be.

Scene 5

10f. осмелюсь доложить, 'I (shall) venture to observe (lit. report)'. For this obs. formal variant of доложу, see II.8.111.

12. Note the enclave то есть, a syntactical feature found several times in the play. Here it comes after a slight pause, caused by the Governor's embarrassment about saying польза.

13. Благочиние (obs.), derived from чин in the old sense of 'order', means 'public order and decency'. From 1782 the police department in provincial capitals was called the Управа благочиния.

14. внимание, 'regard', 'good opinion'.

19. поесть: here 'to eat well'. Cf. пожить, 'to live well'.

19f. срывать цветы удовольствия 'to pluck the flowers of pleasure'. This remark, first introduced in R5, sums up Khlestakov's hedonistic outlook on life. Like its Eng. counterpart, Herrick's 'gather ye rosebuds while ye may', it is widely quoted, but usu. to condemn a person who selfishly enjoys himself, showing no concern for others.

22. подбегая. In his *Предуведомление* G. describes the corpulent Zemlyanika running forward here 'as light as a 22-year-old dandy' (с лёгкостью двадцатидвухлетнего франта) and answering close to Khlestakov's face.

лабардан (obs.): a borrowing, probably via German, of Dutch *labberdaan*, 'salted cod', a word derived from Labourdain, the ancient name of the area around Bayonne, a port used by Basque fishermen, who were among the first to catch cod. The word, which came into English as 'haberdine' (obs.), needs great care in translation since the fish, lately a gastronomic novelty in Russia, is regarded by Khlestakov as a treat and its exotic name delights him; he declaims it rapturously, almost amorously, twice at the end of III.6. As nothing could sound more unappetizing or banal than 'salted cod', the word is best rendered by a suitable French culinary term, such as *meunière* or *bonne femme*.

25. Так точно, 'Yes (indeed)' or 'Quite right'. This stock affirmative response used by subordinates, esp. in the army, is repeated four times by the Postmaster in IV.4, to good comic effect.

33. все как мухи выздоравливают: an inept comparison, reversing the common expression мрут как мухи, 'they die like flies'. Zemlyanika's darkly humorous Freudian slip reveals the true state of affairs. Most of the poorer town-dwellers in Russia at that time had no medical care and of those few who were admitted to charity hospitals a large proportion died from insanitary conditions. Cf. I.1.80–4.

34. лазарет, 'infirmary': obs. sense. The word 'lazaret' or 'lazaretto', denoting a hospital for diseased poor, esp. lepers, is derived from Lazarus of the New Testament.

37f. Уж на что... головоломна, 'Terribly tricky (lit. head-breaking)'. The construction (уж) на что, lit. 'by how (very) much', originally used with a comp., serves here as a coll. intensifier, like Eng. 'ever so'.

38f. Столько лежит всяких дел [sc. **на его ответственности**], 'There are so many things of all kinds he is responsible for'.

40. наиумнейший, 'very cleverest'. A superl. adj. in -ейший is rather bookish today, and the addition of the intensifying prefix наи- makes it even more so.

42. Иной городничий, 'Some governors': pl., as in иной раз, 'sometimes' (l.57). In Russian a sing. noun is often used in generalizations, where English usu. has the pl.; cf. француз, 'the French' (I.2.14).

43f. когда ложишься, всё думаешь, 'when you (= I) go to bed, you keep thinking'. The 2nd pers. sing. verb forms are used here to express an action performed habitually not by people in general (see I.1.77), but by the speaker. Cf. the fut. pf. freq. forms плюнешь (l.72), уморишься, вбежишь, and скажешь (III.6.113–15).

45. ревность here = рвение, 'zeal': obs. sense.

47. в его воле, 'is in its power', i.e. rests with them (the authorities).

49f. то чего ж мне больше [хочется]? 'then what more do I want?'

51f. пред добродетелью всё прах и суета, 'beside virtue all is dust and ashes (lit. vanity)'. The Governor's sententious observation in the lofty style of a *raisonneur* is sheer hypocrisy coming from his lips and thus, by a neat twist of irony, a perfect illustration in itself of прах и суета, i.e. a hollow sham.

54f. Дал же бог [ему] такой дар! 'And God gave him a gift like that!' i.e. the gift of being able to 'paint a glowing picture' (расписывать). The pcle. же adds a touch of disapproval.

57. заумствоваться, 'to give my mind free rein' or 'to lose myself philosophizing'. The Governor's rather unexpected emergence as a 'moralizer' prompts Khlestakov at once to set up as a 'philosopher' himself, and to go one better by claiming to philosophize in both prose and verse.

58. стишки выкинутся: fut. pf. freq. The close resemblance of this phrase to штуки выкинутся ('tricks will be played') is an unconscious hint on Khlestakov's part as to the true nature of his philosophizing. But the verb (replacing напишутся of R1 and 2) springs to his lips probably because it belongs to the language of card-playing (e.g. выкинулся туз), which he is about to speak of. The same associations would be suggested by the Eng. rendering: 'I trick it out in verse'.

61. наукам учился, 'he's an educated gentleman', lit. 'he's studied the branches of learning'. Cf. V.2.22.

65f. знаем... в чей огород камешки бросают! 'we know who you're digging at!' This idiom usu. has the sing. form камешек в огород, lit. 'a pebble into someone's kitchen garden', i.e. a dig at someone, and бросают is used here obliquely for бросаете.

66f. The Governor's expression of mock horror is occasioned by the fact that card playing was officially disapproved of, indeed it had been prohibited by law in 1649, 1696 and 1717. The Устав благочиния of 1782 forbade the setting up of gaming houses and imposed penalties for betting in card games based on pure chance, but allowed card games played for money where skill was required. However, despite the risk of a fine and even imprisonment in serious cases, the passion for gaming continued unabated in Russia.

67. здесь и слуху нет о таких обществах, 'such clubs are quite unheard of here'. Cf. the common phrase ни слуху ни духу о (+ prep.), 'not a word has been heard of'.

70. увидеть... какого-нибудь бубного короля, 'to see . . . some king of diamonds'. Note that the names of face cards and the ace (туз) are treated as animate.

71. такое омерзение [на меня] нападёт (fut. pf. freq.), 'I am seized with such loathing'.

74. Бог с ними! 'To hell with them!' This common expression of dismissal may be rendered variously as 'blow them', 'never mind them' and 'good luck to them' (ironical).

74f. драгоценное время убивать на них, 'to waste valuable time on them'. The expression убивать время, like its Eng. counterpart 'to kill time', a calque of Fr. *tuer le temps*, is loosely used here for зря тратить время.

76f. у меня... выпонтировал, 'he won from me (at cards)'. The verb is compounded of понтировать, 'to punt' and вы- in the sense of 'winning or obtaining by means of'. Cf. выслужить, 'to obtain as a result of service' (II.8.124).

80. вы напрасно [sc. **это говорите**], 'you are wrong to say that' (lit. 'you say that unjustly') or 'I wouldn't say that'.

82f. Если... забастуешь тогда, как (= когда) нужно гнуть от трёх углов, 'If you stick when you should risk your stake and all your winnings'. In faro, bank and stoss, then among the most popular gambling card games in Russia, a punter would declare that he was sticking by saying баста (from Italian *basta*, 'enough'); hence the verb (за)бастовать, later used with the broader meaning 'to cease doing something' and finally in its modern sense 'to strike'. In these same games of chance the punter would bend over a corner (гнуть or загибать угол) and then a second and third corner of his winning card to indicate that he was doubling his stake plus gains (so-called 'paroli') on the next turn, trying to end up with 4, 8 and 16 times his stake respectively (his actual winnings being 3, 7 and 15 times the stake). He could thus win up to four times in succession with the same card if it made a double with that placed to the left by the banker at each turn of two cards.

Scene 6

This so-called сцена вранья is the most famous scene of the Russian theatre and probably the most brilliant piece of sustained враньё ('story-telling', 'romancing') in Russian literature. Mérimée compared Khlestakov's boastful lying in it with that of Falstaff in Shakespeare's *Henry IV*, Part One (Act II, Sc. 4). However, Khlestakov, unlike Falstaff, is motivated solely by a desire to impress, not to deceive, indeed he is so carried away in his ecstasy of mendacity that he believes his own lies, intoxicated more by his imagination than by the wine he has consumed. He is in any case only tipsy, certainly not roaring drunk as he is sometimes represented to be. Referring to Khlestakov's speech and behaviour in this scene, G. wrote: "He is plain stupid; he prattles away merely because he sees that people are disposed to listen; he lies because he has had a hearty lunch and drunk a fair amount of wine ... Every word he utters, every phrase and expression, is a quite unexpected improvisation and hence to be delivered jerkily. It should be borne in mind that towards the end of this scene the wine gradually begins to have its effect on him. But on no account must he sway about in his chair; he should only look very flushed and express himself in an even more unexpected fashion, his voice getting louder and louder as he goes on" (Letter of 10 May 1836, to M. Shchepkin).

G. made many alterations in this scene, especially to Khlestakov's speeches at ll.19–24, ll.106–49 (his great monologue) and ll.162–4. The first draft was expanded in R2 with the addition of much anecdotal material, notably a long tale told by Khlestakov of how at a hotel he once cheated a fellow guest by eating a partridge while the other man slept, after they had agreed that it should go to whichever of them had the best dream. This and other matter was excluded from R4 and fresh details were introduced, but many of the best phrases first appeared only in R5, as indicated below.

4. Раскланиваться means 'to bow on meeting' (as here) or 'on taking one's leave' (as at IV.4.41).

5. в своём роде, 'in its way (lit. kind)'; here 'as it were'. This inept phrase, added in R5, lends an unintentional irony to Khlestakov's would-be gallant remark. The whole exchange of civilities at the beginning of this scene is a parody of the empty forms of politeness used in fashionable society.

8. Помилуйте, 'Mercy me' or 'Pardon me'. The word is used in a pseudo-deprecatory way, as an exclamation of polite protest. When used by Anna (l.16), it could be rendered as 'Lud, sir'. Cf. II.8.39.

10. Как можно-с! 'You are too kind, sir (you really shouldn't)!' Another pseudo-deprecatory exclamation.

14. если вы... непременно хотите, 'if you absolutely wish it' or 'if you insist'.

18. вояжировка, 'voyageuring': a pretentious derivative of вояжировать (from Fr. *voyager*), which latter word, like вояж, is used only facetiously now, though not in G.'s time. Anna's fondness for words of French origin is characteristic of upper-class women in Russia at that time.

19–24. These lines furnish a good example of G.'s evolving technique of composition. In R1 the speech reads: Да, признаюсь, как выехал, я заметил ощутительную перемену. Даже вам, может, несколько странно, — в воздухе этак в городах... Всё как-то говорит: «Да это не то». Например, общества какого-нибудь, бала великолепного, где была бы музыка, на дороге уж вы не сыщете. Ну, конечно, рассеяние, развлечение. Зрение, можно сказать, очаровано: с одной стороны этак вдруг являются горы, какое-нибудь этак приятное местоположение, проезжающие в колясках и каретах; этак что-нибудь вас вдруг займёт: проезжающие экипажи... игра природы... всё видишь — а недоволен. All the last part concerning the sights one sees when journeying was replaced by a condemnation of ignorant postmasters in R2, which runs: Чрезвычайно скучна. Знаете, сделавши привычку жить в свете, пользоваться всеми удобствами, и вдруг после этого в какой-нибудь скверной дороге. Везде такая чепуха; не встретишься с образованным человеком, с которым бы можно поговорить о чём-нибудь; станционные смотрители такие невежи, народ без воспитания... Если бы, признаюсь, не случай такой, который меня вознаградил совершенно, то я не знаю, что бы со мною было. This was little altered in R3, but in R5 it was halved in length and the reference to ignorant country-dwellers condensed to the laconic phrase мрак невежества.

20. comprenez-vous: another refinement introduced in R5. From the middle of the 18th century French was widely spoken among the Russian gentry, after being adopted at court. Khlestakov, posing as a cultured man of society, lets drop a French phrase to impress his listeners, especially the ladies; on stage it is usu. pronounced with a heavy Russ. accent.

21. грязные трактиры, мрак невежества. This is a subtly comic juxtaposition of the concrete and the abstract, evoking the phrase грязь и мрак, which can be either literal ('mud and gloom') or fig. ('squalor and obscurity'). Thus the мрак of the common phrase мрак невежества ('benighted ignorance') acquires a semi-physical sense by association with the filthy inns.

33–5. в деревне: Anna means в глухой деревне, 'in the depths of the country', 'in a provincial backwater (глушь)'. Khlestakov, taking her to mean lit. 'in the country', points to the consolations of the countryside, which '*also* has its hills and brooks'. In R3 his words here were деревня тоже имеет приятности: ручейки, хижинки, зефиры! ... By simply deleting приятности G. produced an illogical use of тоже, yet one more gem of verbal ineptitude. He discarded хижинки ('cottages') and зефиры ('zephyrs', i.e. 'gentle breezes') in favour of пригорки, probably because he felt they were too obvious a dig at the literary sentimentalists.

36f. Вы, может быть, думаете, что я только переписываю, 'Perhaps you think I am only a copying-clerk'. Khlestakov, as an official of the lowest grade, would indeed perform such humble duties as those of a copying-clerk (obs. чиновник для письма; cf. ll.41f.).

38. начальник отделения, 'the head of the department'. In Russia's civil service the департаменты ('offices') of each ministry were divided into отделения ('departments'), which were in turn divided into столы ('sections'), headed by a директор, начальник and столоначальник respectively. Petty officials often sought to impress their provincial brethren by claiming the friendship or favour of those in high places.

41. Это вот так, это вот так [sc. **делайте**]**!** 'Do this so, (and) do that so!'

42. крыса has the derog. sense of 'humble servitor' (in Eng. terms a mouse, rather than a rat). Here it means канцелярская (or чиновная) крыса, 'office drudge', 'quill-driver'.

только here signifies только и слышно, 'all you can hear is'.

43f. Хотели было даже меня... сделать, 'They were even going to make me'. The pcle. было indicates unfulfilled intention. Cf. I.2.67.

V. Gofman errs in treating даже here as comically inappropriate, for although the rank of коллежский асессор ('collegiate assessor') was, as he says, only a *middle* grade, being eighth in the Table, younger officials strove eagerly to reach this point of promotion since it was the first to secure them hereditary membership of the gentry (see II.8.124). It should be added that Khlestakov, unaware that he has been taken for a government inspector, unwittingly reveals here that he is not, for a genuine inspector would have been either a military general or a senator – and senators were then appointed exclusively from officials and officers in the top three grades (see IV.7.66).

44. сторож: see V.8.83f.

52. Без чинов, 'No ceremony'. This expression goes back to the times of Muscovy when the tsar would dine informally with some of his boyars, waiving the order of precedence (местничество) which usually governed the seating at such assemblies.

58. In R1 and 2 Khlestakov says he was taken for Field-Marshal Dibich, commander-in-chief of the Russian army (this name was removed at the request of the censor and replaced in R3 by 'the Turkish ambassador'). There is no good reason to suppose that G. was really making a thrust at Field-Marshal Paskevich, who succeeded Dibich on the latter's death in 1831 (see G. A. Gukovsky, *Реализм Гоголя*, 1959, p. 471). G. is concerned here not with the person of the commander-in-chief, but with his exalted rank, which Khlestakov momentarily – if mistakenly – occupies. Incidentally, this story about being mistaken for the C-in-C contradicts Khlestakov's assertion, immediately before this, that he is recognized everywhere he goes.

59. Гауптвахта, 'guardhouse', comes from Ger. (*Hauptwache* or –*wacht*), like many Russ. military terms.

сделали [честь] ружьём, 'saluted (with their guns)', i.e. presented arms (a similar ellipse, сделал ей [знак] ручкою, occurs in *Невский проспект*). When a high-ranking officer approached a guardhouse the sentry rang a bell, whereupon the soldiers seized their muskets, formed up outside and presented arms at the command of the officer in charge.

64. In R2 and 3 this speech began: Да, меня уже везде знают. Я на всех гуляньях бываю; в театре... By suppressing these words, which show the natural progression of his hero's thoughts, G. made the speech more typical of the man, producing an abrupt jump in thought that exemplifies Khlestakov's лёгкость в мыслях (see I.79).

65. Я ведь тоже разные водевильчики... 'I do various vaudevilles too, you know'. In R1 this sentence contained пишу, in R2 and 3 даю на сцену ('write for the stage'), but was finally left unfinished, in a manner typical of Khlestakov. He would certainly be acquainted with the vaudeville, a form of entertainment that was brought to the Russian stage from France early in the 19th century and soon won enormous popularity. It was a one-act comic sketch, often interspersed with songs and dances, generally given as an afterpiece to round off the evening following a tragedy or melodrama. There is a poignant irony in the fact that G., who disliked this light genre and deplored its domination of the theatre, saw his own *Ревизор* first performed at the Alexandrinsky Theatre largely in the farcical style of a vaudeville.

66f. Бывалю, часто говорю ему, 'I've often said to him'. The pcle. бывало is used with a verb in the pres. (historic), past impf. or, most commonly, the fut. pf. freq. to indicate a repeated, esp. habitual, action in the past.

67. Ну что...? 'How are you ...?' Cf. the different sense ('Well?') at II.4.6.

67f. Да так, брат, — так как-то всё, 'Oh, so-so, old boy, – all sort of so-so'. This banal, almost meaningless reply is richly absurd, purportedly coming from Russia's greatest poet, esp. when followed by the comment that he is 'a great *original*', i.e. a real character. This part of the speech, referring to Pushkin, was added in R5, after the poet had died. In R2 Khlestakov tells his listeners that Pushkin always gets a bottle of rum before composing his works and 'when he starts writing his pen just goes scratch, scratch, scratch' (this last phrase was later transferred to the copying-clerk; see ll.41–3); he had recently written a play, *Лекарство от холеры*, which set one's hair on end and even sent one official mad.

69f. Как это должно быть приятно сочинителю! The word сочинитель is used in the obs. sense of 'author', but a Russian audience may read into it the other meaning – 'story-teller', 'fibber'.

Anna's exclamation bears a close resemblance to the words of Magdelon in Molière's *Les Précieuses ridicules*, Sc. 9; Je m'imagine que le plaisir est grand de se voir imprimer. In the same scene Mascarille boasts of having composed 200 songs, as many sonnets, 400 epigrams and more than 1,000 madrigals, quite apart from riddles and sketches, adding that it is beneath his rank to write and he does so only in response to pleas by publishers; compare Khlestakov's words at ll.75–7.

73. «Женитьба Фигаро». *Le Mariage de Figaro*, the famous comedy by Beaumarchais, was first performed at the Comédie Française in 1784. It appeared on the Russian stage, in French, the following year, and two years later in a Russian adaptation by A. F. Labzin. A production of it at St. Petersburg in 1829, using a new translation by D. N. Barkov, caused something of a furore in the theatrical circles of the capital, a fact which would not have escaped G.'s attention.

74. «Роберт Дьявол»: see II.3.11f.

«Норма». V. Bellini's romantic opera *Norma*, which had its premiere at La Scala, Milan, in December 1831, soon achieved great popularity. It was first performed in St. Petersburg by a German opera company in October 1835, and two years later in Russian.

In the earlier versions Khlestakov claimed to be the author of *Сумбека*, a ballet by A. Blache first staged at the Alexandrinsky in November 1832, and *Фенелла*, a russianized version of D. F. Auber's grand opera *La Muette de Portici* (1828), which appeared at the same theatre in 1834, both works being first modified in accordance with the Tsar's wishes. In R5 these two titles were replaced by the much better-known *Norma*.

79. У меня лёгкость необыкновенная в мыслях, 'I have an uncommonly easy flow of ideas (*or* rapid turn of mind)'. Khlestakov boasts of his ready invention – no idle boast, but Russian audiences inevitably make a connection between the two nouns, recognizing the легкомыслие ('light-mindedness', 'frivolity') which is one of his chief traits. The phrases лёгкость в мыслях and лёгкость мыслей необыкновенная, taken from this famous remark, are now synonymous with легкомыслие.

80. Baron Brambeus was a pen-name of Osip Senkovsky (1800–58), an orientalist who from 1834–48 edited the monthly magazine *Библиотека для чтения*, at that time Russia's most widely read periodical, esp. popular with provincial readers. One such was G.'s mother who, ironically enough, attributed the works of Brambeus to her own son until he disabused her, calling them 'sordid compositions which only appeal to the lowest class'. G. despised the man and was clearly tilting at him by making Khlestakov appear briefly in his guise. In earlier versions of the play more was made of Senkovsky; thus in R1 and 2 Khlestakov claims acquaintance with Senkovsky's friend Bulgarin, a journalist who was one of G.'s harshest critics.

«Фрегат Надежды» (correct title «Фрегат «Надежда»): a tale published in 1833 by A. A. Bestuzhev (1797–1837), who wrote under the pen-name of Marlinsky. A major figure in Russia's short-lived Romantic movement, he was one of the most widely-read writers of the 1830s. His works were esp. popular with military men and minor officials.

81. «Московский телеграф»: a fortnightly journal published in St. Petersburg from 1825. It was closed down by the authorities in 1834 when its editor, N. A. Polevoi, wrote an adverse criticism of a play which, unknown to him, had pleased the Tsar on account of its patriotic tone. After this Polevoi shed his liberalism and began to write patriotic plays himself.

The idea of the same person being responsible for both the *Moscow Telegraph* and all the works of Brambeus, notably *The Library for Reading*, would have been amusingly absurd to G.'s contemporaries; the former was a serious journal, regarded by Belinsky as the best Russia had produced, with contributions from such writers as Pushkin and Zhukovsky, while the latter was a product of slick, superficial journalism, in G.'s words 'a fortress of vulgarity', offering pieces written mostly by literary mediocrities.

82f. In 1833 Senkovsky published two tales – both plagiarized – under the pen-name of Baron Brambeus, and then a collection of tales entitled *Фантастические путешествия барона Брамбеуса*. The following year Pavel Pavlenko published a tale entitled *Барон Брамбеус* and, as A. S. Dolinin suggests, it may well be this last work that Anna Andreyevna is thinking of. Pavlenko's tale, whose hero, a dashing, dark-eyed lancer, falls in love with the daughter of a dull-witted landowner and wins her hand by claiming the title of Baron Brambeus, is the kind of literature that would greatly appeal to Anna. However, given the Munchausenesque character of *The Fantastic Journeys of Baron Brambeus*, there seems little doubt that G. had Senkovsky in mind, at least as far as Khlestakov is concerned.

84. я им всем поправляю статьи (**стихи** in some editions). Senkovsky was a notoriously unceremonious editor who shamelessly tampered with most of the material submitted to him, sometimes mutilating articles out of all recognition and stitching together stories by two or three different authors. G. strongly objected to this and scornfully denounced Senkovsky for such editorial high-handedness in an article he published anonymously in the first issue of Pushkin's *Современник* (April 1836), though he had no axe to grind as he never contributed to *Библиотека для чтения* himself.

85. Мне Смирдин даёт за это сорок тысяч [sc. **рублей в год**]. A. F. Smirdin (1795–1857), founder of *Библиотека для чтения*, was the leading Petersburg publisher in the 1830s, and his bookshop on Nevsky Prospekt was frequented by all the notable writers of the day. One of the first to pay fees to authors, he was noted for his generosity in this matter, which eventually bankrupted him. G. deliberately exaggerated the amount Senkovsky received annually as editor. The true figure is given by A. V. Nikitenko in his diary (8 January 1834): . . . наши почтенные литераторы взбеленились, что Смирдин платит Сенковскому 15 тысяч в год. Even this, however, was an unprecedentedly large salary for such work at that time, hence the indignation it aroused.

86f. «Юрий Милославский»: a patriotic historical novel by Mikhail

Zagoskin (1789–1852), which appeared in 1829–30. The book, written in the romantic manner of Walter Scott and set in Russia's Time of Troubles (Смутное время) at the beginning of the 17th century, became a best seller in its day, being read, according to N. Grech, 'in drawing-rooms and workshops, by the common people and at the Emperor's court'. Zagoskin, a prolific author who wrote comedies as well as novels, was Director of Moscow's Imperial Theatres from 1831–42 and directed the Maly Theatre production of *Ревизор* in May 1836.

95f. Khlestakov's bland lie that there is another *Yury Miloslavsky*, which he wrote, could well contain an oblique reference to the practice of title-snatching, i.e. the appearance on books by unknown authors of titles taken from works by popular writers such as Marlinsky and Zagoskin.

99. Я... литературой существую, 'I live for (*not* by) literature'.

103. прошу [вас зайти] ко мне.

балы даю. During the winter season well-to-do members of society often held balls and routs in their town houses, starting abut 9 or 10 p.m. and going on sometimes till dawn.

104. там refers not to Khlestakov's imaginary house, the best (первый) in St. Petersburg, but to the capital itself.

106. Просто не говорите, 'My word, yes'.

107. в семьсот рублей арбуз, 'a water-melon costing 700 roubles'. Water-melons, grown and consumed in vast quantities in Russia, were dirt-cheap, costing but a few copecks each, even in St. Petersburg, where food prices were high. This fantastic exaggeration recalls the water-melons of monstrous size mentioned in *Иван Фёдорович Шпонька и его тётушка* and *Мёртвые души* (The Tale of Captain Kopeikin).

107f. Khlestakov's claim that 'the soup came direct by steamboat from Paris' (the gastronomic capital of the world) is exaggerated only in that the soup came not in a tin, but in a tureen, piping hot. Thus, K. Bulgakov, writing to his brother in the 1830s, said: "We ate turtle soup that had been prepared in the East Indies and sent to me from London by Vorontsov. Such a degree of perfection has now been reached in regard to food that dinners made by Robertson's in Paris are sent in a new type of tin container which preserves them from spoiling." Canned foods could not be openly imported into Russia under Nicholas I, and hence were very dear.

108f. [когда] откроют крышку — [слышен] пар: the ellipses render the description more graphic. Cf. ll.124, 127–30.

110f. вист here means партия в вист, 'four(some) at whist'. Note the alliteration in вист, свой and составился. This run of sibilants doubtless put G.'s contemporaries in mind of the word свистун, 'whistler', also an old derog. term for a shallow or idle fellow. Cf. K. Fedin, *Гоголь*: Хлестаков сделался непревзойдённым эпитетом для всяческих свистунов, бахвальщиков, пустозвонов, не брезгующих и смошенничать и словчить.

111f. Count Nesselrode, Russia's Foreign Minister (1816–56), a man passionately fond of cards, could have made up a four at the time of the play with the French ambassador Marquis Maison (1834–5) and the German (i.e. Austrian) ambassador Count Ficquelmont (1829–39), but from 1832–5 England had no ambassador in St. Petersburg, being represented by a *chargé d'affaires*, J. D. Bligh, after Nicholas I had refused the appointment of Stratford Canning.

113f. просто ни на что не похоже, 'it's simply shocking (lit. like nothing)'. Cf. I.5.3.

114f. на четвёртый этаж. Khlestakov accidentally reveals that he lives on the top floor, where the apartments are the cheapest, but hastily corrects this to the first floor (бельэтаж), the best and most fashionable. The latter touch was added in R5.

115. скажешь только кухарке, 'you (= I) just say to the cook', i.e. I haven't the strength to say more. Cf. III.5.43f.

Маврушка (coll. dim of Мавра): a common name of servant-women. When stressed on the first syllable it is affect., on the second – slightly supercilious; the latter tone would be used by Khlestakov.

115f. шинель: in that period a long, heavy overcoat with a broad shoulder cape and ample sleeves, similar to the Inverness cape. This so-called Николаевская шинель was part of a civil servant's uniform.

117. У меня одна лестница стоит... 'My staircase alone is worth –'. Khlestakov's gift for invention fails him here.

117–19. Those seeking some favour of a high official had to be in his antechamber (передняя) by 6 a.m. to secure a position of advantage near the entrance to his reception-room (приёмная), though the grandee himself rarely deigned to appear before midday.

119. графы и князья. The title of count (граф, from Ger. *Graf*) was introduced by Peter the Great in 1706, whereas that of prince (князь) was an ancient one, going back to Kievan times. Nobles bearing these titles took precedence over other members of the aristocracy as well as the gentry.

120. Иной раз и министр [sc. **заедет**, as in R2–3]. 'Sometimes even a minister (will call in on me)'.

122. Ваше превосходительство, 'Your Excellency': the title then used to address officials and officers of the third and fourth grades.

124. И странно [sc. **это случилось**], 'And it came about in a strange way'.

125. пошли толки, 'people started talking', lit. 'rumours started'.

126. Многие из генералов, 'Many of the top brass', meaning high-ranking officials. Civil servants in the top four grades were customarily referred to as 'generals', i.e. by the equivalent military rank, which was held in higher esteem. Thus the Governor, in Act V, Sc. 1 and 7, aspires to become a civilian general (штатский генерал), whereas Khlestakov, earlier in the present act, could be taken for either a military or civilian general.

126f. брались [за дело], 'undertook the task'.

127. но [когда] подойдут, бывало, 'but when they got down to (lit. approached) it', i.e. each in turn. Cf. ll.66f.

мудрено, 'it's too complicated'. Cf. II.8.156.

127f. Кажется и легко на вид, 'It *looks* easy enough'.

128–30. Note the pregnant use of ellipse: [когда] рассмотришь, 'when you look at it closely'; ко мне [обратились], 'they turned to me'; по улицам [скакали] курьеры, 'couriers galloped through the streets'.

131. The 35,000 couriers, one of the boldest exaggerations in all G.'s works, are a case of 'galloping' hyperbole. In R1 there are no couriers, in R2 one courier, in R3–4 fifteen, then finally – and unbelievably – thousands.

131f. Каково положение? — я спрашиваю. This is not an enquiry Khlestakov made of the couriers ('What's the position?' I asked), but a rhetorical question addressed to his listeners ('What a situation, I ask you!').

134. вышел в халате. There is probably a recondite punning allusion here. In *Moscow Observer* (June 1834) the historian N. Pavlishchev criticized an article by Senkovsky, entitled *Брамбеус и юная словесность*, and demonstrated that this declared enemy of French writers had shamelessly plundered their works. G., taking up the theme of Senkovsky's plagiarism, likened the book that made him a celebrity to a dressing-gown stitched together from shreds of material supplied by others (из каких лоскутов барон Брамбеус сшил себе халат) and spoke of the brazen self-praise in Senkovsky's article as an act comparable to appearing in public casually attired in his dressing-gown with a pipe between his teeth (как будто бы вышел он в публику в своём домашнем халате с трубкою в зубах).

135. дойдёт до [сведения] государя, 'it will come to the notice of the sovereign'. This is not an absurd suggestion, for Nicholas I did in fact take a close interest in his administration at all levels.

послужной список, 'service record', i.e. the personal file kept on each official by the clerk of his department, a copy of which was held by the appropriate ministry.

138. только уж у меня: ни, ни, ни!.., 'only just (no nonsense) with me – my word no!' A twice or thrice repeated ни expresses an emphatic prohibition.

Уж у меня ухо востро [sc. **держите**, as in R2 and 3]**!** '(You'll have to) keep a sharp look-out (*or* be on your toes) with me!' Cf. I.4.37f., where there is no verb ellipted.

139. уж я... [вас], 'I'll show you'. Here уж has the threatening force of ужо.

145. государственный совет, 'the Council of State'. Instituted by Alexander I in 1810, this was the highest consultative body of the Russian Empire. Its members, appointed by the crown, examined draft legislation and made recommendations on it, but the Tsar, whose power was absolute, quite often ignored their advice or issued decrees without consulting them.

Да что в самом деле? 'And why not indeed?'

146. я не посмотрю ни на кого, 'I won't have regard for anyone', i.e. I'm no respecter of persons. Cf.II.1.50.

147. Я везде, везде. Mikhail Chekhov, in Stanislavsky's 1921 production of the play, delivered these words with great declamatory vehemence, conveying the impression that the spirit of Khlestakov is to be found everywhere. This finds support in G.'s *Отрывок из письма*: И ловкий гвардейский офицер окажется иногда Хлестаковым, и государственный муж окажется иногда Хлестаковым, и наш брат, грешный литератор, окажется подчас Хлестаковым. Словом, редко кто им не будет хоть раз в жизни...

дворец, i.e. the Зимний дворец (Winter Palace), the Tsar's residence in St. Petersburg, where he and his family spent the winter season, from New Year's Day to the eve of Lent. Built by Rastrelli in 1754–62, the Palace now forms part of the famous Hermitage Museum.

147f. The only persons to visit Nicholas I's palace almost daily at that time were Gen. Benkendorf, Head of the Third Section, and Prince Paskevich, the army's commander-in-chief (see I.58). Khlestakov's lie here is very similar to the remark made about Verkholet in Knyazhnin's *Хвастун*, II.1:

> Подумай, он какой случайный человек!
> Он только при дворе проводит весь свой век.

148f. Меня... произведут... в фельдмарш[алы], 'I shall be promoted field-marshal'. Note the use, with verbs denoting entry or promotion into a class of persons, of the construction в + acc. pl., with the animate noun in the same form as the nom., a survival from Old Russ.

Prince Paskevich and England's Duke of Wellington were the only Russian field-marshals at that time, the Tsar being extremely chary of appointing to this, the highest military rank. Khlestakov's vision of being made the third is not only ludicrous fantasizing; it contradicts his earlier statement that he was about to be made a collegiate assessor (ll.43f), for he could not be an army officer and an official at the same time. But this, like his other lapses, goes unnoticed by his listeners.

157. Не разберу ничего, 'I can't make out a word': fut. pf. pot.

159. Ва-ва-ва... шество, 'Yu-yu-your – ency'. Ва-шество was a common contraction in speech of ваше превосходительство, as милостигсдарь was of милостивый государь ('kind sir').

160. не прикажете ли отдохнуть? 'would you care to take a rest?' Cf. I.2.30 and II.1.4f.

163f. Я доволен, я доволен. Лабардан! лабардан! These expressive repetitions were added in R5, but there the latter appeared as отличный лабардан (twice). In 1851, making a last alteration to the play, G. pruned away the adjs., thereby giving the exclamation greater declamatory force and exposing Khlestakov's shallowness even more effectively.

Scene 7

3. оно: redundant pron. used as an emphatic pcle. Cf. I.1.177.

жисть: a pop. corr. of жизнь, 'life'.

5. со страху: synonymous with от страха, but more coll.

6. в рассуждении чина (obs.), 'as regards rank'.

7. чуть ли не does not mean the same as чуть не ('very nearly'), but 'most likely' or 'I'm almost sure'.

8. А я так думаю, 'But I (on the contrary) think'. Here так is an intensive pcle. with adversative force.

8f. генерал-то ему и в подмётки не станет! Idiom: 'a general is not fit to tie his boot-laces (*or* to hold a candle to him)!', lit. 'will not do for the soles of his boots'. For this sense of стать cf. II.1.7.

9. когда: coll. = если. Cf. IV.15.40; V.7.82.

10. генералиссимус, 'generalissimo', a title conferred very rarely, chiefly on generals who commanded several armies. In the 18th century Russia had three (Prince Menshikov, Prince Anton Ulrich and Gen. Suvorov), but in the 19th century – none.

12. Прощайте, 'Farewell'. Here, as elsewhere in the play, not до свидания, but the homelier, more traditional valediction is used.

16f. А мы даже и не в мундирах. Zemlyanika is concerned lest he be reprimanded for not wearing his uniform during hours of duty, as all officials were required to do.

17. как: obs. and pop. = если.

17f. махнёт донесение, 'he dashes off a report' (fut.). This coll. sense of махнуть, 'to do something hastily (with a sweep or flourish)' is found also in подмахнуть, 'to sign hastily' or 'to sweep up hurriedly'.

Scene 8

3. милашка: here 'nice (*or* attractive) man'. Though, strictly speaking, the noun applies to a woman, it may also be used of a man (with masc. agreement). The use of fem. forms in reference to males, e.g. in fam. and dim. masc. names, as a mark of friendliness or affection, is characteristically Russian.

4f. Но только какое тонкое обращение! 'But oh, what refined manners!' Here только is a pcle. emphasizing но. Cf. I.4.10.

5. Приёмы, '(His) manners' or 'bearing': obs. sense.

7. Молодые люди can mean 'young people' or 'young couple', but mostly means 'young men', as here. Cf. Fr. *jeunes gens*.

я просто без памяти [от него], 'I'm simply smitten (with him)' or 'he's quite bowled me over'.

12f. с своим вздором подальше! 'get away with you and your nonsense!' Here подальше means 'a long way away' and has imp. force.

15f. Боже сохрани, чтобы не поспорить! 'God forbid you should ever agree (lit. not argue)!' or 'You will argue, won't you!'.

16. да и полно! (coll.), 'and that's that!' Cf. полно! 'that's enough!' (II.2.41).

16f. Где ему смотреть на тебя? 'Why should he look at you?' Cf. II.1.39.

23. да и то так уж, лишь бы только, 'but even then only just to (sc. be polite)'. Note the remarkable string of eight pcles.

24. дай уж посмотрю на неё! 'I think I'll just give her a glance!' The imp. sing. дай with the 1st pers. sing. fut. pf. expresses a decision to do something on the spur of the moment. The pcle. -ка is used in a very similar way, as at IV.4.27.

Scene 9

6. Да как же и не быть правде? 'And why shouldn't it (lit. how could it not) be true?' For the dat. with быть cf. II.2.12.

6f. Подгулявши, человек всё несёт наружу, 'When he's had a drop too much, a man comes out with everything'.

7f. что на сердце, то и на языке corresponds exactly to the Eng. saying 'what the heart thinks the tongue speaks'. It is a shortened variant of the dictum У пьяного что на уме (or душе), то и на языке, 'What is on a drunken man's mind is on his tongue'.

8f. не прилгнувши, 'without embroidering'. This gerund does not relate to the subject of the main clause (речь) but is used with adverbial force. The sentiment of the whole remark accords with that of the proverb Красно поле рожью, а речь — ложью, 'A field is adorned by rye and speech by a lie'.

16. высшего тона, 'of the highest breeding' or 'of the most refined manners'.

16f. о чинах его мне и нужды нет, 'his (great) rank is of no consequence to me'. The pl. чины is used in the old sense of 'high rank', and нужды нет is a coll. expression meaning 'it doesn't matter'.

18. Ну, уж вы — женщины! 'Oh, you women!' Cf. II.10.58.

Всё кончено, 'That's it'. Cf. IV.3.29f., where the same phrase may be translated 'That's done it.'

19. Вам всё — финтирлюшки! 'To you everything is fiddle-faddle!' The form финтирлюшки is a variant of the coll. word финтифлюшки, 'knick-knacks' or 'silly nonsense'.

20. ни из того ни из другого = ни с того ни с сего, 'without rhyme or reason'.

21. мужа и поминай как звали. Idiom: 'it's the last you'll see of your husband' (lit. 'remember what your husband's name was'), i.e. I'll be sent to prison.

24. The use of the вы form by Anna to her husband signifies coolness or displeasure.

25. Мы кой-что знаем такое... 'We know a thing or two –'. Cf. II.6.21.

27. The stage direction *один* is rather misleading: the Governor is soliloquizing, but the ladies remain present.

Ну, уж с вами говорить!.. 'Oh, it's no use talking to you!' The pcle. уж here has the same sense as да что, and the independent inf. expresses the futility of the action.

28. Эка в самом деле оказия! 'What an odd business, to be sure!' Cf. II.7.7f.

32. Чудно всё завелось теперь на свете, 'Everything in the world has turned topsy-turvy (lit. strange) nowadays'.

33. хоть бы народ-то уж был видный, 'if only people looked distinguished', i.e. portly, in both senses. Important officials were expected to be large and stout, hence the Governor's remark at II.8.138f. (А ведь какой...

низенький) and his words in R2 (at V.8.199): Был бы он хотя по крайней мере толст в теле, как прилично знатному человеку...

а то [когда человек] худенький, 'but when a man is thin' i.e. like Khlestakov.

34f. Ещё военный всё-таки кажет из себя, 'a military man (sc. in uniform) still looks somebody all the same', i.e. even if not stout. Казать is a pop. verb meaning 'to show', and из себя is a coll. equivalent of собой, 'in one's person' (cf. III.2.41).

35. фрачишка (now -ишко): derog. dim. of фрак, 'tail-coat'. Cf. II.1.43.

37f. заламливал такие аллегории и екивоки, 'he concocted such riddles and taradiddles (lit. allegories and quibbles)'. Заламливать is a coll. form of заламывать, 'to crack *or* snap', here fig. 'to fabricate', and екивоки (from Fr. *équivoque*) is now spelt экивоки.

38. век... не: here in the obs. sense of ввек не, 'never in one's lifetime'; it is still used in coll. speech to mean 'not for ages'.

40. человек молодой implies молодо-зелено, 'he's a greenhorn', 'he has much to learn'.

Scene 10

1. кивая пальцами (obs.), 'beckoning'. Cf. I.3.65.

7. полно вам! 'that's enough from you!' or 'that'll do!' Cf. III.8.16.

12. слишком... много, 'a great many', not 'too many'. The use of слишком to mean очень is one of G.'s (hitherto unnoticed) stylistic idiosyncrasies, symptomatic of his hyperbolism. Cf. *Отрывок из письма*: Черты роли Хлестакова слишком подвижны, более тонки и потому труднее уловимы (i.e. than those of the Governor).

22. чин какой на твоём барине (= у твоего барина)? 'what is your master's rank?' This use of на + prepl. in relation to rank is old-fashioned. Cf. D. Lensky, *Лев Гурыч Синичкин*, II.2: На мне четырнадцатый класс.

23. Чин обыкновенно какой (i.e. какой обыкновенно имеют), 'the usual sort of rank'.

25. поговорить = сказать. This transitive use of поговорить is unusual.

27. распекать: a verb widely used in military and official circles in tsarist times. The expression распекать на обе (or все) корки, originally a baker's term for freshening stale bread or cakes by covering them with a damp cloth and heating them on both (all) sides, came to be used in the fig. sense 'to haul over the coals', 'to give a wigging to'. The last part of the expression was dropped here, but survived in similar ones derived from it, such as бранить на все корки, 'to give it someone hot' and драть на обе корки, 'to tan the hide off'. Today распекать had the milder sense 'to tick off'.

28f. Уж ему [sc. **нравится,**] **чтобы всё было в исправности**, 'He really likes everything to be just so', i.e. running smoothly.

33. там, i.e. в Петербурге, as at III.6.104.

35. Здесь нужная вещь, 'This is a serious matter'.

дело идёт о жизни человека, 'a man's life is at stake'. In the expression дело (or речь) идёт о + prepl. ('it is a matter of') the noun has lost its substantival sense, serving in effect as a pron. Compare the impers. subject in Fr. *il y va de* and Ger. *es geht um*.

37. не мешает, 'it does no harm', lit. 'it does not hinder'.

37f. The Governor's use of the forms чайку (gen. sing. of чаёк, from чай, 'tea') and стаканчик, '(nice) glass' illustrates the Russ. fondness for friendly dim. nouns relating to food and articles connected with eating and drinking (cf. бутылочка for 'bottle', водочка for 'vodka').

39. целковик: obs. = целковый (coll.), 'one rouble' (originally in silver coin).

на чай. It was considered more refined to give drinking-money 'for tea' than 'for vodka' (на водку).

41. всякого здоровья, 'every good health': part. gen.

53f. Любит он, по рассмотрению, что как придётся [sc. **ему по душе**], 'He likes things according to (lit. by consideration) how each takes his fancy', i.e. it all depends. Here что has a distributive sense (cf. I.1.75), and как is a deferred conj. (cf. I.1.138).

57f. Вот уж на что я крепостной человек, 'What though I be (*or* I may only be) a serf'. Here уж на что means 'however much'; contrast its use at III.5.37f.

60f. ваше высокоблагородие (a calque of Ger. *Euer Hochwohlgeboren*), 'your Worship': the title used to officials and officers of the sixth to eighth grades. The Governor, thus addressed at V.7.3, holds one of these ranks (probably the 8th) but Khlestakov, in the lowest grade, is properly entitled only to ваше благородие, which Osip uses at IV.16.61.

64f. дело ты говоришь, 'you talk good sense' or 'you are right'.

75f. Идите себе! 'Off you go now!' The pron.-pcle. себе here suggests 'in your own time' and softens the imp. Cf. II.1.32.

80. О, уж там наговорят! 'Oh, won't they just talk (i.e. plenty) in there!' Наговорить means 'to talk a great deal *or* too much' (cf. III.9.39).

81. поди (= пойди)... да послушай, 'if you went . . . and listened'. The imp. sing. is used idiomatically to express the conditional, either generalized as here, or in reference to a specific subject as with заговори (IV.1.38).

Scene 11

3. так и валится, 'he just comes tumbling in'.

сорок пуд, 'forty poods (= approx. 1440 lb.)'. The 'forty' is purely conventional, as at I.5.28. The gen. pl. пуд, instead of пудов, was normal in the first half of the 19th century. Several masc. nouns denoting units of measurement (вольт, ампер), like some for nationals (грузин, турок) and soldiers (солдат, партизан) still have the gen. pl. identical with the nom. sing.

4. Где вас чёрт таскает? 'Where the devil have you been?' lit. 'Where is the devil dragging you about?'

6f. Эк как каркнула ворона! Probably an allusion to Krylov, *Ворона и Лисица*: Ворона каркнула во всё воронье горло.

12. и ни с места [sc. **не двигайтесь**]! 'and don't budge (from the spot)!' The ellipse of не and the verb is normal in this expression, as with ни души and ни слова (больше) and ни шагу дальше.

14. Только here = как только, 'as soon as'.

ACT IV

This act, the longest, gave G. greater trouble and underwent more alteration than any other in the play. Two scenes in R1, in which Khlestakov is visited by landowners, were omitted from R2; three scenes in R2, between Khlestakov and the Director of Schools, Rastakovsky and Dr. Hiebner respectively, were omitted from R3. In R4 major changes were made to the opening scenes; a new scene showing the officials conspiring to bribe Khlestakov was put at the beginning; Khlestakov's monologue, in a much shorter and altered form, followed; and a new fifth scene, with Khlopov, was added. Substantial changes were also made between R1 and 5 in the wooing scenes with Anna and Maria. Finally, some material was shuffled round, the order of scenes 3 and 4 being reversed, and words originally spoken by one character being put in the mouth of another.

Scene 1

In his *Отрывок из письма* G. wrote: "During the performance I noticed that the beginning of the fourth act was cold; it seemed as if the play, which had hitherto flowed smoothly, was suspended or was dragging sluggishly here. I confess that even during the reading a knowledgeable and experienced actor remarked to me that it was not well contrived to have Khlestakov asking for loans first, and it would be better if the officials offered him money themselves. While respecting this quite perceptive observation, which had some justice in it, I nevertheless saw no reason why Khlestakov, being Khlestakov, should not ask first. But the observation had been made, 'therefore', I said to myself, 'I have not made a good job of this scene'." The main change G. made in the light of this criticism was to start Act IV with the so-called conspiracy scene (сцена сговора). The R4 version of this consisted of 108 lines, which were reduced in R5 to exactly half that number.

5. полукружием: obs. = полукругом, 'in a semicircle'.

6. скорее [станьте] в кружок, 'hurry up and form a circle'.

8. на военную ногу, 'in military fashion'. Cf. на широкую ногу, 'in grand style'.

12. Воля ваша, 'Say what you will'. The phrase, which also means 'as you wish', is often used to express a doubt, reservation or mild remonstrance, like present-day Eng. 'with respect'.

16. Подсунуть [ему деньги]? 'Grease his palm?' lit. 'slip him some money?' G. may well have taken heed here, and at ll.20–4, of Bulgarin's objection that bribery was not shown properly in the first stage version. The word bribe (взятка) was always avoided, Bulgarin pointed out, and the bribery was committed cleverly, often taking the form of presents given to a man's wife, so discreetly that no one guessed.

17. хоть и may be rendered here as 'why not?' after the verb.

19f. раскричится, 'he'll raise hell (*or* Cain)'. For the 'intensive' sense of verbs with the prefix раз- and the reflexive suffix -ся cf. расчихаться (I.1.77).

20. государственный человек, not 'statesman', but 'person in a high office of state' (as also at IV.8.3).

23. мол, 'we could say'. This coll. pcle. of citation, derived from молвит ('he says'), may be used of any person, sing. or pl., and report real or, as here, imaginary words. Cf. II.2.32.

26. по почте, 'by post-chaise', an oblique way of saying 'by police waggon' and a punning reference to the literal use of the phrase ('by post') by the Postmaster.

подальше, 'a very long way away', i.e. to Siberia. Cf. III.8.12f.

29. между четырёх глаз (obs. Gallicism: *entre quatre yeux*) = с глазу нá глаз, 'in private'. Note the arch. use of the gen. with между in this expression.

30. там is a pcle. serving here merely as a verbal filler.

33. Так лучше ж вы [начните], 'No, you'd better go first'. This adversative use of так contrasts with its opposite sense of 'yes', as at II.4.22.

34. вкусил хлеба, 'has broken (lit. partaken of) bread': part. gen.

38. заговори = если заговорит, 'if . . . starts to speak'. For the conditional use of the imp. sing. see III.10.81.

39. у меня просто и души нет, 'I go quite to pieces' or 'I simply lose my head'.

40. язык как в грязь завязнул (now в грязи завяз), 'my tongue sticks to the roof of my mouth (lit. is stuck as in mud)'. The standard Russ. expression today for being tongue-tied is язык прилип к гортани.

43. некому [sc. **взяться за дело**].

43f. У вас что ни слово, то Цицерон с языка слетел, 'With every word you utter (lit. whatever your word,) Cicero trips from your tongue'. Cicero, the famous writer and statesman of ancient Rome, was noted for his great powers of oratory.

46. Смотрите. . . ! 'Good gracious . . .!' Cf. II.8.60.

49. вы и о столпотворении [вавилонском умеете говорить], 'you can also talk about the Tower of Babel'. According to the Old Testament (Gen. XI, 4–9), the Babylonians tried to build a tower up to heaven and God punished them for their hubris by scattering them and causing the proliferation of languages, – hence 'babel' (столпотворение), meaning 'a noisy, confused medley of voices'. The freethinking Judge would speak sceptically about such Bible stories; cf. the Creation (сотворение мира), mentioned at I.1.138f. and also referred to here in R4, but deleted by the censor.

50. Отец, 'guide and protector': obs. coll. sense.

53. откашливание, 'a clearing of the throat'.

54. наперерыв: arch. = наперебой, 'vying with each other'.

59f. Отпустите. . . хоть душу на покаяние, 'Set at least my soul free to repent', a rather old-fashioned expression meaning 'Let me breathe' or 'Leave me in peace', now mostly used in a jocular way.

61. Выхватываются, 'Burst (lit. are snatched) out'.

62. комната остаётся пуста. G. here flouted the rule of Classical drama that the stage should never be left with no one on it.

Scene 2

In R1–3 Khlestakov's monologue opened the act and was longer, including comments on the stupidity, as well as the kindness, of the Governor, from whom he conceives the idea of requesting a further loan in order to try his luck again at gambling. This proves unnecessary, since the Governor himelf offers to lend him more money (see Sc. 16, ll.15f.).

4. мне подсунули чего-то [sc. **прекрепкого**, as in R4], 'they slipped me something (really strong to drink)'. The same verb is used in Sc. 1 (l.16) for slipping bribes, appropriately, since the drink and the bribes serve the same corrupt purposes.

9. и матушка такая, что ещё можно [было] бы. . . [приволокнуться за ней: R2 variant], 'and the mother is the kind one might still . . . (start flirting with)'.

10. я не знаю [как другие, as in R4], 'I don't know about anyone else'.

Scene 3

3f. [у меня] коленки и ломает, 'I feel weak at the knees', lit. 'my knees are aching'. Physical and emotional states are often expressed by an impers. verb form with a direct object, e.g. [меня] тошнит, 'I feel sick' (II.5.19), or with a complement in у + gen., as here.

6. коллежский асессор: see III.6.43f.

8f. С восемьсот шестнадцатого [года] был избран, 'I was elected from 1816'. In expressing the year it is common to give only the last part, omitting the century.

Earlier, at I.3.150f. the Judge states that he has been on the bench for 15 years. From these two statements it may be concluded that the play is set in the year 1831. This tallies with the statement in R1 and 2 by Rastakovsky, in a scene later deleted, that he had applied for a supplementary pension in 1801 and had been waiting 30 years for a decision. It conflicts, however, with the mention, in those same versions, of *Robert the Devil* and *Fenella*, neither of which was performed in St. Petersburg till 1834. In R1 and 2 Khlestakov claims that he is a contributor to both *The Library for Reading*, the first issue of which appeared on 1 January 1834, and *Moscow Telegraph*, which was closed down on 3 April 1834. This evidence puts the play in the early part of 1834. It seems likely that G. had the year 1834 in mind and either overlooked the discrepancy between this and the Judge's statements or intended the 'fifteen years' to be only an approximate figure. But in R5, inadvertently no doubt, G. introduced the anachronism of Khlestakov claiming to be the author of *Norma*, which had its Petersburg premiere in 1835 (see III.6.74).

12f. представлен к Владимиру четвёртой степени, 'I've been put up for the (Order of) Vladimir, fourth class': see II.8.126. In R1 and 2 the Judge said he had been *awarded* the decoration; the verb was altered by the censor, who objected to a corrupt official being shown as the recipient of this distinction.

13f. со стороны ('on the part of') is redundant and pompous here.

16f. Анна третьей степени уже не так, 'the (Order of St.) Anne, third class, is not nearly as good'. This order was founded in 1735 by Karl

Friedrich Ulrich, Duke of Holstein-Gottorp, in memory of his wife Anne, daughter of Peter the Great. It was introduced into Russia in 1743 by their son, who later became Peter III, but it was made an official Russian order only with the accession of Paul I in 1797. The St. Anne, 3rd class, was three degrees lower than the St. Vladimir, 4th class. These two orders were the ones most often awarded to civil servants, but the St. Anne was commoner. In R4 Khlestakov, referring to the latter, added at this point: Слишком уже, знаете, обыкновенно: и регистратор и все носят и столоначальники.

20. Точно горячие угли под тобою (= подо мною), 'I feel as if I were on hot coals'. Cf. the expression сидеть как на (горячих) углях, 'to be on tenterhooks'.

23. ассигнации, 'assignats', i.e. treasury notes. Paper money was first circulated in Russia in 1769, but from 1788 it depreciated in relation to silver, esp. during the first decades of the 19th century. During the 1830s the value of paper roubles in relation to silver ones fluctuated between 3·5 to 1 and 4 to 1.

25f. Никак нет: a respectful, now obs. way of saying 'no', the negative counterpart of так точно (III.5.25).

26f. тележку подвезли схватить меня! 'the (police) waggon has come (lit. been brought) to pick me up!' A тележка (from телега, 'cart') was the springless carriage regularly used as a post-chaise and mail-carriage, also by couriers, police and others. The Judge's words here have the same sort of sinister ring as the phrase 'the tumbrils are rolling'.

34. пресвятая матерь, 'Most Holy Mother', i.e. Mother of God (мать божия). The form матерь is the Ch.Sl. acc. sing., which, like the nom. мати, served also as a voc.

35f. то да сё, '(what with) this and that'. Cf. II.3.12f.

37. как можно! 'you mustn't think of it!' or 'I won't hear of it!' Cf. III.6.10.

37f. и без того, 'as it is'. Cf. IV.11.32; IV.12.51.

38f. слабыми моими силами, 'to the best of my poor abilities': here an expression of mock modesty.

39. усердие, 'zealous devotion': obs. sense.

41. руки по швам, 'thumbs by seams', lit. 'arms along seams (of trousers)'. Cf. II.8.4. Note the nom. absolute construction, a rarity in Russian.

41f. беспокоить своим присутствием, 'to intrude on you', lit. 'to disturb with my presence'. A similar formula is used by Khlestakov's other visitors before taking their leave.

43. Какого приказанья? 'Any orders?' *not* 'What kind of orders?' Khlestakov is repeating the end of the Judge's question, in which какого = какого-нибудь.

44. не дадите ли, 'do you wish to give'. See I.2.30.

46f. In some editions this speech ends with the additional words: нет, ничего. Покорнейше благодарю.

Scene 4

4. надворный советник, 'court councillor', the seventh grade in the tsarist civil service, equivalent to the military rank of lieutenant-colonel.

When G. first saw the Maly production in October 1839 he reproached F. S. Potanchikov, who was playing the Postmaster, for making himself up to look old. The actor pointed out that to attain the rank of court councillor required many years of service, unless one started with a good education. When G. reminded him that Maria fancies the Postmaster is dangling after her (I.6.18), Potanchikov argued that this is not because the Postmaster is young, but probably because he is the only bachelor among the officials. G. graciously conceded the point.

5. милости просим! 'you are welcome!' lit. 'we beg the favour (i.e. of receiving you)'.

10. не так многолюдно. The observation is historically accurate, for district towns in Russia had small populations at that time, a fact which would strike a visitor from the capital.

11. Не правда ли. . .? 'Isn't that right . . .?' This very common question tag, indicating that an affirmative answer is expected, mostly comes at the end of the sentence, as on l.22 ('don't you agree?'). Не так ли? 'Isn't that so?' (ll.14 & 35) serves the same function.

13. бонтон (from Fr. *bon ton*), 'good manners *or* breeding'. Khlestakov's concern with 'tone' finds further expression in his use of моветон (V.8.132) and задать тону (II.7.12).

14. Гусь means 'goose' in the sense of 'simpleton' here, as at II.5.16.

27. А попрошу-ка я у этого почтмейстера взаймы! 'Yes, I'll ask this postmaster for a loan!'. The pcle. -ка, when used with the 1st pers. sing. fut. pf., expresses a firm decision or intention, usu. after some hesitation; cf. напишу-ка я (IV.8.4f.).

In this aside, one of only two he speaks in the play, Khlestakov characteristically has a sudden brainwave, suggested by his unexpected piece of luck when the Judge nervously dropped his money in the previous scene. This psychological subtlety was achieved in R4, where G. introduced the money-dropping incident (not in R1–3) and made the Postmaster come in after the Judge (in R1–3 he came in before).

31. Почему же? 'But of course': the same meaning as как же (III.6.84).

31f. почту за величайшее счастие, 'I should (lit. shall) deem it a very great pleasure'. Почитать/почесть за + acc. has been superseded by считать/счесть + instr. Cf. IV.12.85.

Scene 5

2. Сзади его (now него). In G.'s time 3rd pers. personal pronouns did not have the prosthetic н- when used after secondary preps., i.e. those derived from other parts of speech. This is the case today only with вне and внутри (+ gen.), preps. of adverbial origin that govern the dat., such as вопреки, подобно, and compound preps. like вследствие, по поводу.

Чего робеешь? 'What are you afraid of?' Obs. construction with gen.

5. титулярный советник, 'titular councillor', the ninth grade in the tsarist civil service, equivalent to the military rank of captain. Khlopov is the lowest ranking of the town officials, the only one not to have attained membership of the hereditary gentry (see II.8.124). His modest rank is associated with the meek, humble servitor, such as Akaky Akakievich in *Шинель*. The very word титулярный (often without советник) was treated with ridicule; it is spoken with contempt by the Governor at V.1.58.

8f. Вот тебе раз! 'Well, I never!' Cf. I.1.11.

12. не то, что в Петербурге, 'not like the ones you get in Petersburg'.

13. куривал: from куривать, coll. freq. form of курить, 'to smoke'. Cf. I.1.18.

по двадцати пяти рублей: in spoken Russ. today по in this distributive sense is generally followed by the nom./acc. form of numerals, exc. один, which still stands in the dat., as do nouns (cf. по метле, 'a broom each', at I.4.34).

14. сотенка: pop. dim. of сотня, 'a hundred'.

24–30. I. Vishnevskaya suggests that Khlestakov is here sounding out the Director of Schools with a view to procuring some girls, it being a well-known fact that seminaries sometimes provided pupils for the pleasure of the well-to-do. For all his love of physical delights, however, Khlestakov would never be so calculating. His wooing in Sc. 12–14 is entirely impromptu, like everything else he does and says.

28. Не смею знать, 'I dare not say (lit. know)'. Cf. Не могу знать, 'I couldn't say'.

29. не отговаривайтесь! 'Don't try to get out of it!' or 'Don't wriggle!'

34. какая-нибудь брюнетка сделала вам маленькую загвоздочку, 'some brunette has put you in a bit of a quandary'.

39. ваше бла... преос... сият... Khlopov, uncertain how to address

Khlestakov, stammers out the first syllables of благородие, преосвященство, сиятельство, '(your) Honour, Grace, Highness'. The last two forms forms of address are used to a bishop and to a prince or count respectively.

40. Продал проклятый язык. . .! 'My damned tongue has played me false . . .!' Cf. the saying Язык мой — враг мой, 'My tongue is my enemy'.

41f. In R4 this sentence continued: — магнетическое, не правда ли? The phrase was risky, for Nicholas I was known to speak of his own eyes as 'magnetic' and contemporaries such as Queen Victoria spoke of their awesome quality.

50. Вот те штука, если нет! 'A fine thing if it (the money) isn't there!' For те = тебе cf. I.1.11.

Scene 6

9f. вверенных моему смотрению, 'entrusted to my care'. For obs. смотрение see I.1.78f.

13f. Рад стараться на службу отечеству, 'I'm glad to do my best in the service of my country'. The phrase рад стараться was the stock response of soldiers in the Russian army when complimented by a superior.

21. исполняю службу, a concise, rather old-fashioned way of saying исполняю служебные обязанности, 'I perform my duties'.

23f. в большом запущении, 'in (a state of) gross neglect'.

24. посылки, usu. 'parcels', here means 'mail'.

26f. в присутственных местах: see I.1.90.

35f. все. . . как вылитый судья, 'they are all the (spit and) image of the judge'.

39f. This speech began in R2 with a further remark about the Judge: Да и безбожник: больше десяти лет, как не исповедывался. The censor deleted these words on the grounds that they might offend the religious feelings of the audience.

41. якобинец, 'a Jacobin'. The Jacobins were members of the club of Parisian revolutionaries formed in 1789. The name was adopted in Russia, where it was used by their political opponents to designate extreme radicals and freethinkers. Chatsky, the hero of Griboyedov's *Горе от ума*, is described by Princess Tugoukhovskaya as a Jacobin.

42. неблагонамеренные правила, 'subversive principles'. The adj. неблагонамеренный (lit. 'ill-intentioned') was used by the tsarist authorities to describe persons known or thought to be hostile to the regime, hence politically unreliable.

43f. Zemlyanika's remark reveals the bureaucratic mentality. An English contemporary, Linney Gilbert, wrote: "It is the invariable custom in all parts of Russia, both with high and low, that all engagements [i.e. matters], whether of importance or of the most trifling nature, are 'reduced to writing', for the Russian proverb says: 'What is written with a pen cannot be erased by an axe' [Что написано пером, того не вырубишь топором]", *Russia Illustrated*, London, 1843, p. 194.

59f. There is a characteristically Gogolian comic touch here, expressed in an unexpected deviation from the norm. A series of very ordinary Russian names, Nikolai, Ivan, Elizaveta and Maria, is completed with the rare, old-fashioned name Perpetua.

67f. **в другое тоже время...** [sc. **навещайте меня**].

77. **как кстати**, 'how convenient'.

Scene 7

Bobchinsky and Dobchinsky, unlike the officials, do not come to offer Khlestakov bribes, as is clear from the fact that they can scrape together only 65 roubles between them when asked for a loan. Dobchinsky comes to make a request concerning his son; Bobchinsky, who comes only because he and Dobchinsky are inseparable, requests that his existence be brought to the notice of the high and mighty in St. Petersburg.

3. **Иванов сын** (= Иванович). From this combination the word сын was dropped, giving Иванов, originally a patronymic, later a surname.

9. **присох**: here coll. for подсох, 'it has stopped bleeding (*or* started to heal)'. Присохнуть strictly means 'to stick while drying', e.g. of a bandage.

11. **Денег нет у вас?** 'Have (*not* haven't) you any money?' 'Haven't you ...?' is Разве у вас нет...?

18f. **приказ общественного призрения**, 'the office of social welfare'. These bodies, set up under Catherine II in each provincial capital, managed various charitable institutions. They raised funds by acting as savings banks (there were no private clearing banks in Russia till the middle of the 19th century).

27. **Да вы поищите-то получше**, 'Now do look a bit harder (lit. better)'. The pcle. -то here adds a touch of familiarity, like -ка.

32. **Я ведь только так** [sc. **спросил**], 'I just thought I'd ask, you know'. Cf. I.1.118.

33. **пусть будет шестьдесят пять рублей**, 'sixty-five roubles will do (lit. let it be)'. Cf. Пусть завтра, 'Tomorrow will do' (IV.9.15).

42. **То есть оно так только говорится**, 'I mean it's only in a manner of speaking'. For the redundant оно see I.1.93.

45–7. Dobchinsky's request was not merely a matter of propriety, for illegitimate sons of the gentry were barred from entering government service. It also had topical point, for Nicholas I refused to legitimize children born out of wedlock, whereas his predecessors had frequently done so. The speech originally concluded: Теперь это запрещено, я знаю, но потому только, что об этом просят большею частию маленькие люди, а если большой человек попросит, то оно сейчас сделается. This suggestion that a double standard was being applied was expunged by the censor.

52. расскажет, 'he can recite': fut. pf. pot.

53. если [ему] где[-нибудь] попадёт ножик, 'if he comes across a penknife anywhere'. Here попасть is coll. for попасться (в руки).

53f. дрожечки (dim. of дрожки), 'toy droshky'.

66. сенаторам: the Senate was created by Peter the Great in 1711 as the highest judicial and administrative organ of the Russian state, but its powers were curtailed under later tsars. In the time of Nicholas I it was little more than a court of appeal. Its members were appointed from among officials and military men belonging to the top three grades of the service.

68. Так и скажите, 'Just say that'.

71. если... и государю придётся [sc. **услышать об этом**], 'if the sovereign should come to hear of it by chance'.

72–4. The statement 'In such and such a town there lives a man called Pyotr Ivanovich Bobchinsky' was duly taken note of by Nicholas I, who repeated it later to the actor who had played that part.

81. выпровожает (obs. = **выпроваживает**) **их**, 'bundles them out', or 'gets rid of them'. Contrast the use of провожать at IV.6.66, where Khlestakov shows Zemlyanika out politely.

Scene 8

G. reworked this short monologue in each version. The most significant change, introduced in R3, is Khlestakov's late realization that he has been taken for someone of importance; yet though he correctly concludes he is regarded as a person in a high office of state (государственный человек), he mistakenly believes he is mistaken for a governor-general, not an inspector (see V.8.49f.). Conceited words by the hero about his appearance were introduced in R3 and 4, then dropped. In R5 the speech was almost halved in length compared with the R4 version and the remarks pertaining to Tryapichkin were moved from the last to the first part.

2. Здесь много чиновников. In reality there would have been *more* officials in a district town than are shown in the play. Missing are the district исправник ('police chief'), стряпчий ('crown attorney'), казначей ('treasurer') and other members of the local administration, such as the предводитель дворянства ('marshal of the nobility'), though the latter is mentioned at I.1.165. G., however, was not aiming to show a complete collection of officials, only a typical selection.

4. я... им подпустил пыли [в глаза], 'I showed off in front of them'. Like the Eng. expression 'to throw dust in someone's eyes' (i.e. to mislead or confuse), пускать пыль в глаза ('to show off') comes from Fr. *jeter de la poudre aux yeux*, which has both meanings.

Экое дурачьё! 'What a bunch of boobies!' Collective nouns in -ьё, other examples of which are дубьё, трапьё, солдатьё, are mostly coll., with a derog. shade of meaning. Дурачьё, however, is softer and friendlier than дураки.

4f. Напишу-ка я, 'I know, I'll write' (cf. IV.4.27). Note the use of -ка no fewer than five times in this short scene. The mixture of spontaneity and jauntiness that it expresses makes it the Khlestakovian particle *par excellence*.

5. Тряпичкин: this invented surname, derived from тряпичка, a dim. of тряпка, 'rag', is most apt for one who writes cheap satirical pieces, esp. squibs. The name has become a byword for a журналист-болтун ('gossip columnist') and has given rise to the abstract noun тряпичкинство.

5f. он пописывает статейки, 'he writes short articles from time to time' (i.e. of the type described above). In Ushakov's dictionary both verb and noun (a dim. of статья) are qualified as ironical here, but Khlestakov is not speaking ironically; on the contrary, he admires Tryapichkin and later talks of following his example (see V.8.139f.).

6. пусть-ка он общёлкает их хорошенько, 'just let him lampoon them thoroughly'. Before he hit on the *mot juste* общёлкать (lit. 'to flick off'), G. used first обкритиковать ('to roundly criticize') and then отбрить ('to make cutting remarks about').

7. чернилы = чернила, 'ink'. The use of -ы for -а in the nom. pl. of neut. and irregular masc. nouns, common in the 18th and 19th centuries, is now arch. and pop.

8. произнёсши: obs. = произнеся. Cf. I.1.153.

9. если кто[-нибудь] попадёт [ему] на зубок, 'if anyone gets the rough side of his tongue'.

10. берегись = пусть бережётся, 'let him beware'. Cf. II.8.64f.

отца родного не пощадит для словца, 'he wouldn't (lit. will not) spare his own father for (the sake of) a quip': a variant of the saying для (or ради) красного словца не пожалеет родного отца.

10f. деньгу... любит, 'he's fond of the shekels'. In pop. speech the sing. де́ньга, originally the name of a small coin worth half a copeck, is used with final stress to mean 'money'. Cf. зашибать деньгу́, 'to coin money'.

16f. Ну-ка...! 'Now then!' or 'Come on!' An exclamation of challenge, invitation or encouragement.

18. кто кого, 'who gets the better of whom', i.e. at another game of cards (see II.3.5–9). In this common idiom some such verb as побьёт or одолеет is understood.

Scene 9

G. significantly altered the beginning of this scene. In R1 and 2 Khlestakov decides to leave of his own accord, but from R3 it is Osip who urges him to depart without delay. This change follows the convention of classical comedy, whereby the servant is quicker than his master to grasp the true situation (see *Characters and Costumes*, ll.31–2).

9. Да так, 'Oh, no reason'. Cf. III.2.38.

Бог с ними со всеми! 'Blow the lot of them!' (cf. III.5.74). When все or всё qualifies a personal or demonstrative pron. governed by a prep., the latter may stand before both pronouns (cf. у всех у них and обо всём об этом). The repetition of a prep., with nouns as well as pronouns, is a feature of Old Russ. syntax preserved in folk literature.

11. Плюньте на них! 'Don't give a damn about them!' lit. 'Spit upon them!' Cf. II.6.8f.

не ровён час. Idiom: 'you never know (what might happen)'. The end-stressed pronunciation ровён was used in G.'s time.

13. так бы [мы] закатили! 'I'd so love us to be bowling along!' Cf. II.1.56.

17. всё = всё-таки. Cf. I.1.103.

23. пожалуй, 'you may as well'.

24. возьми, 'take', *not* 'fetch'. When Khlestakov arrives in town he keeps his travel document (подорожная) and needs to show it only when ordering horses for his departure.

25. Ямщики were peasants who worked as drivers for the postal relay service, providing their own horses. This service was first set up under the Tatars (the word ям being Turkic for 'posting-station').

26. фельдъегеря: coll. pl. = фельдъегери, 'imperial couriers' (from Ger. *Feldjäger*). These officers traversed the Russian Empire in every direction on various errands, travelling not on horseback but in a тележка (see IV.3.26f.).

29f. с человеком здешним, 'by their man'. The use of человек and люди for 'servant(s)' is obs.

37f. Тройка here, as at V.8.154, means 'team of three horses', i.e. to draw the post-chaise. Osip orders more horses than his master's rank entitles him to. Officials of the lowest six grades were entitled to two horses, those in the 6th to 8th grades to three, and those in the top five grades to six. The fastest horses were supplied to couriers, hence the designation курьерские ('express').

39. казённый here = на казённый счёт, 'paid for by the treasury (казна)', i.e. gratis. Officials travelled on business at public expense.

Да [скажи ему,] чтоб всё живее [делалось], 'And tell him to look lively about it all'. For this use of the comp. живее see I.4.16.

40. Стой, 'Wait' or 'Hang on'. Cf. IV.11.9.

41f. Любопытно [мне] знать, 'I'm curious to know' or 'I wonder'. Cf. любопытно, 'you'd be interested' (III.6.117).

42f. в Почтамтской или Гороховой [улице]. In G.'s time в was used with most street-names in St. Petersburg and на with most of those in Moscow (V. V. Vinogradov, *Русский язык*, 1947, p. 692).

44. недоплачивать, 'not to pay the rest' (of his rent). Tryapichkin is in the habit of doing a moonlight flit.

46. печатает = запечатывает, 'seals': obs. sense. The letter is rolled up, addressed on the outside and sealed with wax; no envelope is used.

47. Куда лезешь...? 'Where d'you think you're going . . .?' Here лезть has the coll. sense 'to try and enter without permission'. Cf. IV.11.67.

борода, 'you with the beard' or 'beardy' (an example of synecdoche). Russian merchants, like peasants, all wore beards.

48. никого не велено пускать (= впускать), 'no one is allowed in', lit. 'it is forbidden to admit anyone'. In the construction не велеть, 'to forbid', lit. 'not to order', the negative logically belongs with the following verb.

51. за делом: obs. = по делу, 'on business'.

62. К твоей милости прибегаем, 'We appeal (lit. have recourse) to your Worship (for help)'. The same honorific title occurs in Sc. 10, ll.3 & 42, and Sc. 15, l.44.

63. Прикажи... принять (obs.), 'Please accept'. Cf. II.1.4; II.5.14.

67. развёртывает, 'unrolls': the petitions (просьбы) are in the form of scrolls.

68f. Его Высокоблагородному Светлости Господину Финансову, 'To His Most Noble and Serene Highness the Lord Treasurer (lit. Master of

Finances)': a pompous, fanciful title no doubt intended to signify the Finance Minister. The adj. should agree in the fem. with Светлость, rather than with Господин.

70. Чин, 'office': obs. sense.

Scene 10

Russian merchants, who formed a separate social class below the gentry and clergy, at that time wore long dark caftans or frock-coats and baggy trousers tucked into knee-boots. The language of the merchants in this scene smacks of almost feudal servility.

3. Челом бьём вашей милости, 'We humbly greet your Worship'. Suppliants bowed low, touching the ground with their foreheads, and thus the phrase бить челом meant 'to humbly greet *or* beseech'. Hence the nouns челобитье and челобитная, 'petition'.

5. Обижательство: pop. = обижание, 'infliction of wrongs' or simply обиды, 'wrongs', 'injuries'.

10f. Постоем совсем заморил [нас], 'He's utterly crippled us with billeting troops (on us)'. From the time of Peter the Great civilians were required by law to house and feed soldiers stationed in areas where there were no permanent barracks, an obligation from which the gentry were exempted by Catherine's Charter of 1785.

11. хоть в петлю полезай (pop. = лезь), 'we're at the end of our tether', lit. 'you may as well climb (i.e. put your head) into a noose'. For this use of хоть with the imp. sing. to express resignation or despair cf. хоть брось, 'it's no good', lit. 'you may as well throw it away'.

11f. Не по поступкам поступает, 'He doesn't treat us with the treatment (sc. that is right)': a tautological construction typical of uneducated speakers.

12. татарин, lit. 'Tatar', here in the coll. sense of 'barbarian' or 'infidel', a meaning that goes back to the time in 1240–1480 when the Tatars held sway over much of Russia.

13. [Другое дело,] если бы, то есть, чем-нибудь не уважили его, 'It would be different, I mean, if we failed to respect his wishes in any way'. The merchants are fond of using the parenthetic phrase то есть as a verbal filler.

14. порядок всегда исполняем, 'we always do the right thing'; an illiterate, euphemistic way of indicating that they supply the Governor with goods free of charge.

15. Супружница: pop. = супруга, 'spouse', 'wife'.

15f. мы против этого не стоим: obs. = мы ничего не имеем против этого, 'we don't object to that'.

17. что ни попадёт (= попадётся) [sc. **ему на глаза**], 'whatever he claps eyes on' (cf. IV.7.53). In his *Предуведомление* G. wrote: В нём [Городничем] есть только желание прибрать в руки всё, что ни видят глаза.

18f. суконце (coll. affect. dim. of сукно), 'nice bit of cloth'.

20. без мала (= малого), 'nearly', 'not far short of'. Мала is the old gen. sing. masc. and neut. short form of малый, 'little'. Cf. от мала до велика, 'both young and old'.

аршин: gen. pl., as at V.2.18. Cf. пуд at III.11.3.

23. никто не запомнит, 'no one can remember': fut. pf. pot., *not* impf., as Ushakov mistakenly indicates.

24. Так goes with и as an intensive ('simply'). Cf. I.3.81.

25f. не то уж говоря, чтоб какую[-нибудь] деликатность, 'not just (to speak of) some delicacy'. Note the illit. confusion of two constructions: не то, чтоб, 'not (just)', and не говоря уж о. . . 'not to mention'. Деликатность in the sense лакомство ('dainty food') is obs., as is деликатный in the sense 'dainty', 'choice' (of food) at V.5.14f.

26f. лет. . . по семи: see IV.5.13.

27. сиделец (obs.), 'shop assistant'.

28. он целую горсть туда запустит, 'he will stick his whole hand in (the barrel)', i.e. grab a handful (though горсть here actually means 'cupped hand', not 'handful').

28f. Именины его бывают на [день святого] Антона, 'His name-day is on (the feast of St.) Anthony' (17 January). Before the Revolution each Russian was christened with the name of a saint, whose date in the Orthodox Church calendar was his or her name-day (именины). It was this feast-day, rather than the birthday, that was traditionally celebrated with presents.

29. уж (pcle.), 'indeed', 'really'.

30. подавай, 'you have to give'. Cf. ты доставай (II.1.40).

30f. на Онуфрия, 'on (the feast of St.) Onufrius (= Humphrey)', which falls on 12 June.

35f. А если что[-нибудь возразишь], велит запереть двери, 'And if you say anything (i.e. protest), he'll order the doors to be locked', meaning 'lock you up in his house', not 'close down your shop' or 'lock up your house', as all the translators put. The sense is made clearer in R1–4, where the phrase reads: позовёт к себе, да и двери велит (тебе) запереть.

36f. From 1742 most Russian merchants were divided into three guilds, according to the amount of their capital. Members of the first two guilds, and those of the third guild who held any municipal office, were exempt from corporal punishment.

37. пыткой пытать, 'torture with torture': another illit. tautology.

38f. ты у меня... поешь селёдки! 'I'll make you eat some herring!' (cf. II.8.140). The use of torture, except in certain cases, was proscribed by Catherine II in 1763, and it was forbidden under all circumstances by Alexander I in 1801, but continued in various forms. The torture described here, viz. giving the victim salty food and no water, was widely practised by the tsarist police. Cf. A. Herzen, *Былое и думы*, I, 10: И во всей России... людей пытают; там, где опасно пытать розгами, пытают нестерпимым жаром, жаждой, солёной пищей.

40f. Да за это просто в Сибирь [sc. **его нужно послать**]. Many criminals and political prisoners were sent to penal colonies in Siberia.

42. запровадит: obs., coll. = спровадит, 'will pack off'. Cf. V.2.36.

43f. подальше, 'as far away as possible': absolute comp.

44. Не побрезгай, 'Do not spurn', lit. 'do not be squeamish about': a coll. polite form of invitation.

хлебом и солью, i.e. our gifts. Bread and salt, placed on a wooden platter draped with a cloth, were traditional offerings to guests among Russians and other Slavonic peoples, hence хлеб-соль came to mean 'hospitality'. The ancient custom came to be used at times as a form of bribery and the offering of these or other gifts to officials was banned by an ukase of Alexander I in 1801, but to no avail.

44f. кланяемся тебе сахарцом и кузовком вина, 'we humbly offer you (lit. bow to you with) sugar and a basket (with bottles) of wine'. Sweet products, such as sugar and honey, being highly taxed luxuries, were often given as presents or bribes. The merchants use the dim. forms сахарец, кузовок and подносик (l.55) to ingratiate themselves with Khlestakov and to suggest that their presents are harmless.

50. отец наш! 'kind sir!' The use of отец and coll. батюшка to address a person in authority reflects the then still prevalent patriarchal attitude, whereby the lower classes were regarded, and even referred to, as children. Cf. IV.1.50.

51. Да что триста! 'But why only (lit. what is) three hundred!' Что, often followed by там or тут, is used to express the smallness or insignificance of something.

Уж does not intensify лучше, but adds hortatory force to the imp. (возьми), as at ll.55, 57, 66, i.e. 'go on'.

52. я ни слова [sc. **не скажу против этого**].

57f. за одним разом: obs. = заодно, 'at the same time' or 'while you are about it'.

61. головы [сахара], 'sugar-loaves'.

64f. [если] тележка обломается... подвязать можно, 'if the chaise breaks in any part (*not* 'breaks down', which would be сломается) . . . you can tie it up'. For example, with a length of cord and a piece of wood one could splice a broken shaft.

68. уж не знаем, как и быть, 'we just don't know what to do (lit. how to be) at all'.

73. самому, 'to himself'. This coll. use of сам for 'master' or 'boss' corresponds to the use of 'himself' in Irish English.

75. матушка, 'my good woman'. Cf. I.6.9.

76f. Милости твоей... прошу! 'Grant me (lit. I beg) your favour!'

78. Пропустить её (for **их**): an error arising from the fact that there was only one petitioner in R1–4 (see below).

Scene 11

In R1 the N.C.O.'s wife presented herself alone in this scene. In R2 both petitioners appeared but the N.C.O.'s wife was excluded by the censor Oldekop, apparently because he mistook her for an officer's wife, whose flogging would have been too scandalous. She was restored, however, in R5.

1. слесарша и унтер-офицерша, 'the wife of a locksmith (слесарь) and the wife of an N.C.O. (унтер-офицер, from Ger. *Unteroffizier*)'. For the suffix -ша see II.1.27f.

2. кланяясь в ноги, 'bowing down to the ground', as opposed to кланяясь в пояс, 'bowing from the waist'.

7. мещанка, 'townswoman', specifically a member of the urban lower middle class, comprising small traders, craftsmen, junior officials and the like.

8. Петрова = Петровна. Members of the lowest social classes often still used the old patronymic form in -ов(а) after they began to adopt surnames early in the 19th century. Cf. IV.7.3.

11f. на городничего челом бью! 'I wish to petition (*or* make a complaint) against the governor'. Cf. IV.10.3.

12. Пошли ему бог, 'May God send him'. Cf. побей бог его, 'may God smite him' (ll.20f.). See I.1.186f.

12f. A чтобы-clause, without an introductory verb of wishing, is often used with exclamatory force to express an imprecation, as here and later in the scene, or a categorical command, e.g. Чтобы этого больше не было! 'No more of that!'

14. прибытку: old gen. sing. of прибыток (pop.) = прибыль, 'profit', 'gain'.

16f. забрить лоб в солдаты (obs.), 'to enlist in the army'. Every alternate year the Russian peasantry and lower citizenry (мещане), i.e. the taxpaying classes, were required at that time to furnish from every 200 males between the ages of twenty and thirty-five one conscript to serve with the colours. At the recruitment boards a patch was shaved above a man's forehead if he was accepted and at the back of his head if he was rejected, the chairman simply pronouncing either the word лоб or затылок. As the procedure was to shave the forehead (забрить лоб) and send for a soldier (отдать в солдаты), the expression забрить лоб (в солдаты) was used in the sense 'to call up', 'to recruit'.

17. очередь-то на нас не припадала: obs. = была не наша очередь, 'it wasn't our turn', i.e. to supply a recruit. Potential conscripts were selected either by drawing lots or on a rota basis, each family taking its turn.

18. The locksmith's wife is wrong in claiming that the law exempted married men from conscription. Recruitment boards were instructed to choose a younger son before an elder, a son without children before one with, a bachelor before a married man, and to avoid ruining a family by taking its sole breadwinner. Nevertheless, married men were sometimes torn from their families, of which they were the chief prop and stay.

19. как же, 'how ever' (emphatic).

21. и на том и на этом свете! 'both in the next world and in this!'

23. чтоб... он... околел, 'may he die like a dog'. The verb околеть, like издохнуть, means 'to die' of animals; both words are used of people only abusively.

25. пьянюшка, properly пьянюжка (pop. dim. of пьянюга), 'rotten drunkard'. The suffix -ка, usu. affect., is derog. here.

26. присыкнулся (pop. and dial. = **пристал) к**, 'pestered' or 'kept on at'.

27. подослала к, 'sent (secretly) to'. Today the dat. alone is used with this verb, as with писать (cf. I.2.49).

28. На что... тебе муж? 'What d'you need your husband for?' Cf. II.2.7.

32f. его... возьмут в рекруты, 'he'll be taken for a recruit'. See III.6.148f.

33. Да мне-то каково (= как) без мужа...! 'What d'you think it's like for *me* without my husband . . .!' As the term of military service was 25 years, conscription was dreaded as a great evil for a man and his family. Cf. R. Lister Venables: “Every domestic tie is severed for him who becomes a Russian soldier, as much as if he were dead; his home is lost; his wife a widow; his children are orphans; his parents childless . . .”, *Domestic Scenes in Russia*, London, 1839, p. 323.

34f. Чтоб всей родне твоей не довелось видеть света божьего! ‘May none of your kin come to see this (lit. God’s) world!’ i.e. may they all be stillborn. Cf. явиться на божий свет, ‘to be born’.

48. задрались (coll.), ‘started to fight’.

49. да и схвати меня, ‘and they went and seized (i.e. arrested) me’. For the ‘impulsive’ imp. sing. cf. Fonvizin, *Бригадир*, IV.2: Теперь Игнатий Андреевич напади на меня ни за что ни про что. See I.3.69.

так отрапортовали, ‘they gave me such a reporting’: a euphemism for flogging, often carried out after a report on a person had been submitted to those in authority.

два дни: see I.1.35.

In R1 and 2 the N.C.O.’s wife told a different story. The Governor had her flogged, she says, because he believed – erroneously – that she had acted as matchmaker between a merchant’s daughter and an officer lodging in the town whom the Governor wanted Maria to marry. The story given in R5 makes the punishment an injustice based on mis-identification and an action more in keeping with the character of the Governor, who is not a vindictive man (see V.2.50). In R1 and 2 the N.C.O.’s wife also offered to show Khlestakov the stripes on her body, but this was cut out, presumably on the grounds of impropriety.

53. штрафт: corr. of штраф (from Ger. *Strafe*), ‘fine’, meaning here ‘damages’ (убытки).

54. Мне от своего счастья неча (= нечего) отказываться, ‘There’s no point in me turning down my good luck’. Her ‘luck’ consists in the fact that she has been unjustly flogged and hopes to turn her misfortune to good account by claiming compensation.

60. Не нужно, ‘Don’t (do it)’. Не нужно and не надо can mean either ‘one need not’ or ‘one must not’. Cf. IV.14.20.

Надоели [они мне], ‘I’m sick of them’.

64f. во фризовой шинели, ‘in a frieze overcoat’. Frieze (from Fr. *drap de frise*, ‘Friesian cloth’) is a coarse woollen cloth with a rough nap, usu. on one side only. Coats made of this cheap material were worn by the poor (cf. ‘frieze-coat’, a nickname for an Irish peasant).

66. в перспективе, ‘in the background’, i.e. upstage.

69. захлопнув за собою дверь, ‘slamming the door to after him’. A past gerund, which normally indicates an action prior to that of the main verb, may also, as here, describe an action immediately following it.

Scene 12

This and the following two wooing scenes are a parody of the love-scenes found in conventional comedy, with the suitor going down on bended knee, swearing everlasting love, and threatening to kill himself if he is not accepted. The comic device, whereby two women are courted simultaneously or in rapid succession, was not original on G.'s part; it is used in Molière's *Don Juan* and in a number of vaudevilles by D. T. Lensky, F. A. Koni and others.

In R1 Anna and Maria appeared together and Khlestakov asked first for the mother's hand, then the daughter's. In R2 the ladies were wooed separately, first Anna, then Maria. In R3–4 only Maria was wooed and most of the words spoken by Anna in the first scene of R2 were given instead to her. In R5 the double wooing was re-introduced, with Khlestakov now courting first Maria, then Anna, and finally Maria again.

13f. To effect an entrance by making the character pretend to be looking for someone else was a stock device of 18th-century drama. G. adds his own touch of originality in Khlestakov's absurd insistence on knowing why Maria was 'not going anywhere'.

22. **принесть**: arch. = принести.

23. **Вы говорите по-столичному**, 'You speak like a man of the world (lit. in the manner of the capital)'.

26. **вам должно не стул, а трон**, 'you should have not a chair, but a throne'. The arch. impers. form должно is used here transitively, in the same way as надо, видно, слышно; cf. Мне надо книгу, 'I need a book'.

29. **платочек** (affect. dim. of платок, 'shawl' or 'kerchief'): here 'scarf', 'fichu'. Khlestakov naturally resorts to dim. forms when referring to Maria's dress and person; hence also шейка for 'neck' (l.34) and губки for 'lips' (l.38).

30. **Вы насмешники.** For the obs. polite pl. form of the noun see III.2.3.

30f. **[вам] лишь бы только посмеяться**, 'you only wish to mock'. Cf. III.3.12.

32–4. Such sentiments ('Would I were your scarf . . . that I might embrace your lily-white neck') are typical of the romantic style. Cf. Shakespeare, *Romeo and Juliet*, II.2:

> O! that I were a glove upon that hand
> That I might touch that cheek.

40. Вы всё эдакое говорите... 'You do keep saying such things ...' Эдакий is a pop. variant of этакий (see III.1.17f.).

41f. на память, 'as a keepsake' or 'to remember you by'.

46. Какие-нибудь эдакие —, 'Oh, any kind –'.

48. Да что стихи! 'Poems – that's nothing (i.e. easy)!' Cf. IV.10.51.

51. Да к чему же говорить? 'But what's the point of reciting them?' K чему? 'What for?' also occurs on l.70.

55f. О ты, что в горести напрасно на бога ропщешь, человек!.. 'O thou, man, who in thy grief dost murmur vainly against God!' In response to Maria's request for a *new* poem Khlestakov quotes the opening lines of *Ода, выбранная из Иова*, by the famous 18th-century poet Mikhail Lomonosov. In those days most Russian schoolboys learnt this ode by heart.

61. что за любовь = что такое любовь,'what this thing (called) love is'.

61f. Отдвигает: obs. = отодвигает, 'moves away'.

82. это уж слишком... 'now you go too far ...'

88. Я так только, 'I didn't mean it'.

Scene 13

3. какой пассаж! 'such goings-on!' Пассаж in this sense ('a strange or unexpected turn of events') is obs. Cf. I.2.42.

18. что такое мне суждено, 'what my fate is to be'. Судить is used in the arch. sense 'to destine'.

21f. Делать декларацию is an obs. Gallicism, *faire une déclaration*, i.e. to propose marriage, declaring one's love.

24f. Если вы не увенчаете постоянную любовь мою, 'If you will not reward (lit. crown) my undying love', i.e. marry me. This is a Gallicism (*couronner mon amour*) drawn from the elevated style of French classical drama. Cf. Corneille, *Cinna*, V.3: Et que demain l'hymen couronne leur amour.

25f. С пламенем в груди, 'With heart aflame', lit. 'with a flame in my breast'. The word пламя, like Eng. 'flame', took on the fig. sense of Fr. *flamme*, i.e. 'passion', 'sexual love', found in classical literature.

27f. я в некотором роде... я замужем, 'I am in a manner of speaking (lit. in some sort) – I'm married'. A similar comic use of this qualifier is found elsewhere in G.'s works, e.g. in *Мёртвые души*, II, where Manilov objects to taking money for souls (i.e. male serfs) 'who have in a sense terminated their existence' (которые в некотором роде окончили своё существование). Cf. also III.6.5.

29f. Для любви нет различия, 'Love knows no barriers (lit. distinction)'. The power of love to transcend all social distinctions is one of the main themes of the sentimentalists, whom G. is satirizing in this scene.

30. N. M. Karamzin (1766–1826) was the leader of the sentimental school of literature, his tale *Бедная Лиза* (1792) being the most popular literary work in Russia for a good quarter of a century. By the 1830s, however, sentimentalism was considered *passé*, suitable only for lower-class and provincial readers.

«Законы осуждают». These words come from a young man's lament for his beloved in Karamzin's *Остров Борнгольм* (1794). The first stanza of this song, much in vogue during the 1830s, runs:

Законы осуждают
Предмет моей любви;
Но кто, о сердце! может
Противиться тебе?

30f. Мы удалимся под сень струй. . . 'We shall retreat to the shade of the waters . . .' This would-be romantic *cri de coeur*, combining the poetic words сень and струя in a precious piece of absurdity, trivializes the noble ideal of a simple life in the bosom of nature, preached by Rousseau in the 18th century. The style of the sentimentalists had been mocked by Russian playwrights before G., notably by I. Krylov in *Пирог* (1802) and A. Shakhovskoi in *Новый Стерн* (1805), but nowhere to such good effect as in this brief but brilliant phrase. G.'s translators, by making this deliberate nonsense meaningful, rob the words of all their point and piquancy.

Scene 14

2. папенька: see I.6.13.

3. увидя: arch. = увидев.

6f. как угорелая кошка, 'like a scalded cat'. Угорелый lit. means 'poisoned by charcoal fumes (угар)', given off, for example, when a stove was not properly tended. People made dizzy or sick by such fumes would often rush about 'like creatures possessed' (как угорелые).

7f. что тебе вздумалось? 'what's got into your head?'

9f. не похоже на то, чтобы, 'you wouldn't think that', lit. 'it does not look as though'.

12. как прилично: obs. = как подобает, 'as befits'. Cf. III.3.5.

13. хорошие правила, 'good principles (of conduct)', i.e. good manners.

13f. солидность в поступках, 'sedate behaviour', 'decorum'.

17f. У тебя вечно какой-то сквозной ветер разгуливает в голове, 'Your wits are scattered by every puff of wind', lit. 'Some draught is forever going round in your head', i.e. you are empty-headed. This is a picturesque variant of the stock expression у неё ветер (гуляет) в голове.

19. Что тебе глядеть на них? 'Why should you look to (i.e. copy) them?'

20f. Anna's claim to be a model of propriety echoes Famusov's remark to Sophia in Griboyedov's *Горе от ума*, I.4:

Не надобно иного образца,
Когда в глазах пример отца.

26. Так вы в неё [sc. **влюблены**]**?..**

29. Дрянь corresponds to 'hussy' or 'baggage' in English comedy of that period.

31. стоит, чтобы я нарочно отказала, 'it would serve you right if I deliberately refused'. The impers. стоит is used in the old sense 'it is deserving *or* worthy', and is equivalent here to ты стоишь.

34. Вперёд (coll. = **впредь**) **не буду** [sc. **этого делать**], 'I shan't do it again'. It is normal to omit the last part of this expression, which usu. takes the form больше не буду.

Scene 15

6. Честью, 'On my honour'.

6f. наполовину нет того, что они говорят, 'not half of it is (true), what they say'.

7. обманывают и обмеривают, 'cheat and chisel (lit. short-serve)'. Note the Governor's alliteration, repeated at V.2.24–6.

9f. Она сама себя высекла, 'She flogged herself'. This remark, which has become proverbial, recalls the saying Сама себя раба бьёт, коли плохо жнёт, 'The slave woman beats herself (i.e. condemns herself to a beating) if she reaps badly'.

11. Провались (= пусть провалится) унтер-офицерша, 'The sergeant's wife can go to hell' or, in this context, 'hang herself'. Cf. Провались! 'Get lost!'

11f. мне не до неё! 'I'm not concerned about her!' Cf. I.2.55.

15. известны за лгунов = известны как лгуны, 'well-known (as) liars'.

16f. такие мошенники, каких свет не производил, 'the biggest swindlers the world has ever known', lit. 'such swindlers as the world has not produced (before)'. G. was fond of using this expression; cf. *Мёртвые души*, V: он только что масон, а такой дурак, какого свет не производил.

19. удостоивает: now spelt удостаивает.

21. Куда! 'Never!' or 'How could that be!' Cf. II.1.39.

22. Не извольте гневаться, 'Pray do not be angry'. Cf. I.3.27.

29. свихнуть с ума, 'go off my chump'. This coll. expression, used disparagingly of another person, is ineptly applied by Khlestakov to himself.

32f. отдать руки, 'to bestow (your daughter's) hand'. The gen. руки is dependent on the preceding не согласитесь. The acc. руку would be equally correct, since the negation is here indirect, i.e. it belongs to the auxiliary verb.

40. я решусь на всё, 'I'll stop at nothing'.

Khlestakov's resort to emotional blackmail, threatening to kill himself if the Governor will not give his daughter's hand in marriage, is not to be taken seriously, of course, but there are examples of such a threat being used in earnest. The poet Ryleyev, for example, won consent to marry his beloved by putting a pistol to his head and threatening to blow his brains out if he was refused.

42f. Я. . . не виноват ни душою, ни телом, 'I am not to blame in any way (lit. neither in soul nor in body)'.

45f. Такой дурак. . . сделался, 'I've become such a fool'. Today a noun complement of (с)делаться is expressed in the instr., but an adj. may still stand in the nom. Cf. III.4.5f.

48. благословляй! 'give your blessing!' According to Russian custom, a young couple engaged to be married came to the girl's parents, who held up an icon, a crucifix or the right hand and pronounced a blessing on them.

50. Да благословит вас бог, 'Let God bless you'. The pcle. да, used with the 3rd pers. pres. or fut. pf., forms an imp. of a more elevated style than пусть, expressing a solemn wish or hope. Today it occurs mainly in the combinations да будет and да здравствует. Cf. V.2.49f. and V.3.12.

55. Точный жених! 'A real fiancé!': obs. sense of adj.

57. Вона, как дело-то пошло! 'My, look how things have turned out!' i.e. what a stroke of luck. The pop. form вона (= вон) here expresses jubilant surprise.

Scene 16

12. я вдруг [вернусь], 'I'll be back in no time'. Cf. II.8.76f.

17. к чему это? 'why speak of that?'

22. столько же, 'the same amount'. Cf. сколько угодно, 'any amount' (V.8.59).

25. как нарочно, 'as luck would have it'. This phrase properly means 'worse luck', as at II.7.11f. and III.1.6, but G. often uses it in a positive sense, to mean 'luckily'. Cf. *Коляска*: Как нарочно, время было тогда прекрасное, каким может только похвалиться летний южный день.

27. новое счастье, 'good luck': one cannot say 'new luck' in English. Cf. V.4.6.

37f. ангел души моей: a Gallicism, *ange de mon âme*.

40. на перекладной [тележке], 'by post-chaise', i.e. in a springless waggon drawn by relay-horses (перекладные). The Governor is surprised that Khlestakov is travelling in a bumpy public conveyance and does not have a carriage of his own. Cf. IV.3.26f.

43. Тпр. . . i.e. Тпру! In this interj., as in Брр!, the 'r' represents the sound produced by vibrating the lips. In German this sound is appropriately called the *Fuhrmanns-r* ('the coachman's r').

47. это пустое, 'it's nothing' or 'nonsense'.

50f. [тот,] что по голубому полю, 'the one with the blue ground', i.e. a patterned rug. The omission of the antecedent pron. or noun in expressing 'the one (thing or person) that . . .' is common in coll. Russ. Cf. Который приходил вчера, 'The man who came yesterday'.

57. давай-ка. . . сена, 'come on, let's have some hay': part. gen. Hay and rugs were placed round passengers in post-chaises, which had no seats as such, not only to provide warmth, but also to soften the ride.

60. Славно будет! 'That'll do fine!'

69. вы, залётные! 'you flyers!' Russian coachmen used a great variety of epithets in speaking to their horses. In the language of folk poetry залётный (lit. 'far-flying') means 'swift', 'dashing'.

ACT V

Scene 1

Maria is silent in this scene and is not once spoken to by either parent. Indeed, the Governor never addresses a single word to her throughout the whole play.

3. Экой богатый приз, 'What a rich prize'. The spelling экой (for экий) reflects the older pronunciation. Cf. всякой (II.1.31).

3f. канальство! (obs., coll.), 'knavery', here a mild, jocular oath: 'by thunder!'

5. Городничиха (coll.), 'wife of a governor'.

6. с каким дьяволом породнилась! 'what a devil (of a fellow) you're connected with!'

8. Это тебе в диковинку, 'It's a matter of wonderment to you' or 'You find it something to marvel at'.

11. как подумаешь, 'when you come to think of it'.

12. какие... птицы: now какими птицами (see IV.15.45f.). The image of the птицы, 'birds', i.e. 'persons', is completed with высокого полёта ('high-flying').

13. Постой же, 'Just you wait'.

14f. я задам перцу всем этим охотникам подавать просьбы, 'I've a rod in pickle for all those people so eager to hand in petitions'.

18. Вот я их [sc. **проучу**]**. . .!** 'I'll teach them . . .!'

19. иудейский народ! 'pack of Jews!' In Russia, as elsewhere, at that time 'Jew' was used as a term of abuse. Most merchants were in fact of non-Russian origin, but in G.'s time Jews were banned from living in central Russia.

20f. Прежде я вас кормил до усов только, а теперь накормлю до бороды, 'I only had you by (lit. fed you up to) your moustaches before, but now I'll have you by your beards'. The Governor's threatening words were perhaps suggested by the saying кормил (сына) до уса, корми и до бороды, 'once you've fed him (your son) till he's got a moustache, you can feed him till he has a beard', i.e. is fully grown-up.

22. Писака (coll.) does not have the modern pejorative sense of 'scribbler', but the obs. meaning 'scribe' or 'clerk' (писец). See following note.

23. которые закручивали им просьбы, 'who devised their petitions for them' (закручивать is used in the pop. sense хитро составлять). The merchants and other illiterate townspeople paid clerks to write their complaints for them. Cf. N. A. Polevoi, *Ревизоры, или славны бубны за горами*, Sc. 1: Но теперь у нас в городе гулящие писцы обогатеют от писанья просьб и доносов на имена господ ревизоров.

24. дескать: pop. pcle. indicating reported speech, derived from де and скать, a shortened form of сказать. Cf. II.2.32.

25. выдаёт дочь свою [**замуж**], 'he is giving his daughter in marriage'.

26. что: a coll. indeclinable substitute for the pron. какой, which would stand in the gen. sing. here.

28. Кричи во весь народ, 'Shout it from the house-tops'.

28f. валяй в колокола, 'set the bells a-ringing'. The imp. валяй ('go to it') is more graphic and idiomatic than звони or бей.

29f. Уж когда (= если) торжество, так торжество! 'If we're going to celebrate, then let's (really) celebrate!' Cf. I.5.44f.

32. Так вот как, 'There now then', i.e. look how things are now.

36. в Питере так в Питере, 'Petersburg you say, then Petersburg it shall be'. Cf. I.5.44f.

36f. оно хорошо [было] бы и здесь, 'it would be nice here too'. Cf. I.1.93 & 189.

37f. городничество, 'governorship', 'office of town governor'.

42. можно большой чин зашибить, 'I could land myself a high rank'. The coll. verb зашибить ('to knock') is much more expressive than получить. It occurs also in the expression зашибить муху, 'to hit the bottle'.

43. он запанибрата со всеми министрами, 'he hobnobs with all the ministers'. The coll. word запанибрата is a russianized form of Ukr. за панібрати, which comes from Polish *za pan brat* (often expressed in the voc. *panie bracie*). Cf. панибратский, 'familiar'.

45. и в генералы влезешь, 'you (= I) will even rise to be one of the generals', i.e. a high-ranking official. The metaphor is that of climbing the ladder of promotion in the civil service. Cf. III.6.126 & 148f.

49. Кавалерию повесят тебе через плечо, 'A ribbon will be hung across your chest (lit. shoulder)'. The badge of Russian orders of the first class was a star and a broad ribbon, the latter suspended diagonally from one shoulder and fastened at the waist. Both the order and the ribbon were known colloquially as a кавалерия.

49f. какую... лучше [sc. **получить**].

50f. красную или голубую? 'The red ribbon belonged to the Order of St. Alexander Nevsky, fourth in point of seniority, instituted in accordance with the wishes of Peter the Great just after his death in 1725, and the blue ribbon to the highest order, that of St. Andrew, founded by the same sovereign in 1698. Here the Governor is indeed 'reaching for the stars', since these decorations were awarded only to the most high-ranking officials, even among the so-called 'generals', one of whom he now dreams of becoming.

55. случится, поедешь куда-нибудь, '(if) you happen to be travelling anywhere'. Note the paratactic construction, with both verbs in the fut. pf. freq.

55f. Imperial couriers and aides-de-camp, who rode ahead to arrange for the provision of horses at each stage, were given priority over other travellers at the post-houses. Cf. II.8.120.

57. всё = все. Cf. II.1.21.

58f. ты себе и в ус не дуешь. Idiom: 'you don't care a rap'.

59. у губернатора, 'with the governor (of a province)'. See I.1.26.

60. там refers not to the provincial governor's house, but to one of the [почтовые] станции ('posting-stations' or 'post-houses') mentioned on l.57.

стой, городничий! 'the governor of the town has to wait', lit. 'wait, governor!' In this phrase, which has defeated most English translators, the Governor is referring not to himself, but to some imaginary governor whom he – in his mind's eye now a 'general' – keeps waiting his turn for horses. Cf. *Предуведомление*: [Сквозник-Дмухановский] предаётся буйной радости при одной мысли о том, как понесётся отныне его жизнь среди пирований, попоек, как будет он... требовать на станциях лошадей и заставлять ждать в передних городничих...

заливается [смехом], 'bursts into peals of laughter'.

63f. жизнь [тебе] нужно совсем переменить, 'you (will) have to change your way of life completely'.

65. судья-собачник, 'judge who loves riding to hounds'. The word собачник, which usu. means 'dog-lover', here signifies любитель псовой охоты.

67. все светские, 'all the fashionables'.

73. там = в Петербурге. Cf. III.6.104.

74. Рыбица is a coll. affect. dim. of рыба. For this kind of 'gastronomic' dim. see III.10.37f.

75. ряпушка и корюшка, 'houting (akin to the sig) and sparling (*or* smelt)'. These fish, found in the lakes and rivers of N. Russia, both belong to the salmon family and were thus esteemed great delicacies.

слюнка потечёт, 'it makes your mouth water', lit. 'the saliva will flow'. The pl. is normally used in this expression.

77. Ему всё бы только рыбки! 'All he wants (*or* can think about) is fish!' Cf. II.8.71f.

79. амбре, originally an amber perfume (Fr. *parfum ambré*), here has the coll. meaning of 'fragrance'. Nowadays it is used only in an ironic sense to mean 'a bad smell'.

Scene 2

2. соколики! 'my fine friends!' This affect. dim. of сокол ('falcon') is here used ironically, like голубчики (1.4).

3. Здравия желаем, 'our greetings': a common salutation used to a superior, esp. in military circles. Здравие is the Ch.Sl. form of здоровье.

5. Самоварник can mean 'maker *or* seller of samovars', 'lover of the samovar (i.e. of tea)', or, in derog. usage, 'tea-swiller', as here. A similar range of meanings is found in other words of the same type, e.g. картошник, 'potato-grower *or* -seller' or 'lover of potatoes'.

аршинники (obs. coll.), 'hucksters'. This derog. name for petty cloth merchants comes from the old unit of length аршин, in which their material was measured.

6. Архиплуты, протобестии, 'Arch-villains, out-and-out blackguards (*or* cardinal sinners)'. These hybrid words have a humorous quality deriving from the incongruity of prefixing nouns denoting rogues (плут and бестия) with Greek morphemes chiefly associated with names of religious dignitaries, such as архиепископ, 'archbishop', архимандрит, 'archimandrite', and протоиерей or протопоп, 'archpriest'.

надувалы мирские! 'worldly swindlers!' Some editions have морские, which makes no sense here, whereas мирские ('secular', 'worldly') contrasts with the foregoing 'ecclesiastical' titles ironically conferred on the merchants.

7. много взяли? 'have you had much profit of it?' This may be taken in a double sense, referring to the profit derived by the merchants from their trade and to the gain they expect from their complaints to Khlestakov, i.e. getting the Governor put in prison.

8f. семь чертей и одна ведьма вам в зубы, '(I cast) seven devils and a witch in your teeth'. The number seven, like forty, was regarded as magical because of its frequent occurrence in Scripture. Seven devils were cast out of Mary Magdalene (Luke, VIII,2).

10f. какие ты... слова отпускаешь! 'the words you come out with!' Note the detached какой (cf. II.1.28).

15. Теперь я вас... This unfinished threat was made explicit in R1–4, where it runs: Теперь я вас всех скручу так, что ни одного волоска не останется в ваших бородах.

15ff. This characterization of the merchants is borne out by much contemporary evidence, of which the following is an example. "The ordinary Russian tradesman is generally mean and dishonest in the highest degree; he begins by asking for his goods often twice what he eventually takes, and he will, whenever it is possible, impose an inferior article on his customer . . ." (R. Lister Venables, *Domestic Scenes in Russia*, London, 1839, p. 318).

16. Сделаешь. From this point the Governor uses ты to the merchants, treating them as a collective personality. They, in their turn, speak with one voice, like the chorus in ancient Greek drama.

16f. на сто тысяч надуешь её, 'you swindle it to the tune of a hundred thousand (roubles)': fut. pf. freq.

18f. да и давай тебе ещё награду за это? 'and you expect to be given an award (i.e. medal, *not* reward) for it as well, do you?' For this sense of давай ('one must give') cf. I.3.146.

These words about cheating the treasury (i.e. the government) recall those spoken to Chichikov by Gen. Betrishchev in *Мёртвые души*, 2,II: Обокрадёт, обворует казну, да ещё и, каналья, наград просит!

19. так бы тебе. . . Here again the earlier versions are more explicit. R1 adds петлю дали, 'they'd give you a noose', i.e. a rope to hang yourself; R2 and 3 add петлю навесили (вместо медали), 'they'd hang a noose round your neck instead of a medal'. The latter words were deleted by the censor.

19f. брюхо суёт вперёд, 'he sticks his belly out', i.e. puts on side (or rather 'front'). Толстопузый ('pot-belly') was a term of abuse commonly applied to merchants in the 19th century (cf. I.26).

21. ах ты, рожа! 'you ugly swine!' The coll. word рожа means 'mug (= face)', 'ugly mug' or 'person with an ugly mug', as here.

22. да за дело, 'yet it's for a purpose' or 'but it's in a good cause'. Beating, which was considered an efficacious means of inculcating knowledge into children, was then generally practised in Russian schools, as in those elsewhere. Cf. Anuchkin in *Женитьба*, I.20: [Отец] и не думал меня выучить французскому языку. Я был тогда ребёнком, меня легко было приучить, стоило только посечь хорошенько. . .

25. «Отче наша» не знаешь, 'you don't know your "Our Father" (i.e. the Lord's Prayer)'. Отче, the Ch.Sl. voc. of отец, and наш are rolled together here and treated as a masc. noun, hence the gen. sing. ending -a.

26. как (= когда) разопрёт тебе брюхо, 'when you've put on a great paunch', lit. 'when your belly is bursting asunder'. Разопрёт is here impers., with брюхо its direct object. However, what G. actually wrote was not разопрёт but разодмёт, a non-existent russianized form of Ukr. розідме (from роздути, 'to swell'), which was corrected in R5.

27. так и заважничал! 'how you start (lit. started) swaggering!' The coll. use of the pf. past, instead of the pf. fut., in a statement of habit produces a stronger, more dramatic effect by putting the action firmly in the sphere of real time. Cf. II.1.24f.

27f. The samovar (hot-water urn) became a feature of everyday life when tea-drinking was introduced into Russia in the latter half of the 18th century. In G.'s time tea was retailed in the streets and merchants, who usually drank it from a can or a saucer, instead of a cup or glass, were notorious for their vast consumption of the beverage.

29f. я плевать на твою голову и на твою важность! 'I don't give a damn for you (lit. I spit upon your head) and your swagger!' This yoking of the same verb, which has both a literal and a fig. meaning, to a concrete and an abstract noun is a striking example of syllepsis. Cf. II.6.8f.

36. также, i.e. besides the other things I could do now that I am so highly connected.

38. Богу виноваты, 'We are guilty before God'. Виноватый is now constructed with перед + instr.

39. Лукавый попутал [нас], 'The Evil One beguiled us' or 'It's all the devil's doing'. This is a typical expression of self-exculpation, using the devil as a scapegoat. Лукавый ('the sly one') is one of several euphemisms for the devil, others being враг, нелёгкая, нечистый, comparable to Eng. deuce, old Nick, the Fiend. Cf. V.8.205.

40. Уж какое хошь удовлетворение [готовы сделать, as in R1–4], '(We're ready to give you) any satisfaction you like'. Хошь is a pop. allegro form of хочешь; cf. слышь (I.4.17).

42. моё взяло: an ellipse of моё дело взяло верх, 'I've got the upper hand'. Cf. Наша [сторона] взяла [верх], 'We've come out on top'.

43. а будь хоть немножко [сила or **перевес] на твоей стороне**, 'but if things were even the least bit in your favour'; in view of the following words an apter rendering would be 'if the boot were on the other foot'. For будь as the equivalent of если бы был(а) cf. III.10.81.

43f. ты бы меня... втоптал в самую грязь, 'you'd trample me in the dust (lit. right in the mire)'. The expression bears both a literal and metaphorical meaning.

49. Я бы вас... 'I've a good mind to ...' This unfinished threat, like those in ll.15 and 19, was made plain in R2–4: Я бы вас в тюрьму [sc. посадил].

50. Я не памятозлобен (obs. = злопамятен), 'I bear no malice'. D. Mackenzie Wallace observed that Russians are 'individually and as a nation singularly free from rancour and the spirit of revenge' (*Russia*, London, 1877, Vol. 2, p. 231).

51. держи ухо востро! 'mind your P's and Q's!' Cf. III.6.138.

52. чтоб поздравление было... [приличное, as in R1–4], 'see that your congratulations are . . . (appropriate)'. Cf. IV.11.12f.

53f. Балычок: dim. of балык, 'cured fillet of sturgeon'.

54. Ступай с богом! 'Go in peace!' A gentle, conciliatory form of dismissal. Cf. I.3.135.

Scene 3

3f. Верить ли [мне] слухам...? 'Am I to believe the rumours ...?' Cf. I.1.95.

4f. к вам привалило необыкновенное счастие? 'have you had exceptional good fortune heaped upon you?' The prep. к is now omitted from this expression.

8. Подходить к ручке (+ gen.) was then the standard way of saying 'to (go and) kiss someone's hand'.

11f. The inversion is introduced solely for effect, to sound more grand.

Scene 5

8. С благополучным происшествием! '(I congratulate you) on the happy event!' Bobchinsky's use of the word происшествие is comically inept. The Eng. rendering 'happy event' (associated with the birth of a child) makes it even more so.

19. Червонцы, the name given to foreign gold coins in pre-Petrine Russia, came to denote gold pieces worth 3 roubles, and later 5 or 10 roubles. Here, as at V.7.63, it is merely a synonym for 'money'.

энтакого: obs. pop. = этакого. Cf. I.3.49.

Scene 6

10. Луканчик (affect. dim. of Лука), 'Luke dear'.

17. Уже here has the unusual sense of аж, 'so much so that'.

18. Настенька: affect. dim. of Настя, a fam. form of Анастасия.

19f. слёзы так вот рекой и льются, 'the tears are simply streaming down my face'. Так and и are to be taken together, as at I.3.81 and IV.10.24.

Scene 7

4. многие лета: an arch. form used in wishing a person long life, with the old nom. pl. stress ле́та.

10. The parenthesis то есть refers here not to the word дело, but to the phrase as a whole.

12. собственнолично (obs.), 'in person'.

17. самых благороднейших правил, 'of the very highest (lit. noblest) principles', i.e. a perfect gentleman. In Russian, unlike English, a double superl. is not regarded as a solecism, but the combination of самый and an -ейший suffix with an adj. stem is much less common today than it was in the 19th century. Cf. III.5.40.

18. мне жизнь — копейка, 'life to me is (not worth) a copeck'. In Act IV Khlestakov did say this to Anna in R1–4, but it was cut out of R5.

я [sc. **прошу вашей руки**].

23. не в своё дело не мешайся! 'don't meddle in matters that don't concern you!' This singularly inappropriate remark parallels that of Akulina Timofeyevna to her son in Fonvizin's *Бригадир*, V.1: Наше дело сыскать тебе невесту, а твоё дело жениться. Ты уж не в своё дело и не вступайся.

24. изумляюсь. . . [вашим достоинствам, as in R2–4].

28f. отвечать моим чувствам, 'to respond to my feelings', i.e. return my love. Today this would be отвечать на мои чувства.

32. об (= о) тебе. The use of об before words beginning with a consonant, common in older Russ., is now, exc. in certain expressions such as об пол, рука об руку, confined to pop. speech.

33. я ничего этого не отвергаю, 'I don't decline that in the least'. Here ничего is used as a coll. equivalent of нисколько, 'not at all', and отвергать, 'to refuse', 'to reject', is misused for отрицать, 'to deny'.

37. Экая штука! 'What a thing (to do *or* say)!' Cf.II.8.63.

38. подлинно, 'indeed' or 'truly': obs. sense, as at V.8.197.

судьба уж так вела, 'it is the hand of fate', lit. 'fate has so directed'.

40. судьба — индейка, 'fate is an ass (lit. turkey)'. This comes from the well-known adage Судьба — индейка, а жизнь — копейка, the second part of which is quoted above (l.18).

41. Этакой свинье лезет всегда в рот счастье! 'A swine like that always has the luck fall into his lap (lit. thrust into his mouth)!'

44. мне теперь не до кобельков, 'I've better things to think of just now than dogs'. Кобелёк is an affect. dim. of кобель, '(male) dog'.

45. не хотите: cf. I.1.99.

54–6. Anna and her husband say that Khlestakov has gone to visit his uncle in order to obtain his blessing on the proposed marriage with Maria, but Khlestakov himself gives no such reason for visiting his uncle, not even in the earlier versions. If he were seeking such blessing, it would be from his father in any case.

58–60. The 'chorus of congratulations' (поздравительный гул) is occasioned by the Governor's sneezing. The first time it is probably a buzz of 'Bless you!' (Будьте здоровы!), but the second time the good wishes are mingled with curses.

59. Много благодарен! 'Many thanks!' lit. 'much grateful!'.

61. Здравия желаем, 'Good health'. Here it is not a greeting, as at V.2.3, but an equivalent of Будьте здоровы! 'Bless you!'

63. Сто лет и куль червонцев! '(May you live to) a hundred and (have) a sack of sovereigns!'

64. Продли (= да продлит) бог [ваш век] на сорок сороков! 'God prolong your life to forty times forty!' i.e. for very many years. The idiom сорок сороков ('forty forties'), much used in folk tales, simply denotes a large number.

65. Чтоб ты пропал! 'May you perish!' Cf. IV.11.12f.

70f. деревенский уж слишком! 'much too countrified!' The adverbial qualifier is given special emphasis when placed after the adj.

78f. Большому кораблю — большое плавание, 'Great ships are made for great voyages'. This saying, now proverbial, comes very close to the Eng. saw: 'A great ship asks deep waters'.

80. По заслугам и честь, 'Honour to whom honour is due'. The same construction is found in other sayings, such as По трудам и отдых, 'As you labour, so shall you rest'.

81f. Вот выкинет штуку, 'a fine spectacle he'll make of himself'. The expression выкинуть штуку means 'to do something odd or stupid'.

82f. Вот уж кому пристало генеральство, как корове седло! 'A general's rank suits *him* as well as a saddle does a cow!' The expression пристать (now подходить) как корове седло, still current, may be compared with the obs. Eng. 'as meet as a sow (*not* cow) to bear a saddle'.

84. до этого ещё далека песня, 'you're still a far cry from that'. In present-day Russ. далека песня would be replaced here by далеко.

почище тебя, 'better men than you'. Cf. II.6.26.

87. уж и в генералы лезет! 'he's even seeking to be a general (i.e. high official) now!' Cf. V.1.45.

Чего доброго, 'I'm afraid' or 'I've a nasty feeling'. The idiom expresses anticipation of something unpleasant.

может: coll. = может быть, 'maybe'. Common parentheses are esp. liable to phonetic reduction, their unstressed part being shortened or suppressed. Cf. Eng. 'course' for 'of course'.

88f. лукавый не взял бы его, 'devil take him', lit. 'the Evil One wouldn't take him'.

92f. не оставьте [нас] покровительством, 'don't deny us your patronage'. For this obs. construction cf. Pushkin, *Капитанская дочка*, I: я, дескать, надеюсь, что он не оставит Петрушу своими милостями.

95. на пользу государства, 'for the good of the state', a rather grand way of saying 'to enter the civil service'.

101. тебе (pop. = **у тебя**) **не будет времени**, 'you won't have time'.

106f. не всякой же мелюзге оказывать покровительство, 'you can't be giving your protection to all sorts of lesser fry'. The negated ipf. independent inf. expresses lack of necessity to perform an action, rejecting it as undesirable or unthinkable.

108f. как она трактует нас? 'how she refers to us?' Трактовать is now used only in the sense 'to treat (a subject)' or 'to interpret (a role)'.

111. This remark, a barely disguised way of calling Anna a pig, alludes to the proverb Посади свинью за стол, она и ноги на стол, 'Sit a pig at table and it will put its feet on the table'. It may be rendered here as 'what do you expect from her (i.e. a pig) but a grunt?' (Eng. saying).

Scene 8

3–5. This dramatic announcement, which matches the Governor's at the beginning of the play and precipitates the denouement, was added in R5. In the earlier versions the Postmaster merely says on entering that he has something surprising to announce.

12. «в Почтамтскую улицу». The Postmaster is alarmed by the fact that Khlestakov's letter is addressed to 'Post Office Street', so called because the почтамт ('head post office') was situated there in St. Petersburg. Cf. IV.9.42.

13. беспорядки, 'irregularities' or 'abuses': obs. sense.

14. Взял да и распечатал, 'I went and opened it'. The verb взять, put in the same form as the main verb, which it precedes, and linked with it by да (и) or и, indicates a sudden or impulsive action. In the p.t. it has the same force as the idiomatic use of the imp. sing. (cf. I.3.69).

17. Призвал было уже курьера, 'I was just about to call a courier'. Cf. I.1.165.

18. с эштафетой, 'with express mail'. The word эштафета (now эстафета) comes from Italian *staffetta*, 'courier', a dim. of *staffa*, 'stirrup'. It was borrowed twice in the 18th century, first in the form штафета, from Ger. *Staffete* (via Polish *sztafeta*), then in the form эстафет(а), from Fr. *estafette*, hence the mixed form эштафета. In Russian it orginally meant 'express mail delivered by mounted messenger', then, since this was usu. done by relays, 'mail carried by relays of couriers'. From this it acquired its modern sense of 'relay-race' or 'baton' used in such a race. Thus it has run a semantic course from stirrup to stick.

20. [меня] тянет, 'I feel drawn (to it)' or 'something draws me on'. This impers. use of тянуть, 'to draw', expresses a strong urge or yearning. Cf. Меня тянет домой, 'I'm longing to go home'.

так вот и here, as on the following line, has the same intensive force as так и ('simply', 'absolutely'). Cf. V.6.19f.

20–23. The Postmaster's inner tug-of-war between fear and curiosity recalls the contrary voices speaking to Launcelot Gobbo in Shakespeare's

The Merchant of Venice, II.2: "The fiend is at mine elbow, and tempts me, saying to me, 'Gobbo, Launcelot Gobbo, . . . use your legs, take the start, run away'. My conscience says, 'No; take heed, honest Launcelot; . . . do not run . . .'"

21f. пропадёшь, как курица, '(or) you'll cook your goose' or 'you're a dead duck'.

24. по жилам огонь [пробежал], 'fire coursed through my veins' or 'my blood felt on fire'.

мороз: a terse, graphic way of saying кровь застыла в жилах, 'my blood froze (*or* turned to ice)'.

25. всё помутилось [sc. **у меня в голове**], 'my head swam'.

27. такой уполномоченной особы? '(written) by a person of such rank and consequence (lit. authorized person)?' Особа here signifies 'important person', 'personage'.

28. В том-то и штука, 'That's just the point'.

34. Я вас под арест. . . [sc. **велю взять**], 'I'll have you arrested'.

37. Коротки руки! 'You haven't the power!' lit. 'your arms are (too) short!' The Postmaster is correct in saying that such an action is *ultra vires* (cf. I.2.30).

39f. я [вас] в самую Сибирь законопачу? (prefaced in R2–4 by и если захочу), 'I'll pack you off right to Siberia (if I want)'.

46. какие со мной чудеса [sc. **приключились**], 'what wondrous things have befallen me'.

50. Генерал-губернатор, 'Governor-general', an official of the highest grade, was the administrative head of one large province or, more often, several provinces grouped together. The post, instituted by Catherine II in 1775, was abolished by a reform of 1837 in all provinces save those of Moscow, St. Petersburg and the border regions.

51. жуирую, 'I'm having a high time'. Shansky cites this as the first recorded use of жуировать (from Fr. *jouir*, 'to enjoy').

напропалую, 'recklessly', 'with abandon'. This was corrected from напропало, a russianized form of Ukr. напропале, which G. used here, as elsewhere, e.g. in a letter to his friend A. S. Danilevsky of 2 February 1838: Рим гуляет напропало.

53f. кажется, [она] готова сейчас на все услуги, 'she seems ready to oblige in any way at once'. The suggestion that Anna would willingly bestow her favours was followed in R2 by the censored words: и я сегодня или завтра намерен поставить городничему препорядочные рога, 'and I intend today or tomorrow to fix a right proper pair of horns on the governor', i.e. to cuckold him.

55. наширомыжку (obs. pop.), 'at other people's expense', 'by scrounging'. Cf. широмыжник, 'sponger' (II.2.34).

57f. на счёт доходов аглицкого (= английского) короля? '(charged) to the King of England's account?' This is an old jocular way of saying 'without paying'. Similar expressions were на счёт китайского императора and на шереметьевский счёт (the Sheremetievs being the wealthiest of all Russian landowners). The American equivalent is 'charge it to Uncle Sam'.

58. Теперь [дела приняли] совсем другой оборот, 'now things have taken quite a different turn', i.e. gone quite the other way.

59. От смеху: now со смеху.

61f. глуп, как сивый мерин, 'stupid as a donkey (lit. grey gelding)'. The same poor beast is sometimes used also as a measure of comparison for idleness and mendacity; cf. ленив (врать), как сивый мерин.

67. Как же бы я стал писать? 'How on earth could I have written it?' The verb стать here has inceptive meaning ('how would I ever *begin* to write?').

73. как будто оно там и без того не стоит, 'as if we hadn't heard that (lit. it wasn't there) already'.

80f. когда (= если) уж читать, так читать! 'if you're going to read it, then read it!' Cf. V.1.29f.

82f. Позвольте, я прочитаю. The reading of a letter aloud by more than one person is found in earlier comedies. Mérimée claims that here G. was freely imitating the last scene of Molière's *Le Misanthrope* (1666), while Kenevich, who edited Krylov, believed that G. was drawing on Sc. 9 of his one-act comedy *Пирог* (1802). Similar episodes occur too in the anonymous *Злодумный* (1788) and Zagoskin's *Добрый малый* (1820). In all these plays, however, the letter incident was introduced artificially, whereas in *Ревизор* it came about naturally, as a result of what is said and done before.

83f. Почтмейстер точь-в-точь департаментский сторож Михеев, 'The postmaster is our office porter Mikheyev to a hair'. This is the porter referred to at III.6.44.

86f. мальчишка: here derog. ('whipper-snapper'), but elsewhere in the play simply 'lad' or 'youngster'.

92. нечёткое перо, 'it's not a clear hand'.

100f. Прочитать я и сам прочитаю, 'I'll read it myself, thank you'. The use of the inf. with a finite form of the same verb expresses emphasis. Cf. Я и думать не думал, 'I never even thought of it'.

103. читано: see III.2.21.

113f. совершенная свинья в ермолке, 'a perfect pig in a skull-cap'. Zoological comparisons occur quite often in G.'s works. Thus, in *Записки* *сумасшедшего* the hero Poprishchin is described as 'a perfect tortoise in a sack, i.e. ill-fitting suit' (совершенная черепаха в мешке).

119. протухнул насквозь луком, 'reeks to high heaven of (lit. is rotten to the core with) onions'. Today verbs in -нуть denoting a change of state always lose the suffix -ну- in the p.t. Thus, instead of протухнул, one would have протух. Cf. завязнул for завяз (IV.1.40).

126. чёрт ли в нём, 'there's not a damned thing in it' or 'it's not worth a damn'. For this expressive use of чёрт cf. Я ни чертá не понимаю, 'I don't understand a damned thing'.

127. дрянь этакую читать,'what's the point of reading such rubbish?' For this use of the independent inf. cf. III.9.27.

130. уж читайте! 'go on, read it!' Cf. IV.10.51.

132. моветон, '*movays tone*', i.e. ill-mannered. This obs. word, which comes from Fr. *mauvais ton*, properly means 'ill-breeding' but is used here in the transferred sense of 'an ill-bred person' (человек дурного тона).

140. наконец, 'after all'; this sense derives from Fr. *enfin*.

140f. Пища для души ('spiritual nourishment') is a stylized way of referring to good literature (the kind that sustains the soul). Cf. Pushkin, *Разговор Книгопродавца с Поэтом*:

> Кто просит пищи для сатиры,
> Кто для души, кто для пера. . .

143. Подкатиловка, the fictitious name of Khlestakov's country estate, evokes echoes of the phrase подкатить этаким чёртом, 'to roll up in grand style' (II.5.8). A similar 'theatrical' place-name is Разгуляево, the estate belonging to Count Vetrinsky in D. Lensky's *Лев Гурыч Синичкин* (1840), the only vaudeville to remain in the repertoire of the Russian theatre.

144. Милостивый государь was used as a polite form of address ('sir' or 'good sir') and at the beginning of letters ('Dear Sir'). On the outside of a letter it corresponds to the old courtesy title 'Esquire'.

146f. в доме под нумером девяносто седьмым would now be expressed as дом номер девяносто семь. G. used the house number and position of the flat he was living in when he first wrote the play, changing only the street-name (Малая Морская).

147. поворотя: obs. = поворотив or повернув. Cf. I.1.32.

148. реприманд (obs.), from Fr. *réprimande*, is variously interpreted here as 'surprise', 'nasty shock', 'unexpected or unpleasant turn of events', 'setback' and 'lesson'. It could perhaps be rendered as either 'a pretty pass' or 'a slap in the face'.

149. Вот когда зарезал, так зарезал! 'There, he's done for me, utterly done for me!' Cf. I.5.44f. and V.1.29f.

151. рылы: obs. = рыла, 'snouts' (cf. IV.8.7). In G.'s world pigs, often seen in Russian folklore as the devil in disguise, are evil forces disrupting human affairs. The pigs' snouts thus symbolize the true nature of the officials.

153. Куды воротить! 'Bring him back indeed!' Cf. II.1.39.

154f. чёрт угораздил дать и вперёд предписание, 'and damn me if I didn't go and send orders in advance', i.e. to other postmasters, telling them also to give Khlestakov the best horses. For this use of угораздить, 'to make one do something foolish or unnecessary', cf. the saying Угораздила меня нелёгкая, 'The devil put me up to it'.

157. конфузия: obs. pop. = конфуз, 'embarrassing situation' or 'pretty pickle'.

160f. Zemlyanika gave Khlestakov not 300 roubles, but 400 (see IV.6.74–6). He may be deliberately understating, or it may be an oversight on G.'s part, since in R3–4 the amount given *was* 300.

165. на ассигнации: obs. = ассигнациями, 'in assignats'. Cf. IV.3.23.

167. Как это, 'How on earth'. Here это is an emphatic pcle.

170. Выжил... из ума! 'My wits have addled with age!' The expression has an exact equivalent in the verb 'to dote' in its original sense, i.e. 'to become feeble-minded, esp. with age'.

172. мошенников над мошенниками: either 'swindler upon swindler' (the literal rendering, but with sing. nouns), or 'swindlers of the highest degree' (the sense given in Russ. dictionaries). This use of над is obs.

174. поддевал на уду (obs. = удочку), 'I've taken in', lit. 'I've caught with a (fishing-)rod'.

174f. Трёх губернаторов обманул! 'I've hoodwinked three governors!' i.e. of our province. Tenure of office by governors in any one province was generally quite short, on average four years under Nicholas I. With such frequent changes it is not surprising that they were often hoodwinked and abuses at the district level went undetected.

175. Что губернаторов! 'Governors – pooh!' Cf. IV.10.51.

179–202. The Governor's big speech was expanded in R5 to double its former length. Most notable is the addition of a tirade against writers (ll.188–95), in which G. turns the tables on those who had denounced the play in 1836, by putting in the Governor's mouth the kind of abuse they had flung at its author.

179f. Кукиш с маслом — вот тебе обручился! 'Engaged my arse!' Кукиш ('fico' or 'fig') is an indecent gesture in which the thumb is thrust between the index and middle fingers, and the pop. expression кукиш с маслом ('a greased fico') is used to signify that absolutely nothing has been achieved.

180f. Лезет мне в глаза с обрученьем! 'She thrusts the engagement in my face!' The obs. expression лезть в глаза (+ dat.) means 'to importune', 'to make a nuisance of oneself'. Today one would use тычет instead of лезет.

183. [Скажите or **дайте] дурака ему**, 'Call him a fool': an obs. expression.

184. Эх ты, толстоносый! 'Oh, you fat-nosed fool!' In R2 it was Anna who spoke disparagingly of the Governor's bulbous nose. After her words at IV.15.36f. she added: Ну, что ты с своим носом стоишь? только мотает им, рад, что толстый нос.

184f. Сосулька, lit. 'icicle', has here the obs., coll. sense of 'squit', 'dandiprat', i.e. puny, insignificant person.

186. заливает колокольчиком! 'he's jingling along!' lit. 'he's filling the air with (the sound of) his coach-bell!' Harness-bells were an indispensable part of all post-chaises in imperial Russia.

188. щелкопёр (obs.), 'scribbler'. This word, much beloved by G., derives from the expression щёлкать пером, 'to flick (= sharpen) a pen'. In the 18th century it denoted a humble official who trimmed quill pens. Once he had sharpened his quota he left the office and had time to loaf around, hence the word came to mean 'idler'. Later it signified 'scribe' or 'pen-pusher', hence 'scribbler' (of a poor author); also 'rogue', 'braggart' or 'ne'er-do-well'.

бумагомарака: obs. = бумагомаратель, 'ink-slinger', 'hack'.

190f. These famous words ('What are you laughing at? – You're laughing at yourselves!') may have been suggested by the literary almanac *Мнемозина* for 1824, in which a piece by V. Odoyevsky had by way of illustration a picture of an old man standing before a mirror and the caption read: Чему смеёшься ты? — Твоё изображение.

Though there is no stage direction to say so, the Governor's words are usually addressed directly to the audience, creating a brilliant *coup de théâtre*. In Stanislavsky's production of 1921 Ivan Moskvin came to the front of the stage, planted one foot on the prompt-box and delivered the words straight at the spectators, with all the house lights turned on.

191f. со злости, 'in a fury'. This is one of a small number of phrases in which the prep. с + gen. may be used in a causal sense instead of от + gen. Cf. умрёт со смеху, 'he'll die laughing' (IV.9.27f.).

193. либералы проклятые! At that time the word либерал, like вольнодумец, was an opprobrious label attached by the Russian authorities and their supporters to writers and others who voiced even the mildest criticism of the government. *Ревизор* was condemned by many in 1836 as the work of a dangerous 'liberal' and G., smarting at this unjust charge (for he was blaming persons, not institutions), hit back at his detractors with these words spoken by the Governor, added in R5.

чёртово семя! 'spawn of the devil!'

194f. да чёрту в подкладку [сунул]! в шапку туды ему! 'and shove you up the devil's lining! into his cap, that's where!' i.e. into the lining of the devil's cap. Туды is an obs. pop. form of туда, as куды is of куда.

195. суёт кулаком [себе в грудь], 'he jabs his fist (at his chest)', i.e. beats his breast in anger.

197f. если бог хочет наказать, так отнимет прежде разум, 'whom God would ruin (lit. if God wishes to punish,) He first deprives of reason'. This well-known saying is traced to a Latin translation of one of Euripides' *Fragments*: Quos Deus vult perdere, prius dementat.

199. Вертопрах (coll.), 'feather-brain', belongs to the same rare type of noun formation as щелкопёр (l.188), consisting of the verbal stem верт- and the noun прах, the Ch.Sl. equivalent of пыль, 'dust'. Originally, in the 18th century, it meant 'an empty-headed dandy', one who tried to cut a dash (пускать пыль в глаза).

200. ни на полмизинца, 'not a whisker' (of resemblance), lit. 'not to the extent of half a little finger'. Cf. ни на волос,'not the least bit'.

201. все [sc. **кричат**].

204. хоть убей: see I.1.56f.

205. туман какой-то ошеломил [нас], 'some sort of fog stupefied us'. The fog here is spread by Khlestakov (cf. Какого туману напустил! at II.8.64). Fog, as a symbol of confusion, is found in many of G.'s works. Thus, when Piskarev, in *Невский проспект*, pursues a beautiful stranger, who proves to be a prostitute, все чувства его горели, и всё перед ним окинулось каким-то туманом.

212. Разумеется, 'Of course', a common shortening of the phrase само собой разумеется, 'it stands to reason'.

214. Нашли важную птицу! 'Some bigwig you found!' The p.t. of найти is quite often found in ironic remarks. Cf. Нашёл с кем знаться! 'A fine acquaintance you've made!'

219. рыскаете: coll. = рыщете, 'you roam'.

220f. сороки короткохвостые! 'bob-tailed magpies!' This is a singularly apt description of Bobchinsky and Dobchinsky, who go about as a pair, wearing tail-coats contrasting with the colour of their hair, and chatter incessantly.

222. Пачкуны, 'Blundering idiots'. Пачкун usu. means 'sloven' or 'dauber'.

223. Колпаки! 'Nincompoops!' This coll. sense of the word arose by metonymy from дурацкий колпак, 'dunce's cap'. Cf. околпачить, 'to make a fool of'.

224f. Сморчки короткобрюхие! 'Short-bellied shrimps!' The two squires have little pot-bellies, but are not fat. Cf. *Characters and Costumes*, ll.34ff.

230. первые: obs. = первый. Cf. III.2.3.

Last Scene

1. жандарм. The Corps of Gendarmes, a special force of security police commanded by the head of the Third Section, was formed under Nicholas I in 1827. Its officers wore light blue uniforms with epaulettes, white belt, gauntlets and shoulder-straps, trousers with footstraps (but not boots), and a plumed helmet.

I. L. Vishnevskaya (*Гоголь и его комедии*, 1976, pp. 146–8) sees the Gendarme's appearance as a fantastic, unreal element in the play. She points out that gendarmes were stationed in provincial, not district towns, and that it was not part of their normal duties to accompany inspectors, though they may have done so in exceptional cases, but there is no evidence of any particularly grave abuses in this town to warrant such action.

Yet there is surely no great mystery in all this. It was one of the chief tasks of the gendarmerie to root out corruption among officials, and corruption must have been suspected here for the authorities to have sent an inspector. Moreover, the gendarme who accompanies him comes from the provincial town and, according to N. Kotlyarevsky (*Н. В. Гоголь*, 1908, p.314) is not a commissioned officer but an N.C.O., the most junior rank, as in the ordinary police (cf. I.1.3). He is thus not too grand a person to perform the office of announcing the real inspector's arrival; indeed, in *Мёртвые души* it is a gendarme who comes and summons the guilty Chichikov to appear before the governor-general. Finally, if this had been unusual or unknown in real life, we may be sure that some of G.'s contemporaries would have commented on it, for they were quick to point out such errors in his works. Since this is not the case, it must be concluded that here G. was accurately reflecting the reality of his time.

2. по именному повелению, 'by imperial command', i.e. an order issued in the name of the tsar (от имени царя).

3. сей же час, 'forthwith'. Cf. I.6.34.

6. излетает из (obs. = **слетает с**) **дамских уст**, 'escapes the ladies' lips'.

7. в окаменении, 'transfixed', lit. 'in (a state of) petrifaction'.

Dumb Scene

G. attached great importance to this final tableau, on the correct staging of which, in his view, the success of the whole play depended. Having seen it badly mishandled in the original production, he added detailed directions in R5, insisting that the scene be performed exactly as specified. He provided further comments on it in two letters to Shchepkin, in his *Предуведомление* and *Отрывок из письма*. In this last he stressed the need to show the organic unity between this scene and the rest of the play, and for the main actors to express their fear in different ways. He wrote: Испуг каждого из действующих лиц не похож один на другой, как не похожи их характеры и степень боязни и страха, вследствие великости наделанных каждым грехов... Одни только гости могут остолбенеть одинаким образом, но они даль в картине... Словом, каждый мимически продолжит свою роль...

Something akin to the dumb scene is found near the end of A. Klushin's comedy *Смех и горе* (1793) and at the end of Pushkin's *Борис Годунов* (1831) in the words Народ *безмолвствует*, but these brief episodes serve a different purpose and lack the significance of G.'s symbolic finale. Closer parallels to the dumb scene appear in G.'s own works. There are several examples in the early tales of people being struck dumb and rooted to the spot in the face of something unexpected and incomprehensible. The greatest similarity, however, is to be found in the scene in *Мёртвые души* where Manilov is dumbfounded by Chichikov's proposal to buy dead souls: Манилов выронил тут же чубук с трубкою на пол и как разинул рот, так и остался с разинутым ртом в продолжение нескольких минут. Оба приятеля... остались недвижимы, вперя друг в друга глаза...

8f. с самым сатирическим выражением лица, 'with a most sarcastic (lit. satirical) expression'.

10ff. At the end of his *Предуведомление* G. gives substantially the same directions for this scene, except in the case of Zemlyanika, who is described, less characteristically, as being с приподнятыми кверху бровями и пальцами, поднесёнными ко рту, как человек, который чем-то сильно обжёгся.

14f. произнесть: arch. = произнести.

15. Вот тебе, бабушка, и Юрьев день! 'Now we're really in the cart!' lit. 'So much, granny, for St. George's Day!' This old pop. saying originally expressed the bitterness of the Russian peasants at being deprived of their ancient right to change masters, provided all their dues had been paid. At the end of the 15th century the right was restricted to the week before and the week after St. George's Day, which fell on 26 November. From 1581, under Ivan the Terrible, this right was suspended during certain years, and from 1603, under Boris Godunov, it was suspended annually. Thus immobilized, the peasants gradually became serfs, bound to the soil and to their masters, a situation that was formally recognized in the Legal Code (Уложение) of 1649.

21. остаются просто столбами, 'remain simply like posts' (instr. of comparison). Cf. стоять столбом, 'to stand motionless'.

Почти полторы минуты, 'Nearly a minute and a half'. G. variously prescribed the length of time this scene should last, from 2–3 minutes in *Отрывок из письма* to nearly one minute in *Предуведомление*. Even one minute, however, proves too long in the theatre, where the curtain is usually rung down after only 10–15 seconds.

BIBLIOGRAPHY

(a) Studies of Gogol in English:

Erlich, V. *Gogol*. New Haven & London, 1969.
Fanger, D. *The Creation of Nikolai Gogol*. Harvard U.P., 1979.
Gippius, V. V. *Gogol*. Ann Arbor, Michigan, 1981. (Russian original pub. Leningrad, 1924.)
Karlinsky, S. *The Sexual Labyrinth of Nikolai Gogol*. Harvard U.P., 1976.
Lavrin, J. *Gogol*. London & New York, 1926, and *Nikolai Gogol (1809–1852). A Centenary Survey*. London, 1951.
Lindstrom, T. S. *Nikolay Gogol*. New York, 1974.
Magarshack, D. *Gogol: A Life*. London & New York, 1957.
Nabokov, V. *Nikolai Gogol*. Norfolk, Connecticut, 1944.
Peace, R. *The Enigma of Gogol*. Cambridge U.P., 1981.
Rowe, W. W. *Through Gogol's Looking Glass*. New York U.P., 1976.
Setchkarev, V. *Gogol: His Life and Works*. London & New York, 1965. (German original pub. Wiesbaden & Berlin, 1953.)
Troyat, H. *Divided Soul: The Life of Gogol*. New York, 1973.(French original pub. Paris, 1971.)
Zeldin, J. *Nikolai Gogol's Quest for Beauty*. Regents Press of Kansas, 1978.

(b) Gogol's dramatic works:

Anikst, A. A. 'Гоголь о реализме в драме', *Театр*, 3 (1952), 41–52.
Anikst, A. A. 'Н. В. Гоголь о драме', in his *Теория драмы в России от Пушкина до Чехова*, Moscow, 1972, 106–31.
Danilov, S. S. *Гоголь и театр*. Leningrad, 1936.
Dokusov, A. M. *Драматургия Н. В. Гоголя*. Leningrad, 1962.
Durylin, S. N. 'Гоголь и театр', *Бюллетень АН, серия истории и философии*, IX/2 (1952), 144–64.
Durylin, S. N. 'От «Владимира третьей степени» к «Ревизору»', in *Ежегодник Института истории искусств*, Moscow, 1953, 164–239.
Gorbulina, E. V. 'Литературно-критическая борьба вокруг драматургии Н. В. Гоголя в 30–40-х годах XIX в.', *Ученые записки Ворошиловского пед. института, серия историко-филологических наук*, т.XXIV, вып.1 (1957), 67–116.
Gourfinkel, N. 'Gogol et le théâtre', *Revue d'histoire du théâtre*, 3 (1952), 189–219.
Gourfinkel, N. *Nicolas Gogol, dramaturge*. Paris, 1956.
Khrapchenko, M. B. 'Драматургия Гоголя', *Октябрь*, 1 (1952), 141–74.
Kremlev, A. N. 'Драматические произведения Гоголя и взгляды его на значение театра', *Образование*, 4 (1909), 42–59.
Kryzhitsky, G. 'О драматургии Гоголя', *Театр*, 12 (1952), 114–18.
Kupreyanova, E. N. 'Гоголь-комедиограф', *Русская литература*, 1 (1990), 6–33.
Mann, Yu. V. 'Парадокс Гоголя-драматурга', *Вопросы литературы*, 12 (1981), 132–47.
Matskin, A. P. *На темы Гоголя: Театральные очерки*. Moscow, 1984.
Nemirovich-Danchenko, V. I. 'Тайны сценического обаяния Гоголя', *Ежегодник императорских театров*, вып.2 (1909), 28–35.
Pfulb, A. 'Comment Gogol concevait le théâtre', *La Pensée. Nouvelle série*, 44 (1952), 105–10.
Piksanov, N. K. *Гоголь-драматург. Стенограмма публичной лекции*. Leningrad, 1952.

Pokusayev, E. I. 'Гоголь об «истинно общественной» комедии', *Русская литература*, 2 (1959), 31–44.

Romashov, B. S. 'Великий художник русского театра', *Театр*, 3 (1952), 3–17.

Rozanov, V. V. 'Гоголь и его значение для театра', in his *Среди художников*, St. Petersburg, 1914, 264–71.

Stepanov, N. L. (Ed.) *Гоголь и театр*. Moscow, 1952.

Stepanov, N. L. *Искусство Гоголя-драматурга*. Moscow, 1964.

Thiess, F. *Nikolaus W. Gogol und seine Bühnenwerke*. Berlin, 1922.

Varneke, B. V. 'Гоголь и театр', *Русский филологический вестник*, 2 (1909), 307–36.

Vishnevskaya, I. L. *Гоголь и его комедии*. Moscow, 1976.

Volkova, L. P. '«Русский чисто анекдот» — структурообразующий принцип гоголевской драматургии', *Вопросы русской литературы*, 55 (1990), 3–12.

Worrall, N. *Nikolai Gogol and Ivan Turgenev*. London, 1982.

(c) 'The Government Inspector':

Aleksandrovsky, G. V. 'Этюды по психологии художественного творчества. «Ревизор» Гоголя, *Ежегодник коллегии П. Галачана*. Kiev, 1898.

Belyayeva, L. A. 'К вопросу о положительном пафосе комедии Н. В. Гоголя «Ревизор»', *Ученые записки Московского областного пед. института им. Н. К. Крупской*, т.XVI, вып.4 (1958), 33–47.

Berkovsky, N. Ya. 'Комедия империи', in his *Литература и театр*, Moscow, 1969, 517–35.

Bertensson, S. 'The Première of "The Inspector General"', *Russian Review*, vii, I (1947), 88–95.

Bodin, P-A. 'The Silent Scene in Nikolaj Gogol's "The Inspector General"', *Scando-Slavica*, 33 (1987), 5–16.

Bogolepov, P. K. *Изучение комедии Гоголя «Ревизор»*. Moscow, 1958.

Börtnes, J. 'Gogol's "Revizor"—a Study in the Grotesque', *Scando-Slavica*, 15 (1969), 47–63.

Brodsky, N. L. 'Гоголь и «Ревизор»', in his *Н. В. Гоголь, «Ревизор»*, Moscow, 1927, V–LVII. Revised in his *Избранные труды*, Moscow, 1964, 40–84.

Brown, N. *Notes on Nikolai Gogol's 'The Government Inspector'*. Nairobi, 1974.

Bryantsev, A. A., Gippius, V. V. *et al. О «Ревизоре». Сборник статей*. Leningrad, 1936.

Burakovsky, S. Z. *«Ревизор» Н. В. Гоголя. 1836–1886 гг. Опыт разбора*. Novgorod, 1886.

Corbet, C. 'Le "Révizor" de Gogol devant la critique journalistique parisienne', *Revue de littérature comparée*, 33 (1959), 481–99.

Danilov, S. S. *«Ревизор» на сцене*. Kharkov, 1933. Revised ed., Leningrad, 1934.

Danilov, S. S. *«Ревизор» на Александринской сцене 1836–1936*. Leningrad, 1936.

Danilov, V. V. '«Ревизор» со стороны идеологии Гоголя', *Родной язык в школе*, 10 (1926), 13–21.

Debreczeny, P. 'The Government Inspector', in "Nikolay Gogol and his contemporary critics", *Transactions of the American Philosophical Society*, Vol. 56, Pt. 3 (1966), 17–29.

Degozhskaya, A. S., Chirkovskaya, T. V. *Комедия Гоголя «Ревизор»*. Leningrad, 1958.

Derzhavin, N. S. *Н. В. Гоголь: «Ревизор», комедия в 5 действиях. Сценическая история в иллюстративных материалах*. Moscow, 1936.

Dokusov, A. M., Marantsman, V. G. *Изучение комедии Н. В. Гоголя «Ревизор» в школе*. Moscow-Leningrad, 1967.

Dolgikh, A. I. 'К вопросу об индивидуализации и типизации речи персонажей. (Материалы сличения речи Городничего по трем редакциям комедии Н. В. Гоголя «Ревизор»)', *Русский язык в школе*, 2 (1959), 46–51.

Dolgikh, A. I. 'К вопросу об изобразительных возможностях синтаксиса русской разговорной речи. (Материалы сличения редакций комедии Н. В. Гоголя «Ревизор»)', *Ученые записки Орловского пед. института, кафедра русского языка*, т. 21, вып.6 (1962), 17–29.

Dolgikh, A. I. 'Типы диалога в комедии Н.В. Гоголя «Ревизор»', *Ученые записки Липецкого пед. института*, вып.3 (1963), 146–70.

Dolgikh, A. I. *Речевая характеристика персонажей в комедии Н. В. Гоголя «Ревизор». (При сопоставлении различных редакций произведения)*. Abstract of dissertation. Moscow University, 1964.

Dolgikh, A. I. 'Структура диалога в комедии Н. В. Гоголя «Ревизор». (Средства связи реплик и их характерологические функции)', *Известия Воронежского государственного пед. института*, т.66 (1966), 5–22.

Dolinin, A. S. 'Из истории борьбы Гоголя и Белинского за идейность в литературе', *Ученые записки Ленинградского государственного пед. института*, т.XVIII, факультет языка и литературы, вып.5 (1956), 26–58.

Ehre, M. 'Laughing through the Apocalypse: The comic structure of Gogol's "Government Inspector"', *Russian Review*, 39 (1980), 137–49.

Eleonsky, S. F. 'Шесть редакций комедии Гоголя «Ревизор»', in his *Изучение творческой истории художественных произведений*, Moscow, 1962, 231–99.

Fedorenko, E. W. 'Gogol's "Revizor": A reexamination of language characteristics', *Russian Language Journal*, 106 (1976), 39–50.

Gerigk, H. J. 'Zwei Notizen zum "Revisor"', *Russian Literature*, IV/2 (1976), 167–74.

Gippius, V. V. 'Работа Гоголя над образами «Ревизора»', *Рабочий и театр*, 1 (1935), 20–2.

Gippius, V. V. 'Проблематика и композиция «Ревизора»', in *Н. В. Гоголь. Материалы и исследования*, Moscow-Leningrad, 1936, Vol. 2, 151–99. (English translation by R. A. Maguire in his *Gogol from the Twentieth Century*, Princeton, 1974, 216–65.)

Gippius, V. V. 'Заметки о Гоголе. III. Вариант Хлестакова', *Ученые записки Ленинградского университета, серия филологических наук*, т.76, вып.11 (1941), 9–12.

Gofman, V. A. 'Язык «Ревизора»', *Литературная учеба*, 6 (1934), 74–101.

Gofman, V. A. 'Язык и стиль «Ревизора»', in his *Язык литературы*, Leningrad, 1936, 301–38.

Grinkova, N. P. 'Из наблюдений над языком комедии Н. В. Гоголя «Ревизор»', *Русский язык в школе*, 2 (1952), 7–17.

Gukasova, A. G. 'Комедия «Ревизор». (Проблема типического в свете комедийного конфликта)', in *Гоголь в школе*, Moscow, 1954, 280–321.

Gurksy, V. K. *«Ревизор» Станиславского и... Гоголя*. Moscow, 1922.

Ivanov, V. V. '«Ревизор» Гоголя и комедия Аристофана', *Театральный Октябрь*, I (1926), 89–99. (English translation by R. A. Maguire in his *Gogol from the Twentieth Century*, Princeton, 1974, 200–14.)

Kas'yanov, A. V. 'Речевая характеристика персонажей комедии Н. В. Гоголя «Ревизор». (Из материалов наблюдений)', *Ученые записки Армавирского пед. института*, т.1 (1957), 57–109.

Kas'yanov, A. V. *Лексика и фразеология комедии Н. В. Гоголя «Ревизор»*. Dissertation. Московский государственный пед. институт им. В. И. Ленина, Moscow, 1958.

Kas'yanov, A. V. 'Лексика и фразеология комедии Н.В. Гоголя «Ревизор»', *Ученые записки Армавирского пед. института*, III/1 (1958), 183–230.

Kas'yanov, A. V. 'Особенности лексики и фразеологии комедии Н. В. Гоголя «Ревизор»', *Русский язык в школе*, 3 (1959), 20–7.

Kas'yanov, A. V. 'Речевые средства юмора и сатиры в комедии «Ревизор»', *Литература в школе*, 2 (1961), 58–61.

Kas'yanov, A. V. 'О речевых средствах юмора и сатиры в комедии Н. В. Гоголя «Ревизор»', *Ученые записки Армавирского пед. института*, т.4, вып.2 (1962), 3–19.

Kostelyanets, B. 'Еще раз о «Ревизоре»', *Вопросы литературы*, I (1973), 195–224.

Krestova, L. V. 'Зрители первых представлений «Ревизора»', *Научные труды Индустриально-педагогического института им. К. Либкнехта, серия социально-экономическая*, вып.8 (1929), 5–23.

Krestova, L. V. *Комментарий к комедии Н. В. Гоголя «Ревизор»*. Moscow, 1933.

Kupreyanova, E. N. 'Авторская «идея» и художествеиная структура «общественной комедии» Н. В. Гоголя «Ревизор»', *Русская литература*, 4 (1979), 3–16.

LeBlanc, R. D. 'Satisfying Khlestakov's appetite: The semiotics of eating in "The Inspector General"', *Slavic Review*, 47 (1988), 483–98.

Lotman, Yu. M. 'Историко-литературные заметки. 2. Городничий о просвещении', *Ученые записки Тартуского университета, литературоведение*, т.IX, вып.184 (1966), 138–41.

Lotman, Yu. M. 'О Хлестакове', *Труды по русской и славянской филологии*, Tartu, 26 (1975), 19–53. (English translation by R. Sobel in A. Shukman, *The Semiotics of Russian Culture*, Ann Arbor, 1984, 177–212.)

Maimin, E. A. 'Сюжетная композиция в драматическом произведении. Построение сюжета в комедии Гоголя «Ревизор»', in his *Опыты литературного анализа*, Moscow, 1972, 160–83.

Mann, Yu. V. *Комедия Гоголя «Ревизор»*. Moscow, 1966.

Mann, Yu. V. '«Ужас оковал всех...» (О немой сцене в «Ревизоре» Гоголя)', *Вопросы литературы*, 8 (1989), 223–35.

Nikolayev, D. P. 'Конфликт в комедии Гоголя «Ревизор»', in *Н. В. Гоголь. Сборник статей*, ed. by A. N. Sokolov, Moscow, 1954, 139–67.

Nordby, E. L. *Gogol's comic theory and practice in 'The Inspector General'*. Dissertation. Stanford University, 1971.

Pacini Savoj, L. 'Il "Revisore" e la "Follia Mistica" Gogoliana', *Ricerche slavistiche*, 1 (1952), 3–21.

Petrov, V. 'Пьеса и сценарий. К экранизации «Ревизора»', *Искусство кино*, 6 (1952), 108–17.

Pozdeyev, A. A. 'Несколько документальных данных к истории сюжета «Ревизора»', *Литературный архив*, Moscow-Leningrad, 1953, Vol. IV, 31–7.

Shenrok, V. I. 'Комедии Гоголя на сцене', in his *Материалы для биографии Гоголя*, Vol. 3, Moscow, 1895, 505–22.

Shklovsky, V. 'Ситуация, коллизия «Ревизора»', in his *Повести о прозе*, Moscow, 1966, Vol. 2, 112–22.

Smirnov, N. A. 'К литературной истории текста «Ревизора» Гоголя', *Известия Отделения русского языка и словесности АН*, т.6 кн.1 (1901), 235–41.

Smirnov, V. A. 'Комедия Н. В. Гоголя «Ревизор» как выдающийся памятник художественного слова. Опыт изучения средств речевой характеристики городничего и Хлестакова', *Ученые записки Горьковского пед. института*, т.17 (1955), 202–27.

Stender-Petersen, A. 'Gogol und Kotzebue. Zur thematischen Entstehung von Gogols "Revisor"', *Zeitschrift für Slavische Philologie*, 12/1–2 (1935), 16–53.

Stepanov, N. L. 'Работа Н. В. Гоголя над языком «Ревизора»', *Театр*, 3 (1952), 28–40.

Stepanov, N. L. 'Сатира Гоголя на экране («Ревизор»)', *Искусство кино*, 1 (1953), 71–86.

Stolpyansky, P. 'Заметки на полях Гоголя. (Историко-библиогафические примечания)', *Ежегодник императорских театров*, VI (1910), 63–72.

Suprun, A. E. 'К характеристике языка «Ревизора»', in *Сборник научных работ студентов Киргизского университета*, вып.1, Frunze, 1954, 77–86.

Tabakov, O. 'A Soviet actor and director looks at Gogol and "The Government Inspector"', *Journal of Russian Studies*, 35 (1978), 24–8.

Tikhonravov, N. S. 'Первое представление «Ревизора» на московской сцене', *Русская мысль*, V (1886), 84–105.

Tikhonravov, N. S. 'Очерк истории текста комедии Гоголя «Ревизор»', in his *«Ревизор». Первоначальный сценический текст*. Moscow, 1886.

Triomphe, R. 'Une comédie russe: le Révizor ou le jeu du rire et de la vertu', *Bulletin de la Faculté des Lettres de Strasbourg*, 33 (1954–55), 169–84.

Triomphe, R. 'Gogol und die russische Kritik über den *Revisor*', in *Vorträge auf den Berliner Slawistentagung*, Berlin, 1956, 140–61.

Tsitlevich, L. M. 'Сюжетно-композиционная система комедии Н. В. Гоголя «Ревизор»', *Вопросы русской литературы*, 55 (1990), 12–18.

Vishnevskaya, I. L. 'Что еще скрыто в «Ревизоре»?', *Театр*, 2 (1971), 92–104.

Voitolovskaya, E. L. *Комедия Н. В. Гоголя «Ревизор». Комментарий*. Leningrad, 1971.

Vorob'ev, P. G. 'Комедия «Ревизор» в практике изучения ее в средней школе', in *Изучение творчества Н. В. Гоголя в школе*, ed. by L. I. Timofeyev, N. V. Kolokol'tsev, Moscow, 1954, 61–90.

Wiens, H. *Die Geschichte einer Komödie. Die Entstehung von Gogols "Revisor". Seine Beurteilung durch die Zeitgenossen und die Reaktion des Verfassers*. Dissertation. Göttingen, 1946.

Wigzell, F. 'Gogol and Vaudeville', in *Nikolay Gogol: Text and Context*, ed. by J. Grayson and F. Wigzell. New York, 1989, 1–18.

Zelinsky, B. 'Gogol's "Revisor". Eine Tragödie?', *Zeitschrift für Slavische Philologie*, 36/1 (1971), 1–40.

(d) English translations of Ревизор:

Anderson, J. *The Inspector General. A satiric farce in three acts*. London & New York, 1931.

Campbell, D. J. *The Government Inspector*. London, 1947.

Cooper, J. *The Inspector*, in 'Four Russian Plays', London, 1972.

Dolman, J., Rothberg, B. *The Inspector-General* (*Revizór*), *a Russian farce-comedy*. Boston & Los Angeles, 1937.

Ehre, M., Gottschalk, F. *The Government Inspector*, in 'The Theater of Nikolay Gogol', Chicago U.P., 1980.

English, C., McDougall, G. *The Government Inspector*, in 'Nikolai Gogol. A Selection', Moscow, 1980.

Garnett, C. *The Government Inspector*, in 'The Works of Nikolay Gogol', Vol. 6, London, 1926. Revised by L. J. Kent in 'The Collected Tales and Plays of Nikolai Gogol', New York, 1964.

Goodman, W. L. *The Government Inspector*. Adapted by H. S. Taylor. London, 1962.

Guerney, B. G. *The Inspector General*, in 'A Treasury of Russian Literature', New York, 1943.

Hart-Davies, T. *The Inspector. A comedy*. Calcutta, 1890.

Ignatieff, L. *The Government Inspector*. Adapted by P. Raby. Minnesota U.P., 1972.

MacAndrew, A. *The Inspector General*, in '19th Century Russian Drama', New York, 1963.

Magarshack, D. *The Government Inspector*, in 'The Storm and other Russian Plays', London, 1960.

Mandell, M. S. *Revizor, a comedy*. New Haven, 1908.

Marsh, E. O., Brooks, J. *The Government Inspector*. London, 1968.

Mitchell, A. *The Government Inspector*. (An adaptation). London & New York, 1985.

Reeve, F. D. *The Inspector General. A comedy in five acts*, in 'An Anthology of Russian Plays', Vol. 1. New York, 1961.

Saffron, R. *The Inspector General*, in 'Great Farces', London & New York, 1966.

Seltzer, T. *The Inspector-General; a comedy in five acts*. New York, 1916.

Seymour, J. L., Noyes, G. R. *The Inspector. A comedy in five acts*, in 'Masterpieces of the Russian Drama', London & New York, 1933.

Sykes, A. A. *The Inspector-General* (*or "Revizór"*). *A Russian Comedy*. London, 1892.

STUDIES IN SLAVIC LANGUAGE AND LITERATURE

1. Peter I. Barta and Ulrich Goebel, **The Contexts of Aleksander Sergeevich Pushkin**
2. Mark J. Elson, **A Diachronic Interpretation of Macedonian Verbal Morphology**
3. Colin Partridge, **Yuri Trifonov's the Moscow Cycle: A Critical Study**
4. Gareth Williams, **The Influence of Tolstoy on Readers of His Works**
5. A.D.P. Briggs, **A Comparative Study of Pushkin's *The Bronze Horseman*, Nekrasov's *Red-nosed Frost*, and Blok's *The Twelve*: The Wild World**
6. Edward E. Ericson, Jr., **The Apocalyptic Vision of Mikhail Bulgakov's** *The Master and Margarita*
7. Peter I. Barta (ed.), in collaboration with Ulrich Goebel, **The European Foundations of Russian Modernism**
8. János Pilinszky, **Metropolitan Icons: Selected poems of János Pilinszky in Hungarian and in English,** Edited and Translated by Emery George
9. N.V. Gogol, РЕВИЗОР: **The Government Inspector: A Comedy in Five Acts**, Edited by M. Beresford